One Way Home

Whispers of Grace Series

Book One: One Woman Falling
Book Two: One Way Home

One Way Home

Whispers of Grace Series

Melanie Campbell

MBI

Dedication

For my mom...
With love, from your brown-eyed girl
And for my dad...
Who was, is, and always will be my *real* dad

Acknowledgments

It took me years of starting and stopping to write my first novel. But this, my second book, was under contract and had to be written in approximately one year. It sounded like more than enough time at first. But as the months ticked by full of other author-related responsibilities, I found myself up against what felt like an impossible goal to reach.

I want to thank my publisher, Mountain Brook Ink, for giving me the time I needed to finish this book. When a technical glitch caused a significant portion of my work to be lost, Miralee Ferrell gave me grace, encouragement, and much-needed time to rewrite the lost words.

Then when I thought *One Way Home* was done, my editor, Alyssa Roat, gently informed me that it needed some work. I was given *more* time to do that work. Because of Alyssa pushing me to make this story better, Johnny Beckett is now part of *One Way Home.* Once he became part of the story, I knew he was meant to be there.

As always, my husband and children encouraged my writing and were patient with me during the stressful moments. I love them more than words can say.

I want to say a special thank-you to my stepmom, Candy Maidens, who is always willing and excited to read my work, give me feedback, and assist with research. My sister Melissa Salazar has been my go-to legal expert for both of my novels. I appreciate her always answering (or trying to answer) my weird questions. My gratitude also goes out to my other sister, Melinda Maidens, for helping me with all of the racing information and jargon.

My critique group, the Fictitious Five, played a vital role in making this a better story. Thank you, Patricia Lee, Dorcas Smucker, Amanda Bird, and Jacque Gram. You are all a gift.

I'm thankful for my ever-faithful friends and fellow writers, Elisheba Haxby and Jesse Rivas, who are always willing to read what I've written and offer encouragement and ideas. Also, they dropped the name of my first novel, *One Woman Falling*, into the plot of their latest book, *Ninety-Nine Promises*. I can't tell you how much it surprised and delighted me. You two always make me smile.

Above all else, I'm grateful to God for holding my hand through the writing of another story. I don't always understand why the journey is so difficult, but I can trust Him to bring something good out of it.

PART ONE

"The LORD is slow to anger and abundant in lovingkindness, forgiving iniquity and transgression; but He will by no means clear the guilty, visiting the iniquity of the fathers on the children to the third and the fourth generations."

Numbers 14:18 NASB

Chapter One

IT DOESN'T MATTER.

I held the vial, ready to fill it with saliva as the instructions stated. They also said not to drink, eat, or smoke for thirty minutes prior to providing the sample, so last night I set the vial on my nightstand and reached for it first thing this morning. But now my mouth was dry. My skin crawled, telling me it was time for a cigarette. Something in me wanted more than a smoke, but I couldn't go there.

I put the vial down. Closed my eyes. Inhaled. One, two, three. Exhaled. It had been over six months since my last drink. Six months since my last horrible, can't-go-back-and-change-it mistake. It was getting easier, and yet the strain was still there, an itch I couldn't scratch.

It had also been that long since I found out the truth. My mom died only two weeks after her telephone call confessing the part of the family secret she had kept hidden from me. Now I was the matriarch of our little family.

I laughed at the title. Some matriarch. Fifty-four years old and the contents of my life surrounded me in the twelve-by-twelve bedroom of the duplex I shared with my daughter and granddaughter. It was a shrine of my life—pictures and memorabilia. On a shelf out of my granddaughter's reach was the music box. Who knew a simple object could hold such power? Power to unravel everything, to tint every memory of my past in a shade of gray that blurred the lines, obscuring who I thought I was—and who I'd become.

It doesn't matter.

A light tapping on the door made me jump. I slid the vial and instructions under my pillow. The door crept open and

Renee peeked in, one emerald eye visible through the small opening. I held out my arms. The saliva sample could wait. I'd spent my entire life not knowing the truth. It didn't matter, anyway. What mattered was rebuilding my life. Repairing my relationship with my daughter and granddaughter. Making the last part of my life count for something.

Renee ran into my arms. Her hair was a mess of brown ringlets, her eyes bright and ready for a new day. She climbed onto my lap. I swallowed the aching joy in my throat and held her close. Her ability to love me was still overwhelming, amazing. It had kept me going, pushed me forward. Helped me fight the scream of my nerves when I'd passed the liquor store, the convenience store, the alcohol aisle in the supermarket.

I had the day off from my maid job at the hotel. Today I'd take Renee to school and give Cassie a break from her usual hectic morning routine. That daughter of mine was like a machine, working and mothering and making a home like the whole world would fall apart if she stopped and took a breath.

"Grammy, will you sing the song?" Renee looked at me with the deep green eyes I couldn't say no to. The eyes she inherited from her alcoholic father. If only the genetic roll of the dice had been different for me—if I hadn't been born with my father's brown eyes—maybe things would have been different. Maybe the secret could have died with my parents. Who would have even suspected a thing, if my eyes had been blue or gray?

I inhaled. One, two, three. Exhaled. I smiled down at her. "You aren't tired of it yet?" I hoped she'd change her mind. I couldn't sing this morning. At least not the song she wanted to hear.

Renee shook her head enthusiastically. "It's my favorite."

I squeezed her. For my granddaughter, I'd sing the words to the song that haunted me. The song from the music box.

"I can't deny my love for you
It's deeper than the bluest sea
Stronger than the mightiest tree
Darling, say you love me too
Because I can't deny my love for you."

I hummed out the rest of the song as I pulled Renee close and wiped the tears from the corners of my eyes. I couldn't tell anyone why singing the song broke my heart. And who would I tell? My AA friends? Even the thought of telling them felt like I was betraying my mom, her memory. When I had it figured out—when my search yielded results— then maybe I'd tell Cassie. After all, the version of our family history I now knew was only the difference between dark and milk chocolate. Mom had said it was up to me whether Cassie knew the rest of the story. Why she would leave a decision like that in the hands of someone with a history like mine, I had no idea.

It doesn't matter.

I patted Renee on the back. Like my mom used to with me. "It's time to get ready for school, Sweet Pea. We don't want to be late and get Grammy in trouble."

Renee bounced up with a grin. "Will you make pancakes for breakfast?"

"And sausage?" I already knew the answer.

"Yes!" Renee did a little jump

I nodded. "Run along and get dressed. Grammy needs to make her bed."

Renee pranced out the door, humming the tune of "Undeniable Love." I reached under my pillow and found the little vial. I could do this. My mouth wasn't so dry anymore. Humiliation settled on my shoulders as I filled the tube and followed the instructions. I wrote my name on the identifying insert: Sharon Gilbert. Thousands of people had done this. Millions perhaps. Whatever the number, I was among the many who had handed over seventy-nine dollars and a bottle of spit to some lab to find out what their DNA could tell them.

At least a few had done this with the hope—no, the need—to find out who their biological father was, right?

It doesn't matter.

No. It did matter. Because until I knew his story, his reasons, how and if he ever overcame the curse that propelled my mom into blotting him out of our lives, I wouldn't know if there was any hope for me.

That night I made Renee's favorite dinner—spaghetti. Lucky for me and my mediocre cooking skills, it was an easy dinner to make.

"I found another church to try this Sunday." Cassie spun spaghetti noodles around the prongs of her fork.

I nodded, weighing my response. This would be church number three since Cassie began her quest after Mom passed away. She was a wandering sheep and I was no shepherd. I wasn't even a fence post. I worked most Sundays and heard about her experiences on Sunday evenings. My chest ached for my daughter. It looked like finding the right church for her and Renee wasn't as easy as finding waterfalls.

"They say the third time is the charm." A trite response, but the most positive thing that came to mind. "Where did you hear about it?"

"One of the secretaries at work goes there." Cassie shrugged. "It's a pretty big church, which I'm not into, but they're supposed to have a great children's program and she knows some other single moms that attend." My daughter's word showed her typical optimism, but sadness lingered in her voice.

Single moms. I wondered if that was easier to say than divorced mom? Especially at church. "Well, let me know how it goes. If you like it, then I'll join you on my next Sunday off."

"Hmph." A small sound escaped Renee, who sat at one side of the small dining table. Her lips curled into a frown.

"What's wrong, Sweet Pea?"

Renee threw a furtive glance my way, then focused on her mother. "Do I have to go to the kids' church?" Her voice balanced on the line between a whine and a plea.

Cassie set her fork down and turned away, her focus on the dark window at the other end of the table. I studied her profile. So much of her dad remained in her. The wavy brown hair touched with a hint of red. The gentle blue eyes. A wave of nostalgia mixed with the remnants of grief washed over me. Steven had been the love of my life. For the millionth time I wondered what life would have been like if parenthood had quashed Steven's love of dirt tracks and car racing. I wouldn't have been left a widow, and Cassie would have known a father.

Cassie's eyes fluttered as if something outside the dark window had been holding her attention, then she pivoted back to Renee. "The first time we go, you can sit with Mommy. But if we go a second time, I want you to try the kids' church." Cassie leaned toward Renee, her eyebrows raised. "I need you to let me know if the people in charge of the children know what they're doing," she whispered covertly.

I covered my mouth with my napkin, hiding my grin.

Renee's eyes widened, and she nodded. "Okay," she whispered back, apparently satisfied with the role she'd been given. At least for now.

After dinner we fell into our weeknight routine. Renee helped me clear off the table while Cassie ran water in the bath down the hall. I cleaned the kitchen while Cassie supervised Renee's bathing. We sat together afterward on the couch in the living room to watch a rerun of *Full House*. The cheesiest show on earth, in my opinion, and more than a little weird. What two single men would give up their freedom to help raise the three little girls of their friend/brother? Not many.

In my estimation, the last two good men left in this world were dead—my daddy who raised me, and my one true love, Cassie's father, who died when she was so young she didn't remember a thing about him. But the sitcom was sweet, like any other fairytale, and Renee loved it. Sadly, that show was the closest thing she had to a male influence in her life. But no man was better than a bad man. I could testify to that.

After watching the sitcom, Cassie tucked Renee into bed, which always took a while. There was the double-check of the teeth brushing, the prayers, the one last drink of water, and then the reading of a bedtime story.

I used the time to set out my uniform for the next day and get the coffee pot ready for the morning, then stepped outside for a quick cigarette. The smoke rose into the cold drizzle typical of January in the Willamette Valley. The clock ticked toward nine as I sat back down on the sofa and waited for Cassie to emerge from Renee's room. My mornings started early, but something was bothering that daughter of mine, and I wasn't going to bed until I found out what it was.

A door opened and closed softly down the hall and Cassie walked into the living room, looking nearly as tired as I felt.

"You played that one well." I nodded my approval.

Cassie tilted her head. "Played what well?"

"The church question. The job you gave Renee of investigating how the kids' part goes. It reminds me of something your grandpa would say."

Cassie smiled wistfully and plopped down on the couch beside me. "Yeah, every once in a while, maybe I get something right."

I studied her face. It was still there. That hint of sadness and a touch of fear. "What's eating at you, baby girl?"

Cassie sighed and looked at the television, though the screen was blank. We were still working at the mother-daughter thing. It was like chipping away at an ancient artifact. If you dug too fast, you could damage it, and the long-buried treasure would crumble. At the same time, with so much of it covered, it was hard to tell what you'd find.

I patted her knee reassuringly, the way Mom would have. The clock ticked. The familiar itching, crawling feeling under my skin threatened to grow. I inhaled. One, two, three. Exhaled.

Finally, Cassie focused her gaze on me. "I don't know. I'm afraid of messing up with Renee. She's already been through so much. I know we need to go to church, but it almost feels like child abuse or something dragging her from one church to another. I had no idea when I decided we should start going to church that finding one that fits us would be so hard. And then Renee was obviously not happy about trying another one."

The things Cassie beat herself up about. "I understand your fear, but there's far worse things to subject a child to than church shopping." Even as I said it memories surfaced, the ones I had put my own daughter through. The things she'd seen, the nights when she was alone. I shuddered inside.

"I know. You're right." Cassie's eyes met mine. I still

expected them to hold resentment, but they were soft and full of tenderness. "Maybe it's also that Derrick will be out of jail soon, and I don't know what will happen." Her voice cracked, and despite my imaginary caution tape, I put my arm around her.

"He can't bother you anymore without going back to jail. He can't see Renee unless it's supervised by someone he has to pay. It's going to be okay." The last six months of Derrick being in jail had given Cassie a chance to feel safe. I didn't want her to lose that sense of security.

Cassie leaned toward me, resting her head on my shoulder. My heart swelled. I would do anything to take away the fear that still bared its ugly fangs.

"I want to believe that. And I know I need to trust God because He's gotten Renee and me this far." Cassie gave me a quick hug, then stood up, the familiar line of determination on her brow. "I'm going to head to bed and read my Bible for a bit before I go to sleep."

I nodded. "That's a good idea." Cassie had inherited my mom's Bible by default. Undoubtedly, the underlined passages and well-worn pages brought her as much reassurance as the Scriptures themselves.

I wished reading words in a book comforted me. I had tried. But the words usually blurred before I got much out of them. I was glad my daughter was more like her grandma than she was like me.

"I love you, Mom. I hope you sleep well."

I forced myself up off the sofa. "I love you too." Then Cassie was gone, and it was time to turn out the lights and head to my own room.

The silence felt like death. I had an old CD player on my dresser. Music had always been my solace. I switched the radio on and found an oldies station. The reception wasn't the best, and static crackled beneath the music, but the beebop happy tune of a Beach Boys song took the edge off the silent night.

I pulled my calendar from the wall and counted out the weeks. According to what the pamphlet with the DNA test said, it could be three months before I received my results. That meant early April. Ironically, I would have answers in time for Mom's birthday. I was pretty sure my DNA decoding was not what she would have asked for if she were still alive. I took my pen and drew a heart on April 12th. The first birthday since Mom passed. That would be a hard day.

I placed the calendar back up and took my journal out of my dresser. It was only a spiral-bound notebook from Dollar Tree, but it worked. I wrote down my accomplishments for the day. The last one was "Got Cassie to open up to me a bit, even got a hug."

Nighttime was the worst, and I wondered if Cassie's wish for me to sleep well was because she'd heard me wandering around the house at night, searching for a distraction. Sometimes I'd have a bowl of cereal or an ice cream bar at midnight, or I'd go outside for a cigarette. That was another habit I needed to quit. I hated the way Renee's nose scrunched up in disgust when I got too close to her after having a smoke. Before turning off the radio and my lamp, I wrote myself a note and set it on my nightstand. Tomorrow I would call the doctor's office about getting nicotine gum or patches.

"Baby steps are better than no steps at all, right, Mom?" I talked to the ceiling.

The crazy thing was some part of me heard an answer. "Yes, sweetheart. Keep your chin up." Water clouded my vision. I blinked it away and set the alarm on my phone.

No matter how old you are, I mused, you never stop needing your mom to reassure you, even if it's only the echo of her voice in your subconscious.

Chapter Two

No one should have to work as a hotel maid when they're in their fifties. By the second hour of the workday my back always screamed, and by the end of the day—which was never more than six hours in the winter—my entire body ached. Of course, I wasn't in the best physical shape, but I was trim for my age, and despite my smoking habit could make it up a flight of stairs without running out of breath. Still, the work was hard.

Most of my coworkers spoke English as a second language. They were nice ladies who worked harder than most men, in my opinion, but other than being on the same career trajectory, we didn't have much in common. But there was one lady, Janice, who'd become a friend, of sorts.

Janice sighed audibly when we opened the door to Room 204. "Looks like someone partied a little too hard." She looked at me and laughed. "Thank God for rubber gloves, right?"

I scrunched my nose. The room was a disaster. Half-empty fast food containers littered the floor, remnants of cosmetics and spilled drinks streaked the bathroom counter, and a sour, putrid smell wafted from the bathroom. The bed sheets hung half off the bed, and the aroma of the room told me even the abundance of bleach we used in the laundry probably wouldn't erase the stains they held.

"Do we have any face masks?" I zigzagged to the window, weaving my way around the garbage on the floor. Pulling the heavy maroon drapes to the side, I opened the window. Cool, fresh air floated into the room, along with the diffused light of a cloudy day.

Janice giggled. "I'm sure we do somewhere. But we'll be out of here before you can say 'melodious maids made merry in the messy maniac menagerie' seven times."

I put on my gloves and pulled at the sheets, trying not to think about what had caused them to become so disheveled. "I couldn't say that once without hurting my head. I'll strip down the bed if you look for any leftover personal belongings."

"Deal, but if the personal belonging makes me gag, you get bathroom duty." Janice zipped from floor to surface to floor, scooping garbage into a plastic bag. "Gross."

I dumped bedding into the dirty linen bag on the cart and pulled out fresh sheets from a side cubby. "Leftover personal item?" I tittered, guessing at what it might be.

"Not one they would want back." Janice lifted one dark eyebrow and tied the plastic bag. "Melodious maids made merry," she sang off key as she shuffled toward the bathroom.

"In the messy maniac menagerie." I sang the rest of the tongue twister and tucked in the corners of the bottom sheets.

Janice stopped and swung around, her hand on her ample hip. Small beads of perspiration shone on her round, weathered face. "You have a beautiful voice. You should sing more often." Her dark brown eyes twinkled, and I wasn't sure if she was teasing me or if the compliment was sincere.

I used to sing. Often. In another life. These days I usually only sang for Renee and in the car when I was alone.

"If the hotel paid me more, I'd be the most melodious maid you ever heard." I took the window cleaner off the cart and grabbed a clean towel.

Janice laughed. "Well don't hold your breath on that one. But honestly, you have a unique but beautiful sound, and singing makes work merry." Janice happy-feeted her way back to the cart. "That bathroom is going to require extra bleach."

I nodded. I'd expected nothing less. It was amazing our

navy uniforms didn't end up completely spotted with bleach stains. "Lucky me, you didn't gag when you found that personal item." I'd never once seen Janice gag, and we'd found some disgusting things working together. Given the fact that the rooms at the Day and Night Inn weren't the cheapest in the Eugene and Springfield area, I would've expected the guests to have more class.

"We still have six more rooms to clean, and I say you get the next four bathrooms to make up for this one," Janice spoke over the light hum of the bathroom fan.

I didn't argue. My luck always did have a way of running itself out.

My drive home from work used to be a time of relaxing enjoyment as I smoked a cigarette. Now, it was another challenge for me to figure out some other way to unwind. The doctor had been quick to prescribe the nicotine patches for me, and I'd started them before I could change my mind. Now, four days later, I wondered what I'd done to myself.

I pulled into the Quick-Shop-N-Go parking lot. Inhaled. One, two, three. Exhaled. The creaking of the Buick's door as I slowly got out could have also been the creaking of my joints.

When I entered the store, my eyes zeroed in on the beer case: Keystone, Miller, Bud Light, and so many more filled the case from top to bottom. Thankfully, the aisle with gum was nowhere near it. I grabbed three packs of Trident, a box of Red Vines, and some Sweet Tarts and scurried to the counter. The Marlboro sign behind the clerk beckoned me. One more pack of cigarettes wouldn't hurt, would it? Ease my way out of the cycle. Hadn't I jumped off enough bridges?

"Will that be all?" the young clerk asked, barely making eye contact.

I hesitated, shifted my gaze. The beer case shone like a warning in the security mirror to the side of the register. I thought of Renee's crinkled up nose and of Cassie and her disapproving glances when I went outside to smoke. "Yeah," I sighed, "that'll be it."

A strange mixture of disappointment and triumph filled me as I got back in the car. I focused on the positive. Today was a short day and I could pick Renee up early from the afterschool program. That was the nice thing about my schedule in the winter—fewer travelers equaled less rooms to clean. It also meant less of a paycheck, but hopefully I'd make up for it with longer hours this summer. The bad news was I had forty-five minutes to kill before I could pick up Renee. Schools were so regimented these days that without a signed form from Cassie or clearance from the Secret Service, trying to pick Renee up directly from school when it wasn't part of her normal schedule was like applying for a job with NASA.

I opened the box of Red Vines and drove. I messed with the radio dial until it landed on an oldies station that was playing Credence Clearwater's "Bad Moon Rising." It was amazing I could actually listen to songs from that album now and not break down in tears or run for a drink. Credence Clearwater Revival's *Green River* album had been Steven's go-to when he was in his shop working on his stock car.

The song swept me back in time, and I could see Steven's feet tapping together as he lay underneath his beloved modified 1969 GTO as it sat on car ramps. I could hear his low voice singing along with Fogerty. And that's why I loved him. He hadn't been like most other guys my age. He loved old music and old cars and collected antique lanterns like they contained magic. He had a bit of danger about him with his love of racing and his non-parent-approved music choices, but he was nothing but good and true down to his core.

The last bite of Red Vine stuck in my throat and "Bad Moon Rising" came to an end. "At Last" by Etta James started playing, and I switched the dial. The memories were bearable now, but certain ones were too painful to relive. Too much was lost.

Another twenty minutes to kill. I opened a package of gum and turned right. Dollar Tree was my friend. For half an hour of wages, I could spend the next thirty minutes filling a small basket with treasures.

The parking lot by the cafeteria of Sky View Elementary School was nearly empty when I arrived. I parked and made my way to the purple cafeteria doors. The cacophony of dozens of youthful voices poured out of the cafeteria when I opened the door. I checked in with a young man at a table, then waited while one of the teenage helpers fetched Renee. The structured program was quite different than the home daycare Renee had been in before starting school. It'd been tough for both Cassie and Renee to pull her out of the daycare, but it was in a different school district than Sky View, so there was no way of getting Renee there on school days. A small—and guilt-laden—part of me was relieved. Bonnie, the lady who ran the other daycare, had developed a close relationship with both Cassie and Renee. A relationship I should have had with them. I had enough stacked against me without competing with some angel from on high. Granted, the sweet and wise woman had been a godsend right when Cassie and Renee needed her most.

I kicked my toe against the gym floor. What kind of person was I, grateful for someone like that *not* being in my granddaughter's life?

Sometimes I wondered if there was any hope for me at all.

"Grammy!" Renee's squeal pulled me out of my self-loathing. Her arms reached upward, ready for a hug. I picked her up and breathed in. My sweet granddaughter. Innocence and hope. Like a tiny ember left in a pile of ashes, I let her light push away the darkness that threatened to sink into the progress I had made.

"Ready to go home?" Such a wondrous, magical word. Home.

Renee nodded enthusiastically. I led her out to the car, where a few cheap toys from Dollar Store waited for her. Cassie would playfully scold me later tonight for wasting my money on junk. What she didn't understand was that junk was saving my soul.

Baby steps were better than no steps.

Chapter Three

"Are you working this Sunday?"

Cassie's question caught me off guard. I mentally counted off the weeks. Nearly four of them since I sent in my DNA kit. One third of the wait done. My heart quickened with the thought. I kept my eyes on Renee's shirt as I folded it.

"Mom?" Cassie had crossed the small living room and stood next to me.

I cleared my throat. "Sorry, honey. I was daydreaming." I shifted my gaze to my daughter. "Nope. I have this Sunday off." I tried to sound cheerful about it, but I knew where this conversation was going.

"Great!" Cassie plopped down on the sofa, grabbed a pair of pants, and folded them. She always had to stay busy. Something we had in common, but for different reasons. "Do you want to go to church with Renee and me? I like this one so far. They have a good worship band that I think you'd enjoy. It kind of has a rock and roll sound. And the pastor isn't long-winded. He's even kind of funny. And there's three services every Sunday, so we could go early or closer to lunch. And—"

"Cassie—yes, I'll go." I laughed. "You don't need to sell me on the idea. If you want me to go, I'll go." I pulled the last garment out of the laundry basket, a t-shirt that Renee picked out for me for Christmas during a trip to Goodwill. The shirt was light blue with a silhouette picture of Ariel, the Little Mermaid, on the front. "Because it reminded me of you, Grammy," she'd declared, glowing with joyful self-assurance. I wasn't sure what I had in common with a red-headed mermaid, but the gift warmed my heart.

"I'm so glad." Cassie leaned back with a loud sigh. "If you like it, then I think I've finally found a church to call home."

I chuckled. "No pressure, right?" Then the feeling came. The one I couldn't shake. The room shrank a little. I inhaled. One. Two. Three. Exhaled. I'd quit drinking. I'd quit smoking and would soon begin weaning myself off the patches. I wasn't sure I was ready for another change, another commitment.

Cassie seemed to sense my unease and sat up. She put her hand on mine, which I now realized was gripping the laundry basket like it would keep me from sinking. Her hands were soft. Mine were rough, calloused—the side effect of folding overly bleached towels and sheets when I worked in the laundry room at the hotel.

"You don't have to, but I would love if on your Sundays off we went to church together. I know that's what Nannie would want too."

My heart pinched. I let loose of the laundry basket and gave Cassie's hand a quick squeeze. "It's not that I don't *want* to go to church, baby girl." I looked away, searching for the words to explain. It'd been nearly twenty-eight years since I called a church my own. Something broke between God and me on the night Steven died, and the bridge of my devotion to Him was now held together by the tired remnants of my childhood faith. A faith that was planted by the parents I adored. By the mother who held a secret until her dying days.

"I understand." Cassie's tone held love and reassurance. It was like she was the mother and I was the child. "I've been in the same place you are."

I knew she was talking about the terrorizing months when she fled her abusive marriage and fought for custody of Renee. Of how she'd believed God had left her high and dry. But everything had worked out for Cassie. Derrick's alcoholism and abusive behavior had landed him in jail, and Cassie had been awarded sole custody of Renee. As terrible as her experience had been, it was different than mine. I'd let her believe she understood where I was coming from, what ate at me. That's what a mother does, hides her pain. Sometimes so deeply she forgets it's even there.

I squeezed Cassie's soft hand again. "I'm sure if you like this church, I will too." And I would keep going even if I didn't like it, for Cassie and Renee.

Renee was excited about church Sunday morning, and I soon understood why. Donuts. The church building was large and modern with a big, bright foyer full of people. A long table of treats sat to the left of the entry: coffee, hot water for tea, and platters upon platters of pastries, including full-sized donuts. No miniature donuts or donut holes at this church—they went all out. *Go big or go home.* I'd take home, thank you. I laughed at my own silent joke. Renee made a beeline to the pastry table and I followed her while Cassie chit-chatted with the greeter.

"Here, Sweet Pea, let me help you." I grabbed two paper plates and noted that they were thick and sturdy. "What kind do you want?"

Renee studied the table with a furrowed brow, tapping her chin in deep thought. Then she lifted her face up to me with arched eyebrows. "Can I have two?"

I twisted my lips to keep from smiling. "What would your mom say?"

My granddaughter's shoulders slumped. "She only lets me have one."

"Then let's keep it that way." I winked. "But I'll give you a bite of mine." I set a maple donut on one plate. "These are my favorite."

Renee's eyes lit up. "Mine too! But I like the chocolate ones too. And the twists. Oh, and the ones with jelly in them."

I belted out a laugh, but then heard someone clear their throat behind me. A man in a button-down shirt and his young daughter were behind us, waiting their turn. "Let's get you a chocolate donut." I picked out a donut and set it on the second plate, then handed it to Renee.

"Thank you, Grammy."

With my hand on Renee's shoulder, I guided her away from the table just as Cassie approached.

"I see you found the donuts." She put her hand on her hip, giving Renee a mock scowl. "I'm surprised you didn't talk your grandma into letting you take two."

Renee gave her mom a sheepish grin, then took a big bite of the donut. I squeezed her shoulder. "You'd never even think of doing such a thing, would you, Sweet Pea?"

I met Cassie's gaze. We exchanged a knowing, good-humored look. I loved these moments. Times like these made it feel like life could be good, normal, as if I had always been there. Like the days before us were a blank slate on which we would write new experiences, new memories. Good ones.

"Cassie! I'm so glad to see you." A petite blonde woman materialized from the crowd and gave Cassie a quick side hug. "And how are you doing this morning, Renee?" The woman's focus went down three feet to Renee, whose cheeks were full of pastry.

Renee glanced at her mom and then bobbed her head. "Good," she mumbled around the pastry.

The woman then pivoted toward me. "And who is this?" She smiled with bright white teeth. The makeup around her eyes accentuated the creases in them, confessing her age.

"Oh, this is my mom, Sharon." Cassie motioned toward the woman. "Mom, this is Evie. She's the associate pastor's wife."

The look on my daughter's face reminded me of when she was little and had done something she was particularly proud of, like cleaned her room without being asked. I held out my hand. "Nice to meet you."

Evie's smile dropped a tad, but she quickly held out her hand, like she'd been jumpstarted. "Nice to meet you, Sharon. I know Cassie was hoping you'd have a Sunday off and be able to attend."

Something in me rankled at Evie's delayed reaction. Was my Little Mermaid t-shirt not good enough for this church? It was definitely a stark contrast to Evie's attire. With her cream-toned blazer over fitted black slacks and high-heeled pumps, she could have been going to work instead of church. "I'm glad I could make it." I forced a smile I didn't feel.

"I hope you enjoy the service." Evie beamed. "I think you'll like Pastor Dean's teaching. He always brings the Word to life in interesting and unique ways."

"I'm sure it'll be great." I hoped my tone sounded more enthusiastic than I felt.

Evie's attention was drawn to a group at her left. She held up her arm to someone in the crowd and waved them over. "Samantha!"

A woman about my age dressed in a long floral skirt and white cardigan walked toward us. Her sleek dark hair and nearly flawless olive skin seemed familiar. She approached us with smooth, confident strides. "Evie, how are you?"

"I'm doing well." Evie embraced the woman. No side hug for her.

Why did the sound of her voice make my heart skip a beat?

Evie directed her attention toward us. "This is Samantha. She's our women's ministry leader."

Samantha. My stomach stirred and my pulse quickened in response. Why did that name raise an alarm?

Starting with Cassie, Evie made her way through introductions, winding down to me. "And this is Cassie's mother." Evie tilted her head. "Sharon, correct?"

I held out my hand to Samantha and our eyes met. In that millisecond, recognition lit her eyes and raised the hairs on the back of my neck. Samantha pulled back her hand so quickly it was like she'd been shocked by a light socket.

No, no, no.

"You...what are *you* doing *here*?" Women's ministry leader or not, she held back none of the disdain in her voice.

Evie's mouth dropped open and her eyes fluttered as she looked back and forth between Samantha and me. "You know each other? Maybe we can go over—"

"Oh, yes, we *know* each other, don't we, Sharon?" Samantha had regained her composure to a certain extent and pasted a fake, cold smile on her face. Her eyes spoke her real feelings. They were full of a simmering fire that had been fanned to flames. Fanned by the face of someone from her past. The face of her enemy.

By the woman who had unwittingly slept with her husband, nearly twenty-six years ago.

Chapter Four

We drove home in silence.

I couldn't recall one song the worship team had played during service, or what the pastor preached about. The only thing I remembered about Cascade Christian Church was that my past caught up with me. With Renee in the back seat, I knew Cassie wouldn't ask too many questions as she drove us home, but I hadn't expected complete silence. My heart sank to my stomach. I didn't know what was going through my daughter's head, but if she asked questions and I answered them truthfully, she might never talk to me again.

One way or the other, Cassie was going to hear the truth. Better to hear it from me than from Samantha. At least then she'd hear my side of the soap-opera-like story.

Lunch was waiting in the Crock-Pot when we walked in the door of our duplex. I spooned bowls of steaming chili out for the three of us, adding a small ice cube to Renee's to cool it. Cassie set out the Fritos and sour cream. Renee chattered endlessly about the puppet skit at the kids' church. Cassie and I nodded appropriately in response and oohed and ahhed as if it were the most fascinating thing we'd ever heard. I managed to eat maybe three bites of chili. My stomach wouldn't stop burning. Cassie didn't eat much, either. I put the remains of lunch away while Cassie led Renee into her room for a nap. Sunday siesta. That's what my mom always called it.

Cassie returned from putting Renee in bed. "What was that all about, Mom?"

I switched the sink faucet off, the Crock-Pot now full of soapy bubbles. Bubbles that would disappear as the water cooled. Bubbles that would be completely gone if given enough time. But the soap in the water would remain. Turning to Cassie, I motioned toward the kitchen table. "Let's sit down and talk about that."

Cassie sighed and shot darts at me with her eyes. This was not going to end well, but it had to be done. Half-truths did no one any good. I could testify to that. If Mom were here, she'd say the same thing, though she'd be speaking in hindsight. We each took a seat at opposite ends of the small table. I brushed some Frito crumbs away.

"Simply put, Samantha hates me, and she has every right to. I had no idea whatsoever that she went to your church. I didn't even know she was a Christian. Of course, I guess a lot can change in twenty-six years."

"But why does she hate you? What happened between the two of you? She looked ready to kill you, and she's the women's ministry leader. I mean, it must be horrible?" Cassie's voice cracked.

I swallowed and averted my gaze to the table. I couldn't look Cassie in the eyes and tell her this story. I didn't want to see what it did to her.

"It was about a year after your dad died. I was pretty new to the drinking life at that point, I mean compared to later." I ventured a glance at Cassie. Her arms were now folded across her chest. Great. But what else could I expect when I talked about my drinking and the past? "One night I got a little more drunk than usual. I met a guy. I went home with him. I barely remember the details, but I do remember waking up the next morning with someone I didn't know. I felt sick and ran to the bathroom. He didn't stir out of the bed. I was so filled with shame I threw on my clothes and left. The problem was I left my wallet. I didn't even realize I didn't have it until later that afternoon when I went to the store, and at that point I could have left it anywhere. You were with me, but you were only four, so thankfully you don't remember any of this."

"What does any of this have to do with Samantha?" The irritation in Cassie's voice was unmistakable.

The room was getting warmer. I inhaled. One. Two. It was no use. I had to get this over with. "When we got back to our house, Samantha was waiting there. I didn't know who she was. I think we would have ended up in a cat fight though if you hadn't been there. When she saw you, she stepped back a little."

I bit down on my lip, remembering Cassie's young face when the angry woman approached me, yelling obscenities. Confusion and fear mixed with sadness. "Samantha had found my wallet in the guest bedroom of her home...the home she shared with her husband."

Silence. A car drove by. A squirrel ran across the branch of a tree in the backyard. My heart beat so hard in my chest, I thought my ribcage would break. I hung my head, unable to look Cassie in the eyes.

"You slept with her husband?" Cassie whispered like it was still a secret. Or too shameful to say out loud.

Nodding, I braved a look up. Horror filled Cassie's features. Her arms were no longer crossed. Her hands gripped the edge of the table as she leaned toward me. "You slept with the man who is married to the women's ministry director?"

I shrugged. "Sweetie, I seriously don't think they were church attenders then. I didn't know he was married. Not until Samantha showed up and told me who she was and why she was at my house." Acid rose into my esophagus. I was the most despicable person in the world, no matter how you sliced it.

"This has to be some kind of joke." Cassie dropped her head in her hands and rubbed her temples.

"I'm sorry, Cassie." What else could I say? Trying to explain myself was pointless. Nothing I did then was rational. It was one bad choice after another to escape the pain, until I'd created a mess beyond fixing. Sleeping with Dylan, Samantha's husband, had been the culmination of my stupid way of dealing with the emptiness inside me. Once Samantha made me realize I wasn't only promiscuous but also a homewrecker, I thought I'd sunk as low as a person could go. I'd been wrong. Being a promiscuous homewrecker had been only the beginning of my self-destructive path.

Cassie pushed her chair away from the table and stood. "I thought I'd finally found a church for us." Her voice broke, hinting at the emotion she was struggling to keep at bay. "But how can I go back now?"

I shook my head. "I don't know. I mean, maybe—"

"Maybe what, Mom?" Cassie's voice rose. Tears streamed down her reddened face. "There is no maybe. I could never go back there. I'm trying so hard to build a new life for Renee and me, and even for you. But it's one thing after another. I thought since Derrick was out of the picture, I'd have a fighting chance, but no." Cassie squinted her eyes into angry slants. "You managed to ruin it. Will I ever stop paying for *your* mistakes?"

Blood rushed to my head, causing it to instantly ache. The room got smaller, darker, hotter. I forced myself up, standing on quaking knees. Words I wanted to shout swirled in my mind.

You have no idea what I've been through.

I never intended to hurt you.

I'm fighting this battle inside with every ounce of my being.

Instead, I shouted, "Don't you dare talk to me in that way! That's no way to speak to your mother."

Cassie's eyes darkened. "You're..." She cut herself short and looked away.

She didn't have to finish her sentence. I knew the rest of what her heart wanted to scream.

I was no mother.

My skin burned over the aching of my chest, over the barrenness of my soul. An itching deep within me rose to the surface. I walked past Cassie to my room. I grabbed my purse and without looking back, I walked out the door.

I drove straight to the Quick-Shop-N-Go down the street and marched in and bought a pack of Marlboro 100s and a new lighter. I'd stupidly thrown away all my lighters, thinking I could actually kick this bad habit on top of quitting drinking. Guilt nipped at me as the smoke filled my lungs, but the soothing from the shot of nicotine far outweighed the negative. Cassie had been ecstatic about my quitting my smoking habit. Would the smell of cigarettes on me give her even more reason to be angry? I cracked my window, letting the cool February air chase the smoke out so I didn't end up smelling like an ashtray.

Why did I agree to go to church? My gut told me it was too much, too fast. Of course, my gut had nothing to do with Samantha being there, but if I'd listened to it anyway, Cassie wouldn't hate me right now. She'd still have a church, and I'd still have the small amount of dignity I'd regained in her eyes. Now it was gone, swirling away like the smoke escaping out my cracked window.

I drove the main streets of Springfield, then over the river into Eugene. The streets had changed since the last time I'd lived in the area. Fifteen years earlier I'd tried living near my family. Cassie was a teenager and I figured it was my last chance to make a home for her. But I'd gone about it all wrong. I worked in a nightclub. Drank despite my attempts to quit. Let myself fall in love with a guy who broke my heart. I shook my head at the memory. It wasn't long after my relationship with Johnny ended that I gave up on my attempt at rebuilding my life with my family.

A sign caught my attention, and I pulled into a small parking lot. Quite a few cars filled the spaces even though it was a Sunday afternoon. A day for church, for family.

For drinking.

The sign read "The Busted Bottle," next to a lighted picture of a beer bottle with a red crack going through its amber glass like a lightning bolt. I laughed at the irony, at the name. I'd never been here, but it sounded like it was made for me. I shut off the engine and sucked in the last drags of my cigarette. The double door of the tavern beckoned me. I didn't have to be anything to anyone inside those doors. The cigarette had calmed the crawling of my skin, settled my emotional shaking into something more like a small, nervous tremor. One drink could take me down another notch.

You're no mother.

Words not spoken with the mouth but seen in my daughter's eyes. I wiped away the tears that wouldn't stop streaming down my face. I couldn't escape my past. Worse yet, my daughter was still suffering from my mistakes. The years upon years of drinking, too caught up in my own pain to be a mom, leaving my parents no choice but to take her from me when she was nine years old. It didn't take a psych degree to know the hurt I caused Cassie made her end up in an abusive marriage, one that ended in a bitter, frightening divorce.

I was trying to make amends, fighting to stay sober. Now, instead of helping me, God seemed to be throwing everything in my face. What was the point in even fighting anymore?

I pulled my keys out of the ignition and reached for my purse. I shifted the rearview mirror so I could see my face and wipe away the mascara that was probably all over my cheeks by now. I shifted and glanced up, but I'd angled the mirror too low and it was reflecting my chest, not my face. Instead of smeared mascara and fine lines I saw the shirt I was wearing. The mermaid shirt Renee had given me for Christmas.

My throat ached, and I ran my hand over the mermaid's silhouette. *Because it reminded me of you, Grammy.* Me, a mermaid. That was funny, but I didn't laugh. I sighed and set the mirror at its proper angle. I didn't know much about mermaids, but I was pretty sure they didn't go to bars. I rested my head against the seat of my old Buick. I would never win mother of the year, but I still had a fighting chance of being a decent grandma.

Chapter Five

HEADING BACK HOME DIDN'T SEEM LIKE the best idea. Cassie needed time to cool down, and I hoped to allow the cigarette smoke to dissipate and maybe find some inspiration of what I could say or do to make things right. I had nowhere to go, but driving up and down streets that might boast more neon signs was definitely not an option. I found an on-ramp to the interstate and headed south.

I didn't think about where I was going. Even after all these years the drive came automatically to me, like my body had memorized where to turn and when. The closer I got to Cottage Grove, the more my chest ached. But it was an ache I could handle. An old pain, a broken heart yearning for home. Looking for answers that probably couldn't be found this side of heaven.

I took the first Cottage Grove exit and hung a right, drove over the little bridge, then right again. Another right took me to a narrow, tree-lined road that went under a railroad bridge. The road ended at a field and then a parking lot for the Cottage Grove Speedway.

The large chain link gate to access the track was locked to prevent entry by vehicles, but the opening was large enough for me to squeeze through. On the other side of the catch fence, the clay quarter-mile track lay before me. I made my way to the bleachers, breathing in the aroma of the track—the earthiness of the dirt mixed with the sweet and chemical tang of engine oil and gasoline. I found a seat near the top of the stands and closed my eyes. For some reason, smells carried me back in time more vividly than sights or sounds. Alone now, I didn't try to stop the tears from falling.

I rubbed them away from my eyes, forcing myself to take

in my surroundings. I hadn't been here in eons. After Steven died, I hated this track. I hated anything to do with racing, and that bitterness overflowed to the friends we shared who had participated in the sport. I burned bridges faster than a lightning-ignited forest during a drought. In one fateful night my entire life was snatched from me. Everything except Cassie. Then again, if I hadn't been home with her that evening, maybe the tragedy would have been avoided...or if I had been a better wife the night before the race.

I shivered away the thought. No. I couldn't think about that. Those thoughts would take me back to the Broken Bottle bar and I wouldn't be able to stop myself from the solace the double doors promised.

I scanned the racetrack and the bleachers I sat on. Not much had changed in the last thirty years. It was still a small, hometown kind of dirt racetrack, waiting for hot summer nights.

If the races started in spring like they used to, then soon these stands would be full of race fans. The open space to my left—the pits— would be lined by trailers, cars, and their crews. The roar of the engines would fill the air, red dirt would fly, and the crowd would cheer on their favorite racer. The smell of hot dogs and greasy fries would waft from the snack bar through the stands. In between races people would fill the stairs, beelining their way to food and restrooms.

What would Steven tell me to say to Cassie? The thought landed on me unexpectedly, like a ladybug on a warm June day. I laughed out loud. When was the last time I'd even posed that thought—what would Steven do? After my downward spiral, I was so far from deserving anything my loving husband would have said or done, I never let myself think about it.

I'd read in a magazine about a woman who did online

shopping while on Ambien, the sleep medication. She said each day when the UPS driver arrived, she didn't know what she was going to get. It wasn't like Christmas, though, because she had paid for whatever was wrapped in those brown cardboard boxes. My sobriety was a lot like that. The further along I got, the more packages from the past surfaced in my memory. Some good, many bad, and a few bittersweet. And I'd paid the price for all of them.

I stared at the rich green trees that banked the Coast Fork of the Willamette River on the opposite side of the track. I inhaled. One. Two. Three. Exhaled. I could do this. I had to do this.

What would Steven say? My bottom lip quivered. I closed my eyes and imagined him sitting beside me on the bleacher. Imagined the crowd around us, a blur of noise in the background. A warm summer night filled with anticipation. Steven's lean, muscular arm around me, holding me close, keeping me safe, protected. Steven whispering in my ear.

"She's not going to stop loving you just because you ticked her off."

It was almost too real. Steven's voice was straight from my memory, but the words were new. "She'll calm down once she has time to think about it. Our girl's been through hell...all that stuff with her ex-husband and the way he treated her."

I nodded to myself, to the imaginary Steven. Cassie's marriage and divorce were full of pain. She'd fought hard for herself and Renee. She came through it like a champion, even if she didn't see it that way. If only I had been as strong all those years ago.

"I've messed up so bad, I'm afraid there's no coming back from it." My voice sounded loud, reminding me that I was alone and the stands were empty. I shivered and wrapped my arms around myself.

"How long has it been since you've been to a meeting?" Steven's voice again, but the magic of the moment was gone.

I sighed, knowing the answer. Too long. For some reason, ever since I sent in the DNA test, I hadn't managed to go to an AA meeting. I'd been gung-ho on AA meetings when I made the decision to quit. I did the thirty meetings in thirty days. I'd read the *How It Works* book. The meetings were a lifesaver, though I took some issue with their open-ended *higher power* philosophy. I found a temporary sponsor to hold me accountable. I made amends with my mom, and, to some extent, with my daughter. Then Derrick took Renee and we didn't know where she was. And I found out Mom was deathly ill. It was too much. I fell off the wagon and down into the hole of darkness. But I clawed my way out, went back to my meetings in Florence. Found my sponsor and got some accountability. Even when Mom called and told me about the secret she'd kept all these years, I stayed the course. Not one drink. I knew deep down that if I failed again, it would be the end of any chance I had at a relationship with my daughter and granddaughter.

I couldn't let the fallout from a former ill deed let me fail. I needed to start going to meetings again. I stood and took in the view of the track one last time. So many good memories forever marred by one terrible, tragic one.

Back in my car, I used my phone to look up AA meetings. After moving in with Cassie in the fall, I'd found a group in Springfield to attend, but they met on Tuesday nights. I needed something *today*. I searched through the list Google provided for me and found a meeting that started in an hour in Eugene.

I drove back toward Eugene, debating with myself whether I should call Cassie or not. I didn't want to worry her, but I also wanted to give her space. When I arrived at the church where the AA meeting would be held, I had my mind made up.

"Hello?" Cassie answered on the first ring.

"Hey, baby girl, I'm calling to let you know I'll be home in a couple of hours."

"Oh. Where are you?"

I sighed, thankful she hadn't asked where I'd been, only where I was. "I'm at a church in Eugene. There's an AA meeting starting in about half an hour."

"I thought you went to the one in Springfield?"

Cassie hadn't asked much about the ins and outs of AA. That seemed to be a box she was afraid to open, probably for fear of what she'd find. "Usually I do. But it's been a while since I've gone. I have today off, so it makes sense to go." No need for too many details.

The line was silent for a moment. I imagined Cassie analyzing what I meant, turning it over in her mind, deciding if she needed to know more or not.

"Okay." Cassie's voice was soft, hesitant. "I'm sorry about earlier. I...overreacted."

I blinked. Was she only saying she was sorry because she was afraid I'd fallen—or would fall—off the wagon? "I'm sorry too." I sucked on my bottom lip, choosing my words carefully. "You shouldn't have to find out about the skeletons in my closet the way you did this morning."

"No, but that's all in the past. *Now* is what's important." Cassie's voice cracked. "That's what Nannie would say."

"You're right, baby girl. You're absolutely right."

The AA meeting was in the church basement. It was cool and a little damp, with worn-out carpet and a slight musty odor. Obviously not the best room in the place. While I poured myself a cup of coffee at the table in the hallway, I asked the person next to me if the rooms upstairs were reserved for the more prestigious groups, like Gamblers Anonymous. She didn't laugh at my joke. I took a seat in the semicircle of unpadded folding chairs and prayed that the rest of the group had a better sense of humor.

The leader, a middle-aged man with a receding hairline and thick glasses, read the AA preamble and then led the group in the serenity prayer before starting the introductions. This looked like it would be an unstructured discussion meeting, which was fine with me. Those types of meetings were usually dominated by the people who talked the most. I wasn't here, though, to tell my story. My solace came from hearing that I wasn't alone in my struggles.

One woman who spoke up had lost custody of her children and was attending meetings by court order. I said a silent prayer of thankfulness that Cassie had never been removed from my custody by the state. My parents had taken her when she was nine, but never kept me from seeing her as long as I was sober. A man spoke about how he relapsed and lost his job. He was now seven days sober. When I relapsed last summer, I hadn't been working, so I had no job to lose. As each person told their story for the day, I found another reason to be thankful. My heart softened, grew, and remembered how good sobriety had been to me.

Near the end of the hour, a man a few chairs over from me stood up. He had a couple days of stubble and dark circles under his eyes. He was dressed neatly in dark jeans and a button-up plaid shirt. "My name is Sam, and I'm an alcoholic."

"Hi, Sam." the group said in unison.

"I'm trying really hard to reestablish my relationship with my daughter."

Goose bumps prickled my arms as I nodded with the rest of the group.

"Her mom has sole custody because of the mistakes I've

made, but I'm jumping through all the hoops to see her again. I've been sober for five months now. I'm seeing a counselor too. I've arranged for four supervised visits so far, and those were good." Sam looked down at the green and brown carpet, shrugging. "Well, as good as can be expected anyway."

People in the room nodded silently, waiting for Sam to continue.

"It's hard, but I know it's worth the fight." Sam looked up with wet eyes, scanning the faces in the room. "I'm not going to give up."

I shivered and rubbed my arms. It sounded like this guy was in a similar boat as Derrick, Cassie's ex. When Derrick got out of jail, would he fight in the right way like Sam was? Or would he let his daughter slip away from him?

The way I always thought my father let me slip away.

The way Cassie thinks my father didn't fight and left without ever looking back.

If Derrick did the same, Cassie would think she had failed again—that she was perpetuating a family curse. But she didn't have the whole story.

I mindlessly joined the group in thanking Sam for sharing, but thankfulness was not exactly what filled my heart. It was a heavy hammer, ready to chip away yet another piece of the angelic-like image Cassie had of her grandmother.

Sooner or later, I would have to share the last bit of the family secret with my daughter. And after what happened today, sooner was the wisest option.

Chapter Six

DESPITE MY GOOD INTENTIONS, I'D YET to divulge the secret that nagged me, even though a full month had passed. There never seemed to be an opportune moment. My focus was on doing things to help. Deeds that kept my mind away from thoughts I couldn't bear. Simple things within my skill set, like making dinner.

The aroma of breaded chicken wafted from the oven, making my stomach growl in response, despite my edginess. I'd double coated chicken pieces in flour before frying them in an iron skillet. Once browned, I transferred them to the oven to finish. I'd followed my mom's recipe the best I remembered. Hopefully, the result was edible.

My CD player sat on the kitchen counter and the oldies station played an Aretha Franklin song. Cassie and Renee would be home any minute. I sang along to "Think" while I added a final dash of salt and pepper to the mashed potatoes. Singing and cooking were a more productive outlet for my nervous energy than shopping at Dollar Tree.

The front door swung open as I belted out a soulful "Freedom!" Renee ran in, all smiles and verve.

"Grammy, were you singing? I could hear it outside." Renee's eyes were wide with wonder.

I reached for the volume knob on the CD player, dialing it down several decibels. "Nah, that was Aretha Franklin singing, Sweet Pea."

Renee's eyebrows scrunched together. "But I thought I heard you."

Had I been singing that loud? If so, I surely couldn't have blended in with Aretha. I turned to the entryway where Cassie was hanging up her purse. She looked pale, and her shoulders were slumped forward. My mother hen radar told me something wasn't right. It'd been three weeks since the incident at church, and things between us had smoothed out enough that I didn't feel like I had to tiptoe around her.

I shifted my focus back to Renee. "Dinner's almost ready. How about you put your stuff away and wash your hands for dinner."

Renee puckered her mouth briefly, then ambled off and did as she was asked.

I approached Cassie before she headed to her room to change. "You look like you're carrying the whole world on your shoulders."

Cassie faced me, the fear in her eyes confirming my assumptions. "I need to tell you something. In private."

I nodded. "Renee's washing up."

Cassie motioned for me to come closer, then whispered, "I got the call today." Her voice cracked. "Derrick was released this afternoon."

Cassie's fear was palpable. I put my arm around her, desperate to chase the monsters away. "It's going to be okay." I hoped my words sounded more convincing than I felt. "He can't bother you anymore unless he wants to go straight back to jail."

"It's not me I'm worried about." Cassie bit her bottom lip and her brow knitted together. "What if he wants to see Renee? What if he tries to take her again?"

As if on cue, my granddaughter trotted into the living room. It took only a millisecond for her to pick up on her mom's distress. She stopped short, her face now a mirror of Cassie's angst. "Mommy, what's wrong?"

"Oh, nothing." Cassie forced a short laugh, but the tension in her shoulders remained.

I dropped my arm that encircled her, joining in on the charade. "Your mommy had a rough day." I paused, choosing my words carefully. "We all have bad days that make us cry sometimes. Remember a few weeks ago when that girl at school teased you because you kept missing the ball in P.E.?"

Renee nodded solemnly. "Someone was mean to Mommy?"

Yes, and his name is Daddy.

"No one was mean to me, honey," Cassie interceded. "It was a super busy day at work, and Mommy was overwhelmed. But now I'm home with my family, and dinner smells delicious."

I studied Cassie's profile. She was smiling with her mouth, but her eyes told a different story. Hopefully we could talk more later, after Renee went to bed. Though we'd already discussed safety measures to put into effect upon Derrick's release, the reality of the dreaded day being here was clearly weighing on my daughter. To be honest, it weighed on me too. How long would it be before Derrick found out I was now living with Cassie? Would he try using my presence against her and file something in court? He'd have a weak argument, but he didn't think like a rational person. How long would it be before he requested a supervised visit with Renee—and how would Renee respond to seeing her father again?

As I set the chicken and mashed potatoes on the table, one thing was clear—Cassie had enough problems for today. The burden I carried would have to wait to be shared.

Cassie looked beat when bedtime rolled around. After Renee was tucked in, I stood with Cassie in the living room and did my best to reassure her again. "We're safe here. *You're* safe."

Cassie nodded, but her eyes were hollow. "I guess I was kind of getting used to the peace and quiet. Now..." She crossed one arm across her middle, grabbing her elbow.

What should I say? All we could do was hope that Derrick had learned his lesson. But did men like him ever truly learn? I'd already urged Cassie to get a gun and a concealed carry permit, but she refused, saying she was afraid of it getting into Renee's hands. I thought about buying one myself, but Cassie's thoughts and concerns overflowed to me, making me afraid of what could happen. Besides, I was in no mental condition to carry a lethal weapon.

"We'll take it one day at a time." I rubbed Cassie's back.

"That's all we can do. And pray." Cassie's gaze met mine.

I averted my eyes and dropped my hand. What was she trying to say? "Yes, we can pray," I mumbled, ashamed of my lackluster response. It wasn't that I didn't believe prayer worked, but I couldn't pin my family's wellbeing on any prayer of mine.

The effective, fervent prayer of a righteous man avails much. One of Mom's favorite scriptures, one she cited often.

My prayers were heartfelt but ineloquent. What could the prayers of a wayward woman produce?

"Mom, we haven't talked about going back to church." Cassie hesitated, seeming to choose her words carefully.

I waved my hand. "Nah, don't worry about it. I work more Sundays than I have off anyway. You go where you want." I'd had one Sunday off since the incident with Samantha, and I'd begged out of going, claiming I had a headache.

"But I'd love for you to go with us when you can. Cascade is a big church with several services. Maybe we can find out which one Samantha *doesn't* go to. I mean, it's been great so far, but I don't want to leave you out. That would be...pointless."

I searched my daughter's blue eyes. What was she trying to say? Was she worried about my salvation? I laughed, though my irritation was rising. "Seriously, Cassie. I'm fine. I have my AA meetings. Those are kind of like church. You do what's best for you and Renee."

"But before, when Nannie was still alive, it seemed like you wanted to go to church. What's changed?"

What had changed? A little bit of the truth had surfaced. A little bit of me falling off the wagon. A little bit of me realizing I may never truly break the grip addiction had on me. I inhaled. One. Two. Three. A voice in my head screamed, *Tell her! The door is open!* I exhaled. Opened my mouth. Shut it.

Why was this so hard to say? It wasn't even that big of a deal. Simply a slight change in what she already knew.

"Cassie, here's the thing—"

"Mommy, can I have a drink of water?" Renee's voice reverberated down the hall, knocking out the miniscule amount of courage that had risen in me.

"Just a minute, sweetie," Cassie called over her shoulder, then turned back to me. "I'll be right back."

Relief flowed over me. The opportunity had passed. The truth could wait.

Don't put off until tomorrow what can be accomplished today.

Mom's voice again, soft yet reprimanding. Both she and Dad were the proactive type, responsible and sensible. But me? I took procrastination to an art form. Even in kindergarten I was the last one to obey the bell at the end of recess, the last one to finish my morning work page. Mom said I was stubborn, but Dad called me strong-willed.

Whatever you called it, maybe it was a trait I had inherited from my father. I swallowed the lump of dread in my throat.

Cassie returned to the living room. "So, what was it you were starting to say?"

I closed my eyes and pinched the bridge of my nose. The time was now.

"Let's sit down. This might take some time." I lowered myself to the couch, and the blood in my body seemed to pool at my feet. I inhaled. It was only the difference between dark and milk chocolate. One was only a little sweeter than the other.

And one could be bitter.

Cassie took a seat beside me, her brow now wrinkled. "I'm listening," she whispered.

I cleared my throat and nodded. Someday, when I looked back on this day, would I see it as the "Day of Confession," or the "Day of Disaster?" Only time could tell.

"Nannie didn't tell us the entire truth about the music box."

Chapter Seven

"WHAT DO YOU MEAN?" CASSIE LEANED forward, a hint of panic in her eyes.

I exhaled. For better or worse, my secret spilled out between us. Dark and widening.

"There's more to the story than she told us. The basics haven't changed. The music box was a gift from my biological father, something that had belonged to his deceased mother. He and Nannie *did* have a love affair. He *did* leave after she found out she was pregnant, and she never saw or heard from him again. Then Grandpa came back from college and married her. Those things remain the same."

Cassie shook her head. "I don't understand. What else is there to know?"

Poor Cassie. It was less than a year ago she learned the story behind the music box my mom kept in her room, less than a year ago she learned the grandpa she had loved and admired wasn't biologically related to her. Now this. Better to get the ugly truth out than beat around the bush. "My father...Michael...didn't know Nannie was pregnant. She never told him."

"So she didn't know she was pregnant until after he left?"

My fingers dug into the edge of the couch. Nerves. But also something else—an emotion I didn't want to admit.

"No. She knew. The night she went to tell him, he was drunk. Belligerent. Instead of telling him she was pregnant, she broke up with him."

Cassie sat up straight, her mouth pinched. "But that doesn't make sense. Why did she lie about that part?" Cassie paused. "Wait...did you know about this all along?"

I shook my head, my shoulders heavy. "I knew the same version as you, up until a couple of weeks before Nannie passed. She confessed to me on the phone." My throat constricted at the memory. "I think she knew her time was drawing near."

"Which version did Grandpa know?" Cassie's face had paled, and she bit down on her lower lip. The fairytale was slipping out of her grasp.

The heaviness on my shoulders grew. Sharing it with my daughter wasn't what I wanted, but deceit was worse. I could testify to that. "She told him what she had told us. I think that's one of the reasons the lie persisted." I sighed, imagining the scene in my head. My mom pregnant and alone, having sent the father of her child away. Then the man she'd loved for years, the one who had always been there for her, returned. He was her only hope of a good future, both for herself and for me. Desperate to take some of the shame away from her situation, to make herself look more like a victim than a person who had make a mistake, she twisted the truth a tiny bit. She had no choice. The wolf was at her door. "She had her reasons, Cassie."

"Reasons to lie?" Cassie's voice cracked. "To lie to Grandpa of all people?"

"You know Nannie was raised by her aunt."

Cassie held up her hands. "So, what does that have to do with anything?"

"Do you know why she lived with her aunt?"

Cassie's hands dropped, and she shrugged, her brows knitted together. "Because her parents hit hard times and sent her there."

"The reason her parents—my grandparents—hit hard times was because their drinking had left them without a home."

Cassie rubbed her temples. My stomach hurt, realizing

how much my daughter was getting hit with today. Her abusive ex-husband's release from prison. More family secrets to tarnish the golden memories of her beloved Nannie. The knowledge that alcohol was the demon of her family tree, coming at her from both sides.

"Nannie didn't want to marry a man who might be an alcoholic. To have her child raised by an alcoholic father. In her eyes, it would have been better to face the world alone."

Quiet filled the air between Cassie and me and grew around us. I could hear my heart beating in my ears, fast and hard. The refrigerator hummed. Cassie shifted in her seat. She looked up, lines etched across her brow.

"I hate this." She frowned. "Why did Nannie wait so long to tell you? Now she's gone, and I can't make what you're telling me line up with the grandma I knew." Cassie looked up at the ceiling and exhaled, then turned her focus to me. Her eyes searched my face, and revelation flickered in her eyes. "You grew up believing your biological father wanted nothing to do with you, abandoned you. But he never even knew you existed."

Chills ran down my arms. I nodded, swallowing down the unwanted emotion rising from my stomach. "Yes, that's true. But I had Grandpa."

"Why did Nannie even tell you anything? All the secrets could have died with her. It's like she left us with a ghost."

"I've already told you." It was one of the first questions Cassie had asked me after my mom passed and we started talking again. Why reveal a painful secret at all? When I was young, it had been a matter of practicality. My mom and dad weren't the only ones who knew my origins. A few family members knew the dad who raised me wasn't my biological father. And then there was the question that popped up, the one that shed light upon the lie to anyone who knew a thing about genetics. My daddy's eyes were blue. Mom's were gray. Mine were a deep brown.

Cassie raked her hands through her hair. "Still, why would Nannie choose to have you believe you were abandoned by your father? How is that better than telling you your father had been an alcoholic, so she never told him she was pregnant?"

I looked away and rubbed the side of my neck. I'd asked myself the same question, but in those final days of my mom's life, I'd never demanded an answer. "I think because it was what she told my dad." I sighed and shook my head. "I think once a lie is planted it grows. The longer it goes on, the harder it is to cut it down and reveal the truth." My insides twisted at my revelation. I understood all too well how a lie could stand the test of time. "Besides, knowing...believing...my biological father abandoned me made me hate him. I didn't want anything to do with someone who gave me up." I shrugged, focusing on my hands. They were dry, with lines and bulging veins. "I think I would have tried to find him if I'd known the truth."

"Mom."

I looked up at Cassie. Her angst had changed to concern, curiosity.

"How do you feel now? Knowing the truth."

I looked away and laughed. Forced and fake. Fighting against the burning in my chest. I didn't want to admit how I felt. But I could admit what I was doing.

"I want to find him," I said as flatly as I could.

Cassie nodded, understanding in her eyes. "Do you know where to look? Do you have anything more than his name?"

"Not much." My mouth twisted into a sheepish grin. For some reason what I was about to admit suddenly seemed funny. "I ordered one of those DNA kits."

"Oh...wow." Cassie's eyes widened. "I've heard of people discovering relatives they didn't even know about because they got matched through DNA. But wouldn't he have to be in the system? It doesn't seem likely that some old man in his seventies would have done a DNA test."

"True." I shrugged. "But odds are he had more children. Perhaps one of them, or one of *their* children, has done it. It would at least give me a starting point. Something more to go on than the name Michael Smith."

Cassie bit her lip. "Someone out there could be in for quite a surprise."

Ain't that the truth.

Chapter Eight

I SAT AT THE DINING TABLE, making a grocery list. The clouds blocked the sun today, which was typical for late March. Renee would be returning to school Monday, after having spent her spring break at a YMCA day camp. Part of me had hoped Cassie would ask me to at least watch Renee on my days off during the school break, but it didn't happen. It stung a little, even though I'd expected it.

Baby steps, sweetheart.

Mom's voice, tender, patient. That's what I kept hearing each time frustration grew.

"Grammy, tomorrow is church day." Renee approached me, seemingly from nowhere.

I pushed away my melancholy. My ability to get lost in my thoughts was disturbing.

I smiled at my granddaughter. "Yep, tomorrow is Sunday."

"Mommy said you don't work tomorrow, but she won't ask you to go, but I can." Renee touched my arm.

A tiny needlelike pain stuck in my chest. My daughter couldn't even ask me to church herself. Or had she sent Renee to ask me because she knew I couldn't say no to my granddaughter?

I pulled Renee into a hug. "Yes, I'll go, Sugar Bug."

Renee pulled back, a glint in her eyes. "We can have donuts again!"

Bending close to her ear, I whispered, "Maybe even two, right?"

Renee giggled, then bobbed her head up and down like a happy puppy.

I woke up before my alarm went off the next morning,

even though dread lay like a heavy blanket over me. Would we see Samantha at church again? And what about her husband, Dylan? Was she still married to him? I didn't see him at church with her. At least this time I'd be prepared for having my past in the building, and I had nothing to hide from Cassie.

Except the things you've buried.

My arms shivered and I pulled the blanket around me. There were no more secrets. Cassie knew the family story. She knew how low I'd gone during my drinking years. Maybe not every detail—no one needed to know that much detail. I hadn't fallen off the wagon since last July, and other than the one measly cigarette I had weeks ago, I'd quit smoking. Still, the nagging feeling was there, eating at my insides. I threw the blanket off, forcing the feeling away with the action. I'd keep the pain in my heart to myself, thank you very much.

The church was the same as I remembered. After Renee and I chose our pastries, we met Cassie at a seating area near the entrance to the sanctuary. We sat on a modern, firm sofa the color of coffee with too much cream. Cassie fidgeted, looking around furtively. My stomach knotted, and the sweet dough I tried to swallow stuck in my throat. Had she seen Samantha?

I managed to swallow, then took a sip of water from the plastic cup I'd filled at the beverage table. "Cassie, honey, is everything okay?"

My daughter nodded, a nervous grin causing her cheeks to dimple unnaturally. "Yep. It's just that this is kind of like going to a new church. A different service time means different people. I'm scanning the crowd for a familiar face."

"Sorry." What else could I say? Despite my best efforts, I'd still messed things up for Cassie.

A group of teenagers walked by, their loud voices and

laughter distracting me from my guilty conscience. They must've caught Cassie's attention too, because her head jerked their direction and didn't turn back for a few long moments. Or maybe she simply didn't want to look at her mom and reveal her true feelings.

When she did shift her attention back to me, her eyes were bright, inquisitive. "Mom, look over there." She tilted her head back toward the direction the teens had come from. "Is that who I think it is?"

My stomach lurched. I inhaled. One. Two. Three. Exhaled. Some things you couldn't escape. I scanned the area Cassie had indicated. Where was the long dark hair? The flowy dress? Nothing caught my eye. Except...there was a man standing near a door, in front of a wall with a sign that read "Youth Room." Something was familiar about him. Spiked blonde hair. Lean build. I stared, waiting for him to turn my direction. When he shifted to shake the hand of a passerby, my heart rate spiked from the shock. It was Pastor Matt. My mom's pastor from her church in Stayton. What was he doing *here?*

"Should we go say hello?" Cassie stage whispered.

I shrugged one shoulder and glanced down at Renee. She'd almost finished her donut. I couldn't deny the fact that seeing Pastor Matt brought a wave of memories from our last and only meeting—at Mom's funeral. Would I be able to hold myself together?

"You go on. I'll stay here with Renee."

Cassie's face dropped into a frown. "Please? It's awkward. I don't know what to say. And..." She lifted her eyebrow. "Maybe he knows more about the things that were kept secret."

I studied my daughter's face for a heartbeat. Cassie had a big heart, and no doubt she wanted to know more about her grandma's past, but there was something in her eyes that was more than goodwill and curiosity. Despite my own emotions, the corners of my mouth twitched into a smile.

"All right then." I patted Renee on the knee. "Give Grammy your plate." I stacked Renee's paper plate with mine and stood. "Let's go see your Nannie's old pastor."

We sauntered over to Pastor Matt. We were a good twelve feet away when he turned toward us, and recognition lit his face. He beamed, simultaneously displaying dimples and crow's feet. "Cassie? Sharon?" He stepped toward us, reaching out for a handshake.

Cassie stepped forward and took his hand, smiling bashfully like a girl who was meeting a movie star. Was it admiration, or something more in her eyes?

"I'm so surprised to see you here." Cassie dropped her hand, and Matt spun toward me, offering the obligatory handshake. Then his gaze dropped to Renee. "How are you, Miss Renee? Have you been enjoying the pastries?"

Renee's head bobbed up and down with a grin, and for the first time, I noticed chocolate frosting on her upper lip. Cassie was already reaching in her purse for a tissue, and within moments was bending over Renee, wiping her mouth.

"It's good to see all of you." Pastor Matt nodded toward me, empathy in his eyes. "Have you been coming to Cascade Christian for long?"

"A little over a month or so." Cassie tucked the dirty tissue back in her purse. "What about you? Are you visiting here?"

Pastor Matt chuckled and put his hands in the pockets of his gray trousers. "Nope. I'm taking up permanent residence." He motioned with his head toward the Youth Room sign behind him. "I've been hired as the youth pastor."

"Oh." Cassie's face fell. "So, you left your position as the pastor of the Hope of Stayton?"

"I'm afraid so." Pastor Matt's expression turned serious. "Ever since my wife passed away, it hasn't felt right."

Cassie nodded sympathetically. She seemed to have some idea what he was talking about, but I was in the dark.

"Besides, nothing will keep you young like a bunch of teenagers." Matt smiled, but the sadness still tinged his eyes.

"Or they'll turn your hair gray and make you want to run away to Mexico," I piped in, hoping to lighten the mood.

Everyone laughed, even Renee, who couldn't have had a clue what I was talking about. Warmth spread through my chest at the sound of her contagious laugh. That was definitely something worth fighting for.

We made small talk for a few moments, then music drifted from the sanctuary, our cue that it was time to find a seat.

"It was so nice to see you all. I know Eula would be tickled pink to know you were going to church."

The statement was meant for all of us, but Pastor Matt's eyes rested on me. Unease shimmied through my insides. "I'm sure she would."

Cassie didn't move. I could tell there was more she wanted to say. Or ask. No doubt this was not the time. Besides, if Pastor Matt was the youth pastor here, she'd have plenty more opportunities to see him.

"Will you ladies be attending the church's Easter potluck the weekend after next? It'd be great to catch up with you in more detail."

"Yes!" Cassie rocked on her heels. "I'm planning on it." She looked at me. "Mom, you should request the day off so you can go too." Her eyes met mine, pleading.

I nodded. "Sounds like a plan. I'll see what I can do."

I'd just gotten off work and was sitting in my car, giving the old clunker a chance to warm up before backing out of my parking space. Nothing else to do but listen to the radio and check my phone. Seeing the email preview stating, "Your DNA results are ready to view" on my home screen turned my insides to Jell-O. Sitting in the parking lot of the hotel was not the place to potentially find a long-lost relative on my father's side.

By the time I calmed my nerves enough to put the car in reverse, the back window was fogged up. No doubt my heart rate was the same as someone climbing stairs at a full run, and my breathing was trying to keep pace. I cursed under my breath and put the car back in park, jumped out and opened the door to the back seat. Using my bare hands, I rubbed the fog away.

"Surprised you're still here."

The familiar voice came from behind me. My coworker, Janice, a.k.a. Happy Feet. I sighed and pulled myself out of the back of the car. I wasn't in the mood, nor did I have the time, to talk. I wanted to be at home, in my room, and alone when I read the results. A drizzle fell from the sky. It was nothing that required an umbrella or even a hood, but it added to my annoyance.

"Yeah, window got fogged up. I'm jetting home now to get some stuff done before I make dinner." I grabbed the handle of the driver side door and pulled it open.

Janice didn't budge. The drizzle settled in her hair, bringing out the black, shiny curls. "Well, listen, there's this bar down off Gateway. It's kind of a dive, but it has karaoke on Friday nights. A couple friends and I are going tonight, if you want to join us." Janice gave me her big puppy grin. "I'm telling you, girlfriend, your singing will knock people out. It'll be a blast."

I sighed and closed my door. No need to get my seats wet and make my car smell even worse. "Thanks for inviting me." I paused, looking for a valid, believable excuse. Many recovering alcoholics told everyone and their mother's brother they were in recovery, like it was some kind of combat badge. Not me. I'd never been one to divulge too much to new people, and admitting I battled addiction was at the top of my "don't ask, don't tell" list. Now my secrecy had left me in a predicament. The last place I should be was in a bar. "Cassie's going out tonight and I said I'd watch Renee." An outright lie, but the best my already frazzled brain could come up with.

A pained expression flitted across Janice's features, like she knew I was lying. Guilt nipped at my already quivering gut, and the creeping, edgy feeling that was all too familiar shot through all my appendages. I inhaled. One. Two. Three. Exhaled.

It did no good. My adrenaline was in overdrive. "I gotta go." I jumped in my Buick before Janice could respond. As I shifted into reverse, I glanced over my shoulder and waved in the friendliest way I could muster. Janice stepped back a few paces and waved, the sadness in her eyes not lessened by the tentative smile she offered in return.

I drove straight home, passing Quick-Shop-N-Go on the way. Its blue letters beckoned me. Inside were the things my nerves screamed for. Cigarettes and beer were off limits. Some Red Vines sounded good, and they were something I *could* have. I hit my blinker to turn, until a voice inside me screamed, *you know you'll get more than candy if you go in there right now.* I switched the blinker off and jerked back into my lane, eliciting a honk from the driver behind me. I glanced in my rearview mirror at some young man in a luxury car. *Go fly a kite, kid, you've got no idea.* I rolled my eyes and stepped on the gas. I had to get home.

I pulled up to the curb of the duplex and yanked the car into park before coming to a complete stop. My transmission made some unholy sound as I was jolted against the seatbelt. I cursed for the second time that day, this time at myself. The last thing I needed was a big mechanic's bill.

The sprinkling rain had escalated into a full-blown shower. I exhaled and closed my eyes. Why did it feel like everything in the universe was trying to keep me from reading the darn email? Shaking my head at my own stupidity, I grabbed my purse and jog-walked to the front door, my knees screaming in protest. After fumbling with my keys, I unlocked the door. The old grandfather clock that had belonged to my parents—one of only a handful of my parents' possessions that I'd kept after Mom moved to a retirement home—greeted me with a tick-tock and Roman numerals. It was only three in the afternoon. I had a good two hours before Cassie and Renee made it home. After grabbing a Diet Coke out of the fridge, I headed to my room.

I plopped down on my bed and set my purse on the floor, then reached for my reading glasses. They were my newest purchase from Dollar Tree, and I hated wearing them. Being a grandma was great, but I wasn't quite ready to look like one. I unlocked my phone and hit the Gmail icon. The MyGeneology.com email was sitting at the top of my email list. My finger hovered over the subject line.

Was I ready for the places these results could take me? What if it only led to my worst fear coming true? What if my biological dad was still an alcoholic? In prison, dead from liver failure, or homeless?

Yeah, Sharon, like some homeless guy is ordering DNA tests.

I laughed at my own thoughts. The odds of one of my matches actually being my bio dad were slim to none, but I might find a sister, or an uncle, or a cousin. Any of those relations could point me to the location of my birth father.

Unless they don't want you to know.

Goosebumps shot down my arms. Could I handle the rejection of a family I didn't know?

My gaze shifted up to the shelf where the music box sat. Intricate gold leaves entwined around its edges, two lovebirds in flight on its top. Though it wasn't opened, the melody it contained played through my head, ghostly and sweet.

I can't deny my love for you
It's deeper than the bluest sea
Stronger than the mightiest tree
Darling, say you love me too
Because I can't deny my love for you.

Whoever Michael Smith, my biological father, had been, whatever he had done, one thing was plainly obvious. He had loved my mom. Loved her enough to give her a music box that once belonged to his mother. One that played a song about endless love.

Even if he turned out to be a loser, even if I was rejected by whatever other family I was genetically tied to, could I ever be at peace without knowing who this man was and what had become of him? Without knowing what parts of me came from him? The parts that had never seemed to fit in anywhere at home. The part of me that was empty and hollow and longed for a drink.

Before I could ask myself any more questions, I hit the email and let it pop open on my screen.

Chapter Nine

With trembling fingers, I typed in the password.

The browser opened to a page declaring it held my DNA results. The top half of the page reported my heritage. As I'd expected, I had a healthy dose of English and Welsh, as well as Irish. My heart skipped at the next two areas with the highest percentage—Eastern European and French. I'd never heard anything about being part Eastern European or French from my mom. She'd bragged of our family's deep roots in the south, all the way back to the founding days of the country. Ancestors on my mom's side were English and Irish. Not Eastern European. Not French. That heritage had to have come from my father's side.

I scrolled down to a button labeled DNA Matches. My finger hesitated over the button, my heart beating a fast and loud rhythm against my chest.

Quit jumpin' on the binders. I shivered at Steven's voice, telling me to quit putting on the brakes and go. I hit the button.

Matches were listed according to relation. At the top was a section titled First Cousin with one person under it. I scanned down the rest of the page and saw the relations only became more distant as the list continued, going all the way to fourth cousins.

There were no Parent matches. Nothing under a Sibling heading. My heart sank so fast the room swirled. I put the phone down. I'd waited all this time for nothing.

Except...first cousins were a pretty close relative. I picked my phone up again and looked at the match under First Cousin. Whoever it was hadn't used their entire name as a username and was instead listed simply as

"Rbowers99." The pink icon next to the name indicated the person was female. The cogs in my brain started spinning again, this time slowly enough it didn't hurt.

Mom's maiden name was Brown. She'd had one sister who never had much to do with the family. Did she marry someone by the last name of Bowers and have a daughter? No matter how hard I tried to remember, I couldn't recall what her married name had been. Besides, if my female cousin had married, Bowers could be *her* last name.

I exhaled loudly and looked farther down the page. There were several second cousins. I noticed some Millers and Thorntons, both names I knew to be on my mother's side. There weren't any other Bowerses. When I got to the bottom of the second cousins list, though, one username caught my eye: RJSmith00. His user information included an actual picture next to the blue icon. It was small, but RJSmith00 was obviously male and fairly young.

Smith.

Like my father.

Could he be a descendent of my father's family? I tapped on his name and was taken to a page with more information. There was no family tree as part of his profile or any kind of indication of his age. I noticed a tab labeled Shared Matches. I tapped on it.

A new page appeared. "The people below share DNA with both you and RJSmith00." Directly under that was the top match: first cousin, Rbowers99. Scanning the rest of the page, I saw no Millers or Thorntons. I set the phone down and gazed up at the music box. The rain had stopped, and sun was breaking through the clouds, shining stubbornly through my thick drapes and into my room, illuminating the golden box.

I was no Einstein, but it looked like I might have found a

cousin on my father's side. If I could figure out who and where this Bowers was, I might find my father.

After all, wouldn't most people know where to find their uncle?

"How was your day?" Cassie had arrived home with a bag of groceries and set it on the counter.

"My day was...interesting. I got that email I've been waiting for."

Cassie stopped putting the groceries away and faced me. "And?"

I turned the burner down to low and set the spoon on a plate. "Well, I didn't find *him.* But I might have a lead." I shrugged, refusing to let the disappointment show.

"A sibling?" Cassie's eyebrows arched, her eyes lighting.

My throat tightened. I'd only been thinking of myself when the results weren't what I'd hoped for. Looking at the anticipation in my daughter's eyes, I realized she too wanted to know more. She longed for family. A great aunt or uncle for Renee, maybe even second cousins—or a grandpa.

I shook my head. "No, not a sibling. A cousin." I summarized what I'd read on the website and what I'd gathered by the matches and names.

Cassie lowered her chin. "I bet we can track her down, whoever she is."

"I don't even know where to start. There's an option to send a message through the MyGenealogy website, but I'm kind of afraid of scaring her off."

"Yeah, it's probably best to do a little more research before you contact her." Cassie reached into the paper sack and took out the last two items—a bag of apples and bunch of bananas. "Did Nannie give you any more information on Michael's family? How many siblings did he have?"

I sighed. When I was younger and first learned about my birth father, after I'd gotten over the initial shock and hurt, I'd asked a few questions. Mom had been extremely guarded, giving me as little information as possible. My questions also made me feel guilty, like by even wondering about my birth father I was betraying the dad who had raised me and whom I adored. The combination had quieted me from giving voice to my ponderings. When Mom was dying and had confessed the rest of the story about my father, I'd been too upset about her failing health to pester her with questions. Now I had almost nothing to go on.

"He had two brothers, if I remember correctly. Michael was the oldest."

"Do you know their names?"

I tapped my chin with my finger, trying my best to recall the conversation of my youth. "I *think* Nannie said their names were Richard and Anthony. But I wouldn't bet my life on it."

Cassie nodded, seeming encouraged. "What about his parents?"

My mind went through the painful catalogue of memories. All I could see was the uncharacteristic lack of emotion in my mom's face. All I felt was the guilty burden of not being my dad's real daughter. I knew Cassie could understand the pain it had caused me to learn the news. She'd gone through similar emotions last year when she learned the secret about my dad—her beloved grandpa—not being related to us by blood. But she could never fully understand the rejection I lived with from a young age by believing that my father's reaction to finding out about my mom's pregnancy was to leave town and never look back.

"I believe his father's name was Joseph. I'm not sure about his mom." I shrugged my shoulders. "I was twelve years old when I found out. Kids don't think about those details so much."

Cassie sighed. "That makes sense." She looked at me thoughtfully, her blue eyes full of sympathy.

I looked away. The last thing I wanted was my daughter feeling sorry for me.

"If we can figure out what year Michael was born, I might be able to find something through an online service we use at work."

Of course. Because she worked for lawyers, Cassie had access to things most people didn't. "Will your work let you do that?"

"Technically, no." Cassie puckered her lips. "But I know my friend Missy has done it before. I'm sure she'd be happy to help."

I smiled at the mention of Missy. I'd only met her a few times, but she was quite a character. She was the one who had encouraged Cassie to see all those waterfalls.

"If Michael and Mom and Dad were all childhood friends, then he'd have to be the same age. I'd guess he was born around the same time—1942 or 1943."

Cassie grabbed soup bowls out of the cupboard, glancing toward the hall. I followed her gaze. Renee was coming our way. "It'll be a long shot." Cassie spoke matter-of-factly. "But I'll see what I can find out."

Chapter Ten

Waking up on my mom's birthday Saturday morning was like trying to pull myself out of a deep pit. Of course, my head still reeling from the DNA results probably didn't put things in the best perspective. I hated that I had to work today and was not looking forward to dragging myself to the hotel. Some people would find the distraction helpful, but I wasn't sure how I was going to make it through the day without breaking down in tears. How had I made it through the first of everything when Dad passed away?

The answer was so obvious I laughed out loud at myself. Dad died during my drinking days. Nothing takes the ache out of sorrow like a Jack and Coke. It was a recipe I concocted after Steven died. Sometimes I added little twists, but it was always basically the same. A glass full of ice, two shots of Jack Daniel's whiskey, four shots of Diet Coke, mix thoroughly with a spoon. Drink it fast, washing away regret and heartache and sorrow. Repeat until everything goes black.

A knock at the bedroom door pulled me out of my self-pity. "Yes?"

Renee poked her head in, her eyes big with concern. "Mommy's crying."

Was Cassie hurting as much as I was today? "Come here, Sweet Pea." I reached out to my granddaughter. Renee ran to me, and I pulled her up next to me on the bed. "Can you make yourself a bowl of cereal while I go check on Mommy?"

Renee nodded solemnly. "She was in the living room but then she went to her bedroom and closed the door. But I saw her crying before she went in there. When I knocked, she sounded funny and told me to go get dressed." Renee's brow furrowed. "Is Mommy okay?"

I nodded and planted a kiss on her forehead. "Mommy is fine. Today is just a hard day."

Renee cocked her head. "Why?"

How much would a six-year-old understand? "You remember Nannie?"

Renee nodded, a broad grin on her face.

I swallowed the lump in my throat. "Today is her birthday, and your mommy and I are sad because she isn't here to celebrate it with us."

"But she gets to have birthday cake with Jesus." Renee's answer was matter of fact and happy, as if she were confirming maple syrup belonged on pancakes. How could I argue with that?

"That's right, Sweet Pea, but we still miss her."

"I miss her too." Renee frowned and looked at the floor.

I patted her on the back. "You go ahead and get dressed and have breakfast. I'll check on your mommy."

Renee obeyed, and I walked slowly to Cassie's bedroom, pausing before knocking. I put my ear to the door, and hearing nothing, tapped on it lightly. "Cassie?"

"Yeah." The voice that came through the door was both high-pitched and hoarse.

I opened the door and peeked in. Cassie sat on the edge of her bed, head in her hands, a section of newspaper rumpled at her feet. Had Cassie forgotten what today was until she saw the date on the newspaper?

I walked gently to the bed and eased myself down beside her, the heaviness in my own heart like an anchor in my stomach. I put my arm around my daughter, and she fell into my arms, sobbing like a little girl. There was no holding back my own tears now, and they cascaded down my face like they'd been held back by a flood gate.

"It's okay, baby girl. Today's a hard day, but we're going to get through it together." I rubbed her back gently. While ninety percent of me grieved, another small part of me rejoiced. I was a mom to Cassie again, holding her while she cried.

Cassie's sobs slowed, and she sat up, embracing me with a strong hug. "The first thing on my mind when I woke up was that today is Nannie's birthday."

I nodded, tears welling up again. "Yeah, me too."

Cassie cleared her throat and pulled away, her gaze on the newspaper crumpled on the floor. "Before the day even started, it went from bad to worse."

Realization dawned on me. "What was in the paper?"

Cassie wiped away the tears on her face with the back of her hand. "I guess that's what I get for signing up for a free promotion for a newspaper subscription. Worst timing ever."

Frustrated with her beating around the bush, I picked the crumpled paper off the floor. It was the vital records section—obituaries, births, marriage announcements. Had someone else she knew recently died?

"What's going on?"

She turned to me, her eyes bloodshot and puffy. "I woke up early this morning and couldn't fall back to sleep. I had Nannie on my mind. So of course I ended up reading through every stupid thing in the paper." Cassie drew in a breath. "I even read the vitals."

I patted her hand, urging her to continue.

Cassie lip quivered. "Derrick's remarried."

My mind spun in circles. How long had he been out of jail? And he was already remarried? I understood why Cassie was upset, but she should be glad that the no-good, poor excuse for a man was someone else's problem. Looking at Cassie, though, it was obvious she wasn't thinking the same thing. Her heart was hurting. Bad. Words to comfort her escaped me. This wasn't what I was expecting when I saw her tears. I put my arm around her and squeezed. "I'm sorry, baby girl."

"He's only been out of jail four weeks. You know what that means?"

I shrugged, still shocked at the unexpected news. "That some poor woman out there is exceptionally stupid?"

The corners of Cassie's mouth lifted into a hesitant smile. "Well, there is that...but also." Cassie inhaled and exhaled slowly, the tears forming again in her eyes. "He must have been seeing someone before he went to jail. Maybe even before we were divorced."

"He's a piece of work." My jaw tightened. How did he explain his arrest and time in jail to this other woman? What lie had she been fed to keep her waiting for a man jailed for domestic violence and a DUI?

And how much more could my poor daughter's heart take?

"I know it's hard not to have the answers to what happened." Boy, did I know what it was like to not have answers. "But this doesn't mean anything about your worth. All it does is set you free."

Cassie looked away. "It makes things more final, that's for sure."

Now it made sense why Cassie had not heard from Derrick since his release from jail. His focus was elsewhere. Maybe as long as it stayed there, Cassie and Renee's lives would be peaceful and safe. Though my daughter was hurting from another shot of loss, I saw only her freedom and a future of possibilities.

If only I could see the same for myself.

I pushed the thought away. This wasn't about me. I took Cassie's face in my hands and turned her head toward me. "You're free, Cassie. It's like stamping a giant 'The End' on your past and opening a whole new book."

"I know." Cassie's eyes fluttered with emotion. "I'm sure it's for the best. Well, for me at least."

Silence lay between us now, thick with unanswered questions. Would having a new wife prompt Derrick to seek out his parenting rights with Renee? Would he use his marriage as supposed proof of his reformation and take Cassie back to court for unsupervised parenting time with Renee—assuming this woman even wanted another woman's child in her home? Or would this new addition to his life make him completely let go of his daughter? And if he never came back to the role of father in Renee's life, who would fill that gap?

My grief over the loss of my mom took a detour, and my heart ached for the life Renee would never have.

"You should've been there last night for karaoke. My friend Cindy sang 'I Wanna Dance with Somebody.'"

I sighed and tucked in the bottom corner of the sheet on the bed I was making. Room 124 hadn't been a bad one. Something to be thankful for in my day. "That's a good song."

Janice laughed, her eyes twinkling as she wiped down the nightstand. "Yeah, it is. Except Cindy can't sing *or* dance...and she was trying to do both on stage."

I snorted. There'd been a time in my life when karaoke in a bar sounded like a good time. Those days were gone. "I think the whole point of singing in a bar is to make people laugh, not dance."

"You've got a point." Janice stopped working and looked at me, her hand on her hip.

I smoothed out the bedspread and then swiveled toward her, discomfort sinking into my core. *Please don't invite me to karaoke again.*

"What's bugging you today? You're not yourself." Janice's voice was soft with concern, her usually jovial expression now serious.

Ugh. I'd have been better off being asked to a night of comedic singing. "Nothing. I'm fine."

Janice chortled. "You're speaking to another woman here. I know what 'fine' stands for."

I rolled my eyes. "And what's that?"

"Well..." The sparkle returned to Janice's eyes. "You're either telling me to shut up because you don't want to talk about it, or you're saying that you're freaked out, insecure, neurotic, and emotional."

"*The Italian Job*. That was a good movie." Apparently the line from the movie had stuck with me through the drinking.

"You're changing the subject." Janice wouldn't give up.

"I'd say the answer is yes—to both options." My stomach did a little flip-flop on me. I guess it was as surprised by my both mean and revealing response as I was. *Nice one, Sharon.*

"Okay." Janice walked away and loaded our supplies back on the cleaning cart.

Nagging guilt raked at my gut.

Your catch fence is so high you're keeping everyone out. Maybe it's time to lift a little. What was it these days with Steven's voice in my head, talking to me in racing terms?

I met up with Janice at the cleaning cart. "Look. I'm sorry. Today is a hard day."

Janice's eyes met mine with a mixture of concern and curiosity. "Want to talk about it?"

No. I didn't. Yet, I needed to. "Today is my mom's birthday. The first one since she passed. Then this morning Cassie found out her ex got remarried already. She was pretty torn up."

"That's enough to put anyone in a bad mood." Janice squeezed my arm gently. "I'm sorry."

I nodded and looked away, unable to respond through the tightening in my throat. Talking about this stuff at an AA meeting was one thing. It was almost anonymous, in a room full of people with problems as big as or bigger than my own. Talking to Janice was different. She was a coworker with what seemed like a fairly normal life. We exited the room, pushing the cart ahead of us to the next door on our list of rooms to clean.

"Are you doing anything to mark the day?"

"What do you mean?" Cassie and I had agreed to take flowers to Mom's grave today after I got off work. Other than that, I just wanted to get the day over with.

"My pastor lost his daughter a few years ago." Janice waved the card lock key in front of the next door and pushed it open, pulling the cart behind her. "Drug overdose."

"That's terrible." A pastor losing his daughter to addiction seemed especially tragic. This conversation was getting depressing. I didn't even want to imagine how horrible it would be to lose Cassie.

"Yeah, it was." Janice flipped the light switch, then stopped, her full attention now on me. "But every year on her birthday, he and his wife cook their daughter's favorite meal and bake her favorite cake. They eat together and talk about their fondest memories of her."

Doing something like that sounded downright torturous. It would be like pouring salt on an open wound, then following it up with a cup of vinegar. "I think I'd rather hide in a dark cave and wait for the day to be over."

Janice nodded sympathetically. "I thought the same thing, at first. But my pastor pointed something out that made me look at in a different way. By taking the time and purposely honoring the loss of their daughter and their grief over her death, they were healing. Each year it gets easier. I think if you keep hiding from it you can't ever get past the loss."

"I think that's easier said than done." I'd tried facing the loss of my husband eons ago, and I ended up an alcoholic. What would happen to me if I tried fully facing the loss of my mom?

You know that's not true, Sharon. You hid from the truth.

I shivered as goose bumps spread through my body.

"I'm sure it is hard." Janice paused, pursing her lips. "If you need anyone to talk to, I'm here. Believe it or not, I've been *fine* before too."

"Freaked out, insecure, neurotic and emotional?"

"Yes, ma'am." Janice winked. "And I've had a time or two when I've told a friend to mind their own business."

"But I bet you didn't mean it."

"We never really do, girlfriend. We never really do."

We stopped at a florist on the way to the cemetery. When we entered the shop, Renee went straight to the sunflowers. "Nannie loved yellow, right, Mommy?"

She was right. Amazing a little one could store such detailed memories.

"Yes, honey, but I think her favorite flowers were roses." Cassie pointed to the blooms.

"Yellow roses," I spoke up, but my voice cracked.

Cassie looked my way. "Of course."

We ordered a dozen yellow roses for Mom and a single sunflower for Renee.

Mom and Dad had chosen a flat gravestone in their planning. Seeing Mom's name engraved in it —Eula Belle Bradford—still made my heart sting, as if I had discovered all over again that she was gone. Dad's name was engraved on the left side of the stone, his date of death preceding Mom's by three years. We set the roses in a holder on the corner of the grave marker and stood in silence. A light breeze blew through the graveyard, blowing my fine hair into my eyes. Oddly, Cassie and I had only been here together once since Mom passed. I'd come alone three times since. It was at those times that I talked to Mom as if she were sitting across from me. Part of me actually believed she could hear me.

Renee wiggled her way between Cassie and me and grabbed my hand, clutching the sunflower in her other hand. She looked up at me with sorrowful eyes. "I miss her too, Grammy."

I swallowed the prickling pain in my throat. "Of course you do, sweetie."

Renee let go of my hand and stepped closer to the gravestone, setting the sunflower on top of it, the bloom next to Mom's name, the stem underlining Dad's. The position of the flower seemed appropriate. Their relationship had been loving, respectful, and stood the test of time. Yet their only descendants didn't seem to have such luck. I was widowed and couldn't see myself ever loving again. Cassie was divorced.

A thought settled on me, as gentle as a butterfly kiss. The memory of how Cassie had looked at Pastor Matt when she saw him at church. I smiled. There was no hope of love for me, but maybe someday Cassie could steer the family ship back to solid ground.

Chapter Eleven

"IT'S A GREAT DAY FOR AN Easter egg hunt." Cassie carefully set the Crock-Pot of potato soup she had made for the church potluck in the back of the car, stabilizing it with a few rolled-up towels.

I wished I shared her enthusiasm. All I could think about were the odds of Samantha or her husband being there, and what I would do or say if I had to face her again.

When we arrived at Cascade Christian Church, the parking lot teemed with cars. People milled into the church, excited children laughing and being corralled by their parents. What a madhouse.

We made our way inside. Upbeat Christian music carried through the chatter and laughter of the people. Spring-themed floral arrangements brightened the foyer. The doors to the sanctuary stood wide open. Entering the sanctuary, we found the usual chairs gone, replaced by long pop-up tables spread with white disposable tablecloths. On the left side of the sanctuary on a tiled area of the floor, long tables groaned under the weight of various dishes. We turned that direction, and I kept my gaze in front of me as I held Renee's hand.

"Cassie! Sharon!" A welcoming male voice rose above the murmur of crowd noise. Pastor Matt waved at us from a spot near the food table.

I nodded toward him. Mother's instinct drew my gaze toward Cassie. Her face lit up, and my heart warmed at the spark I saw there. Odds were nothing would come of it, but it was good to see her happy, especially after the brokenhearted tears shed the other day.

Pastor Matt helped Cassie find a place to put her Crock-

Pot. Renee and I followed and set the condiments and serving spoon next to the soup.

"Can I help you ladies find a seat? It'll be some time before we eat, but it's good to claim your spot early."

Cassie nodded. "Great idea."

"Let's go over there." Pastor Matt motioned toward a table near the corner of the sanctuary.

Renee skipped along with a big grin. I was surprised she hadn't asked when the egg hunt would start. Was she as curious as the rest of us about Pastor Matt?

We reached the table. "If you ladies don't mind some teens sitting nearby, I'd love to join you for the meal." Pastor Matt smiled broadly, though a hint of uncertainty lingered in his eyes.

"That'd be great!" Cassie piped, almost too enthusiastically. "Should we save a few spots?"

"If you don't mind." Pastor Matt looked around. "The youth I've seen so far look like they're going to sit with their parents, but I like to make sure I save a space near me for the ones who show up alone or who prefer not to sit with their parents and younger siblings."

"I'm surprised a teen would show up to a potluck of their own volition," Cassie said.

Volition. That daughter of mine and her fancy words. Was she trying to impress someone? I chuckled to myself.

"What's funny, Grammy?"

I sucked in my cheeks. "I was thinking how great it is that teenagers would come to an Easter potluck." *Of their own volition.*

The corner of Pastor Matt's mouth raised in a crooked grin, and I had the uncanny feeling he could tell what I was thinking. An uncharacteristic heat ran up my neck.

"How much space should we save?" I asked, changing the subject.

"Three or four should be a safe bet." Pastor Matt shifted his focus to Renee. "The egg hunt for preschoolers will start soon. It'll be about fifteen minutes before the big kids' egg hunt, *but*," Pastor Matt raised his eyebrows, "I heard the big kids get the best prizes."

Renee giggled and bounced on the balls of her feet.

We took our seats, and I soon learned Pastor Matt was a master at small talk. Within five minutes he knew Cassie and I shared a home, where she worked, where I worked, and where Renee went to school. We also learned that he lived in a small apartment in Eugene, a downsize from the home he had owned in Stayton, but since it was only him now, he didn't mind at all.

Renee fidgeted in her seat. No doubt she was restless. So was I. Seeing Cassie's interest in Pastor Matt brought me joy, but it also made my heart ache. The last time I'd looked at anyone with even half of the fondness she showed for Pastor Matt was long ago. Johnny Beckett had been the last man I'd let myself get flustered over. My heart still did a stupid little flip when his face came to my mind. Never again.

"Maybe I could take Renee to the play structure outside while we wait for the egg hunt?" I offered, desperate for a distraction.

"Sure, that'd be great." Cassie's genuine smile made my heart sing.

Renee bounced out of her seat and grabbed my hand. "Let's go, Grammy."

Pastor Matt's eyes sparkled. "The egg hunt is right beyond the play structure. It's roped off, but I bet from the top of the slide you can get a good view."

"Wouldn't that be cheating?" I asked.

Pastor Matt laughed. "It's more an Easter dash than a hunt. There's not many places to hide eggs on a flat green lawn."

"When they announce it's time, I'll head out there and find you guys," Cassie said.

Renee and I exited the sanctuary to the foyer, taking the side exit that led to the play area, which contained Noah's Ark-themed equipment and a huge slide. The playground bustled with children. My heart squeezed. Maybe I shouldn't have brought Renee out here. I'd lose sight of her in the swarm of children.

Renee hugged my leg. "I love you, Grammy."

My chest warmed. It wouldn't be too many more years before the lovingness of childhood was replaced with the snubbing of adolescence.

"Want to see me go down the slide? It goes super-fast." Her eyes were wide with excitement, free of the fear and worry I'd seen so many times before, especially during Cassie's divorce.

"Of course!"

Renee ran off toward the Noah's Ark slide, and I followed, positioning myself near the bottom to wait for Renee's descent. Children waited in a short line on the stairs going up the slide. I took my phone out of my purse so I could snap a picture as Renee slid down. The MyGenealogy app icon stood out like a red beacon, but I ignored it. Now was not the time to check for updates. The screams and laughter of the children competed with the upbeat Christian song blaring through the outdoor speakers. I glanced around, feeling out of place. Shimmering black hair caught my eye. My pulse jackrabbited.

Samantha stood at the other end of the Noah's Ark, closer to it than I was. Still as a statue, she didn't look my way. Her eyes remained hawk-like on the slide. Had she already spotted me and was now trying to avoid eye contact? Or was she watching a child come down the slide? A little boy slid down the slide, and as soon as his feet hit the ground he ran around to the back of the line. Samantha remained frigid, her face emotionless.

Was she waiting for her own grandchild? Or was she helping with the kids as a church staff member? I hadn't thought about any of those possibilities when I volunteered to watch Renee play. Strike one.

A cold ball of lead settled in my stomach. I couldn't handle another face-to-face with Samantha. As soon as Renee got to the bottom of the slide, I'd talk her into going back to the table. As if on cue, I heard the unmistakable squeal of my granddaughter as she flew down the slide. I smiled, but the joy of the moment was overshadowed by the woman with black hair. I held up my phone to take a picture but was too late, snapping it when Renee was already at the bottom.

Renee ran toward me, strands of hair standing every which way from static electricity. "I want to go again."

"I don't know, sweetie, we should get your mommy. It's almost time for the egg hunt."

"But she said she'd come out here." Renee's brow furrowed.

I was torn between guilt and self-preservation. "I supp—"

A little girl who had just landed at the bottom of the slide ran up to us. "Hi, Renee! Let's go down again, but together."

I bit my lip, ignoring the tautness of my nerves from having Samantha nearby. Renee was making friends at this new church, just like her mom.

Renee nodded, giggling, reaching for the girl's hand. "Okay."

"Isabella! Come here." A sharp female voice cut through the air.

I looked up to see Samantha marching our way. *You've got to be kidding.*

The little girl turned. "Grandma? What's wrong?"

Samantha reached us and grabbed Isabella's hand. "What are you doing?"

"Renee and I are going to go down the slide again." Isabella's freckled face was full of joy as she looked up at her grandma.

"I don't think that's a good idea."

"Why? I've only gone two times."

Renee added to the plea. "Please?" Her gaze flitted between me and Samantha.

Guilt won out. No reason to make my innocent granddaughter suffer because I was uncomfortable. "It's fine with me, Sweet Pea, but only once more."

Renee squealed and pulled on Isabella's arm to go, but Samantha quickly tugged the opposite direction, making a human tug-of-war rope out of her granddaughter.

Samantha's eyes were hard. The sunlight on her stonelike face deepened the shadows under her cheekbones, accentuating the lines around her eyes and mouth. Her olive complexion didn't completely hide the signs of age under the light of the sun.

"I don't think that's a good idea." Samantha's tone was icy, ungiving.

Isabella frowned. "But whyyy?"

Renee dropped Isabella's arm, realizing the battle was lost. Fire shot through my veins. I pulled Renee toward me. Was Samantha not letting her granddaughter play with Renee simply because she was related to me? What a coldhearted, unforgiving, and downright evil woman. No man, woman, or child was going to treat my grandbaby like that because of something I did before she was even a sparkle in her mother's eye.

"You small-hearted piece of work." Bitterness oozed out of me like pus from a festering wound. Ugly and nasty.

"Excuse me?" Samantha's eyes widened and she pulled her shoulders back.

"It doesn't take a rocket scientist to figure out what's going on here."

"I don't know what you're talking about. We need to get ready for the egg hunt. That's all." Samantha leveled her eyes on me, shooting darts, and her lips pulled into a tight smirk.

Walk away, Sharon, walk away. Little eyes are watching.

That sounded like Mom's wisdom more than my own. I bit down on my lip, holding in words no child should hear. "Come on, Renee. Samantha is right. It's time to go." I grabbed Renee's hand and whirled away before Samantha could breathe another syllable.

Before we made it back inside, the music on the speakers was interrupted by a man's voice announcing the egg hunt for kindergarten through second grade. I stopped, telling Renee we would wait for her mom. I'd been looking forward to seeing Renee hunt eggs, but now all I wanted to do was get this ordeal over with and get out of this place.

Cassie found us and we went to the roped-off area for the egg hunt. Renee was handed a bag by a volunteer, and the next thing I knew, she was running off to look for eggs. Instead of watching her, I found myself glancing around me, looking for Samantha and Dylan. I didn't see them anywhere but caught a glimpse of their granddaughter running with the other kids, nowhere near Renee.

Almost as soon as it started, the egg hunt ended, and we meandered back in with the crowd. Renee chattered happily about her egg finds, but her voice blended in with all the others around me. I couldn't focus on anything—my nerves were too fired up. I inhaled slowly as we walked, counted to three, exhaled. I couldn't let my run-in with Samantha ruin this day.

Pastor Matt sat at the table, now joined by a couple of teenagers, two teen girls no older than fifteen. Both girls were intently listening to Pastor Matt, their eyes sparkling. Starstruck. Silly girls and their crushes. Hopefully, Renee never got that dumbfounded by a man.

You used to look at me that way.

I shivered. Sounded like Steven in my head, but different. My heart rate was still spiked, and I was lightheaded. Maybe I should go to a doctor. Was I having some delayed alcohol deprival hallucinations?

Cassie beamed when she saw Pastor Matt, oblivious to the turmoil inside of me.

Renee tugged on her mom's hand. "I'm hungry and Grammy is acting weird, Mommy."

Good grief, throw me under the bus, kid. I shrugged. "She didn't want to quit playing earlier."

Cassie reached for Renee. "We're going to eat now, honey." Cassie glanced at me and turned back to Renee. "Grammy looks fine to me."

"How about if I save your spots and when you get back, Avery, Piper, and I will get our plates?" Pastor Matt spoke to Cassie, his smile showing off dimples.

My little family and I got in line for the food. I glanced around, hoping beyond hope not to see Samantha. If I did, I wasn't sure I could control myself. Her granddaughter's face flickered in my mind. A little girl with freckles and red hair didn't look like she belonged to someone like Samantha, but who knew? Genetics were a mystery to me.

"It looks like you and Pastor Matt are pretty friendly."

Cassie blushed. "Well, he's a nice man. I understand why Nannie was fond of him."

"Mmm-hmm." I spooned bean salad onto my plate, followed by a helping of ham.

"He's so easy to talk to. He has a way of making people

feel comfortable and safe." Cassie put a huge serving of green salad on her plate, and, against Renee's protests, added some to her plate too.

"That seems like a pastor-like quality."

"Yes, I'm sure it is. But he's not intimidating like I imagine many pastors could be."

"Sounds like you're taking after Nannie."

Cassie stopped her progression in line and twisted toward me, a quizzical lift to her eyebrows. "How's that?"

"Your fondness for Pastor Matt."

"Mom!" Cassie's face turned bright red.

I laughed. Though I felt a little bad about embarrassing my daughter, the lighthearted teasing took the sting out of my exchange with Samantha. At least momentarily.

"I told him about what you're going through." Cassie spoke with hesitation.

"You did what?" I almost dropped my plate.

Cassie glanced around her, then leaned closer to me and whispered, "I told him about the DNA test and stuff."

"Why on earth would you do that?" Irritation made my voice rise, and the woman in line behind me took a tiny step back.

"Mom," she whispered, her eyebrows raised. "I didn't think you'd mind."

I inhaled slowly and exhaled even slower, counting to three. The crawling under my skin was more than an itch, the raking at my heart more than humiliation at the revelation of my secret—our family secret.

I spoke through clenched teeth as we made our way back to the table. "I honestly don't know what you think you'd accomplish by sharing that bit of info with Nannie's *pastor* of all people."

Cassie blinked, hurt flashing in her blue eyes. She stopped and touched my arm with her free hand. Renee stopped with us, watching with big-eyed curiosity. "I'm sorry. I didn't think of it that way. I thought...maybe...Nannie had told him something. Maybe he had more information than we do."

People moved around us, going to their seats. This was not the time or place for a long conversation. What Cassie said made sense, but it still irked me. "I understand. Look, let's talk about it later. At home."

We moved back toward the table. I dreaded the idea of sitting down and making casual conversation with someone whose knowledge of me could be summarized as a maid who lived with her daughter and was the result of an out-of-wedlock love affair and a long-kept secret. Strike two for me.

My list of reasons for *not* going to Cascade Christian Church was growing. One more strike, and I was out.

PART TWO

"But the mercy of the Lord *is* from everlasting to everlasting on those who fear Him, And His righteousness to children's children."

Psalm 103:17 NASB

Chapter Twelve

"I SUPPOSE IT'S A START." I pushed away the paper Cassie set in front of me at the dining table. Renee was tucked into bed and the house was quiet.

Missy had returned from her vacation Monday morning and got right to work helping Cassie look up information through the websites the law office had access to. By the time Cassie left, she'd printed out a few pages of information. None of it was a golden ticket to finding my father.

"It's hard without more to go on." Cassie flipped to the second page of the sheet in front of me. "But look, this is an address for an Anthony Smith, *and* it lists a Mike Smith and a Riley Smith as possible relatives."

My heart skipped a little beat. Maybe this was a breadcrumb. Mike was short for Michael. Riley might be the "R" in the "RJSmith" in my DNA matches.

"But no relatives for anyone with Bowers as a last name?"

Cassie frowned. "No."

"I don't know what to do." I rubbed the spot between my eyebrows. This whole thing seemed hopeless.

"I was thinking about that. If you message R.J. Smith or the R. Bowers on the website, they may ignore you. I think it's easier to brush an email off and not respond. But if you show up at Anthony's doorstep"—Cassie pointed to the address for Anthony Smith—"he might talk to you. It's a lot harder to turn someone away in person."

"Maybe." I shrugged. If my father's family wanted to deny my existence, there was nothing I could do to change their minds. If Anthony ended up being a dead end, I'd have no choice but to send out a couple of emails through the MyGenealogy website and hope for better results.

Cassie tapped her fingers on the table, seemingly lost in thought. *What crazy idea was that daughter of mine cooking up?*

"Mom, can I look at your account on the MyGenealogy website?"

"Sure. Let me get my phone."

I went in my room and grabbed my phone off the dresser. It wasn't like I had anything to hide from Cassie. I looked up at the music box on my shelf. How had Mom kept such a secret for so long? The burden of carrying it had to have been exhausting. Depressing.

You're no stranger to keeping things under the hood.

Maybe. But nothing like Mom did.

Are you sure about that?

I hurried out of the room and handed Cassie my phone. Cassie opened the app and scrolled through the screens.

"Look at this." Cassie scooted beside me at the table, holding the phone screen up. "This says RJSmith hasn't been on this app since October of last year."

I glanced at the screen, noting the date Cassie pointed out. "So, you think he's dead?"

"Well, I don't know. He probably hasn't been on the app for a while, which makes me wonder how useful it would be to send him a message through it."

"I guess not." More discouragement. "Wouldn't it go to his email?"

Cassie wrinkled her nose. "It might, but who knows. It could end up in his junk folder. What I'm saying is, someone who's not actively using this app may be more difficult to get in touch with. They might never read your message."

I nodded. "Makes sense."

Cassie flipped through screens again, this time landing

on the R. Bowers page. She tapped on another tab, and a date came up. December first. About a month before I mailed off my DNA test. "See, this person here, your first cousin. She's used the app more recently. Given her closeness in relation and how recently she's used it, she's our best bet."

"What should I do then? Write a letter to this Anthony guy, who may or may not be my uncle, or email this Bowers lady and find out if she knows something? Or go for broke and do both?"

Cassie blew air through her teeth. "I don't know. I guess we should pray about it and then make a decision."

"You go ahead, kid. Let me know what you find out."

Cassie pursed her lips, concern in her eyes. "You seem...angry lately."

Angry? I didn't know if that's what I'd call it. Anxious. Frustrated. *Fine.* I laughed out loud, remembering my conversation with Janice.

"Why are you laughing?"

"It's nothing, baby girl. I don't know what I am." I looked toward the window. The days were getting longer, so some light still shone on the horizon, a deep pinkish purple.

Cassie put her hand on mine. "I don't completely understand why you want to find your father. But I know what it's like to have unanswered questions." She squeezed my hand. "We'll find him, Mom. One way or another, we'll find him."

I did pray. Maybe not the same way Cassie did. Definitely not the way my mom would have. Tuesday after work I went for a drive, rolling down my windows and letting the fresh spring air wipe away the staleness of old cigarette smoke in my car. The radio blared classic rock and roll, and I sang along to my favorites. Janis Joplin. Steppenwolf. Credence. Songs entirely different from the hymns I sang in church during my youth, but ones that matched the strings of my heart and momentarily soothed the broken substance of my soul.

I blared the music as loud as my speakers would go without crackling and sang with gusto. While lyrics came from my lips, words circled in my mind.

Lord, there's something broken in me I can't fix.

Lord, finding my father seems like the only answer. I'm not sure what I'll do if he remains a mystery.

Lord, I know I'm my own worst enemy. Help me be a better person.

Lord, take this loneliness away.

The Lord didn't answer my pleas or questions. Not that I expected Him to say much. I kept driving and found myself on a country road heading toward Marcola, a road I'd driven down so many times with Steven. Marcola was where he grew up. A small-town boy if ever there was one. Quiet and sweet, yet funny and charming. Tough as nails when needed, gentle as a whisper when we were alone. Our love of old music knitted us together. Sure, we listened to the '80s music of our contemporaries, but we loved the old music of the '60s, even some songs all the way back to the '50s.

Steven sang off key, so I sang louder. I danced like no one was watching, so he watched over me. He told me he loved me for the first time when we danced to "At Last" by Etta James, playing through the static on his old radio in the garage where he kept his 1969 GTO, the car that became his first race car.

My heart ached too much. The itching came. Strong. I inhaled and exhaled. Counted to three. Counted again. All this not knowing and waiting to decide was killing me. I needed to do something with the information I had, and I needed to do it *now.*

I pulled the car over and parked under the shade of a giant fir tree. Switching the radio off, I put my hands on the steering wheel and lowered my head. Cassie said I'd been angry lately. Something was stirring in me. It was like a bubbling brook, but it was fiery, and I couldn't control it as it ignited into a river of fire. The thing was, I wasn't even sure who I was angry with. My mom? Steven? My unknown father?

Myself.

Maybe there was no right answer, or maybe there were one hundred wrong ones. I mulled the conversation I had with Cassie over in my mind. Should I write to Anthony with the hope he actually was my uncle? Or email some lady I didn't know? Both seemed doomed to failure.

Even if you don't hit the groove, you'll still make it around the corner. Just make a choice.

Resolve washed over me at the sound of Steven's voice in my head. Today was the day to make a decision, to commit to the turn. I knew what I had to do.

I had a good hour before Cassie and Renee walked in the front door. Settling myself on my bed, I took out my phone and opened the MyGenealogy app. After tinkering around, I found R. Bowers, and then the tab for sending a message. I pecked out my message with shaking fingers.

Hi,

My name is Sharon Gilbert. I was born Sharon Bradford. I knew growing up that the daddy who raised me wasn't my biological father, but I didn't know until recently that my birth father didn't know about me. My mom didn't tell him. It's a long story. Anyway, I'm hoping to find him. I don't expect anything of him or his family. I just want to know if he had a good life. I'd like to know what he looks like. Stuff like that. His name is (was?) Michael Smith. He lived in Springfield sometime between 1943 and 1955, and I guess he came back to visit sometime around 1965. I think he had two brothers. That's about all I know. If you have any information about him, I'd sure love to hear about it.

Thanks,

Sharon, Your cousin according to DNA

I read over my email. It sounded ridiculous, but I wasn't sure what to change. I hit the Send button.

"What are you going to do if she doesn't respond?"

I'd waited until Renee was in bed before telling Cassie about the message I'd sent to R. Bowers.

"I haven't thought that far." I didn't want to think about hitting a dead end.

We sat on the couch with the television on a cop show neither of us was interested in watching, but it helped create background noise for our conversation. Renee had enough in her life that didn't make sense without trying to explain what was going on in mine.

Cassie pulled her knees up under her, like she was settling in for a long, intimate conversation. She was wearing yoga pants and a t-shirt, her hair pulled into a messy bun. I couldn't believe she was thirty already. I was getting old. My parents' grandfather clock ticked in the background. Time seemed to move faster the older you got. "I was praying about it, and I think we should work on this together. As a team."

I guessed God *had* talked to her. "Isn't that what we're doing?"

"Yes." Cassie stretched her arms over her head, cracking her knuckles. "But it seems to me you feel like you're in this all alone. You're not. I have something at stake in this too."

"I know, Cassie, but you don't need another thing to worry about."

"I'm not worried. I'm curious."

That made sense. Cassie had less skin in the game, so to speak. "Well, what do *you* think I should do next?"

Cassie pursed her lips and exhaled. "Let me contact Anthony."

"You think I'll mess it up?" She was probably right. My track record for success at anything wasn't in my favor.

"No, but I did some research online about how to go about these things—"

Of course you did. Smart girl.

"—and some people say it's best to have a third party contact a long-lost birth father, especially if he doesn't know you exist."

"But Anthony isn't my birth father. He *might* be my uncle."

"True, but it's still less intimidating, I think, to have someone with less at stake contact you out of the blue. I'm not unrelated, but the relation is further down the line. I'm looking for my grandpa, not my dad. It seems less...vital."

"That still won't stop him from lying if he wants to protect his brother from a love child's family. For all we know, Michael Smith is rich, and we could look like gold diggers." An unlikely scenario, but one of many that had crossed my mind.

"True. I read the blog of a woman who tracked down her adoptive father in a bolder way. She showed up and knocked on his door, once she was sure she had the right one. She'd found pictures of him online, and the resemblance was uncanny. She figured it'd be harder to deny someone was your child if you saw them face to face and it was like looking in the mirror."

Butterflies erupted in my chest. I looked very little like

my mom. How much did I look like my father? Mom didn't have pictures of him. All she had ever said about his looks was that he was muscular and had brown eyes just like mine. Could he deny my existence if he saw me in person?

If he was even still alive.

"We can drive to Medford and back in a day, right?" My mind whirled with possibilities, the information about him from the printout Cassie had shown me already burned into my memory.

"Absolutely." Cassie smiled, her eyes shining with hope.

"How accurate is this record thing you used at work? Is there any way to tell if he still lives at the address it gave us?"

Cassie's brow creased. "Hmm. Maybe." She was silent for a moment, seemingly lost in thought. Suddenly she straightened, like she'd been jolted awake. "If he owns his home and I can access the property records for whatever county Medford is in, then I could confirm he still lives at that address."

Facing a long-lost uncle would be far less intimidating with someone by my side. I leaned forward, putting my now clammy hand on Cassie's knee. "If you confirm it's the right address, then maybe it's worth the trip."

"It most definitely is—and I bet I can find a great waterfall to stop at on the way."

That daughter of mine. Always looking on the bright side. If I didn't love her it'd be annoying.

Chapter Thirteen

I PULLED INTO THE QUICK-SHOP-N-GO parking lot, needing a pick-me-up to get through the rest of the afternoon after a bustling day at work. It seemed my whole life was on standby, making me ridiculously tense. Waiting to hear back from R. Bowers, whoever she was. Waiting for a Saturday off so we could make a trip to Medford and find Anthony Smith. I felt like I was holding my breath waiting for answers that may never come.

I beelined to the candy aisle and grabbed a package of Red Vines and a Snickers, then breezed to the soda cooler for a Diet Coke. I caught a glance of myself in the bowl-like security mirror and winced. My uniform had shrunk—or I had grown. My hair tie was loose, making my fine dishwater blonde hair fall in my eyes. At least the loose hair helped hide my crow's feet. I opened the door of the soda cooler, the cold rush of air a welcome chill to my overworked body.

"Sharon, is that you?"

I jumped at the male voice behind me.

"Sorry if I startled you." The smoky tone was familiar, like an old song.

Closing the cooler door, I spun toward the voice, then felt my jaw drop like some starstruck teenage girl. Talk about a blast from the past. "Johnny?" Though I said his name as a question, I had no doubt about the identity of the man in front of me.

Johnny grinned, creating deep lines on the edges of his goatee and moustache. "Guilty." He shook his head, sky-blue eyes twinkling. "How long has it been? Twelve? Wait, no—fifteen years?"

I nodded, suddenly feeling awkward with my hands full of candy and soda. "Something like that."

Johnny's gaze softened. "You look the same." He gave me an almost shy grin.

I blushed. I didn't look the same. The years of drinking and smoking had made wrinkles appear around my mouth and across my forehead. My blonde hair hid most of my gray, but soon I'd have silver streaks unless I started coloring it. Johnny, however, had aged well. If anything, the white accents in his beard and eyebrows added depth to his light brown hair. His hairline had receded, but it only made his blue eyes stand out more.

"You haven't changed much either." I wasn't about to tell him he looked even better than he had when he up and left me fifteen years ago.

Johnny looked down at the load in my hands. "Need some help with that?"

Good gravy. Talk about great impressions. "Nah. I just need to pay for this and get home."

Johnny stepped out of the way and let me by. I noticed he held a six-pack of Budweiser beer. My heart fell. Looked like some things remained the same. He walked beside me as I made my way to the counter.

"I wondered if you still lived in Springfield."

I snorted. "Yep. Just moved back here last fall." I handed my card to the cashier, not wanting to see the expression on Johnny's face and hoping he didn't ask any more questions. "What brings you to Springfield? Seattle not treat you well?" I cringed at the bitterness in my voice. Things had not ended well between Johnny and me, to say the least.

Then again, relationships never did end well for me.

Johnny chuckled. "Seattle's ancient history. I was working in Portland most recently. Now I'm in Springfield for a spell, until my new job down south starts."

I laughed. Still the same ol' Johnny. The cashier handed me back my debit card and I faced Johnny again, intending to bid him farewell. The gentleness in his expression stopped me short.

He set his six-pack of beer on the counter. "I'd love to catch up with you while I'm in town."

I looked at the Budweiser, then at Johnny. "Lots of things have changed."

Johnny glanced at the brown paper bag in my arms. "No doubt about that." He grinned sheepishly.

Why did his smile still make my heart flutter, after all these years?

"See ya later, Johnny." I hurried past him and out the door, my chest aching. Maybe I'd been harsh, but my ex-boyfriend's job story and the six-pack of beer he was buying at three in the afternoon were all I needed to know about what Johnny was up to these days.

Why then did the air feel colder and the clouds overhead look darker when I walked away from him? I got to my car and fumbled with my purse, pulling out my keys. Johnny walked out of the store, his hands empty, and ambled up to me.

I tried my best not to let my eyes linger on him too long, but I couldn't help but notice he still had a muscular build under the flannel shirt he wore, though the bulging of his midsection softened his overall appearance. "Looks like you forgot something."

He shrugged. "It can wait." An uncharacteristically serious expression lined his brow. "I know things between us didn't end on a high note, and I can only imagine what you've summed up about me in the last three minutes." He sighed. "How about this." Johnny reached in his back pocket, pulling out a wallet. He took a card out and handed it to me. "Here's my business card. I'm going to be in town for the next month. If you want to grab a bite to eat or a cup of coffee or even go for a drive and catch up, give me a ring."

Johnny's jovial smile—the same one that had won me over all those years ago—returned. "Or text. That's what people do these days, right?"

I took the card and met Johnny's gaze, which was full of nothing but tenderness and good humor. I put the card in my bag. "Take care of yourself, Johnny."

I got in my car and watched Johnny walk away. Surprisingly, he didn't go back in the store. Instead he got into what had to be a brand-new Ford F-350 pickup, the kind of truck that had a payment equal to some people's rent.

Thoughts of Johnny filled the rest of my afternoon. When I got home, I looked over his business card. Apparently, he was an independent trucker these days. The phone number on the card had a 503 area code—Oregon, probably the Portland or Salem area. It even had an email. I couldn't help but grin at the email address: JohnnyBGood@longhaultruck.com.

To my annoyance, my stomach was too full of butterflies to eat the Red Vines. Women in their mid-fifties shouldn't get all flustered over a man. Especially when said man had broken the woman's heart. Peeling myself out of my uniform, I berated myself. Johnny had been great...until he wasn't. I'd met him after I'd moved back to Springfield to be closer to Cassie and my parents. He was a bouncer in the night club where I tended tables. Things were great for nearly a year. Then he changed. Johnny never harmed me physically or emotionally, he simply...stopped, for lack of a better word. Stopped working. Stopped paying the bills. Stopped coming home every night. Then one day, he said he'd found a job in Seattle and was moving. Sure, he'd invited me to go with him, but how could I? My relationship with my family had already been shaky, marred by my drinking. If I moved to another state, my relationship with them would be nonexistent. Plus, even as messed up as I was then, I knew Johnny wasn't reliable. He was an alcoholic, like me.

Johnny was the last thing I needed in my life right now. Yet I couldn't bring myself to throw his card away. Instead, I put it in the bottom of my nightstand drawer, hidden under my journal.

After days that moved so slowly I felt like I was living in a world of cold molasses, the Saturday we set for our little adventure arrived. Cassie had been able to access the Jackson county property records, which confirmed that an Anthony Smith owned a house at 1126 Fir Acres Lane in Medford. According to the other information she found, Anthony was seventy, the right age to be my father's younger brother. It was enough to justify a one-day trip to Medford.

We loaded a cooler containing a picnic lunch and plenty of water in Cassie's Explorer. Unfortunately, all the waterfalls between Springfield and Medford were quite a drive from the I-5 corridor, so Cassie elected to skip waterfall hunting this time. I could tell she was a little disappointed.

The drive south was beautiful. The rolling lush green hills dotted with oak trees gave way to steep mountains covered with majestic conifers. Renee played on her tablet in the back seat, humming along to the Christian pop music blaring from the radio. I'd brought some Lifesavers and popped one in my mouth within fifteen minutes of leaving home. Riding in a car was still hard to do without smoking. If I was driving, I at least had something to do with my hands. Being a passenger left me too idle.

"Sing, Grammy!" Renee's voice piped up from the back.

Surprised by the request, I turned to Renee. "I don't know this song, sweetie." I spoke the truth. All Cassie listened to these days was contemporary Christian music, songs mostly unfamiliar to me. I preferred my old-time rock and roll, thank you very much.

"But Grammy, I love it when you sing." Sadness tinged Renee's voice.

Cassie glanced at me. "I remember you singing me to sleep when I was young. It's one of my favorite memories."

"Yeah, I keep that to myself these days." I shifted in my seat.

"I know. I'd forgotten all about it, honestly. But the other day I heard you singing when we walked in the house. It was good, Mom. It kind of pulled me back into the past for a minute." Cassie smiled, but sadness filled her eyes.

"I'm sorry." I gripped the handle on the passenger door as my chest tightened. The last thing I wanted to do was remind my daughter of all the hurt I'd caused her.

"Why? It was a good memory."

I turned to Cassie. "It was?"

Cassie chortled. "Yes, Mom. It wasn't all bad times. Lately I've been able to focus more on the good. It's almost like the more time that passes between when—you know, what happened last year—and now, the clearer perspective I gain on my past."

"I'm glad to hear that, baby girl." I inhaled, soaking in the beauty outside the car window. Cassie was healing from the abuse Derrick had inflicted—it was as clear to see as the crystal blue sky outside the window.

Since moving in with Cassie and Renee, I had found myself singing again when others weren't around. Somewhere along the path of alcoholism, I'd quit altogether. I hated my voice almost as much as I hated who I was. When I quit drinking almost two years ago, I started singing in my car one day. My voice was crackly at first, but the more I used it the more my vocal cords seemed to realign and remember what to do. After moving in with Cassie and

Renee, I found myself singing when others might hear, like at work when no guests were around, or at home when I was making dinner. Hope nudged my heart, saying it was possible for me to keep getting better. That, like Cassie, I could heal from my past. Maybe if I located my birth father and found the answer to my questions, I could begin to feel like a real person again, whole and full of promise.

We stopped at a park in Grants Pass, a serene little place along the Rogue River. We took the picnic lunch to a park bench in the shade.

"This is what I think we should do." Cassie spoke between bites of her turkey sandwich, made with nutty whole wheat bread. "When we get to the house, you and Renee stay in the car. I'll go knock on the door and introduce myself and tell him who I'm looking for."

I took a sip of my Diet Coke. "What are you going to do if he says he *does* have a brother named Michael?"

"Well, first off, I'll try not to jump up and down with joy." Cassie gave me a crooked grin. "Then I'll ask him if his family lived in the Springfield area sometime around the early 1950s. If that's answered affirmatively, I'll ask him if he knows whether or not his brother came back to visit Springfield sometime around 1964. I'll probably also ask him if he remembers Nannie."

I nodded. Cassie had the years right, based on what we knew. Michael and his family had lived in Springfield until he was twelve. They'd moved away, but Michael had come back alone to visit when he was about nineteen.

"What if he doesn't remember her?" I set my drink down. "Why not just ask him where Michael is?"

"Think about it. If some stranger showed up at your door and asked you where your sibling or some other relative lived, would you tell them?"

I tilted my head. "Good point."

Cassie put down her sandwich and opened her purse and rummaged through it, pulling out a small white envelope. "I'll show Anthony this, to help jog his memory." She took out a black and white photograph and handed it to me. A picture of my mom when she was about eighteen. Her ash brown hair was cut in a cute bob, and her gray eyes seemed to sparkle in the photograph, even though it lacked color. A wave of grief washed over me.

"And if he remembers Nannie, what will you say?"

Cassie glanced at Renee, who was eating her apple slices but listening intently. "Well..." She shifted her gaze back to me, her mouth askew. "Then I'll tell him the rest of the story, and where I fit into the saga."

"What's a saga?" Renee's eyes were wide with interest. The older she got, the harder it was to shield her from grownup matters. At some point we would need to tell Renee the family history. No more keeping secrets.

You're not the flagman in Renee's life. It's Cassie's main event.

Goosebumps erupted on the back of my arms. It would be Cassie's choice of when and what to tell Renee. Would she learn from my mistakes? Or would the legacy of secrets continue? The Diet Coke in my stomach felt like acid.

"A saga is a big story," Cassie replied without missing a beat.

"Why are you in a saga, Mommy?"

Cassie ruffled Renee's hair. "We're all in a saga, honey. It's called life."

Great way to avoid answering the real question. "Are we ready to get back on the road?" I put the picture of my mom into the envelope and handed it to Cassie.

We found the house easily enough, a tan '50s-era bungalow

with a few nice shade trees and a long driveway with extra parking space on the side. Not fancy, but well kept. Cassie parked on the opposite side of the street.

"What if he's not home?" It was a question so obvious I wasn't sure why neither of us had asked it before.

"I thought about that. If he's going to be home, Saturday midday is as likely a time as any. If he's the guy we're looking for, he's probably retired and home more often than not."

"Good point." I looked at the house. "I can't believe we're doing this."

Cassie laughed. "Me neither. I feel like I should be on one of those reality TV shows or something."

"Where are we?" Renee asked from the back seat.

Cassie turned toward Renee. "Mommy needs to talk to the man at this house. I won't be there very long. You and Grammy can stay here."

After grabbing her purse, Cassie exited the car. As I watched her walk up to the house, anticipation mixed with dread made my heart bang into overtime and perspiration broke out under my arms. Inexplicable fear seized my entire body and everything in me wanted to yell at Cassie to get back in the car and get out of there. Instead, I sat stiff as a statue, trying to keep myself from hyperventilating. I inhaled slowly. One. Two. Three. Exhaled. What had I gotten myself into?

The door opened shortly after Cassie knocked, answered by a petite woman with short curly dark hair. Was she Anthony's wife? She looked far too young, probably younger than me. Maybe this wasn't the Anthony's house I was looking for after all. Relief and disappointment cooled my body, slowing my wild heartbeat.

I expected Cassie to come back within a couple of moments, but she stayed on the porch, talking to the woman. My heart jackrabbited. I sucked in my breath. Who was this woman? What were she and Cassie talking about? Was the woman in the door a relative of mine? Of Cassie's?

I gripped the door handle. I had to get my nerves under control. I inhaled and exhaled slowly, counting to three. Over and over. My pulse slowed, but my body felt weak, as if I'd run a marathon already.

And it was barely past noon.

"Grammy, are you okay?"

Renee had been such a trooper for the car ride and now waited patiently for something she didn't understand. "Yes, Sweet Pea." I looked at my granddaughter seated behind me. She held the tablet in her hands, her favorite game lighting the screen. How had she known anything was wrong? "Why do you ask?"

Renee shrugged, her mouth in a frown. "You're breathing funny. And you're quiet." Her sad eyes looked at me with concern. "You aren't the same."

Guilt washed over me, replacing the fear. I remembered Cassie's remark about my seeming angry lately. The last thing I wanted to do was not be present for my granddaughter. She'd been through and lost enough.

We all had.

Though all I wanted to do was watch Cassie's conversation with the stranger across the street, I forced myself to refocus. "Do you want to play tic-tac-toe?"

Renee bobbed her head up and down. "We can draw it on my tablet."

"Sounds good. You go first."

I used the minute it took Renee to switch programs on her tablet to glance up at Cassie on the front porch. She was still talking to the woman.

Renee and I made it through seven games of tic-tac-toe before Cassie opened the driver's door and got back in the car, her face unreadable.

"Well...how'd it go?"

Cassie turned to me, her brow crinkled but a smile on her face. "The good news is, I think we found the right guy."

My breath caught in my throat. "What's the bad news?"

"He's not here."

I exhaled and tried to conceal my disappointment.

Before I could ask questions, Cassie continued. "He's rented out the house for the last three years. He spends his retirement traveling in his RV. In the summer and fall, he comes back here, but there's no telling when. He keeps some of his things in a room in a storage shed behind the house here, but pretty much lives in his RV year-round."

The information swirled in my mind and I tried to make sense of it. "Is there a way to contact him?"

Cassie shook her head. "I asked for his cell phone number, but Carol—the lady who is renting the house—didn't feel right handing it out, which I understand. She did say she would give him my number and let him know I stopped by. She also said he tends to go to the same places at different times of the year. Come June, though, he's never consistent about where he goes."

Talk about elusive. "How are you sure we have the right guy?"

Cassie waggled her eyebrows. "I asked Carol if she knew whether or not Anthony had lived in Springfield when he was a kid. She said, 'As a matter of fact, I think he did. My son interviewed him last year for a school paper about farming in the 1950s.'"

Cassie took a breath, then continued. "I guess his family owned a small farm. I asked her if he had a brother named Michael, and she said she couldn't recall the names but did remember him mentioning he had two brothers. However, they had all gone their separate ways in adulthood."

Mom had never said anything about my biological father

living on a farm. "I don't know, Cassie, it's still a long shot." I couldn't get my hopes up. Or let my inexplicable fear get a foothold because of some vague clues.

"Sooooo." Cassie lowered her chin, scolding me momentarily with her eyes. "I asked Carol if she happened to have a picture of Anthony. She was actually quite excited about it, because of the report her son had written based on his interview with Anthony." Cassie smiled. "She is definitely a proud mom. She had the report in a binder on the bookshelf and got it out for me. There was a picture in it."

Cassie pulled her phone out of her purse and held it up to me. "Believe it or not, she let me snap a picture of the picture."

I looked at Cassie's phone and pulled my head back, wishing I'd remembered to bring my reading glasses. It was a black and white photo. A man, a woman, and three boys were standing in front of a modest farm-style house. I peered at the boys. The oldest looked to be a preteen. His hair was light, probably a sandy blond, like mine. An eerie sense of familiarity flowed over me. The width of his nose. The way it pointed at the end. His eyes were brown, easily determined even in black and white. The thin lips. The strong cheekbones, wide-set jaw. It was like looking at a picture of me when I was young, except male, taller, and muscular. All my life I hadn't looked like anyone around me, including my beautiful mom. Even Cassie hadn't inherited many of my features. But the boy in this picture looked like me.

"There's definitely a similarity." My voice was raspy.

Cassie nodded. "I agree."

"I'm surprised she divulged so much information to a complete stranger." I handed Cassie's phone back to her.

Cassie shrugged with one shoulder. "I had to hedge the truth. When she told me he was gone and wouldn't be back until August or later, I knew I had to come up with an alternative approach. I told her I was doing a research project, putting together a history of my family who migrated to Oregon from the Midwest. I told her the Smiths were relatives on my mother's side and not much was known about them."

I shook my head. "That was a long shot. But I guess if she didn't know the family history it wouldn't matter where you said they were from."

"It was actually my road in. Since Carol's son had already done a research project and knew a little about Anthony's history, the statement about the Midwest struck her. I guess his family *was* from the Midwest. Illinois, in fact."

"That's an amazing stroke of luck."

"That's not luck, Mom. That's godly intervention."

Goosebumps erupted on my arms. Call it what you want, I wouldn't argue with some good fortune for a change.

We talked more about Anthony Smith on our drive home. From what Cassie had learned, he was probably driving from an RV park in Arizona to one in Moss Landing, California. Carol had taken Cassie's number and offered to call Anthony and let him know she was looking for him, but Cassie told her there was no hurry. Carol said Anthony rarely called her, so if she didn't call him, he may not get the message until he returned to Oregon.

"Don't you think we should have had her contact him, then?" I was mildly irritated. Didn't Cassie understand all this waiting was agonizing?

"I'm not sure." Cassie stared straight ahead, focusing on the road.

The Christian radio station crackled, then the signal was completely lost and the Explorer filled with silence. I was surprised Cassie didn't try to tune to another station. "You could've given her my phone number. Maybe we can turn around." Letting this lead go nowhere was not an option.

Cassie's jaw tightened and her brow wrinkled. "I had an idea." She glanced over her shoulder, checking on Renee, then got the look on her face that every mother since the dawn of time has when the child who they hope is sleeping is actually asleep.

"I'm all ears."

"I've been at my job for a year now and have paid vacation coming. What if we go on a little family vacation to California?"

"What about Renee's school? And the cost of gas and food and a hotel?" I couldn't ask my family to sacrifice money and schooling for my benefit.

"Renee has a three-day weekend coming up. It wouldn't hurt for her to miss one day of school and make it a four-day weekend. She's only in kindergarten. We could easily drive to Moss Landing and back in four days. It's not that far."

"Seems like a lot to do for something that still may not lead to answers. There's better things to spend money on." I looked out the window. I had seven hundred dollars in my savings, but I was putting it away for Christmas and the inevitable auto repairs on my old clunker.

"I have some money saved."

"No! You're not using any of your hard-earned money for my sake. It's more than enough that you drove down to Medford for me." After all I had done to and hadn't done for my daughter during most of her years, the last thing I needed was for her to do so much for me.

"Mom! Believe it or not, it's not all about you."

Those were fighting words and stung. I pursed my lips together to keep my mouth shut and continued to stare out the window.

"Look." Cassie's voice softened, full of tenderness, increasing my guilt. "Renee and I could actually use a little getaway. Life hasn't exactly been a walk in the park for the last year."

She was right. Cassie and Renee had been through the wringer. Though things were calm now, life for Cassie seemed to be all about working and keeping life going from day to day, with little time for special outings and definitely no vacations.

I turned to my daughter. When had she aged? Tiny lines formed around her eyes, and the fullness from her cheeks had lessened. Yet when I looked in her eyes, I saw the hope of a child. My child. "Okay, let's say we call this a family vacation with a little side trip. Is Moss Landing where you would really want to go?" The idea of visiting California beaches was a dream for me, but Cassie was a mountain and waterfall girl.

"Are you kidding me? It'll be amazing. California. Beaches. Adventure!" Cassie opened her mouth wide with exuberance, but something about her expression seemed forced.

Unease washed over me. "I don't know. When is this three-day weekend?" I didn't know how long I could handle waiting. Even now, the all-too-familiar and tense feeling of wanting to be out of my own skin was trying to take over.

"In two weeks." Cassie frowned. "It isn't a trip you should make alone, you know."

Could she feel me chomping at the bit? Two weeks wasn't too terribly long to wait. I'd waited months for the DNA test results. A couple more weeks wouldn't kill me.

"If you really want to make this happen, I'm game."

Chapter Fourteen

WITHIN TWO DAYS OF RETURNING FROM our trip to Medford, Cassie had arranged time off from work and researched RV parks near Moss Landing.

"There's only two RV parks in Moss Landing." Cassie had called me from work during her afternoon break, almost breathless with excitement.

I sat outside in a cheap plastic chair and watched Renee play on the lawn. Cassie had arranged for me to pick her up from her afterschool daycare early so Renee could enjoy some of the warm and sunny spring day.

"That's a lucky break." I continued before Cassie could once again chide me about how there was no such thing as luck. "Are we going to go to both and knock on every door until we find him?"

"Of course not."

I gave a little laugh. "Is there another way?"

Cassie sighed. "When I was talking to Carol and she told me about how Anthony spent his time at RV parks, I said something like, 'Oh, he must have one of those KOA memberships,' and she said, 'Oh no, he's not a fan of KOA.'"

Renee rolled a Barbie Mustang over the grass, making car sounds as she went. I smiled at both my daughter's cleverness and my granddaughter's playfulness.

"Let me guess. Out of the two RV parks near Moss Landing, one is a KOA and the other isn't."

"Bingo!" Cassie nearly squealed, clearly excited about her discovery.

I pushed the edginess creeping up on me down to the pit of my stomach. This couldn't end badly. I could handle my own disappointment—one way or the other. I *wouldn't* be able to stand seeing my daughter let down if our search proved unsuccessful.

"Sounds like we have a plan. My coworker Janice said she'd switch days with me if needed, so I can get the time off." I forced my voice to be nonchalant, though not one bone in my body was that carefree right now.

"It'll be our Mother's Day family getaway," Cassie said matter-of-factly.

Mother's Day was that close? Dread clung to me, pushing away the hope. The first Mother's Day without my mom, and I was going on a hunt for my biological father. How was that for irony?

I did all I could to keep busy while we waited for our weekend getaway to arrive. I even went to a couple of AA meetings. I fought the itching feeling under my skin and the tautness of my nerves by making one too many trips to Dollar Tree and eating one too many candy bars. My expanding waist threatened to bust a seam in my jeans. I needed to find a better way to ease my tensions before I required a new wardrobe from Goodwill.

One night after dinner, I went to my room early, unable to find comfort in anything. Lying in bed, wide awake, I remembered my run-in with Johnny. Was he still in town? Johnny had always been a good listener. In the year we were together, I'd opened up to him more than any man I'd met since Steven died.

It'd be nice to have someone to talk to now, someone who understood at least part of my past. Someone who might listen to my longings and hopes without judging me. I rolled over and opened my nightstand drawer, pulling out his business card. The black card with the phone number in red type called my name. Grabbing my phone, I punched the number in, then my finger hovered over the green button to finish the call.

What good would talking to Johnny do? Sure, he was a great listener, but what about his drinking? What if he invited me over? Would I say yes? Would he be drinking? And if he was, how could I resist a drink?

My stomach sank. I couldn't take the chance. Too much was at stake with my relationship with Cassie and Renee. Even finding my birth father could be sidetracked by whatever happened with Johnny. Exhaling my disappointment, I moved to push the end button, but something caught my finger like a lick of fire. The next thing I knew, I'd pressed the Add New Contact button instead. With trembling fingers, I typed in "Johnny Beckett" and saved it. Who knew? Maybe I'd need a trucker friend in the future. Best not to burn bridges.

"I wish you didn't have to work today." Cassie sleepily gazed at me over her cup of coffee as I gathered my purse, ready to head to work.

"You and me both." I frowned dramatically, hoping Cassie believed me. The truth was, I counted working on Sunday as a blessing. I still hadn't told her about my run-in with Samantha during the Easter potluck, and as long as I stayed away from church, I didn't see a point in bringing it up.

Cassie's brow pinched. "I hope you can go when we get back from our trip. I think it would do you good."

What was that supposed to mean? I had two minutes before I had to be out the door, but I couldn't avoid the bait. "Why's that?"

Cassie shrugged. "You've seemed kind of edgy and sad...ever since Nannie's birthday."

A gut-punch of a statement, though I knew Cassie didn't mean it to be. "I'm sorry. I guess I miss her some days more than others. It's hard to explain." My response was true, but there was more. How could I explain the sadness and anger intertwining within when I didn't even understand it myself?

"See you this afternoon." I left before Cassie asked any questions.

The bad thing about working Sundays was it meant no Janice. We worked together well, and her sense of humor and at times annoying optimism made the days go faster. My coworker ended up being one of the Latina ladies who spoke limited English, so conversation was sparse.

On my break I checked my cellphone, looking at the MyGenealogy app. R. Bowers hadn't responded to my message, but according to the app she also hadn't logged in since I sent it. Cassie was right. Reaching out to her was probably pointless. I looked through what little information I could find about her on the app, which was nothing more than our relationship and our shared ancestry. Finding my father through her seemed about as likely as winning the lottery.

My only hope seemed to be finding this long-lost uncle of mine that Cassie had tracked down, partly by pure luck.

It's not luck, Mom.

I wished I had my daughter's faith. Her optimism.

A summer storm greeted me as I left work. Normally I loved the smell of rain hitting dry pavement, but now all I could focus on was the darkness the clouds created. Driving home, a different kind of dark cloud invaded my head, casting a shadow over every thought.

I'd never find my father.

Running into Samantha at church was proof I would never escape my mistakes.

The unending urge to drink would eventually be more than I could bear.

I would, eventually, mess up this second chance with Cassie.

Then I would lose everything.

The next thing I knew, I pulled into the parking lot of an outdated strip mall. A line of shops was before me. One of them was a cannabis store. Not my thing. Three doors down from it was a liquor store. That *was* my thing. My pulse jackrabbited, making me dizzy. I needed more strength than I possessed. I needed someone to talk to about the battle inside of me. Every recovery book I'd read would say I should go to an AA meeting, but the thought of talking to a group of strangers about my problems only deepened the scathing wound of loneliness inside of me.

I needed a friend.

I reached in my purse and pulled out my cell phone. I brought up Johnny's number. The thought of talking to him instantly brought a spark of soothing hope to the pain growing in my heart. It also caused an onslaught of baby butterflies in my chest. I remembered his email and smiled. "JohnnyBGood." Could he truly be good now? Had he changed?

I pushed the green button. It was worth finding out.

<h1 style="text-align:center">Chapter Fifteen</h1>

"HELLO?" THE SAME HUSKY VOICE I'D heard in Quick-Shop-N-Go greeted me.

I held my breath, ready to hang up. I'd never set up my voicemail, so if Johnny called back, he wouldn't know it was me.

"Sharon?" His voice was both soft and expectant.

Pretty bold of him to assume it was me. Yet his saying my name into the void of the phone call...it was somehow flattering. Had he been thinking of me?

"Yeah, it's me. Lucky guess." I laughed awkwardly and punched myself in the leg at the same time. There I was again, acting like a dumb teenage girl.

Johnny chortled and my chest warmed. I'd forgotten how good his laugh sounded. It had both a mysterious and musical quality to it.

"I'd kind of given up on you calling. Was still hoping you would, though."

"Yeah, well, you know me. I hate being predictable. I think that was one thing we had in common." *One of two to be exact.*

"Hmm. I'd have to agree with you on that, but..." Johnny paused, but I could hear movement. "I like to think of myself like a good bottle of whiskey. I get better with age."

The mention of whiskey made my stomach do a little flip. Was comparing himself to whiskey a sign he was still a heavy drinker? "I don't drink whiskey," I replied, my voice flat.

"As I recall, you were a Jack and Coke kind of woman." A hint of reverie lingered in his voice.

"Not anymore. Now it's just Diet Coke for me." If that

didn't give him the hint of where I stood these days, then age had made him dumb.

Johnny didn't miss a beat. "I hear you. My partying days are over." He laughed again. "I'm guessing we've both changed a whole lot since the last time I saw you."

He couldn't have changed *that* much. The six-pack of Budweiser he was toting in the mini-mart was proof. Then again, he'd also left it behind.

"My life is completely different than it was when you left, that's for sure." Could he hear the bitterness in my voice? We were ancient history, but seeing him again had brought back the memories like a springtime flood.

Johnny didn't respond right away. "What are you up to today?"

I laughed. Great way to avoid the land mine I dropped. "Well, I just got off work from my dazzling job at the Day and Night Inn and now I'm heading home." *And sitting in the parking lot of a liquor store, trying to talk myself out of walking in and buying a bottle of Jack.*

"Can I buy you dinner?"

My breath caught in my throat. Dinner with Johnny? I'd called him because I needed someone to talk to, but having dinner with him sounded more like a date. "My daughter has dinner waiting for me at home." It was three p.m. and Cassie and Renee had undoubtedly already eaten Sunday dinner. I'd arrive to leftovers in the fridge and the two of them napping, most likely.

"Your daughter is living with you?" He sounded mildly surprised.

"My daughter and granddaughter." The thought of Renee made me smile, and I could hear the change in my tone.

"How about that?" Johnny made a low whistling sound. "It sounds like everything worked out the way you hoped it would, at least in some respect."

Not exactly. It'd been a long time in coming, and there were lost years I could never get back. But I knew what he was thinking—my not following him to Seattle had worked out for me.

Why, then, did I *not* feel like I was living in a happily-ever-after? "It's a road I'm still navigating, to tell you the truth."

"Hmm. I see."

I stared at the liquor sign, having nothing left to say and yet wanting to tell him everything.

"Since you're having an early dinner with your family, how about meeting for a cup of coffee later this evening? I'd love to catch up and hear about everything you've been up to the last fifteen years."

I closed my eyes. I couldn't deny I wanted to see him in person. Hearing his voice only solidified the longing. Coffee sounded innocent enough, and I did need someone to talk to. "As long as wherever we go has decaf."

I agreed to meet him at six p.m. at Shari's, which he assured me had decaf—and pie. My heart fluttered as soon as the significance of his restaurant choice registered. The first time Johnny and I met outside of work had been at Shari's, where we'd had coffee and a slice of pie. I navigated my car out of the parking lot and headed home. The urge to drink had vanished, thanks to Johnny.

By the time I got home, I'd almost talked myself out of meeting Johnny. What was the point? He was practically a stranger to me now. A stranger soon heading out of town. Why get attached to him, only to say goodbye in a few weeks? I'd be better off going to an AA meeting and spilling my guts to a room of strangers.

I found Cassie in the living room reading her Bible. My

mom's Bible. I'd made it through Mom's birthday, but now Mother's Day was coming up. Leaving flowers on her grave would never make up for all the Mother's Days I'd broken her heart by not being there.

"How was church?"

Cassie beamed. "It was good. I wish you could've been there."

I nodded. "Me too." If only Samantha could disappear, going to church might be enjoyable—or at least tolerable.

How long are you going to keep what happened with her under the hood?

I shook away the sound of Steven's voice. It had an almost foreign sound to it after listening to Johnny's on the phone.

"Leftovers are in the fridge." Cassie shifted on the couch and closed the Bible. "I was thinking we could watch a family movie tonight." She glanced out the window at the overcast sky. "Perfect weather for it."

She was right. It would be a great night for a movie. "I don't know, baby girl. I'm thinking about going to a meeting tonight."

Cassie frowned briefly, but then her mouth lifted into a sad smile. "I'm glad you're keeping up with your AA meetings."

Guilt grew in me like a weed sprinkled with fertilizer. The truth was I hadn't been going to meetings as often as I should. The urge to drink still tugged at me like a rope attached to an ox. But worse than all of that was knowing I should go to a meeting tonight, but I was still contemplating meeting with Johnny.

I helped myself to leftovers, but the food turned in my stomach. I wanted to see Johnny. I longed to hear his voice again. I knew he'd listen to my story and my worries without making me feel bad about myself. He'd always had a way of reassuring me. He'd softened my hard edges with his gentleness and humor. I envisioned his soft blue eyes—so much more welcoming than an AA meeting.

But a yellow light flashed in my head, screaming to use caution. If Johnny still drank at all, I couldn't spend time with him unless I could be certain he didn't drink around me. And what if I got attached to him, even if only as a friend? With everything going on in my life, could I handle another loss when he left town?

Even as I showered and got dressed, I debated with myself. When I chose my nicest pair of Levi jeans and my most feminine shirt—a V-cut red blouse with long, flowy sleeves—I knew what choice my subconscious had made.

"You sure look nice." Cassie's eyes twinkled as she looked me up and down. "Is there a man you're aiming to impress at your meeting?"

I sucked in my lips, the unfamiliar taste of lip gloss assaulting my tongue. "A man is the last thing I need."

Cassie nodded. "I agree. It'd only be a distraction."

She was correct. What she didn't understand was how much I needed a distraction. "See you soon." I grabbed my coat and purse and headed out the door, all too aware that I had lied to my daughter. But this was a necessary lie. No need to tell her about a man I'd probably never see again.

Johnny waited for me inside Shari's, standing by a group of people seated on a bench obviously waiting for their names to be called. The place was packed.

He beamed when he saw me, his eyes a diamond-studded sea of periwinkle blue. He closed the distance between us and wrapped me in a bear hug. I stiffened, caught off guard by his show of affection, but at the same time breathed in his scent—Old Spice. The smell transported me in time, and suddenly his arms around me felt familiar and right.

He stepped back, his face uncertain. "Sorry, I didn't mean to catch you off guard." He tilted his head and grinned sheepishly. "You look amazing."

Heat burned my cheeks. "Thanks." I wanted to say he looked amazing too, but my mouth seemed to have forgotten how to form words. He wore a short-sleeved button-up shirt that made it evident he lifted weights. It even somehow hid his wider midsection. The gray in his beard made him look distinguished and wise instead of old.

"Johnny?" A young and bouncy waitress called out. "Your table is ready."

Johnny motioned. "After you."

I followed the waitress, painfully aware that Johnny was probably watching me walk—from behind. Why had I eaten so many candy bars lately? My jeans were too tight, especially in the rear.

The waitress seated us in the corner, at a booth by a window. I slid onto the bench. We ordered our coffee, decaf for me and regular for Johnny. The waitress left us the pie menu.

Johnny set the menu down. "Remember the first time we met here?"

I looked away, unable to suppress a smile—and unwilling to look at the glimmer in his eyes. "How could I forget?"

The memory flooded back, as if it had all happened yesterday. I was working as a cocktail waitress and Johnny was doing security at a nightclub in Eugene. It had been one of the most popular places for music and dancing back in its day.

"I'd been wanting to ask you out but was sure you'd shoot me down. I wrangled my courage when you came back from break that night and I saw tears in your eyes."

I'd forgotten about the tears. No doubt my failure to quit drinking— even after moving back to the area to be closer to my daughter and parents—had caused them. "You'd caught my eye too. I found it admirable you were working nights and going to diesel mechanic school during the day." I shook my head. "You always looked tired."

"I *was* always tired."

"But after all of that, you're driving truck now?" The question had been plaguing me. He'd worked hard to get through school, then moved to Seattle to take a new job.

Johnny sighed. "Yeah, well, I got bored."

"I guess some things never change." I took a sip of my coffee.

"I never got bored of you, Sharon." Johnny's usually twinkling eyes smoldered with sincerity.

I looked away, my cheeks once again on fire. "From your business card it looks like you're an independent contractor. How is it you're moving to take a job?"

Johnny didn't respond right away. Had I offended him by my abrupt change of subject?

"Some opportunities are too good to pass up. Owning your own business isn't all it's cracked up to be."

I met his gaze. "I imagine it's a lot of work, but also gives you a certain amount of freedom."

He looked thoughtful, and for the first time I noticed the lines on his forehead. "Yes, and your financial future is always uncertain. I'm getting too old for that." Johnny lifted one shoulder. "It's well past time for me to be putting money aside for retirement."

Wow, Johnny talking about saving for retirement was something I never thought I'd hear. "Makes sense." My shoulders sank. I had no retirement and no hope of saving for one on a maid's salary.

"I found a sweet truck-driving job down near San Francisco. I'll be making more than I've ever made in my life, even if you consider the increased cost of living there. Plus, I'll get medical and all that stuff."

"San Francisco? My family and I are heading down that way this weekend. I've never been." How coincidental it was the same area where Johnny would soon be moving.

"Really?" Johnny leaned in. "Family vacation? Or are you planning on moving to Cali, too?" The familiar sparkle returned to his eyes.

"Ha! No to moving. It's sort of a family vacation."

"Sort of?"

"It's a long story."

"I'm not going anywhere." Johnny's eyes twinkled.

At least not right away. I sighed. This was what I had called him for. Someone to listen to my struggles. The next thing I knew, I spilled out all the details of my search for my father, brought on by my mother's deathbed confession. I went on to tell him about my quitting drinking and my tenuous relationship with Cassie and Renee. Johnny listened, nodding and encouraging me to continue, with a sympathetic "Oh man" or "That had to be tough" thrown in at all the right places.

The waitress checked on us a couple of times, but Johnny kindly waved her away.

"Whew, Sharon, you've got a lot going on. I'm impressed at how well you're holding yourself together. Many would crack under the weight." Johnny's eyes shone with sympathy.

"I feel like I'm hanging by a thread, and it's getting thinner by the day."

"You're too hard on yourself." Johnny shook his head. "You don't realize how strong you actually are."

My heart warmed, melting my already disintegrating

walls. "Yeah, well, I don't feel strong." I'd spent too much time talking about myself. "There's so much I want to ask you, but one thing I can't figure out."

He smiled. "What's that?"

"Why are you here in Eugene?"

"I came to spend time with my family before I head off to California. It'll be a while before I have vacation time. I've been staying with my sister and her family, but also going up to see my parents in Junction City. Things were rough between us for a while." He ran his finger along the edge of his coffee cup. "Which probably makes you want to ask more questions—and you know I don't respond well to excessive questioning."

I laughed. "Some things never change, I take it."

He shrugged. "I guess so. I always appreciated how you understood the way I thought."

I had never held Johnny's reluctance to questioning against him. Mainly because I was the same way. When I was ready to talk about something, I'd talk. Until then, anyone who tried to make me would face nothing but resistance.

Johnny picked up his menu. "Let's order pie. We can always talk about me the next time we get together."

The next time? My heart pitter-pattered. "But you're moving."

"Not right away. I'm heading back up to Portland this week to settle up a few things. My new job doesn't start until the second week of June."

"That's quite a wait for a new job." He must have a good stash of money put away to be out of work that long.

Johnny nodded. "There's hoops to jump through with getting the California license, finding a place to live, etcetera."

That made sense. "Well, then, I guess we could have

coffee again."

"Or dinner." Johnny winked.

"Sounds like it'll have to wait until after next weekend. You're busy. I'm busy." I lifted my eyebrows, testing him.

"I'm a patient man." His grin was nothing but pure confidence.

I couldn't say no.

Chapter Sixteen

"WHAT IF MY BIO DAD IS DEAD?"

Cassie and I packed our luggage in the back of the Explorer, ready to hit the road. The week had passed slower than a clock running on a low battery, and I was thankful Thursday was finally here. But anxiety had me on edge.

Cassie stopped and put her hand on her hip. "That's a negative note to start our road trip on."

"You're right. Sorry." Truthfully, I *was* a bundle of nerves. I should've been excited for the time away, for the adventure. But the fear of what I'd find—or not find—was a dark cloud over the entire prospect. It didn't help that the sky was overcast this morning, a light drizzle dampening my spirits as well as my hair. Maybe it was an omen.

Renee ran around the house excitedly, even though it was six-thirty a.m., talking nonstop about all the fun we were going to have. The heaviness in my chest lightened. If I could see the day through the eyes of my grandchild, I wouldn't be sad or worried at all.

Once we were on the road, my heart lifted a little. Cassie kept a good pace on I-5, and a few hours later we were driving through Medford and a feeling of déjà vu swept over me. I was overwhelmed for a moment by the absurdity of what we were doing, traveling to another state to find some guy who was probably my uncle but had no idea we were coming. No idea we even existed.

I resisted the urge to text Johnny. We'd exchanged multiple texts throughout the week, but I still hadn't told Cassie about him. I reasoned she only needed to know if I followed through on our dinner plans. I promised myself I wouldn't reach out to him while on this trip with my family.

It was my way of making sure I was putting family first, the way I should've all my life.

By the time we hit Redding, California, Renee was taking a much-needed nap. I wanted to join her but didn't feel comfortable leaving my daughter alone to navigate us through Sacramento and down through the Bay Area to Highway 101. Besides, this was a good time for mother-daughter bonding. Unfortunately, no topics of conversation came to mind. I took a Red Vine out of the package sitting next to me and put one in my mouth.

"I swear you're going to get diabetes." Cassie stuck out her chin.

My insides rankled, but I pushed my own frustration aside. "Nannie had a sweet tooth. She never got diabetes."

"Mom, Nannie liked dessert after dinner. A piece of pie. Some graham crackers and milk. Maybe a cookie or two. You eat candy. There's a difference."

"What's the big deal?" I rolled my eyes and turned to the window, shoving the last of the Red Vine in my mouth.

"Well, for one thing, it's not healthy. For another, Renee is always asking me for candy and I'm always telling her no, at which point she quickly points out, 'But Grammy was eating a candy bar.'"

I sighed. So, I was a bad influence on my six-year-old granddaughter?

"Look, Cassie. Here's the thing. Quitting smoking was a tough one. The candy is my way of dealing with the nicotine cravings."

"Shouldn't they be gone by now? It's been, like, three months."

Laughter rose in me. A twenty-seven-year dirty habit, and she thought it would all be gone and peachy keen in three months. The absurdity of it made my eyes water, and soon a belly laugh had me doubled over.

"Why is that so funny?" Cassie's voice held more than a tinge of irritation.

"Honey, if it were that easy to quit, people wouldn't die from lung cancer." I blew air through my teeth. I knew my daughter was too smart to think quitting smoking was that easy. Something else was going on inside her head. "What's eating at you?"

Cassie shrugged one shoulder, her eyes not budging from the road. "I don't know. I honestly do worry about your health, you know."

I nodded, my heart filling with so much love I thought it would burst. "I appreciate that. It means a lot to me. But I think I'm on the upswing with no more drinking and smoking, don't you?"

Cassie glanced at me, her eyes shining with joy. "I'm so thankful to God for that." After a heartbeat, her expression changed, turning serious. "You're all Renee and I have left in the world. You *have* to take care of yourself, for our sake."

My throat tightened and the bridge of my nose stung. I averted my gaze out the passenger window, watching the farm fields as we passed by. "I'm doing my level best. I promise you."

A melancholic song played on the Christian radio station. "Mind if I change the station?"

"Sure. I guess we've been pretty much listening to the same twenty songs on repeat on the other station."

I snorted. *Ain't that the truth.* "Well, at least we know all the words now."

I reached over to change the dial. Scanning the stations, I found a country music station with an upbeat tune. A few moments later the song on the radio ended. A slower tempo song began playing and a male's baritone voice filled the car. The song sounded like one of those country ballads that was a story. He sang about a dad who drank too much and made a lot of mistakes. His son grew into a man and turned to God to avoid making the same mistakes. The song went on to describe standing at the father's grave, and how the son would choose to pass down both the happy memories and the bad ones to his own child, so the curse wouldn't be forgotten but neither would the blessings of a father's love.

Goosebumps prickled my skin and my chest ached. Of all the songs to come on, why this song *now*, after my daughter told me how she worried about my health? We needed a happy tune to chase the darkness away. I flipped through the dial again and found a pop station playing something danceable with bass. Hopefully the feeling the country song left would be be-bopped away by the new tune.

When I looked at Cassie, though, I knew it was too late. Tears streamed down her cheeks, and she didn't look my way. I fought with every bone in my body not to grab another Red Vine and stared out the window, silent.

We needed to find my father and put this family curse to rest—at least my side of it. No two ways about it. And if we found him and he was still an alcoholic?

No, he couldn't be. God couldn't be that cruel.

As the sun was making its descent, we pulled into the parking lot of our hotel in Salinas.

Two oak trees and a few palms surrounded the simple two-story adobe style building. Not bad for my thirty-five dollar per night rate I'd been able to get us with my corporate discount—one of the few perks of working for a hotel chain. Satisfied pride lifted my spirits. I didn't make much money, but I'd been able to provide our room for this trip.

We unloaded our bags and the cooler and checked into our small but clean two-queen room. We weren't near the ocean, but the view from our window of the expansive blue skyline over the buildings of downtown spoke of warmth and sunshine. Renee jumped on one of the beds, full of pent-up energy and the excitement of staying in a hotel room.

Cassie sat down and looked at her phone. "There's a beach only twenty minutes from here."

"Let's go! Let's go!" Renee squealed.

Laughter bubbled out of me, pushing past the unanswered questions in my head and the heartache from the conversation in the car. "I second that emotion. Let's go to the beach."

Cassie dug through her things and pulled out a couple of beach towels she had brought. I grabbed the bag of cheap sand toys I'd brought from Dollar Tree for Renee, and we headed to the Explorer. Cassie put the address into the GPS and soon we were heading down Highway 183.

After an easy drive, we found a parking lot near Marina Beach and made our way to the sand and down a short but steep hill dotted with low-lying shrubbery. A warm breeze smelling of saltwater blew through my hair, and the tension eased from my shoulders. When we got to the bottom of the hill and stood on the expanse of flat sandy beach, we took our shoes off and carried them with us in a backpack Cassie had worn. Renee ran ahead of us, and Cassie had to call her back twice, but she didn't sound angry or worried when she did. I breathed in the openness of the ocean, the awe-striking beauty, the freshness of the sea air. A person could forget all their problems here, at least for a little while.

Johnny had scored big with his new job if he was going to be living close to a paradise like this. A twinge of jealousy squeezed my chest. Some people had all the luck.

At Renee's request, we rolled up our pants and stepped into the ocean. With Cassie and I each holding one of Renee's hands, we walked into the water and jumped as each wave hit, trying to jump over it. Renee's eyes danced with light, her smile so big it covered her entire face. The brown ringlets of her hair blew every which way. Cassie laughed more than I'd heard since I didn't know when, and I joined her, relishing this moment of family.

For a moment I forgot the entire reason behind our trip. For a moment it even seemed ludicrous to me that finding my father even mattered. Then the lyrics from the country song we'd heard on the way down replayed in my mind, the one about the alcoholic dad. I remembered Cassie's silent tears. I remembered the day I almost walked into the Broken Bottle bar and let everything I was working for slip away.

I couldn't let that happen. I couldn't even let myself come close to it again. As inexplicable as it seemed, I knew the key to fixing this self-destructive void inside of me was in finding my father. The key to my freedom was in finding my roots.

Chapter Seventeen

Hope mixed with dread the next morning as we made our way to Moss Landing. We followed the same highway that took us to the beach, but this time we headed north once we hit Castroville.

When we pulled up to the attendant station at Salty Breeze RV Park, butterflies competed for the Olympic gymnastics trials in my stomach. Cassie talked to the attendant in the booth while I fidgeted in my seat.

"Could you tell me which space is reserved by Anthony Smith?"

The man frowned and scrolled through the screens of his computer. "Space forty-three." He closed the sliding window between us.

He was actually here? My heart rate doubled. Would this be the moment of truth or a dead end? My fingers itched for a cigarette. I reached for a Red Vine despite Cassie's misgivings.

The next thing I knew, Cassie pulled into a nearby parking space. We exited the car and walked through the RV park, looking for space forty-three. Various rigs were backed into spaces that included a tiny square of grass, a picnic table, and rusty barbecues. Not a trashy place, but not the best either. Of course, I had almost no experience with RV parks, so for all I knew, this could be the equivalent of a four-star hotel.

It didn't take long to find space forty-three where a boxy, off-white RV with an orange and brown stripe running along the middle was parked. Obviously an older model, but clean. The door to the RV was closed and there were no signs of recent use of the picnic table. A sudden jolt of fear rippled through my body, and I stopped in my tracks. I couldn't do this.

I grabbed Cassie's arm. "Let's go."

"Why? What's wrong?"

"This is crazy."

Cassie grasped my hand. "You know you don't mean that. If you don't do this, you'll be wondering about it the rest of your life."

Our girl's right, Sharon. This is make it or break it time.

It was the first time I'd heard Steven's voice all week. I breathed in slowly, hoping to slow my pulse. Cassie was right, even though she couldn't possibly understand the significance of it. Steven was right...or whatever that other voice in my head was that sounded like him.

I squeezed Cassie's hand. "I know. I'm getting cold feet, I guess."

We walked up to the door. Cassie stepped in front of me, opened the screen, and knocked.

The sound of movement came from inside the RV. My heart did jumping jacks inside my chest. The door opened and an elderly man stood in the entrance and peered down at Cassie, not seeming to notice Renee and me standing on the pavement behind her.

I couldn't help but stare at him, looking for something familiar, but it was hard to tell with his age. His head was bald, except for short gray hair on the sides that stuck straight out. He had heavy jowls and a large nose, but that was part of aging. Cheeks sagged and noses grew.

"Can I help you?" he asked, looking somewhere between hesitant and concerned.

Cassie cleared her throat. "Hi. My name is Cassie. Your tenant in Medford may have told you about me."

The man nodded. "She mentioned a young lady stopped by wanting to know more about the family, claiming to be some distant relative." He paused and eyed Cassie suspiciously. "You drove here from Oregon?"

"It's a long story. Do you have a few minutes to talk? I can explain everything."

The man jutted out his chin and grunted, looking down at Cassie with uncertainty. "I guess you don't seem like a sales gal. Or a con artist." He cleared his throat. "Give me a moment and I'll join you outside."

He closed the door, and I exhaled. Cassie looked at me with a wide but nervous grin. Ready or not, it looked like we were going to have a sit-down talk with my long-lost uncle.

After a couple of minutes that seemed like twenty, Anthony opened the door and stepped down to the pavement. His gaze fell first on Renee and then on me. His eyes narrowed, then he turned to Cassie. "Let's sit here at the picnic table."

We all took a seat. Renee remained silent and enthralled, seeming to be as expectant and nervous as the rest of us. Cassie had told her what we were doing before leaving the hotel, putting it in simple terms. "We're trying to find Mommy's other grandpa, and the man we are going to see might know where he is." Renee didn't have many questions. Even at the tender age of six, she seemed to sense there were certain things she wasn't supposed to fully understand or question. Things too painful to talk about.

Cassie started talking almost as soon as we sat down. "I'm sorry to show up like this, but I felt like this was better done in person."

The man nodded, his eyes on Cassie. He was silent for a moment, then shrugged. "How can I help you?"

"I don't know exactly how to say this, so I'll just blurt it out."

I noticed Cassie twirling the hem of her t-shirt in her hand, and her foot tapped the ground in a *vivace* tempo. A bundle of nerves. My poor girl, and it was all my fault. Why had she insisted on being the one to talk? I couldn't let her keep this up.

"I think you're my uncle," I announced. No warning, no emotion. Matter of fact.

Anthony sat up straight, his eyes widening. "How's that?"

Cassie rotated her face toward me, her eyes owllike. I hadn't followed the script. I never had followed the rules to a "T." If I followed them at all.

"It's a long story. The short of it is my mom, Eula Bradford—Brown was her maiden name—had a short love affair with Michael Smith. He didn't know she was pregnant with me when they went their separate ways."

"Eula?" Anthony's eyebrows raised. He blew air through his teeth and looked away, rubbing his chin.

"Did you know her?" I asked. It made sense he would. Long before the love affair, Nannie and Michael had been friends. She would have known Michael's little brothers too.

"Yes, she was a sweet girl." He smiled wistfully. "Her and Mikey and...what was his name?" Anthony furrowed his brow in concentration.

"William?" I offered.

"Yes, William." He nodded. "The three of them were as thick as thieves." Anthony met my gaze, seeming to take me in and size me up. I noticed for the first time that his eyes were brown, like mine. "We moved away when I was ten years old."

"Do you know where Michael is?" Cassie piped in. She held onto the bench of the picnic table with both hands, gripping it almost as tight as she had the steering wheel on our drive down.

I wished my stomach would stop flip-flopping like a fish out of water.

Anthony took a deep breath and looked over our heads, his eyes seeming to see a different time, a different place. "No, I'm afraid I don't."

My heart fell to my stomach, taking the little, excited fish down. "You don't? Were you not close?" How could brothers lose track of each other?

"At one time, yes. When we were little. Long before our dad passed away and we argued over the business he left us with. And before..." His voice drifted off, and he shot a sidelong glance at Renee, who remained engrossed in a game on her tablet.

"Before what?" I couldn't help but press, though fearful of the answer.

My newfound uncle looked at me with both sorrow and interest, and something else I couldn't put my finger on. "Mikey and I had a disagreement about whether or not we should keep our family's furniture business or sell it. I wanted to keep it. Our youngest brother, Richard, was only fifteen at the time. I was eighteen but already working in the business full time. Mikey didn't like building furniture or dealing with manufacturers. I guess you could say he wasn't business minded."

Cassie's hands had let go of the bench, and she reached one hand for mine, giving it a little squeeze. That's when I noticed my hands were shaking. We'd come all this way for nothing.

"When did you last see him?" My voice sounded hoarse.

Anthony rubbed his chin. "Guess it would've been 1968. We finally agreed to disagree. Mikey wanted out, and I didn't want to fight about it anymore. I gave him everything we had in savings—three thousand dollars—and he left." Anthony's gaze dropped to the table. "Richard and I ate little more than beans and rice for the better part of a year. Struggled to make the business work. My dad had bought it with my mom's inheritance after she passed away. It went downhill after Dad took over. He was good with his hands, but bad at business—his drinking made him that way." Anthony lifted his eyes, which focused on me. "Mikey had the same problem."

A light breeze blew through the RV park, swaying the big leaves in the palm-like trees. I felt Cassie looking at me, but I couldn't bring myself to turn her way. As Nannie suspected—no, as she *knew*—my biological father had been an alcoholic. From what Anthony said, he was still drinking three years after my birth, and so wrapped up in his addiction he left his younger brothers to fend for themselves after their father's death.

He sounded like a real winner.

An alcoholic. Selfish and self-destructive.

Like me.

"You never heard from him again?" Cassie asked.

I couldn't bring myself to look at Anthony for a reply. My skin crawled, and my insides were heavy and painful. All I wanted was for the pain to go away. For the itching shell of my body to settle, even for a moment, to something that resembled peace.

Anthony spoke, barely above a whisper. "No, I'm afraid not."

"What about your younger brother, Richard? Is there a chance he heard from Michael?"

Another uncle. Maybe he had answers. Good girl, Cassie. Always thinking and searching for possibilities. I raised my head and looked at Anthony, the action sparked by hope.

Anthony's face fell, accentuating his jowls. "If he did, I never heard about it. Richard passed away seven years ago. Cancer."

Hope left, and darkness took its place. I had no fight left.

I bit the inside of my cheek, the pain distracting me from my urge to cry.

"Ma'am." Anthony nodded toward me.

I'm your niece. Didn't you hear? But I had no family title to this stranger. "Ma'am" was good enough for me.

"If I were you, I'd give up looking for Michael. He was a good boy when we were young, but he followed in our father's footsteps. You're better off for never having known him."

Was the statement supposed to make me feel better? I snorted, anger building in me, the weight in my gut intensifying. My mom had made the same decision, deciding I was better off not knowing my biological father. No one seemed to understand that not knowing him was like looking in the mirror and only being able to see half of the image staring back at me. It left me always wondering what the other half looked like. For better or worse, the unknowing had always been there, eating at me, taking one little bite at a time until a wound that I couldn't heal grew and festered.

To know what I knew now—to hear my father had continued drinking and maybe never overcame the demon of addiction—this was worse, because I never got to see any of the good. I heard the evil, the bad, the failure. A stinging reminder of what I had inherited.

"Let's go." I shot out of my seat. My head spun a moment, waiting for my body to catch up. "Thank you for your time."

Cassie frowned but nodded and stood. "I'm sorry we took you by surprise. Here." Cassie reached in her purse and pulled out a piece of paper and a pen, jotted something on it, then handed the paper to Anthony. "If you remember anything that might help us find Michael, could you give me a call? It would mean a lot." Cassie reached for Renee's hand. "To all of us."

We drove in relative silence to the park Cassie had promised to take Renee to—the Dennis the Menace Park. Bright blue and yellow play structures gave the playground an amusement park feel. A cement walkway wound around the park, banked by a lake on the other side. Blue skies and blue water, canopy-like trees mixed with tall poplars, kids running and laughing, parents watching...the stuff of picture-perfect dreams.

Renee grabbed my hand. "Grammy, will you go on the bridge with me?"

A large suspension play bridge, ending at each side on top of a sandy hill, seemed to be one of the main focuses of the park. After the disappointing visit with Anthony, I was in no mood to play, but I refused to let my own self-pity ruin this trip for my family. I inhaled deeply, setting my resolve. "Sure, honey."

Renee and I took off to the suspension bridge. After we wobbled our way across, we went to a long double wavy slide and went down it together. Despite myself, I laughed. Seeing the joy radiating from my granddaughter made me forget for a moment the disappointment that crushed my chest.

When we got back to Cassie, she was talking on the phone. "Yes, we're heading there in a few moments. I can't wait." Cassie glanced at us and held up a finger while she continued her telephone conversation. "I'll let you know what we think." She nodded, eyes twinkling. "Thank you. Okay, talk to you later."

"Who was that?" I asked.

Cassie put her phone back in her purse. "Oh, that was Matt. He told me about this little restaurant down here we should try. He saw it on a T.V. show and thought it sounded great." She smiled sheepishly.

"So, it's just Matt, now, huh? No pastor?" I pursed my lips to keep from smiling too big.

Cassie flushed. "Uhm...well...yes. He asked me to call him Matt and said I could drop the pastor." She shrugged.

"Mmm-hmm." Maybe I wasn't the only one hiding my romantic interest.

We left the park and went toward the wharf, where we had lunch at LouLou's Griddle. Pastor Matt had made a good call. I wasn't a big fan of fish, but their hamburgers were excellent. Even Renee ate all of her fish and chips. After lunch we explored Fisherman's Wharf until Renee whined, complaining her feet hurt. Time to head back to the hotel.

Once we were in the car, Renee fell asleep and all the fun and distractions of the day were gone. The dark, heavy feeling in my chest came back. My lunch turned in my stomach, making me nauseated.

"Are you okay, Mom?" Cassie's voice held more than a tinge of concern.

"I'm fine." It was a fat lie, but what good did *not* being fine do?

"Don't lose hope. We can do more research, and you might hear back from the person you contacted through the MyGenealogy website."

I nodded. Sure. It could happen. For someone other than me. While waiting for the DNA results, every story I heard about someone using the newfound way of finding family members seemed to have a happy ending. The findings of the test and one phone call resulted in cross-country trips to meet unknown family members. Pictures of people with expressions of joyful surprise from finding unknown family seemed to pop up everywhere while I was searching for my own father. It looked like my story would not have a happy ending. I fought against the anger and bitter thoughts. Didn't God know I couldn't keep fighting these urgings in my gut, keep pushing down the aching in my chest, without some help?

Did God even care?

I knew one person I could reach out to who would offer words of solace for my aching heart, but I'd promised myself not to contact him while with my family this weekend. Another pang of bitterness shot through my chest. If Johnny truly cared, wouldn't he have contacted me by now? Even though he knew I was with my family, he could have shot me a text.

Once back in the hotel, we rested for the afternoon and made sandwiches out of the groceries we had brought with us for dinner. Afterward, we took Renee swimming at the hotel pool, then finally it was bedtime. Sleep sounded like a welcome reprieve.

Right after Cassie had gotten Renee bathed and put her into pajamas, Cassie's phone rang. She picked it up expectantly. I assumed it was Pastor Matt. After exchanging a few niceties, Cassie held the phone away from her, and whispered urgently, "Mom, it's Anthony."

She put the phone back to her ear. "Anthony, I'm putting the phone on speaker so my mom can hear."

Cassie took a seat next to me on the couch, holding the phone out in front of her.

"Yes, well…" Anthony's voice came through the phone. "I got to thinking after you gals left. About ten years ago, when I sold the furniture store, I had to get Mikey's signature for a legal document. My attorney tracked him down and sent it to him. Mikey signed it and sent it back." Anthony paused. "I never heard a word from him. But I called Carol in Medford and had her look through the records I have stored in the attic." He cleared his throat. "She found the address. I have no idea if he still lives there, but I thought I could give it to you.”

An address? Adrenaline zinged through my extremities.

“Thank you so much!” Cassie reached for the notepad and pen I still held in my hands. “What’s the address?”

Anthony read it slowly. It was another California town called Susanville.

“I wish you gals the best of luck.” Anthony cleared his throat again, and when he spoke it sounded strained. “If you find Mikey, tell him his little brother Tony said hello and I hope he’s doing okay.”

Cassie thanked Anthony again and ended the call, then looked at me with an ear-to-ear grin. “See, I told you there was hope.”

I returned her smile, but I refused to let hope take me for another ride. “We’ll see.” I studied the address on the piece of paper. “Susanville is in northern California. Maybe I can take another trip. Probably best to send a letter, though, and not waste any more gas and time.”

Cassie sighed with exasperation. “Hold on.” She fiddled with her phone, focusing intently on the screen. “Look, on our way home we can cut through Sacramento and go to Susanville. It’ll only add two hours to our return trip.”

I glanced at Cassie’s phone. “It’s already a nine-hour drive. It’s too much for a six-year-old unless you’re taking her someplace like Disneyland.”

Cassie looked thoughtfully at her phone. “Maybe we could leave tomorrow and stay the night in Susanville. That should cut the driving in half both days.”

“Is there an amusement park in Susanville? A beach? Anything worth dragging Renee on this wild goose chase?”

Cassie lowered her chin and took on a scolding tone. “This could be it. We have an address. It’s the best lead so far.”

I sighed. "It feels selfish to put you and Rene through this." Cassie was a mom now. If nothing else, she should understand the concept of mom guilt.

"Renee is having a blast. And so am I. If we leave tomorrow and drive to Susanville, we'll have a whole new area of scenery to take in. A new place to visit we've never been. It's all part of the adventure. And who knows? It could end with a new family member." Cassie smiled, but sadness mixed with empathy shone in her eyes.

I blew out my held breath through clenched teeth. Maybe she was right. If not now, maybe never. This might be my last chance to find my father. "Okay...I suppose." I looked at Cassie with the sternest expression I could muster. "But if this is another dead end, no more road trips for long-lost relatives."

Cassie sighed. "Never say never."

"I mean it."

"Fine, Mom. No more road trips...unless we have a rock-solid lead."

That daughter of mine. When did she get so stubborn?

Chapter Eighteen

By midday on Saturday we pulled into Susanville, an old-looking town in a vast desert of sagebrush with a barren mountain range in the distance.

The grayness of the mountains against the blue sky reminded me of when Cassie and I had lived in Redmond. We'd ended up there after my breakup with another good-for-nothing boyfriend in Albany. I'd thrown all our things in the trunk and back seat of my Chevy Cavalier, and put my eight-year-old daughter in the front seat with me. Too ashamed to face my parents with another failure, I drove east. Somewhere in my crazy and alcohol-pickled mind I decided we'd move to Boise. New state, new beginning. I'd taken a wrong turn somewhere near Bend and ended up in Redmond around dinner time. To say I was discouraged was an understatement. The wrong turn seemed to be the epitome of every decision I'd made since losing Steven. We pulled into a little diner to eat. A help wanted sign hung in the window. Next thing I knew, I had a job and found a little two-bedroom trailer to rent.

Maybe it could've been a new beginning, out there in a small town in the desert, but I couldn't stop drinking. I tried. Made it five days and four nights. Then I was back at it, slowly at first. A drink or two after dinner. Then a drink before dinner. Before I knew it, I was hitting the bottle by three p.m. each day. With no real friends and no family around except Cassie, I found myself spending more evenings than I should have at the local bar. I convinced myself Cassie was fine alone in the trailer at night. Harmless neighbors. Mature kid. I locked the doors when I left and called it good. I shuddered at the remembrance of my own stupidity.

The things alcohol could make you do.

The way it lured you into its soothing embrace, promising release from the pain.

"Are we going straight there, or stopping for lunch first?" My voice sounded foreign to me, emotionless.

"Probably best to eat something first. Especially for Renee."

We found a McDonald's. Renee ordered a Happy Meal, Cassie got a salad. I ordered a Diet Coke. I had no appetite.

Once we were done at the Golden Arches, the GPS took us straight to the address Anthony had given us. We found ourselves in a neighborhood of homes from the 1940s or 1950s. Simple, small, rectangular houses sat on quiet streets, with neat lawns and poplar trees lining the road.

We pulled up to a plain blue house. A door and three windows faced the front. A little blue Honda was parked in the driveway of a single-car garage. My stomach sank. No old man in his seventies drove a compact Honda.

"We might as well all go together." Cassie parked the car at the curb and killed the ignition.

"What about Renee?"

Cassie glanced over her shoulder. "Renee, we're going to see if a relative of ours still lives here. When we get to our hotel, we can talk about it if you have questions."

I raised an eyebrow at Cassie. "That's a big load for a six-year-old."

Cassie's face pulled into a frown that aged her beyond her thirty-one years. "I don't think there's any way of protecting kids from everything when there's certain family situations."

I lowered my chin to my chest and stared at the crumbs on the car floor. "I guess you're right."

Make this be good, Lord. Give us hope.

God didn't respond, but resolve steadied my nerves. "Let's do this."

Cassie rang the doorbell. The door creaked open. A young woman stood in the entryway with a guarded, concerned face. Her long brown hair was pulled into a loose ponytail, accentuating her high forehead. Thick, dark lashes framed her beautiful blue-green eyes. She offered a hesitant smile with full lips and perfectly straight teeth. "Can I help you?"

There was no way this woman was related to me.

"Hi, my name is Cassie Peterson. I'm sorry to bother you." Cassie paused, throwing me a furtive look. She motioned to me. "This is my mom"—Cassie put her hand on Renee's shoulder—"and my daughter, Renee."

The woman nodded at Cassie, her brow pushed together out of either curiosity or annoyance. She didn't offer her hand or an introduction.

Cassie inhaled and exhaled slowly then poured out words quickly. "We're looking for my grandpa. His name is Michael Smith. My great uncle gave us this address. Does he still live here?"

Nothing like laying it all out.

The look that swept over the woman's face reminded me of when Samantha recognized me at church. Was it surprise? Or fear? Was there something about us that looked threatening? Whatever it was, she regained her composure with apparent ease. "He isn't here." The woman cleared her throat and scanned each of our faces as if committing them to memory. Her eyes settled on me. "What is your name?"

"Sharon. Sharon Gilbert."

The young woman fidgeted with the handle of the door, like she couldn't wait to close it. "My name is Rebecca. I'm...Michael's personal representative. He currently resides in a, um, care facility."

My heart jolted with hope. Michael was alive.

My father was alive.

The smile on Cassie's face told me she shared my hopefulness. "Could you tell us which care facility he's in? We'd love to see him."

Rebecca looked at Cassie like she was crazy. "That's not information I'm comfortable sharing with complete strangers."

"I understand. But we only want to talk to him. Maybe we could call him at the care facility?"

"Like I said, I'm not comfortable sharing that information." Rebecca's eyes narrowed. "Why are you looking for him, anyway?"

Cassie turned to me, her eyes pleading for help. Something told me that even with her resources at the law office, if Rebecca sent us away, we would never find Michael. Yet I couldn't bring myself to tell this woman, a stranger, the complete truth.

"We want to introduce him to his great-granddaughter. He's never met her."

He doesn't even know she exists.

Rebecca shook her head, as if she didn't believe us. "That's interesting. I don't remember him ever talking about a daughter."

"Yeah, well, it's a long story." I was starting to get annoyed with this kid. How old was she? Maybe twenty? Who was a personal representative at her age? My own suspicions grew. No way was I telling her more about me or *my* family.

"How about you give me your phone number, and the next time I see him, I'll let him know you stopped by." Rebecca's voice was businesslike and guarded. We weren't going to get anywhere with her.

"That would be great!" Cassie reached in her purse and pulled out the same notepad and pen she'd used to give

Anthony her number. She balanced the thin notepad on her hand while she wrote our information. "I'm going to put my contact information and my mom's on here." Cassie handed her the piece of paper. "We really appreciate your help. You don't know how much this means to us."

Leave it to Cassie to be prepared and show unwarranted kindness. This Rebecca girl was a roadblock. I glared at her and muttered, "Yeah, thanks for your help."

We walked back to the car, defeat like an elephant on my shoulders. We'd driven to Moss Landing to find rejection and an apparent dead end. A crumb of hope led us on a big detour on our way home. And for what? A young woman who seemed to have a big "Road Closed" sign stamped on her.

My father was alive and yet nowhere to be found.

We found a hotel with an indoor pool, and Cassie took Renee swimming. I stayed in the room. In the quietness, a thought occurred. A convenience store was nearby. California didn't have Oregon's strict liquor laws. I could buy something good at the 7-11. Something to help me forget for a moment the failure of this trip.

You might feel like you're losing the race, but you've still got a chance of qualifying for the main event.

Steven. How different life would be now if he had never decided getting in the race car one last time was more important than his family. I shook away the thought.

A burning in my chest grew stronger. My hands clenched in fists against a feeling I didn't want to admit. One I had avoided for twenty-seven years when it came to my husband.

Anger.

You seem angry lately. Cassie and her observations.

Maybe she was onto something.

I glanced out the window. The sun was setting. I still had time to make it to the 7-11 and get back before Cassie and Renee finished swimming. I'd get some candy too, and tell her that's what I'd gone after if they got back to the room before I did. I could take a few shots in the hotel lobby restroom, store the rest for later in the bottom of my purse. It would be easy.

Realization punched me in the gut. Tomorrow was Mother's Day. How could I do that to my family this weekend out of all weekends? I couldn't. Not if I wanted to keep repairing the bridge between my daughter and me. Not if I wanted to be the grandma my sweet grandbaby deserved. My hands were clenched, holding the thin bedspread on the bed like it would keep me from falling. I inhaled. One. Two. Three. Exhaled. I could hold on for another day.

But I couldn't do it alone.

Digging my phone out of my purse, I sent a text to Johnny before I could talk myself out of it.

I didn't find what I was looking for.

He'd know what I meant. Seconds later, his response came through.

I'm so sorry, Angel Eyes.

Angel Eyes...the pet name Johnny had given me years ago, after he'd called me "baby" and I'd told him I'd punch him in the face if he ever called me baby again. The memory brought a smile, even with the aching in my chest.

Never understood why you chose that of all nicknames. LOL.

His reply was quick. *Because it's what I see when I look at you. Duh.*

I shook my head. *You're crazy, you know that, right?*

Crazy for you...crazy for you, baby.

I rolled my eyes and laughed. The vice that'd been

around my chest fell away. I might actually survive the night.

There you go, calling me baby. You know better.

I'm at a safe distance :)

Not for long.

Good point. I'm sorry you didn't find your dad. I wish I could help.

Me too. The truth was, he already had by making me feel better, even if momentarily.

Looking forward to our dinner.

We still hadn't set a hard date for dinner, and before we did, I needed to tell Cassie, but right now didn't seem like a good time. *Looking forward to it.* I heard a giggle in the hallway, followed by the clicking of the door unlocking. *Gotta go. Good night.*

See you soon.

Chapter Nineteen

Mother's Day.

IT WAS DINNERTIME WHEN WE PULLED into Springfield. I volunteered to treat us to pizza via delivery. Cassie gave a thankful and tired yes to that suggestion. By the time we had our bags inside and had unpacked the dirty laundry, the pizza delivery woman had arrived. We gathered around the dining table, eating sausage and olive pizza.

"When can I give you my cards?" Renee asked, her mouth full of cheese. She turned to me. "I made one for you too, Grammy, because grandmas are moms too."

"As soon as we finish dinner and clean up the table." Love filled Cassie's voice.

The crumbs were barely wiped off when Renee ran back from her room with two homemade cards. Carefully drawn flowers adorned the front of each card, and the endearing script of a six-year-old filled the inside. Mine read, "I hope you have the best Mother's Day ever, because you are the best Grammy there ever was. Love, Renee."

"I guess I better get my gift out of my closet for Grammy, huh?" Cassie winked at Renee.

Renee spun toward me as Cassie left the room. "Mommy wouldn't tell me what she got you, Grammy. She was afraid I'd spill the beans." Renee pouted. "I don't spill stuff, usually."

I sucked in my cheeks, suppressing a laugh. "You certainly don't." I patted Renee on the knee. "Grammy needs to get something out of her room. I'll be right back."

I heard Cassie opening the door of her room as I entered mine. I hurried to my closet and pulled out the two gift boxes. One for Cassie, one for Renee. I'd splurged on having them gift-wrapped. Perfect pink paper and a lavish white bow on each. As I made my way back to the living room, I pondered what Cassie could've bought me. Hopefully nothing too nice. If the gift were anything more expensive than a box of chocolates, I'd feel too guilty to enjoy it.

When I entered the dining room, a large, long box wrapped with purple wrapping paper and topped with a bow lay on the floor by the table.

"What in the world?"

"It's your present." Cassie smiled, looking as satisfied as a fat cat.

What could she have gotten me that required a box that size? Maybe it was a ruse. A big box to hide a small present, like a new DVD or a bracelet. It had to be.

"Are you going to open it, Grammy?" Renee had jumped out of her chair, her eyes dancing with anticipation.

"Well, of course. But first, I have a gift for you and your mommy." I handed one box to Renee, the other to Cassie.

"Mom, it's *Mother's* Day, not daughter's day."

Yep, I'd predicted that one to the "T."

"Single moms deserve extra presents, and you're the best mother I know." I nodded at the package. "I hope you like it."

Renee held her box in wonder and looked at Cassie, her eyes asking permission.

Cassie nodded. "You go first, sweetie."

Renee tore at the paper. I waited, anxious for her reaction. It wasn't a toy, and she wouldn't understand the significance of it until Cassie opened her gift.

"Aww. Grammy, I love this!" Renee picked the t-shirt up out of the box and held it to her chest. My heart warmed at her little-lady-like reaction.

"Can you read what's written on the shirt?" I asked.

Renee held the shirt with a drawing of a crown up in front of her. "Queen!"

Cassie giggled. "Yes, but it says more than that. 'Daughter of a Queen,' to be exact."

"Open yours, Mommy!" Renee put her shirt and box down and clapped her hands.

What a ham.

Cassie gently peeled the paper back. She gave me a little smile, probably because she already had an idea of what was in the box. Her grin widened when she took the lid off. "Do you know what this says?" She showed Renee the front of the shirt.

"Princess!"

"Close. It says, 'Mother of a Princess.'"

Renee giggled. "And you're a queen, Mommy." Renee shifted her focus to me, her face serious. "What does that make you, Grammy?"

"Old," I replied.

We all burst into laughter. I sighed, soaking in the moment. This was what family should be, every day.

"It's time for you to open your present, Mom."

My heart pitter-pattered. Why was I so nervous about the box's contents? "Can you put that up on the table?"

"Sure." Cassie easily lifted the package and put it on the dining table.

At least it wasn't heavy. I ripped the paper, which revealed a plain cardboard box. I smiled, expecting my hunch was correct. A small present inside a big box. "Hmm. I wonder what this could be?"

I found the edge of the rectangular cardboard box and pulled on it, opening one of the ends. Something with black fabric was inside. I grabbed it, feelings its weight. I pulled and got up, bringing the long case out of the box. The shape of it told me what it contained.

"What? Cassie? This is too much!" I held the guitar case in front of me.

Cassie learned forward. "Open it!"

My heart beating wildly, I unzipped the case and carefully lifted out an acoustic guitar. A Gibson. Light brown with a darker neck. A simple design but a good instrument.

"This is beautiful." I swallowed the lump in my throat. How long had it been since I held a guitar, and how could Cassie possibly remember I used to play?

"I hope you like it." Cassie's eyes glistened.

"Grammy, you can sing and play music now." Renee clapped her hands again, grinning ear to ear.

"I haven't played since your mom was in preschool," I told Renee. "I'm not sure I remember how."

"I'm sure it'll come back to you." Cassie squeezed my arm.

"I never told you I used to play." I searched Cassie's eyes. "What made you think to get this? And it's way too much money for you to spend on me."

Cassie put her hand on her hip. "First of all, it wasn't that expensive. I bought it used. Second, like I told you on the trip, I'm starting to remember things I'd forgotten. Good things. One of them is you playing guitar." Cassie relaxed her shoulders. "Then one day, the guitar seemed to disappear."

It hadn't disappeared. I'd hocked it to pay rent. That was my excuse, anyway. The truth was I'd blown all my money on booze. Playing the guitar wasn't the same after Steven died. It only brought painful memories of how much he believed in me.

"I'm surprised you remember. It wasn't long after your daddy died that I got rid of it." No need to tell Cassie the details.

"It's a vague memory. Hearing you sing is what brought it back, I think." Cassie's voice was barely a whisper.

I nodded. My singing seemed to be opening a whole can of worms.

Cassie got up. "There's something else...another reason why I knew I had to get you this, especially for Mother's Day." She went in the living room and came back with Nannie's old, worn Bible.

"You're taking up preaching now?" I teased, trying to lighten the mood.

Renee giggled. At least I got one laugh out of my joke.

Cassie rolled her eyes. "Ha, ha, funny. No. But listen." She sat down and flipped through the pages of the worn Bible.

I swallowed. Seeing the Bible made me miss my mom even more.

Cassie cleared her throat. "'And so it was, whenever the spirit from God was upon Saul, that David would take a harp and play it with his hand. Then Saul would become refreshed and well, and the distressing spirit would depart from him.'" She looked at me with glistening eyes.

"I'm not familiar with that verse." My verse memorization days were ancient history.

"It's from First Samuel. It's about how King Saul was tormented by a distressed spirit. One of his servants said they should get a musician who could play the harp to chase the spirit away. They brought David to play for Saul, and it not only made him well but also made Saul fond of David." Cassie paused, running her hand over the Bible page. "Nannie had the verse underlined and next to it she wrote your name." Cassie tapped her finger on the handwriting. "I think she was acknowledging or praying over your musical gifts."

Something like a rushing river ran through my head, drowning out the sights and sounds around me. A memory. I saw myself barely older than Renee, taking piano lessons. At first, I had enjoyed the lessons and I learned quickly. But it wasn't long before I became bored with the piano music. Listening to country songs on the radio, I longed to play a stringed instrument. I wanted a different sound than the hymns we sang at church. Something with twang, with a beat, with rhythm and soul.

When I asked my mom if I could take up guitar lessons, she'd stiffly refused. I asked her why and her only answer was that it wasn't appropriate. Rebellion and anger grew in me. I refused to continue my piano lessons. Eventually, when I was sixteen, I got a job at McDonald's and saved up enough money to buy myself a guitar. I didn't ask permission and I didn't tell my parents. I only played it when they weren't home, but one day Mom found the guitar in my room. She'd looked at me like I'd hung Jesus on the cross myself and stormed out of the room without a word.

"Mom, are you okay?" Cassie's voice came through the hum in my head.

"Yes, I'm fine. It's just that I don't think Nannie was praying over my musical gifts." I forced a laugh. "She wasn't a fan of me picking up the guitar when I was a teenager."

"Maybe she changed her mind." Cassie's reply was both matter of fact and gentle.

Could Mom have changed her mind? She'd never said a word about it to me if she did. Of course, there seemed to be lot she didn't say...until the end.

"Grammy, you can play the guitar and sing, and I'll dance, and Mommy can take a video." Renee piped up out of nowhere, breaking the somberness.

Could I learn to play again? Maybe, for my granddaughter, I would.

Chapter Twenty

JOHNNY WANTED TO PICK ME UP for our date, but I wiggled my way out of that one and told him I'd prefer meeting him at the restaurant. As wrong as I knew it was, I hadn't worked up the nerve to tell Cassie about Johnny. I had no doubt she'd disapprove, especially after she found out he was an old flame from my drinking days. And besides, why make a big deal of it? He'd be gone in a few weeks. I'd told Cassie I was going to another AA meeting. I wasn't sure what I felt guiltier about—lying to Cassie or skipping out on all the AA meetings I knew I should be going to.

The restaurant Johnny chose was located near downtown Eugene, in an old house that had been converted into an Italian restaurant. Parking was a challenge. I managed to find a spot on the street and made my way inside, my heart pitter-pattering. I'd already worn my best casual outfit when I met Johnny for coffee, so my only option this time was an old summer dress I'd hung onto all these years—floral, short, and made of a thin rayon fabric. If it wasn't for my nervous energy, I'd be freezing.

Johnny waited for me outside the door of the restaurant. I sucked in my breath and hoped he didn't notice my reaction. He wore a gray button-up shirt, with the top two buttons left undone, showing the top of his chest. Over it was a black sports jacket, perfectly cut. Most surprising were the gray slacks he wore. I'd never seen him in anything other than jeans or shorts. I felt underdressed.

"You look beautiful." He spoke softly, but the look in his eyes was intense.

"I don't get dressed up much these days." I stopped about three feet away from him, waiting for him to lead the way into the restaurant.

He held out his arm and touched me lightly on the back, leading me through the door. "I don't get dressed up much myself, but I figured this was a special occasion."

His touch made me break into goosebumps. Now that he was close, I smelled the familiar scent of Old Spice but also something else. The yeasty smell of beer. An alarm went off in my mind, but I let it go. Hopefully he knew better than to order a drink with me around. "Special occasion, huh?" I lifted an eyebrow, waiting for the punchline.

Johnny led us into the restaurant and gave the hostess his name. Apparently, he'd made reservations. "This is something I never thought I'd get to do again, so yeah, it's pretty special." His eyes glimmered playfully.

"You know what they say, 'Never say never.'"

"I'll remind you of that later, if need be." Johnny gave me a mischievous grin.

It'd been forever since I dated. No, that was a lie. It'd been forever since I dated *sober*. In fact, with every first date I had in my career as a widow, I'd taken the edge off with liquid courage. I didn't have that now. I felt naked. Vulnerable. I pulled my arm away from Johnny as soon as we reached our table, unable to come up with a sarcastic or even playful response.

The waitress left us with our menus after telling us about the daily special. I tried to focus on the menu, ignoring the dampness of my palms. Every dish sounded delicious, though I couldn't pronounce the Italian names if my life depended on it. My stomach felt like a little fish was doing acrobats in it. Good grief.

"How are you doing since you got back from your trip?"

I put the menu down. "I'm doing okay." I couldn't focus on food. I'd just order the special.

"You're lying." Johnny's voice wasn't accusatory, only coaxing.

I looked him in the eyes. The earnest interest in them pulled the truth out of me. "I'm discouraged. It was a wasted trip. I feel like every lead I find is a roadblock. They have information but don't want to give it up."

"Why do you think that is?"

Was it a trick question? "I don't know. I guess they take one look at me and figure I'm bad news."

Johnny shook his head. "You're taking it personally. There's nothing bad about you."

I laughed. Johnny had a certain naiveté when it came to me. Or he was a far bigger player than I ever gave him credit for. I'd go with the latter. "You're so full of it, Johnny Beckett."

"I mean it, Angel Eyes." His eyebrows pushed together, and his smile faded. "When did you become so cynical?"

My heart sank. This wasn't going the way I'd imagined. "I'm sorry. Once bitten, twice shy, I guess." As if on cue, the old eighties song by Great White started playing in my head. The truth was I'd been bitten far more than once. Johnny hadn't been as bad as the rest, not even close...but he wasn't innocent either.

Johnny looked down at the table. "Fair enough."

We sat in silence for a few moments. The waitress appeared with a bubbly greeting, ready to take our orders. I told her I'd take the special, even though I honestly didn't remember what it was, only that it had chicken. Johnny ordered something off the menu, and the way he pronounced it made the waitress giggle. She repeated the name back to him in what I assumed was perfect Italian, "Maiale Con Finocchio. Excellent choice." The young waitress smiled flirtatiously and took our menus. "And to drink?"

"I'll take a root beer." Johnny answered without hesitation. He turned toward me. "And a Diet Coke for you, right?"

He remembered. I nodded. "Sounds good." He hadn't ordered alcohol, even though the drink menu on the table looked impressive. My tension eased. Maybe I hadn't smelled beer on him earlier. Maybe I'd expected the worst so much my mind had made it up.

"I really am sorry you didn't find what you were looking for on your trip." Johnny's tone was sincere, subdued.

I needed to be done with the heaviness. He was only here for a few more weeks. No point in dwelling on the past or worrying about the future. I waved my hand. "It was a wild goose chase. Besides, it was good to get away with my daughter and granddaughter. And that California coastline." I inhaled and closed my eyes, the memory vivid. "It was absolutely amazing. I want to go back, someday."

Johnny leaned in, his eyes once again sparkly. "You know, where I'm moving isn't far from those beaches."

I chuckled. "Thanks for rubbing it in. You'll be enjoying sunshine and waves while I trudge through mud puddles and wonder if I'll ever see the sun again."

"You could come visit me, after I get settled in."

Was he suggesting a long-distance relationship? Did he think I'd changed my mind about those? He had to know better. "It's quite a drive. My car is on its last legs."

"I could take a look at it for you."

"Did you go to regular mechanic school after you attended diesel mechanic school?" I said teasingly. We still hadn't talked about what Johnny had been up to all these years.

A tinge of color tinted the skin above Johnny's beard. "Well, no, but I know my way around an engine."

We chitchatted until our meals arrived. My reluctant stomach growled from the enticing aroma. The fancy plated dishes atop the tableclothed table, the flickering candlelight, and Johnny's persistent warmth toward me made me feel like I was in a romantic movie. A welcome escape from the toil of my daily life.

While we ate, I peppered Johnny with light questions. He answered them good-humoredly. I found out his diesel mechanic career had lasted about six years before he became bored with that particular line of business. He'd been working on semis and dreaming of driving across America. He was single and unattached, so it made sense to go to truck driving school and embark on a new venture. After a few years he was able to buy a rig and start his own company.

"It doesn't sound like this new job you're taking will have you traveling far, from what I understand." I touched the napkin to my lips, assuring no tomato basil had been left behind.

"Nope. It'll be day driving only."

"Won't you get bored?"

Johnny lowered his chin. "I'm ready to be a homebody. Part of getting older, I guess."

I pondered his answer, comparing it to what I knew of him before. "You honestly think you could be happy with it? I mean, it'd be the same ol' thing, day after day."

Johnny pushed his plate away. "It'll be predictable, sure." He gave me a lop-sided grin. "But you saw the beaches down in California. The warmer, drier weather. I think it's a fair trade."

"Hmm." I looked him in the eye, wondering if he could ever be settled in one place. I had changed since we broke up. Was it fair of me to assume he wasn't capable of change himself? "I honestly hope it all works out for you." I tried to smile, but my heart ached.

Johnny reached across the table, gently taking my hand in his. "Sharon, I have a confession to make."

Oh great. What was it? He was still a drinking fool? He

didn't really have a job waiting for him in sunny California? He was married? A dozen possible scenarios flashed through my mind.

"I've thought about you a lot over the years," Johnny continued, apparently not needing a reply from me to his last statement.

I swallowed the lump that suddenly formed in my throat. Not what I was expecting him to say. I looked away, unready for the emotion that rose in my chest. "I've thought about you a few times too." Maybe more than a few, but I refused to take his bait—not hook, line and sinker, anyway.

I expected him to laugh, but there was silence. Finally, he cleared his throat. "I always wondered how things would've turned out if you'd gone to Seattle with me." His voice was soft and laced with a feeling I knew all too well— regret.

"Or how things would have been if you never left." The sound of my voice surprised me. It wasn't tinged with anger or sarcasm. Only hurt. Leave it to Johnny to put a nick in a wall I'd built to impenetrable perfection years ago.

Johnny squeezed my hand, and I ventured to look at him again. The sincere longing in his eyes made me tremble.

"I'm sorry. I was a fool."

I exhaled and pulled my hand away. "It's ancient history. If I thought about everything I should've done different in the past, I'd drive myself crazy." I was already driving myself crazy with regret over my daughter. Over Steven. My mom. I couldn't add Johnny to the load.

"Point taken. Still...I wonder if things could have worked out for us, under different circumstances."

Did he mean if we weren't both alcoholics? It was one thing that seemed to have changed for both of us. But it was too late. I shrugged my shoulders. "I guess we'll never know. You're moving in less than a month." My answer surprised me. Did I truly mean it, or was I lost in the moment? If he stayed, would I give him another chance?

"You could come with me."

I met his gaze again, expecting to see the sparkle of humor, a half-grin. What I found was a fiery seriousness. "That's pure craziness."

"Crazy, crazy for you, baby." He sang softly—and almost on key, followed by his characteristic grin.

I laughed. "You're something else."

"So, you'll think about it?"

The nerve. Show up, purely by chance, meet for coffee, exchange a few text messages and share one dinner, and he seriously thought I'd up and leave my life to join him in California? He *was* crazy.

But, as much as I hated to admit it, my heart was enjoying his brand of craziness. "A few more dinners like this might persuade me, but you'd have better luck winning a million dollars on a quarter slot machine."

Johnny's smile spread, accentuating the lines around his eyes. "I'll take the odds."

Chapter Twenty-One

, I came home from work to everything I expected—leftovers from a Crock-Pot meal of turkey roast and vegetables, Renee napping, and Cassie sitting on the plastic chair in the small backyard, reading a book. Peaceful.

Cassie had been disappointed about my missing church yet again. I'd brushed her concern off, blaming work and our weekend away for my not being available on Sunday. What would I do when a Sunday came along, and I wasn't working? I didn't want to face Samantha again, and I didn't want to tell Cassie what she'd said the last time I saw her.

I stuck my head out the sliding glass door to the backyard to say hello to Cassie. When she looked up, her frown stayed a second too long before she offered a halfhearted smile. Uh-oh. What had happened? Ignoring the growling in my stomach, I stepped out onto the patio. Warm spring air and the fragrance of an early-blooming lilac bush next door carried on a gentle breeze.

"How was church?"

Cassie shifted in her seat and lowered her book. "It was fine."

I wanted to tell her I knew what fine meant but got the feeling she wasn't in a joking mood.

"How was the sermon?"

"Good. Pastor Reynolds has been going through the book of Acts."

"And how is Pastor Matt?"

Cassie puckered her cheeks. "He seems to be doing well."

I was almost out of questions, and Cassie hadn't cracked. "Did Renee have fun at kids' church?"

Something flickered across Cassie's expression, gone so quick I wasn't sure if it was my imagination. "She wanted to sit with me today, so she didn't go to kids' church."

Ah, so that was it. Something was bugging Renee. "Is she not feeling well?"

"She feels fine. She wanted to do something different, I guess." Cassie sighed and picked up her book. "I left the Crock-Pot on warm. There's dinner rolls in the cupboard and salad in the fridge."

I guessed our conversation was over.

Later that evening I sat in my room, plucking at the strings of my guitar. I'd bought a couple of music books from Goodwill. My fingers were beginning to develop the calluses they needed for holding the strings in place, and my memory of how the chords were formed was coming back to me faster than I'd expected. Apparently, it was kind of like riding a bike.

It also proved to be a distraction from the MyGenealogy app and its lack of revealing information. Cassie hadn't had any luck finding out more information either. She'd called the care facilities in Susanville under the ruse of trying to deliver flowers. None confirmed having a Michael Smith as a resident. We were at the deadest of dead ends. My only other option at this point was to write to my third cousin match on the app. Since my first cousin match had yet to respond, I wasn't particularly encouraged to try.

I was out of options. For now. I knew I couldn't let the issue lie for too long, though. It wouldn't be long before the emptiness of not knowing grew and overshadowed everything else, like it had after that Rebecca lady had sent us away empty-handed. If it hadn't been for the way Johnny's text made me forget about my troubles, I didn't know what I would've ended up doing that night.

A light tapping on my door sounded over the twang of guitar strings.

The door opened slowly, and Renee stuck her head in cautiously.

"What's up, Sweet Pea?"

"Can I sit with you? Mommy fell asleep on the couch and I'm bored."

"Of course." I set my guitar down and patted the bed next to me.

Renee climbed up, the intensity of her eyes pulling on my heart. Something *was* wrong. I wrapped my arm around her and pulled her close, kissing the top of her head. "What's wrong?"

Renee embraced me and squeezed for a good five seconds before pulling back to look at me. "Mommy said not to say anything about it."

My chest tightened. "About what? What's going on?"

Renee looked down, her voice barely above a whisper. "You promise not to tell Mommy I told you?"

Whew. To keep a secret about a secret. Seemed to be what our family did, and that realization ate at me like termites slowly destroying a house. But I had to know. "I won't tell your Mommy unless you decide it's okay for me to tell her that I know." Hopefully I could convince Renee that whatever she was keeping bottled up wasn't worth hiding.

Renee tilted her head. "Okay."

"So, what's the secret?"

"Remember that lady from the Easter egg hunt? Isabella's grandma who wouldn't let her go down the slide with me again?"

I nodded. I already didn't like where this was going.

"Well, Mommy and I saw her at church when Mommy took me to kids' church, and she was mean to Mommy...and to me."

My blood turned to lava. "What do you mean?"

Renee furrowed her brow. "She told Mommy I couldn't come to kids' church because I had a runny nose. And when Mommy said half the kids in there had a runny nose and she didn't understand, that lady said her granddaughter was in the class and she didn't want her to get sick."

I bit my tongue, knowing there was more to the story. "Then what happened?"

Renee frowned. "Mommy said she thought the lady was being—un...uhm...I can't remember the word—and the lady said, 'I've been here a long time and know what I'm doing. Much longer than you or your child.' And she said it in this really mean voice. And Mommy looked like she was about ready to cry or kick something, and she said fine and we walked away and I sat with Mommy in church." Renee looked at me with sorrowful eyes. "Why doesn't that lady like me, Grammy?"

My pulse beat in my neck with such intensity I thought my jugular would burst open, bathing us in blood. Blood as red as the red I was seeing. "You never mind that rude lady. She doesn't know crap."

Renee's eyes widened at my words. "Grammy!"

It was no way to talk to a child. But neither was the thinly concealed hatred in Samantha's claim that Renee was too sick to go to kids' church. The child wasn't even congested. She simply had a runny nose left over from a run-of-the mill head cold earlier in the week.

I inhaled. Counted to three. Exhaled. "Renee, honey, I need to talk to your mommy about this. What that lady did wasn't right, and we need to make sure it doesn't happen again." My hands clenched in fists as I thought about what I wanted to do to the sour-faced woman.

"But Mommy will get mad. She said she didn't want to upset you." Renee's tiny mouth quivered, her emerald eyes filled with sadness.

Why was Cassie so worried about upsetting me? Did she think it'd be too much for me after the disappointment of our search for my father? That I'd fall back to drinking?

She's just holding the line, Sharon. Cut her some slack.

I closed my eyes, exhaled. Opened my eyes again. "Mommy will understand." I cupped Renee's face in my hands, willing them not to tremble with the rage I held in. "Mommy shouldn't have to deal with this by herself. Grammy is okay. I want to help Mommy."

Renee blinked, one lone tear making its way down her chubby cheeks. "Are you sure?"

"Positive." I pulled Renee into another hug. "I'm so sorry this happened to you, sweetie."

Why did my family still have to pay for my mistakes?

Later that afternoon, I found Cassie at the dining table, going over her checkbook. Guilt pricked at me when I thought about what the guitar must have cost. Even if it was used, it was still more than she should spend on me. I'd have to find a way to replenish her bank account. Another problem for another day. Get in line.

"Can I talk to you?" I sat in the dining chair across from Cassie before she could answer.

Cassie shrugged. "Sure."

This was good. I could tell she had no idea what I was about to say. Did she put that much trust in Renee holding her tongue? That couldn't be, because she hadn't told Renee about the guitar, too afraid she'd "spill the beans."

I might as well get right to it. "Renee told me what happened at church."

Cassie's shoulders sagged. "I figured she would, eventually."

"So why not tell me yourself? Why make Renee carry

that burden?"

Anger flashed across Cassie's eyes. "Like you told me about what happened during the Easter brunch?"

My stomach dropped. What did they call this? Tit for tat? "I'm sorry about that. It was a holiday and you were happy. I wanted to keep it that way."

Cassie shook her head. "But if you'd told me, maybe I would have been prepared for today. Or been able to talk to Matt about it so I knew how to deal with this woman. What to say." The look in Cassie's eyes had shifted from anger to hurt.

My chest was heavy. "I'm sorry, baby girl. I hoped it was a one-time thing." *And I was too ashamed to tell you.*

Cassie stared at the table. "I shouldn't have told Renee to keep it a secret. That wasn't fair to either of you."

"So, what do we do now? That woman can't keep treating my family like second-class citizens because of something I did eons ago." My hands were once again clenched into fists. I forced them to lie flat on my lap.

"I don't know. Since Matt is on staff at the church and so is Samantha, I thought I'd ask him for advice." Cassie shrugged. "I can't imagine the church would be okay with her behaving the way she did, no matter the reason."

I replayed the Easter incident in my mind, along with Renee's version of the exchange between Cassie and Samantha. What would Samantha's version of the story sound like? A few minor changes to what was said, leave out the body language, and it could all sound harmless.

Any woman would know the truth, though. Men never saw the subtleties of female communication. "I know Samantha is the women's ministry director. Who else is on church staff?"

"Well, there's James Reynolds, the lead pastor, of course. Then there's Ben, the associate pastor. Rick and Trish are the children's pastors. There's also an outreach pastor. I think his name is Jeremiah."

"So, other than Samantha, there's one other woman on staff?"

Cassie frowned. "Yeah, I guess so. But does that matter?"

I wanted to believe it didn't. Cassie obviously loved her new church. She was developing some kind of relationship with Matt. Would it lead to more than friendship? I pushed the thought aside. My guts were in a knot. I couldn't have Cassie lose another thing in her life because of me and my mistakes. My veins ignited with fire at the thought.

"I hope someone on staff can set her straight. Otherwise Samantha is going to have to deal with me, personally. And trust me, she's not going to like that one bit."

"Mom!" Cassie's eyes widened. "That's not going to help anything. We need to take the higher road."

"Humph." I turned away. Maybe the high road worked for Cassie, but I knew my way along the low ones much better.

No one messed with *my* family.

Chapter Twenty-Two

I KNEW CASSIE WOULD TALK TO Matt, but I wondered what else could be done about Samantha. Should I find her outside of church grounds and give her a talking to? It sounded good to me. Cassie had been right when she said I seemed angry lately, though I couldn't say exactly who or what angered me. Taking all my pent-up rage out on the likes of Samantha grabbed hold of my imagination.

Going down that road wouldn't win Cassie's heart, though. It definitely wasn't a road my mom would've taken. Or my dad. Which meant only one thing—whatever it was inside me that made that road look appealing had to come from my biological father. It was written in my DNA. Which meant I couldn't help it, right? The thought brought a heavy darkness with it, making it hard to breathe.

I inhaled, forcing the weight on my chest away. One. Two. Three. Exhaled. I needed to go to an AA meeting for real this week. Johnny had invited me out for a lunch date, but I still hadn't told Cassie about Johnny, which meant I needed a cover. Or I needed to let her know I'd started dating someone. But then she'd have questions I wasn't ready to answer.

"Have you talked to Matt yet?" It had only been a day since our conversation, but the situation ate at my very being.

"Yes." Cassie plopped down on the couch. She'd just arrived home from work and looked beat. Mondays were the worst.

"And?"

Cassie sighed. "He said he was sorry about what happened." She looked up at me, her eyes a darker blue than usual. "I had to tell him about why Samantha has a grudge against you."

I nodded. I'd expected as much. How else would she justify the woman's behavior? We'd sound crazy. "Is he going to talk to her?"

"Not directly. He's going to talk to Pastor Ben. He's the one who oversees personnel matters. He said Pastor Ben would probably talk to Samantha first and find out her side of the story. Then he'll contact me and have the three of us come in and talk to him."

My knees felt like putty. Going to church for a sit-down with a pastor didn't sound welcoming. Especially for someone with a past like mine. "It might be best if you go without me. I'll only make you look bad."

"Mom." Cassie paused, drawing in a slow breath. "That's ridiculous. I'll need you to tell him about the Easter incident. Otherwise it's all hearsay."

I lifted my eyebrows. "Yes, Ms. Lawyer. I didn't know it was court."

Cassie sighed. "It's not court. But you're right. I'm looking at this like a legal case. I guess it's ingrained in me, between work and what I went through with Derrick."

I knew my girl had been through a lot at the hands of her ex-husband. How long would the scars from that battle affect the way she viewed the world? If she followed my example, she'd be carrying the heartache around with her far beyond the expiration date most people would apply to it. What could I do to help her? What could I say?

"You're a wonderful mother to Renee." It was a comment totally off subject, but a sentiment that burned in my heart whenever I watched the two of them together.

Cassie raised an eyebrow at first, but then looked away. "I try my best. Sometimes it feels like my best is still not good enough, after everything she's been through."

I tapped my fingers on the table. An uncomfortable itching was trying to overcome me, but I refused to let it have its way or distract me. "I worried about you a lot, after all I put you through. I asked Mom about it. How it was affecting you. You know what she said?"

Cassie turned to me with an angst-filled face. "Probably something wise and comforting, knowing Nannie."

I nodded, smiling. "Yeah. It was. And I didn't believe it at the time. Didn't believe it for a *long* time. But when I look at Renee, I know she was right." I grabbed Cassie's hand, gently. She didn't pull away. Didn't flinch. Her reaction only proved the point. "She said that children always err on the side of love. If you keep filling them up with love, the bad things can't hold onto them and keep hurting them."

"Nannie and Grandpa definitely filled me up with love." Cassie smiled, her eyes distant, seemingly lost in memory. "And so did you, Mom, when I saw you." She squeezed my hand. "It was when I got older that I became angry and bitter. Then Derrick came along. He seemed like the answer to all my hurts." She looked away. "I was so stupid."

Cassie wasn't stupid. I'd been the stupid one. The wrong one. If there was anyone to blame for her ending up in the arms of someone like Derrick, it was me. "You were hurt and in love. I worried about that too. Honestly, so did Nannie. She had more wise words at the time, though."

"What was that?"

"She said every child everywhere comes to their own and has to decide their own path. But the ones who were filled up with more love than loneliness or hate would always come back to the good—to the love and knowledge they grew up with. We simply needed to be there for you when you found your way back."

"Like she was there for you." Cassie's eyes met mine, deep with emotion.

I willed the tears to stay put. "Yes, she was. I wish she

was still here, for both of us."

"But we have each other. Still."

"Yes. And always."

And I wasn't going to let Samantha come between us.

I had Wednesday off. With the weather beautiful and warm, Johnny suggested we grab takeout and find a picnic bench by the river. I knew I should say no. With the Samantha issue bubbling up, I didn't need to add another area of possible drama in my life. Telling Cassie would cause more heartache than it was worth. Johnny would be gone soon. I told myself that if I met Johnny for lunch, Cassie would be at work and never know, and I could go to an AA meeting in the evening. The best of both worlds. Or at least it wasn't tipping any world off its axis.

"I'd love to meet your family one of these days." Johnny popped the lid off the bowl of chicken and mashed potatoes he'd chosen from KFC.

I'd opted for the traditional two-piece. I bit into the buttery biscuit. Cassie would have a coronary. I wasn't only seeing a man on the sly but also eating artery-clogging fast food. "Maybe someday."

"That's what you said fifteen years ago." He laughed, but it sounded forced.

Back then, I knew Cassie didn't need to meet yet another man I'd brought into my life. I was trying to do the right thing. Now, I didn't know what I was doing, except buying time and distracting myself from other things. "When you propose, I'll have you over for dinner." I winked and gave him a mischievous smile. Johnny had made it clear many years ago that he wasn't the marrying kind. To him, it was simply a piece of paper.

Johnny laughed for real this time, and the sunlight

danced off his blue eyes. "I better start ring shopping. It'd be kind of weird for them to not meet the guy you're moving to San Jose with."

I slapped his arm playfully. "Uh-huh. I never said yes to moving." I rolled my eyes and took another bite of my drumstick.

"You didn't say no." Johnny shrugged one shoulder. "I'm still planning on hitting the jackpot."

"That's quite optimistic of you."

The corners of Johnny's mouth dropped, and he looked at me earnestly. "I mean it."

A fluttering in my ribcage took away my appetite. I put the drumstick down and wiped my mouth. Looking in Johnny's eyes undid me. The fiery flame of adoration I saw there melted away the wall around my heart that I thought was built of stone. For Johnny, the wall seemed to be made of little more than wax. But it was too late for us.

"Look, Johnny…seeing you is great. It's fun, but…" I tore my gaze away from him and looked at the tree behind him. "My life is here, in Springfield. I finally have a relationship with my daughter again, not to mention my granddaughter." My heart ached thinking of Renee's sweet face. How could I leave her after all she'd been through this last year? "I can't leave them." I shook my head. "So please, even if you're only joking—which I'm pretty sure you are—stop talking about me moving to California with you. This road I'm on isn't easy. Taking a detour is pretty enticing sometimes."

Johnny sucked in his bottom lip and nodded. "I get it, Angel Eyes. And, quite frankly," he lifted an eyebrow, "I'm not joking, as crazy as it sounds. Or is."

My heart skipped a beat. It would be so much easier if he was joking. Or if he at least pretended to be. We sat in silence for a moment, no sound but the rushing of the river and cars passing on the nearby freeway. Our meal lay before us, half-finished.

Like our relationship.

Johnny took my hand. "I understand what you're saying about your daughter and all of that. I won't bug you about moving anymore—"

Disappointment washed over me. *Don't be stupid. He's doing what you asked him to.*

"—Until we are engaged, anyway." Johnny gave me a Cheshire Cat grin.

I lifted my free hand to hit him on the shoulder again, but he caught my arm in midair and pulled me toward him, closing the distance between us on the bench. The next thing I knew, his lips were meeting mine in a gentle kiss. My eyes closed instinctively and the resistance in my arms was gone. Johnny put his hand on my cheek and kissed me more deeply. I tasted honey and my body filled with a syrupy warmth.

I pulled away and looked at him. I was breathless. Scared. And falling hard for Johnny.

Whether that was a good or bad move for my heart, I wasn't certain.

Although pasting on a smile and facing Samantha at church was the last thing I wanted to do, I felt bad working the next Sunday and knowing Cassie may have to face Samantha alone. Pastor Matt had called her and said he'd talked to Pastor Ben and was waiting to hear back from him about what to do. In the meantime, Cassie would have to brave it alone. I offered to call in sick to work so I could go with her, but she insisted she would be fine.

When I got off work, I came home to an empty house. The Crock-Pot was on low. Stew simmered inside, obviously untouched. My heart jackhammered in my chest. Where were Cassie and Renee? I looked around for a note and checked my phone for missed calls or text messages. Nothing.

I pecked out a short text to Cassie. *Where are you?*

I stared at my phone, waiting for the reply while the three moving dots implied she was typing on the other end. *At the park. Matt took Renee and me to lunch and now we are watching Renee play.*

I smiled so big my nose tingled. Going out to lunch and the park surpassed any sense of pastoral duty, didn't it? I was sure he had more than a church-centered interest in Cassie, and from what I'd seen of her expressions when she talked to him or about him, she had feelings too. Had he talked to her more about Samantha? I settled on the couch, my mind whirling with possibilities. Would they start dating? He was a sweet, handsome man. Honestly, the pastor thing put me on guard, though. Cassie was divorced and had a kid. Did pastors marry divorced women? Women who had their recovering alcoholic mother living with them? I sighed, pushing the thought away. A lunch date was a long way off from a marriage proposal. I suppressed a laugh. Except if it was with Johnny. Oh, that man! I needed to get him off my mind.

I helped myself to a bowl of stew and switched the Crock-Pot off. I'd let it cool and then put it in a container for the refrigerator. I cleaned up the kitchen, but I was restless, waiting for Cassie to come home so I could learn about her afternoon.

I checked the MyGenealogy App. There were no new messages. No new matches. The message I sent to R. Bowers still showed as unread. The familiar, uneasy, pins and needles feeling overtook me. My mouth was dry as dust. I grabbed a Diet Coke and gulped it down, hiccupping when I stopped to take a breath. If only that Rebecca woman had been more helpful. It was like she was trying to hide my father.

A thought hit me like a spark from a Fourth of July sparkler. If she were his representative, couldn't Cassie look it up in some kind of legal computer system? I'd have to ask her about it when she got home.

I grabbed a Snickers out of the cupboard, even though I was still full from lunch. Part of me wanted to text Johnny— to ask him what he thought. When I told him I couldn't take off to California with him, I'd said it was because of Cassie and Renee. It was true. But there was more. I needed to find my father. Johnny wouldn't understand. I didn't even fully understand it myself.

Chapter Twenty-Three

CASSIE FINALLY RETURNED FROM HER OUTING early in the evening, looking kissed by the sun and full of joy. Renee followed her into the house, practically skipping—one hundred percent a contented little girl. My heart swelled.

"Looks like it was a good date."

Cassie dropped her chin, looking at me with uplifted eyebrows. "Mom, it wasn't a *date*." Her attempt at a reprimand didn't take the sparkle out of her eyes.

"Right. Bad choice of words. How was your outing?"

Renee responded before Cassie had a chance. "We went to a restaurant that had yummy noodles of all kinds and a soda machine where you could pick any kind of soda in the whole world." Renee skipped up to me, eyes wide. "Then we went to a fun park I hadn't been to before and Pastor Matt spun me on this round thing super fast." Renee spun in a circle, making me feel faint just watching her. She giggled and fell down. "Then he raced me to the swings, but I won, even though I was dizzy. Then we went and had the best ice cream. They had—" Renee breathlessly turned to her mom. "How many flavors, Mom?"

"Thirty-two, I believe."

"Yeah!" Renee jumped up. "Thirty-two. I tried almost all of them, and Mommy got annoyed, but Pastor Matt just laughed. Then I got a big cone with two scoops."

I chuckled, reveling in Renee's innocent enthusiasm. "Sounds like quite a day."

"It was wonderful." Cassie smiled so big I thought her ears might pop off. "And Renee needs a bath and an early bedtime tonight."

An early bedtime for Renee would be good. Then I could find out more about Cassie's "outing" with Matt.

I sucked in my cheeks. At some point I'd dropped the "pastor" title too. Who would've thought?

After Renee was tucked in, Cassie and I sat on the sofa and watched an old romantic comedy that was already about half over. Before I lost the nerve, I told her my thought about Rebecca's information being in some kind of system because she was Michael's personal representative.

Cassie lifted her eyebrows. "That's a good question. Should've thought of it."

Her widened eyes told me she was sorry. It was the same look she'd get when she was a little kid and forgot to wipe her feet when she walked in the door when it was raining outside. I wondered why she hadn't thought of it, also, but didn't want to say anything. It was almost like her interest in finding my father had faded—or there was something else taking up space in her brain.

I patted her knee, the way Mom would've done. "It's okay, baby girl. It's just that knowing Michael Smith is alive and probably within driving distance, yet not knowing where in Pete's sake he is, is kind of driving me nuts." I laughed, trying to make light of it.

Cassie nodded, but her brow was etched with concern. "Mom...are you going to be okay if you never find him?"

My stomach burned. The idea of coming out of this journey empty-handed made me feel like my life was coming to an end. Cassie didn't struggle with the beast of addiction. How could she know the desperation I felt wanting to know if it truly could be conquered? It was a demon that hadn't touched my mom. It wasn't part of the dad who raised me. It struck me out of nowhere when my heart was broken beyond healing. Wouldn't others have bounced back, found a way of healing without the help of Jim Beam? Cassie had.

Her heart had been shattered by Derrick, yet here she was, a successful single mom with a precious young daughter, and practically dating a pastor, of all people.

I sucked on my bottom lip, trying to find words. "Finding him and knowing how his story went will give me peace. Especially if I find out he eventually overcame his alcoholism." Everything I'd found out so far gave me little hope he had beat the addiction. The only good sign was that he had it together enough to own a home and to have a representative once he was in a care facility. That had to take some responsibility, and alcoholics were notoriously irresponsible, weren't they?

"No matter what became of him, it doesn't control your destiny. You're in control of your life, your future. You and God." Conviction filled Cassie's voice. She reminded me of Mom.

"I know that's true. I know it with my head. But my heart doesn't always agree." I looked away. My faith wasn't as strong as Cassie's newfound devotion. Or my mom's. I was a disappointment all the way around.

"My heart doesn't always agree with what I know to be true, either." Cassie exhaled loudly. "Like today with Matt. I kept telling myself that he was simply being my grandma's pastor, making sure Renee and I were doing okay and trying to be a help to us. But my heart kept saying something different."

I laughed so hard I thought I'd split a muscle in my stomach.

"Wow. Thanks for laughing at me." Cassie sounded more than a little irritated.

"Sorry, baby girl, but your head is wrong and your heart is right. At least in this circumstance."

Cassie sat up straighter. "You really think so?"

"I can't read the man's mind, but it sounds like it to me.

I mean, do you see him asking *me* out to lunch and ice cream? And I was Nannie's daughter for crying out loud."

"True...but..."

"But what?"

"I'm not exactly pastor-dating material. And it's perfectly clear he adored his deceased wife and she's only been gone like a year and half. Do you think someone can recover from losing their spouse that fast?"

I shrugged my shoulders. "Men can. Women are different, I think."

We sat in silence for a moment, my weighty words a statement of the past and present.

"It's good that he expresses how much he loved his late wife. It shows he was capable of deep love and loyalty." My voice cracked, despite myself. "You want that in a husband, trust me."

"Was my dad like that?" The look on Cassie's face spoke a thousand words. She needed to hear her dad was. Luckily, this was one thing from the past that didn't require much sugarcoating.

"Your daddy was the most loving man I'd ever met. Next to your grandpa." My daddy had practically been a saint. No one could compare to him.

"You still miss Dad, don't you?"

Every day. But the reason my heart still burned with his memory went beyond love and devotion. The room closed in on me, pressing down on my chest. I forced myself to breathe in, count to three. Exhale. "I sure do. More than I could ever put in words." Not even Johnny could make that go away.

Cassie put her arm around me and gave me a hug, offering comfort that only led to more of an ache. Steven's death was more than loss. And I would never tell her why, but I could change the subject.

"What did Matt say about Samantha? Any more developments?"

Cassie twisted her lips. "Yes and no. Matt is still new, so he doesn't know everyone's history." Cassie looked away for a moment, then turned back to me. "But he does know Samantha is no longer married to her first husband. They divorced a long time ago, and then she remarried about ten years ago."

"So, what are we supposed to do about the situation now?"

"Matt's still working that out with Pastor Ben. For now, we hang tight, but this is probably going to end with you and me and Pastor Ben sitting down with Samantha. Or..." Cassie paused, looking afraid of what she was about to say. "Pastor Ben may want it to be only you and Samantha who sit down and talk with him."

My stomach squeezed, and I almost shouted, "No!" Doing so, though, would only be another thing for Cassie to hold against me. If it would help my granddaughter, and if it would help strengthen my relationship with Cassie, I might have to subject myself to this whole ridiculous pastoral counseling thing.

It took every fiber of my being to do it, but I muttered, "Yeah, okay."

Maybe it would never happen. Maybe Samantha would say she had meant no harm, and we had simply misread her conversation with us. Maybe she would say Cassie and I were, in fact, a couple of loony ladies who had an inferiority complex.

Right now, being labeled nuts sounded better than sitting across from Samantha, having all my sins revealed.

Monday afternoon when I got home from work, Cassie texted

me. *Can you watch Renee next Tuesday night? I have a thing to go to.*

Interesting. I smiled, guessing what the "thing" probably was. No doubt it had something to do with Matt. Cassie was building a new life for herself. I just hoped she didn't go at it so fast and furious she forgot to check the road for potholes. I'd hit enough of those suckers for both of us. I wondered if she'd had a chance to check on my hunch about Rebecca, but after her telling me how she carried my burdens, I didn't want to bug her unnecessarily. I responded to her text. *I'd love to. See you soon.*

Time to get ready for dinner. I opened the fridge and pondered the options. Chicken breasts and ninety-three percent lean ground beef seemed to be the two meat options. When did they start making beef ninety-three percent lean? I guessed it'd be fine in spaghetti.

As the water for the noodles boiled, I pondered how much Cassie was loosening up when it came to Renee. She let me pick her up from daycare on my days off, more often now than she had three months ago. Now, she wanted me to watch her on a school night so she could go out. It was progress. I felt a little lighter on my toes and soon was humming a song.

My fairy tale reverie didn't last long. I knew I was jumping ahead of myself, but what would happen if—or more likely, when—Cassie remarried? No man wanted his mother-in-law living with him. I'd be booted out. Well, "booted" wasn't the right word. They'd be nice about it. But it would mean no more daily time with my granddaughter, and I'd have to find a place of my own. Afford an apartment on a maid's salary. No one could rent an apartment on minimum wage. I'd need a roommate. My mind reeled. Janice was married. I didn't have any other friends. I heated up the iron skillet and flipped on the exhaust fan.

My heart sank. I didn't have many options. I threw the skinny beef in the frying pan and wasn't surprised when it immediately stuck to the bottom. That's what happened when you didn't have enough fat in the meat. I scraped at it with a rubber spatula. It came off easy enough. Crisis averted. If only not having enough friends were as easy to fix.

Johnny's face flashed in my mind, his mischievous grin, followed by the sincerity in his eyes when he asked me to join him in California. Would he wait for me, if I didn't go with him now?

Stop burning down the house before it's built.

Mom's voice. Calm washed over me. Good grief. My poor daughter was finding her happily ever after, and here I was, thinking about myself and setting things on fire before a stick had gone up.

By the time Cassie and Renee were home, dinner was done, the table set. I poured the Caesar salad mix into a bowl and added the dressing. "Dinner's ready when you are."

Within five minutes, we were all at the table. Cassie asked Renee about her school day. I listened, but I wanted to change the subject. How could we talk about the things that needed to be said while Renee was present though? I ventured a question.

"So, Renee, did you hear Grammy is watching you next Tuesday night so Mommy can go out?"

Renee nodded, her mouth full of food.

"We'll have a good time." I smiled back, then turned to Cassie. "You never said what your plans were, exactly."

Cassie looked at her plate, moving her food around with her fork. "Oh, it's nothing exciting. I'm taking a class."

Not what I expected. "A class?"

Renee, who had swallowed her food, answered for Cassie. "Mommy said she's taking a class to teach her how to be more successful."

Must be work related. "Oh," I responded, searching for words. "That sounds...interesting."

"Boring stuff, that's for sure." Cassie wiped her mouth. "I can fill you in later."

I was a little disappointed, but furthering her career was no doubt a smarter thing to do than getting involved in a relationship. At least for now. Like me finding my birth father. Rebuilding my relationship with him was more important than pursuing a relationship with Johnny—for now.

"What's this class you're taking?" With Renee tucked in bed, Cassie and I settled on the couch. Monday nights were the night we watched our favorite reality TV show together.

Cassie frowned and looked away. "It's not a class, exactly."

"Then what is it?"

"A group, of sorts."

I pressed mute on the TV remote. "A group?"

Finally, Cassie looked at me. The expression on her face was hard to read. She looked guilty. Sad. Even a little angry. But over it all was a guardedness I hadn't seen since I first came to live with her. My stomach tightened.

"It's a group that meets at the church. Adult Children of Alcoholics."

My heart broke a little as it fell to the floor. "But Cassie...I'm not drinking anymore." I paused, searching for words. "I thought we were doing okay."

"We are doing okay, mostly. But I've come to realize that a lot of things I do—the way I react to things, to you—is because I have a faulty way of thinking. Matt asked me when we talked if I had ever gone to the group. I told him no, I didn't need it." Cassie inhaled, as if gathering strength. "He told me about this quiz online. Long story short, I have several of the symptoms of an adult child of an alcoholic."

Dizziness made me put down the remote and grab the edge of the couch. I'd heard of Adult Children of Alcoholics. We talked about that support group and Al-Anon in my AA meetings. But I never thought Cassie needed help like that. My mom and dad had saved her from being damaged by me and my drinking, or so I had believed. I was clearly wrong.

I should've only felt sorrow and compassion. I should've wanted nothing but to encourage my daughter to get the help she needed to be whole and healthy. I did feel those things, but under it was the boiling cauldron of rage that'd been rumbling in me for what felt like eons now.

I bit the inside of my cheek, keeping my emotions and words in check. "Good for you, baby girl." My voice was husky, but I'd done my best.

Cassie grabbed my hand. "You're doing great, Mom. I'm proud of you. When I talked to Matt about what was going on with you living here and then us looking for your biological father, he started asking questions about *me*. How I feel, how I think." Cassie blinked and paused, obviously choosing her words carefully. "I guess I'd never thought about how I was coping with everything. About how I felt. I've been in survival mode for what feels like forever now."

Cassie looked me in the eye, and I held still, waiting for a blow.

"Mom, I'm shouldering too much of what you're going through with recovering from your alcoholism, and even in looking for your dad."

"I never asked for your help." It was getting hard to hold myself in check.

"No. You didn't. But there's a part of me that is so afraid of something setting you off and sending you back to the bottle. It's like I emotionally walk on eggshells."

She walked on eggshells? Did she have any ide0a how

much I tried to be the perfect mother to her now, the perfect grandmother to Renee? Terrified to make one mistake and have her boot me out of her life?

It's a black flag. Pull into the pit. Check your bearings. You don't want to get disqualified.

I breathed in. Counted to three. Breathed out. Felt only a little better. "You don't need to worry about me. I'll always land on my feet."

Cassie tilted her head, narrowing her eyes. At the moment it was the most patronizing look anyone could've given me.

"Hey, I've made it this far, haven't I?" I patted Cassie's arm and shifted my focus back to the television before I exploded. I'd pretend to watch the show, even though there was no way I could focus on it now. I didn't know what else to do or say to make Cassie feel like she wasn't walking on eggshells, afraid to send me back to drinking, but there was one thing I could do. No way I'd be asking Cassie for any more help in finding my biological father. I refused to be a burden.

I could do this on my own.

When I woke up the next morning, loneliness clung to me like a wet blanket. My night was filled with disturbed dreams that were a mixture of my past mistakes and my worst fears. Dreams of Steven and Cassie, Mom and Dad. Renee. Faces from the past I'd sooner forget. Even Samantha made an appearance in my nighttime movie from hell. The overarching theme in my dreams was clear—I needed to stop relying so much on my daughter, for both my emotional support and practical things. Maybe I could even start paying a hundred extra dollars for rent. More than my fair share, but it would be a penance of sorts. Plus, it would help prepare me for a future when I may not have anyone to share household expenses with.

I checked my phone to see if Johnny had texted me. He was one person from my past who hadn't made an appearance in the horror movie of a dream last night. There was nothing. Disappointment washed over me, until I realized I had never answered his last text, asking me how I was doing.

I pecked out a good morning, then told him about my evening and Cassie's revelation of her need for a support group. A long text, but I wasn't up to talking on the phone.

Don't let it get to you. You are going above and beyond for your family. She'll figure that out sooner or later.

Johnny's response made me feel better, but also guilty. It almost seemed like he was saying Cassie was in the wrong. Was that what I hoped he would say? I still hadn't told him about everything Cassie had been through with her ex-husband.

I hope so. I mean, I understand why she's worried. She's been through a lot. Her ex-husband was an alcoholic too.

I'm sorry to hear that. But I wish she understood half of what YOU went through, trying to make your life better for her.

I'd strived to do so, especially when Johnny had known me. But by that time, Cassie was fifteen. I knew I had only three years of her childhood left, and she didn't seem interested in the relationship I tried to build with her. Not to mention, I couldn't quite kick my drinking habit. It wasn't long after Johnny left for Seattle that I left town, eager to escape the pain of rejection and regret.

Would anything be different if I had gone with Johnny to Seattle all those years ago? I shook the thought away. That was a rabbit trail my already taxed brain couldn't take on.

Thank you, Johnny. You always lift me up.

He had lifted my spirits. But he'd also breathed on the fire in my heart.

It was time to get to work.

Work was the same old same old. Janice had the day off, so I sang songs to myself, my Hispanic worker smiling at me every so often. Somewhere out of me came the lyrics of "Last Kiss" by J. Frank Wilson. Then I sang "Fancy" by Reba McEntire. Why that song resonated with me, a woman who had grown up with protective, loving parents, I had no idea. The lyrics to the song simultaneously poured fuel and solace in one heaping bowl over the hurt and anger that chased each other around my chest.

When I got off work, I checked my phone. Hoping for another text from Johnny. Hoping for a notification from the MyGenealogy app. There was nothing from either one. An aching, jagged pain shot through me. I slipped my phone back into my purse. The next thing I knew, I was driving the opposite direction of home—toward the cemetery where Mom and Dad were buried.

It was a clear and sunny day, but it had started out drizzly and cloudy, keeping the temperature moderate but the air thick with moisture. I always kept a few old towels and blankets in my trunk, along with a couple rolls of toilet paper, jumper cables, and a two-gallon container of bottled water—my attempt at emergency preparedness.

I pulled a couple of the old towels out and carried them to Mom and Dad's gravesite. After spreading the towels out like a picnic blanket, I eased myself to the ground. My back was sore from working, and my knees popped as I crossed them into a crisscross seating position. How sad was it that the only person I could talk to right now was on the other side of this life? Maybe that's how it was supposed to be.

My mind brought Mom to life before me. Not the version of her shortly before she died, but the younger one from my growing up years. She'd always taken care of her appearance. Her lips were always covered with Maybelline lipstick, and she never left the house without dabbing on some mascara and blush. When she did yard work, she wore gloves, keeping her silky hands and beautifully long fingers soft. She wore sunscreen long before all the threats of skin cancer, and her skin stayed young and supple long into her golden years. I imagined hugging her, remembering the warmth of her embrace and how she always patted me on the back. I closed my eyes, wishing she were here now. As I did, I recalled something that had been such a part of her, I'd never given it much thought. Her shoulders. They were the stiffest, hardest shoulders I'd ever felt. I used to massage them for her sometimes when we talked in the kitchen and cleaned dishes. No matter how hard I rubbed them, they were like rocks. She never complained about pain, though. She said she was used to her shoulders being that way.

I opened my eyes and studied her name engraved in stone—Eula Jean Bradford. Tears welled up in my eyes, not only at seeing her name etched into a gravestone, but also because for the first time I realized why her shoulders had been impossibly hard. They carried the weight of the secret she kept. A story she had never told anyone. How many times had it kept her up at night? How often had she almost slipped and revealed the entire truth about my birth father? Why had she carried the burden for so long?

Even with her faith in the God I knew she loved and followed, she didn't let go of this one thing. She carried it her entire life, almost to the grave. The burden was hers no more, but my shoulders were heavier now. I didn't realize until my conversation with Cassie how much she was carrying the burden with me.

"Mom." I looked around, self-conscious. No one else was

nearby. Besides, people talked out loud to gravestones all the time. "I've been trying to find my birth father, Michael." I sighed, choosing my words carefully, as if Mom were really listening. "I sure wish you would've left me with more information. Like Michael's birth date, maybe. Or his middle name." What else could have helped, this far after my birth?

I looked around again, making sure I was alone. "Cassie's been trying to help me. I guess it's been more about her trying to keep me sober than her understanding the predicament I'm in." Those weren't Cassie's words, exactly, but it was the sum of their parts, as far as I could tell. "It's put a strain on her, and that's not good for our relationship."

My chin quivered. I didn't want to cry. I hated crying. "It's hard. So hard to stay on the straight and narrow path. I need to know, Mom. It's sounding like you were right. Michael was an alcoholic. From what I've found so far, it doesn't look like he turned into a very good person."

I pulled blades of grass out of the ground, unable to look at the gravestone. "Is that why you never told me? Because you knew he never quit drinking and he'd be a bad influence?"

I shook my head. If that was the case, wouldn't Mom have told me so during her confession? She'd said she believed at the time he was an alcoholic, or on the path to being one, but she never said anything about knowing he'd never change. It had to be a guess on her part.

A safe bet. Alcoholics seldom change.

Yet, she had believed I could.

And it seemed my old flame Johnny had too. Was it fate that he had turned up at this time in my life? Did it mean no matter how hard I tried, it was too late for Cassie and me to have a good, normal mother and daughter relationship? Did it mean I would never find my father and know the answers to my questions? That Johnny was some kind of solace to the wounds that would never be healed inside of me?

Mom didn't answer.

I stood and picked up the towels I was sitting on. They were damp. Once the air hit them, I realized my work pants were a little damp as well. I guessed my preparedness wasn't so good after all. It was a little thing, I knew that, but it seemed to scream at me. Scream what I didn't want to hear but already knew.

I wasn't good enough. I'd been part of a burden my mom had carried, and now I was a burden to my daughter.

I looked down at the gravestone. Part of my past etched in stone.

Sharon, you need to tell Cassie everything. Don't make the same mistake I made.

That warning wasn't about Johnny.

Chills ran down my back, making me shiver. Did you learn the truth about your loved ones when you got to heaven? The memory clawed at the back of my head, begging to come to the front. A memory I'd never shared with anyone, not even my mom. No. I couldn't think about it. And I definitely couldn't tell Cassie. I already had enough strikes against me.

Mom, I can't.

The sound of cars passing by on the nearby road combined with the rustling of branches as squirrels ran in the nearby trees. I waited for more words from my mom. Even for a snippet of racing wisdom from Steven. Anything.

There was nothing but silence among the gravestones.

Chapter Twenty-Four

I HAD SUNDAY OFF AND WAS out of excuses. It looked like I would be going to church and taking my chances with running into Samantha. I'd yet to hear any more about the situation, whether the associate pastor had spoken with her, or if he wanted to have a meeting with Cassie and me to talk about what we experienced. Cassie never said another word, so I didn't ask. Don't ask, don't tell. That was a good motto to live by, if you asked me.

It was the one I was still living by when it came to Johnny. Throughout the week we'd met for coffee twice and a walk by the river once. He was bugging me for another dinner, but I hadn't committed to it yet.

Renee's excitement about my attending church with them again lightened my heart. She seemed to be oblivious to whatever Cassie held against me. I hadn't ruined Renee's life. As far as she knew, I was what all grandmas were supposed to be. Time would change that. She'd get older and figure things out about the past. Ask the hard questions. Until then, I'd enjoy this time of being loved with no black marks against me.

The foyer was full when we got to Cascade Christian Church. Renee and I made our way to the donut table. Maybe I'd avoid Samantha altogether. Wouldn't that be nice? After grabbing a couple of pastries, we joined Cassie.

"Ready to go to kids' church?" Cassie asked Renee.

Renee shrugged. "I guess."

Cassie and I exchanged a look. No words were needed. The entire episode with Samantha had obviously affected Renee negatively.

"It'll be fun!" Cassie exuded fake enthusiasm. "Finish your donut and I'll take you."

"I can take her, if you want." It was probably a dumb question. If Samantha dropped off her granddaughter at the same time, it could be a recipe for disaster.

"Well—"

Before Cassie could finish, a nicely dressed middle-aged man stepped up next to her. "Good morning, Cassie."

Cassie pivoted toward the man, a smile flashing across her face. "Hi, Pastor Ben. How are you?"

He bobbed his head. "Doing well." He turned toward me. "Is this your mother?"

"Oh, yes." Cassie looked flustered. "Mom, this is Pastor Ben. He's the associate pastor of Cascade Christian Church."

Dread climbed up my spine. "Sharon." I held out my hand.

He took my hand and shook it gently. "Nice to meet you, Sharon. I was hoping I'd see you ladies this morning."

I looked at Cassie, who was twirling a strand of hair around her finger. "Is that so?" I asked.

"Yes." Pastor Ben lowered his chin, his hands clasped in front of him. "I heard about the incident with Samantha." His brow lifted, but his eyes held compassion. "I was hoping I could have you and Cassie come to my office and talk about it, along with Samantha." He looked at Cassie and then back to me. "I think we can work this out so that everyone has a better understanding of each other, and there's no miscommunications or hard feelings."

His words swirled in my mind, following a trail I couldn't quite follow. What he was saying seemed plain as day, but every nerve in my body told me there was something between the spoken words. A clue as to how the meeting would end and where I'd stand when all was said and done.

My knees were shaking. For crying out loud, my knees were shaking, and I was in *church.*

I sucked my breath in, steadying myself, then looked at Cassie. She simply stood and stared at me, waiting for my response. Did she know about this? "If that's what you think would be best, then I guess that's what we need to do, isn't it?"

"Um, well, yes, I think it would be best." Pastor Ben cleared his throat. "But you're not under any obligation, Sharon. The choice is yours."

I hoped Cassie would speak up. Say anything. She kept silently twirling her hair. I must've looked desperate though, because she finally spoke.

"Mom, we'll go together. You and me. I think it's for the best." Cassie's voice was soft but unemotional.

What could I say? No? Might as well pack my bags and leave if I did so. I blew out my breath, letting go of the fight within. At least for a moment. "Sure. I'm game."

Pastor Ben smiled broadly and nodded. "This will be a good thing, Sharon. I'm looking forward to it." He shifted his attention to Cassie. "You can call the church office and talk to the secretary. She has my schedule and can find a time that works for everyone." He looked me in the eyes and tilted his head slightly. "It was nice to meet you. I hope you have a blessed day."

The next thing I knew, Pastor Ben was walking away. Music blared from the sanctuary and the crowd around us dissipated as people filtered out of the foyer.

"Did you know about this?" I did my best not to sound harsh but wasn't very successful.

"Yes and no." Cassie blinked. "Pastor Ben contacted me about meeting, and I said I would need to talk to you."

"Well why the heck didn't you say something before we got here?" I hissed.

"Would you have still come today?" Cassie's eyes narrowed.

Cassie's words were a slap in the face. "Are you calling me a coward?"

Cassie glanced around nervously, obviously afraid we were causing a scene. Renee tugged at her hand. "Mommy, don't I need to go to kids' church now?"

"Yes, honey." Cassie clasped Renee's hand.

I looked down at my granddaughter. Her eyes were wide and sad and all too wise. My heart sank. What was I doing, making a scene in front of her? At church? Even if I was cornered and...betrayed. I lowered myself to Renee's level. "Grammy's sorry about this, Sweet Pea. It's all okay though, you hear? You go have a good time in kids' church."

Renee nodded and threw her arms around my neck, giving me a quick hug.

I stood and tilted my chin up toward Cassie. "I'll save us a seat."

She nodded once and walked away, not showing an ounce of remorse.

Tuesday arrived, and for the first time in what seemed like forever, I felt a sense of peaceful anticipation about life. If I let myself think about why I was watching Renee for the evening, my good mood would fall faster than a boulder down a steep hillside. So, I didn't think about it. Instead I planned what Renee and I would do during our evening together. I bought a deluxe frozen pizza and a package of cookie dough. I'd checked with Cassie first to make sure it was okay. Talk about walking around on your tiptoes. I'd also checked with her about picking Renee up early, but Cassie had her enrolled in an extracurricular enrichment program now instead of regular afterschool care. I wasn't sure how Cassie was affording to enroll Renee in a special program, but no doubt she'd pinched pennies somewhere in her budget to make it happen. She was a good mom. The kind of mom I should've been.

But I could be a good grandma to Renee, the one person on this earth who didn't know I was actually a complete failure. Well, not including Johnny. I chastised myself for even thinking about him. Tonight was about Renee. My granddaughter was my last hope. Cassie would never truly forgive me for all I'd done, and I couldn't blame her.

While waiting for five p.m., I fingered through my worn songbooks, looking for a song I hadn't played yet for Renee but thought she'd like. I found "Let it Be" by the Beatles. She might not know it, but it was upbeat and fun, and I could teach her. Practicing the notes brought solace to my heart and light into the room. I could do this. I could be a good grandma.

Cassie hurried through dinner when she got home, wanting to make sure she wasn't late for her meeting. Renee and I cleaned up while Cassie changed clothes and fixed her hair and makeup. I could tell she was nervous about going to the group. My heart ached, hating that she was going through it. Under the ache, anger flickered again. Before I could reflect too much on my feelings, Cassie emerged from her bedroom, dressed casually in jeans and t-shirt. Her sad eyes met mine, and I nodded at her. "You look good, baby girl. You've got nothing to worry about."

"Thanks, Mom." Cassie's voice was soft. "I'm hoping this is a good thing."

Me too, baby girl, me too. Because I'm scared to death you're going to come home and realize you hate me.

"It'll be fine. The first time you go to one of these things is hard, but it gets easier."

My experience was based on AA meetings, but I figured the same principles applied.

Cassie smiled and grabbed her purse. "You two have

fun, but don't stay up too late." Cassie gave Renee a pointed look. "I won't be back until after your bedtime, so you be good for Grammy and don't fight going to bed."

"I won't, Mommy. Promise." Renee stood on her tiptoes, reaching up for a hug.

Cassie squeezed Renee in a bear hug, then turned to me. "I'll see you later."

I nodded. "I'll be up when you get home. You can tell me all about it...if you want."

After Cassie left, Renee chose cookie baking over singing songs for our first activity. I brought a chair to the counter and she climbed up on it. We rolled out balls of dough and put them on a cookie sheet.

"Did you bake cookies with Mommy?"

The question stopped me. "Yes, we did a few times." Thankfully, the cookie sheet was full and I could put it in the oven.

"What was Mommy's favorite?"

"Let's see." I held Renee's hands and had her jump off the chair. "I think she liked oatmeal chocolate chip cookies the best."

"You don't remember for sure?" Renee looked at me curiously.

"It was a long time ago, Sweet Pea. Grammy's memory isn't that good. Want to play some songs now?"

"Okay!" Renee forgot her questions and followed me to the living room.

I sat down on the couch and picked up my guitar. "Grammy's been working on some new songs. Do you want to learn them?"

Renee jumped up and down enthusiastically. "Yeah!"

I chortled. "I'll sing a line of a song, and then I'll play it again and we'll sing together. Sound good?"

Renee nodded and started swaying her hips, as if the music were already playing.

My smile was so big, it took an effort to form my mouth into the words of the lyrics. I strummed my guitar and began the Beatles song. After the first refrain, I stopped and nodded toward Renee. "Okay, now you sing with me." I started the song over and Renee joined in, her eyebrows knit with concentration.

We made it through the whole song, and Renee did well at following along. Her singing wasn't too bad for a kid. My heart swelled with pride. Had she inherited a musical gift from me? I could teach her to play the guitar and help her guide her vocal cords into harmony.

Next I played a children's song, "Home on the Range," which Renee knew. After it was over, Renee clapped and bowed, as if she were both the performer and the audience. I laughed so hard my stomach hurt. "You're a character."

"What's a character?"

"Someone with a lot of personality." I ruffled her hair.

Renee beamed. "Will you play and sing now, Grammy? And I can dance? My voice is tired." She held her hands to her neck, eyes wide in dramatic fashion.

I nodded. "Sure. Don't want you wearing yourself out. Is there any song in particular you would like to hear?"

Renee tilted her head. "One of the ones I heard you sing along with on the radio." Renee sucked in her cheeks. "Like the one about daddies not going away."

My chest stung. "Well...um...I don't have the chords to play that song, sweetie."

"What do you mean?"

I patted my guitar. "I don't have the music to show me which strings to play on my guitar." Truthfully, my musical memory was coming back to me and I could probably figure it out as I went. I'd played that song many times when I was younger, before Cassie was even born. Little did I know how it would play out in our lives.

Renee frowned. "Oh."

My heart sank. "I could give it a try, though, if you can be patient with Grammy starting and stopping a few times."

"Yes! I can!" Renee's frown immediately arced into a smile.

The things we do for our grandkids.

I strummed the guitar and moved my fingers around, trying a few different chords. After a couple of minutes, I was pretty sure I had it right. "Okay, let's see how this goes."

I began the song slowly, but before I knew it, memory took over and my fingers moved up and down the neck of my guitar, finding their place. I sang the lyrics, the sound of my own voice becoming louder and from deep within me as I lost all sense of time and place. All there was in the world was my granddaughter smiling and swaying to the music, the guitar, and me.

When the song was done, Renee clapped enthusiastically. I stood and took a bow, playing into the performance. Then I set the guitar down and sat on the sofa, tired but happy. Renee climbed up next to me. She studied me with soulful eyes. Instead of playfulness, they now held a seriousness and despair that didn't belong to a six-year-old.

"What's wrong?" I reached for Renee, pulling her close to me.

"In that song it says daddies used to never go away."

"Yep, that's what the song says." I swallowed. It's not always true, though."

Renee's eyes glistened. "I haven't seen my daddy in a long, long time."

"I know, honey."

"And we're having a thing at school for Father's Day. Everyone is bringing in something that their dad loves, like a baseball mitt, or a picture of something their daddy loves, like their boat," Renee continued, not stopping for breath, "and we're supposed to draw a picture of it and bring it home and save it for Father's Day. I don't have anything to take...and I don't know if I'll see Daddy to give it to him."

Tears dropped silently down Renee's rosy cheeks. I squeezed her tight and kissed the top of her head. "Have you talked to your mom about this?"

Renee's head was buried in my chest, but she managed to shake it no. I squeezed her again. I didn't know what to say. Every fiber in me wanted to comfort Renee, but I didn't want to step on Cassie's toes by saying the wrong thing. As far as I knew, she'd yet to hear from Derrick since he got out of jail. The last thing I'd heard about him was his marriage to some other woman.

I pulled Renee's face away from me, lifting her chin so I could look in her eyes. "I'm so sorry you're sad, Sweet Pea. Is there anything I can do? I bet there's other kids there who don't have things to bring in, or who don't see their dad very often."

Renee's eyes glistened. "The teacher told those kids they could draw a picture of something for their grandpa, but I don't even have a grandpa, Grammy." Renee's chin quivered.

My chest felt like it was being chopped open with a pickax. This was so unfair. Why did schools even do this kind of thing these days? With so many broken families, wasn't there an awareness of the hurt it could cause?

I looked at the ceiling, sending a silent prayer up to God. The Father of all. How could He let my sweet granddaughter suffer though this? *Lord, we need your help. For Renee's sake.*

Suddenly, an image formed in my head. An item from the past, packed away in a box in my room. "Honey, I think Grammy might have an idea. Let me up a minute so I can go look in my room."

Renee released me, still looking downcast.

"You can have a cookie while you wait for Grammy."

Her eyes lit up. "Okay." She headed to the kitchen.

I hurried to my room and pulled the tote out of my closet. Opening the lid, I was greeted by an array of old pictures I'd yet to put in albums. Pictures of Cassie when she was a baby, pictures of Steven and me all the way back to our dating days. I rummaged through the pictures, not letting myself look at them and get pulled into the past. After digging out a few other keepsakes, I felt the cold metal on my hand. I carefully lifted it out of the tote box. It was crazy I'd kept it this long. The trophy gleamed in the dim light of the room. I ran my fingers over the engraved part with Steven's name. First place in the modified stock car race at Cottage Grove Speedway in the year 1989. It was the last race he won before Cassie was born. The last one where I could honestly say I stood with him proudly, not holding any resentment. I still had the courage of the young who believe nothing bad can happen to them. Invincible. The world was ours.

I sighed as I stood. I'd ditched the bottom of the trophy years ago, keeping only the gold car topper and the engraving of Steven's name. If Renee liked it—and if Cassie agreed—I could send it to school with Renee.

Renee was still at the dining table nibbling on her cookie. I put the trophy down on the table in front of my granddaughter.

"Whoa. What's that?"

"It's a trophy your grandpa won in a car race." Pride swelled up in me at the look of wonder in Renee's eyes.

"My grandpa?"

"Yes, sweetie. Your mommy's daddy. The one who died when she was just a little girl."

"Ohhhhh. Mommy showed me some pictures of him before. She kind of looks like her daddy, I think."

I nodded. "She sure does. And a bit like Nannie too." But not like me.

"My grandpa must've drove really fast." Renee licked the chocolate on her lips.

I laughed. "He sure did. Do you want to take this to school? You could draw this, or if you want, we could find a picture of one of his race cars."

"I want to take this." Renee grabbed the trophy and pulled it to her. "I can put it in my backpack."

I tapped my chin. "We need to make sure it's okay with your mommy."

Renee nodded, then frowned. "But Grammy...I still won't have anyone to give the picture to."

I puckered my mouth, thinking. Could I handle it? It was long overdue, and it would be good for Cassie. Maybe. "You know how we take Nannie and your great grandpa flowers sometimes? By laying them on their gravestone?"

Renee nodded.

"Well, if you want, we could do the same with the picture you draw. Your grandpa has a stone in another graveyard. We could go visit him and leave the picture there."

"Do they get to heaven from there?"

I wish, kid. I'd leave so many things.

"I don't know if they get to heaven, but they might. I do believe God opens a window between heaven and earth, though, and lets the ones we love up there see what we are leaving for them down here." At least that's what I wanted to believe. Had to believe.

Renee let go of the trophy and hugged me. "Thank you, Grammy."

After Renee was in bed for the night, I had a hard time sitting still. What would Cassie say about what I had done?

I was halfheartedly watching an old black-and-white movie when Cassie came through the front door. The tired look in her eyes told me she'd had a long day, but there still seemed to be a bounce in her step.

"How was it?"

Cassie yawned while she took off her coat. "It was good."

She hung her coat up on the coat tree. Silence filled the space between us.

"Do you think you'll go back?"

"Yeah, I think so. They meet every week, but some people only go every other week. It's pretty open."

I nodded, ignoring the uneasy feeling in my stomach. "Was it...helpful?"

Cassie crossed the room and sat next to me on the couch. "Yes. Simply knowing I'm not the only one who thinks the way I do helps. You know what I mean?"

I exhaled. "Yeah." It was the same way I felt when I went to AA meetings, but for an entirely different reason. It was both sad yet almost comical that there was a support group and 12-step program for people like me, and then another program for the people we hurt. Seemed like way too many programs. I guessed sin was like that. It had a domino effect. Maybe we could stop any more from falling before they reached Renee.

And hopefully it wasn't too late.

"How'd it go with Renee? Was she good?"

"She was an angel, as always."

Cassie smiled. "I'm pretty sure she can do no wrong in your eyes."

"You're probably right. We did have a tearful moment though." I shifted on the couch. My palms had turned sweaty.

"What happened?"

I summarized the exchange with Renee about her dad and the Father's Day art activity at school.

Cassie rubbed her temples. "Great. I need to talk to her. I'm not sure what to say, though."

"I know. I did offer her a solution, for now."

"Homeschooling?"

I was glad Cassie was in a good enough mood to make a joke. "Ha. No. But I found one of your dad's racing trophies. I told Renee maybe she could take that to school."

Cassie frowned. "That's not a bad idea, I guess."

The tension eased from my shoulders. She wasn't mad, but obviously uncertain.

"She loved the trophy." I beamed. "I think she is looking forward to showing it off."

"I bet." Cassie offered a half grin. "I guess it'll be okay. Though she won't have anyone to give her artwork to."

"That's another thing." I told Cassie about my idea of taking the artwork to Steven's grave, and Renee's response.

Cassie's eyes welled up. "Oh my goodness. My sweet, sweet Renee." She rubbed the bridge of her nose. "I can't remember the last time I visited Dad's grave. It was always so sad to me. It was all I really knew of him. His gravestone, pictures, and a few stories."

"We don't have to go." Part of me hoped Cassie would agree.

"No. It's a good idea. The whole thing is sad, no matter how you slice it."

Something we could both agree on.

Chapter Twenty-Five

I WAS OFF TO WORK BEFORE Cassie and Renee left the next morning, but the thought of Renee proudly bringing Steven's old racing trophy to school filled my heart with joy all morning.

"You seem to be in a good mood." Janice dabbed at the perspiration on her forehead with a hand towel.

We were in the laundry room unloading towels. The heat from the dryers and steam from the washers was almost suffocating.

I was in a good mood. Last night with Renee had been hard and yet good. Tonight I would see Johnny. It was like having a gourmet dinner with the promise of dessert. "Yeah, I had a good time watching Renee last night." I summarized the events of the evening and even told Janice about the trophy. I didn't tell Janice about Johnny.

"That's so sweet." Janice sighed and shook her head. "Kids are the best."

"They sure are." I looked at the clock on the wall. "Break time."

We went to the break room. I caught a glimpse of the sun through the lobby windows as we passed by. It was a beautiful day. Spring was in full bloom and the promise of warm summer days was in the air. Soon Renee would be out of school. What would Cassie do for childcare this summer?

I pulled my purse out of my locker to get some change and check my phone. A text from Cassie showed on my phone screen. *Pastor Ben contacted me. He'd like us to meet in his office Friday at 5:30 p.m. Does that work for you?*

My heart skipped a beat, and like a deflated balloon, the good mood I'd been riding came gliding to the ground. I set my purse on the table and dug out a couple of one-dollar bills, enough for a Diet Coke. After unscrewing the lid from the bottle, I took a long sip. Janice chattered about something irrelevant, a new store going up in the mall or something. I half-listened and typed out a response to Cassie. *Yes. Friday works. What about Renee?* I couldn't imagine she'd be part of the conversation.

Pastor Ben said she can play in the kids' room. There will be some other staff people at the church and their kids will be hanging out in there.

Hmm. Seemed a little casual for such a large church. Would Samantha's granddaughter be in there too? Unlikely. It wasn't like Samantha was her mom. *OK.* I texted back. No other words seemed necessary. Plus, if I kept typing I wasn't sure what I would say.

"So, what do you think?" Janice's voice registered in my head.

"Oh—sorry. I was texting my daughter. What did you say?"

Janice laughed. "You were nodding the whole time I was talking, but something told me you weren't all here. I was asking if you want to go check out the new craft store that's opening up in the mall."

Crafts? I didn't do crafts. "Um. Well. I could. I mean, I don't usually do crafty things, but I'd go with you to check it out."

Janice gave me a crooked smile. "You never know, you might find a new addiction."

Chills ran down my arms. "What did you say?"

Janice lifted an eyebrow. "I thought you were listening now. I said you might find a new addiction. You never know—you might take up macramé or something."

"I don't like that word." My voice was hard.

"What word?"

Janice looked baffled. What was I doing? She obviously didn't mean a thing by what she said. "Never mind." I waved my hand in the air. "I'm a little edgy, I guess. Maybe I'll get a Snickers." I dug through my purse, looking for quarters.

"Well, they do really satisfy, according to the commercials." Janice paused, seeming to study me for a moment. "Don't take this wrong, my friend, but your mood just took a one-eighty. Is there anything you want to talk about?"

I put quarters in the vending machine. I couldn't look Janice in the eye. "I'm fine."

She didn't say another word, but I swore I could hear her thoughts—*that Sharon, she sure is freaked out, insecure, neurotic, and emotional.*

I couldn't disagree.

I figured I could talk to Cassie more when she got home from work, though I wasn't sure what I'd say. I had the uneasy feeling she knew more about what would take place at our meeting with Pastor Ben than I did. But why would she lie to me? Was she trying to prove something? The thought irked me and kept me on guard like a lingering bad dream.

At least today I was getting to pick Renee up from daycare. Wednesdays were a day free of the extracurricular activities Cassie paid extra for, and she had arranged for Renee to come home right after school. If the trophy didn't meet the teacher's approval, Cassie didn't want Renee carrying her backpack around for too long with a family heirloom of sorts sitting in it.

Luckily, when I picked Renee up from the afterschool program, the trophy was not in her backpack. "What'd your teacher think of Grandpa's trophy?"

"She loved it!" Pride shone on Renee's face.

"Awesome!"

We stopped at the park on the way home. With the temperature hovering in the low eighties, I couldn't say no to Renee's request when she asked, even though I was itching to get out of my work clothes. I'd finally gotten a new work shirt, but my jeans were still too tight. I let Renee play for a bit while I checked my phone.

I'd been checking the MyGenealogy app less often, but it was always in the back of my mind. At some point this R. Bowers person had to get back to me. There were no new messages, so I looked through my matches, checking for new ones. Nothing.

By the time Renee and I got home, it was time to think about dinner. The house was warm, and it was starting to cool down outside, so I opened the windows, letting the spring breeze in, scented by the lavender bush outside the back window. The warmth, the sun, and the spring air lifted my heart, despite everything I could've been discouraged about. I sang freely while I made dinner, and Renee joined in the singing every now and then, making me smile. By the time Cassie got home, I had a savory chicken stir fry ready to set on the table and a light heart. So light, I almost decided not to pry about the meeting with Samantha.

Almost.

While Renee was in the bathroom washing her hands, I blurted out the question that was nagging at me. "Do you know something about this meeting with Pastor Ben and Samantha that I don't know?"

Cassie stopped, fatigue etched in lines around her eyes. Guilt settled in my stomach. I needed to let Cassie be. "Never mind the question. It's okay."

"I know some things, but I think it's best if you hear it from Samantha herself." Cassie's tone was hesitant but neutral.

My guilt was washed away by irritation. "You're keeping something from me?"

"I only know things aren't always what they seem. Samantha has her own story, her own heartbreak she's been carrying around."

"It sounds like you know quite a lot, if you ask me." I put my hand on my hip, dinner forgotten.

"Mom, I can't tell you everything Matt tells me. That wouldn't be right. I think it's best if we all talk about this Friday."

"Why are you doing this to me?" My voice rose, despite my resolve not to yell.

Cassie swallowed and visibly took a breath. "I'm not doing anything but trying my hardest to do the *right* thing."

"And what is that? Betray your mom? Take the side of some woman you don't even know because she looks all holy and perfect?" Even as the bitter words left my mouth, I wished I could take them back.

"I'm not betraying you, Mom." Her voice was barely above a whisper, but the sorrow and conviction in it was unmistakable. "Stop expecting the worst from people."

Before I could respond, Renee walked back in the room, ready for dinner. "What's wrong, Mommy?" Her face puckered in concern.

"Nothing, honey. Let's sit down and eat." Cassie looked away, an audible sigh escaping her lips.

Regret tore at my chest, like a jagged knife through a raw steak. Why had I reacted so harshly to Cassie? My actions only reinforced the negative perception she already had of me—I expected the worst in people.

Was it true?

Maybe, but it doesn't mean you're disqualified from the race. Hold your position and wait for the green flag.

I brushed the racing analogy aside and took a seat at the

dining table, collecting my emotions and stuffing them down to be dealt with later. "Cassie, I'm sorry. I didn't mean what I said. This is a tough spot for me, and I feel like I'm driving blind."

Cassie spooned rice onto Renee's plate and didn't look up. "I understand. I think after we talk on Friday, you'll feel better about everything."

Unlikely, but I'd play along. "I guess we'll see." I'd rather eat worms smothered in pig manure, but I had a day or two to figure out what to do about it.

I faked another AA meeting to get out of the house after dinner. I felt like a teenager lying to her parents. I even stashed makeup and a change of clothes in my car to change into, so Cassie wouldn't see me leaving the house all dolled up. Johnny said he was taking me somewhere nice but not too fancy tonight but wouldn't say where. He wanted me to meet him at the parking lot behind the Valley River Center Mall.

"I want to actually drive you somewhere for a change," he'd said.

I agreed to meet him and leave my car in the parking lot, but I stopped at Walmart first to change my clothes in the restroom and do my makeup. The efforts I was going through were crazy, but it was also exciting. Kind of like something I'd seen in some romantic comedy.

I easily spotted Johnny's truck and parked in the space next to his, facing the river west of the mall. By the time I exited my car, he had jumped out of his truck and made his way to me. As usual, my heart did a little leap at the sight of him.

"So where are we going?" I'd done my best to eat only a small portion of dinner with Cassie, but I wasn't hungry.

Johnny opened the passenger door of his truck and held out his hand. "I thought we'd start with a little drive."

Relief flowed over me. "Sounds like a good idea." I took his hand, warmth spreading up my arm and straight to my chest.

He lifted an eyebrow. "I thought you might like that." He gently closed the door and went around the truck to the driver's seat.

The inside of the truck was as nice as the outside. Spotless. Black leather. Lights and screens everywhere. I tittered. "I wouldn't even know how to drive something this new."

"You'd learn quick." Johnny gave me a lopsided grin. "I'll let you drive later, if you want."

I suppressed a smile. "Maybe next time." Would there be a next time? Johnny was heading south tomorrow to secure his new apartment. It wouldn't be long until he was packed up and moved.

We left the mall parking lot behind and Johnny drove us through downtown Eugene. He pointed at a brand-new building with modern architecture where the nightclub we used to work at once stood. "I remember this place. It's changed."

I huffed. "It hasn't changed. It doesn't even exist anymore." Sadness mixed with reverie. We'd had some good times in that bar.

Johnny didn't respond at first. When he did speak, his voice was tender. "You could say that. The address is still the same. Just a different building."

"And business."

"You're kind of not going along with my preprogrammed script here." Johnny winked.

"Sorry." I sighed. "You're right. Same address. Good memories."

"I think so." Johnny's reply was soft with a hint of sadness.

He continued down the road and took a right on Chambers, which turned into River Road. After a few blocks he took a right on a street I knew all too well. I gave him a questioning look. "Why are we going here?"

"Just driving by." Johnny shook his head but wore a smile. "Relax."

I recognized the house even though it was painted a different color. It was a small olive-colored house, surrounded by a yard overgrown with weeds and a chain link fence. The hollowness in my chest was unbearable. Why was he taking me here? This was the house we had shared, but also the one where he'd left me. It was the last place I lived where I had any hope of getting Cassie back. A reminder of how I had failed.

Johnny drove slowly. "We had some good times there, didn't we?" His tone held reminiscence instead of pain.

"All I remember is how it ended." I looked away, hoping he wouldn't see the pain the memory brought me.

Johnny pulled over, then reached for my hand. "I'd give anything to go back in time. I would've tried harder to get you to go to Seattle with me or waited longer for you to get your daughter back so we could all go." He sighed. "I was shortsighted, no doubt about that."

Did he mean it?

Would he have also given up drinking? Did he understand that was the only way I could've gotten Cassie back?

Did it even matter anymore?

I twisted toward him. The descending sun sent a ray of sunlight directly on his beard, accenting the gray. His eyes held an intensity to them that couldn't be faked. In an odd way, more than the fact that he lamented ending our relationship, it was comforting to be with someone who understood the weight of regret.

His hand still held mine. It was wide, strong, and rough. The kind someone like me needed. My throat tightened. "We can't go back in time. All we have is here. Now."

"And tomorrow." The left side of his mouth lifted in a grin.

I wouldn't put my hope in tomorrow. "Any more memories you want to dig up?" I asked.

Johnny let go of my hand and put the truck in drive. "Nope. Only creating new ones from here on out."

We drove north. The conversation was sparse. The painful memories brought on by the house faded away, surpassed by the mood of the moment. Johnny had a classic rock station tuned in on the radio, and his finger kept a beat against the steering wheel as he drove. Soon we were outside of the town limits and heading toward Junction City, where Johnny's parents lived.

"You're taking me to a restaurant in Junction City?"

"Hmm. Not exactly. It's on the outskirts."

What kind of restaurant was on the outskirts of a small town? Not that I cared about the food. I wasn't hungry, and the sunset was breathtaking. Oranges and reds spread across the horizon. Looking at the sunset made it almost impossible not to look at Johnny, since he was on the west side of the truck. Not that I was complaining. I'd always admired his profile. The strong, straight nose. His upper lip curved into a Cupid's bow, visible even with his close-trimmed mustache. Enough to give even a middle-aged, cynical woman butterflies. If it wasn't for the center console separating our seats, I'd unbuckle and scoot closer to him.

As if reading my thoughts, Johnny looked my way, his mouth slightly opened in a small, playful grin. "What's on your mind?"

"I was admiring the sunset."

He pressed his lips together. "Hmm."

Good gravy. He had me pegged. I turned the tables. "What about you?"

"Just thinking about this woman I know. I call her Angel Eyes."

"Hmm," I replied, barely suppressing a smile. "Are they good thoughts?"

"The best." He glanced at me. "And I think they're going to get better."

We drove through the small town of Junction City, then took a left at the Y in the road. The road that would eventually lead to Johnny's parents' place. "Um. Please tell me we are *not* going to your parents' house."

Johnny's mouth shaped into a half-grin. "Well, not their *house*."

"Johnny Beckett, what in the world are you up to?" Why would he take me to his parents' house? I could kind of see him taking me to his sister's house in Springfield since that's where he was staying. Of course, we'd have no privacy if we went there. I looked at the time on the dashboard. We'd already been gone nearly an hour. How was I going to explain my long absence to Cassie?

"Don't worry, Angel Eyes, I'm not taking you for a reunion with my parents. Not tonight anyway."

I sucked in my breath, my nerves on edge. Were his parents not home? Surprises were great for parties, not so much for dates. A few miles later we took a bend down the dirt road that led to his parents' property. I tapped my foot.

Johnny stopped the truck. "I need you to do one little thing." He opened the center console and pulled out a black handkerchief. "I'm going to put this over your eyes." His periwinkle eyes sparkled, even in the dimming light. "It's part of the effect."

"You're blindfolding me?" I sat back, not liking the idea at all.

"It'll literally be for twenty seconds. You can hold it over your eyes yourself and not tie it, as long as you promise not to peek." His eyes pleaded with me, like a little boy asking for a piece of candy before dinner.

I rolled my eyes and grabbed the cloth from him. "I can't believe I'm letting you talk me into this." I put the dark handkerchief over my face. It smelled like Johnny. I ached to feel his hand in mine again. "Okay, let's go." I felt the truck move slowly and heard the gravel under the tires. Moments later, the truck leaned to the right slightly as it pulled off the road. The truck came to a stop, and Johnny cut the engine.

Johnny exhaled. "It all stayed exactly the way I left it." He sounded relieved. "You can drop the hanky now."

I pulled the cloth away and opened my eyes. It took a moment for them to adjust. There was only the slightest light left from the sun. In front of us was a simple gazebo, constructed of what appeared to be thin poles and covered in a muslin fabric. White lights were strung along it, creating an almost magical room of light in the growing darkness. In the middle of the gazebo was a white-clothed table and two chairs, with a candle centerpiece, casting a soft light over a table setting for two. My mouth gaped open. He'd done all of this for *me*?

"What do you think?" He looked at me expectantly.

"I'm...shocked...impressed...darn near speechless." My nose tingling with the smile I couldn't hold back. "I don't remember you ever being quite this romantic."

"Like I told you, I'm like a good bottle of whiskey—better with age."

Before I could respond, Johnny jumped out of the truck and walked around to the passenger door, opening it and giving me his hand. The cool night air hit me, and goosebumps erupted on my arms. I took Johnny's hand and slid out of the truck.

"Hold on a second." He pulled on a lever in the back of the seat, pushing it forward, and grabbed something. The next thing I knew, soft, woven fabric was draped over my shoulders. "I brought this little blanket from my sister's, just in case."

How thoughtful was that?

He took my hand in his and we walked toward the gazebo. I couldn't help but smile at the table setup. It was obviously a pop-up white table covered with a tablecloth, flanked by two folding chairs. The centerpiece candle was in a hurricane glass vase. The plates looked like they were of decent quality, and there were real utensils and cloth napkins set by each.

Johnny pulled out one of the chairs and motioned for me to sit. I looked around, noticing a firepit filled with wood next to the gazebo. The candlelight danced off a blue cooler to my right, and next to it I made out the shape of a small grill. I wondered what we were going to eat but didn't want to ask. How was Johnny going to pull this off?

After I was seated, Johnny went to the cooler and pulled out two beverages. He put a Diet Coke before me and set a root beer by his plate. Next, he pulled out two individual salad bowls, covered in plastic wrap, along with a bottle of ranch dressing.

"I'll be your chef *and* server tonight." He set the salad in front of me and whipped off the plastic, then bowed. "Excuse me while I get the fire going for the chef's special, El Feast De La Hobo."

I laughed. "Sounds delicious."

After lighting the coals on the grill, Johnny worked on the fire pit, coaxing the fire to blazing flames. We made silly jokes while he waited for the coals to get hot, then he pulled two tin-foil packages out of the cooler and set them on the grill. Afterward he trotted back to his truck and climbed in. A moment later music played from the speakers, not too loud but clear enough to hear the words. He returned to the table, perspiration lining his brow. "Dinner will be ready in thirty minutes. Give or take." He took a seat across from me.

"This is amazing. I don't even know what to say." I picked up my salad fork and set the napkin in my lap.

"Leaving you speechless was the goal." Johnny grinned and poured ranch on his salad.

We chatted easily while we ate salad and waited for the main course to cook. Johnny told me about the trip he was taking to San Jose, beginning the next morning, to get his new place secured and set up. "I'll take pictures. You're going to like it."

I lifted a shoulder. "I'm sure it will be amazing." My stomach sank, thinking of him leaving. I definitely didn't see myself having any more dates like tonight with anyone anytime soon. If ever.

The thirty minutes passed quickly. Johnny used the small shovel to pull the hobo dinners out of the fire, then set them on two clean plates he pulled from a bag behind the cooler. He set them on the table. "We should probably let those sit for a bit before popping them open."

"I agree."

"There's one thing I'd like to do while we wait." He walked back to the bag behind the cooler, grabbed something small out of it, and then held his hands behind his back as he walked back to the table. He took his seat, keeping one hand behind his back.

He looked at the table, seeming nervous. That wasn't like him at all. "Sharon, I have something I want to give you." He brought his hand to the front and set a small black box on the table between us.

A jewelry box.

The kind that held a ring.

My pulse raced. "Wh—what's this?"

He wouldn't.

Would he?

Johnny looked away, seemingly embarrassed. "Yeah, it's not what you think, okay? Not exactly, anyway." He turned back to me and nodded toward the box. "Just open it."

I opened my mouth to say no. My head spun, and the yellow flashing light that I'd experienced before when it came to Johnny flashed behind my eyes. But I couldn't resist the urge to see what was in the black box. I took it in my hands and opened it.

There was a ring inside, but not a diamond one. Not an engagement ring. It was a gold ring with an octagon-shaped setting. An opal sat in the middle. It wasn't like anything I'd seen before. It was simple. Not fancy. My heart dipped, but I was also relieved.

"What do you think?" Johnny's voice was slightly higher pitched than usual.

"It's beautiful. Unique." I picked up the ring and put it on my right ring finger. The candlelight glimmered off the white stone.

"Just like you," Johnny whispered.

My cheeks burned. I groaned inside. Wasn't I too old to get flustered over a man? "I love it, but...what's the occasion?" It clearly wasn't an engagement ring. That would have been crazy anyway.

"You know I'm not a marrying man." Johnny shifted in his seat. "I mean, it's only a piece of paper, right? But I wanted to give you something to symbolize my devotion to you." Johnny took my hand, his brows pressed together. "It's my way of saying, as long as you're in my life, I'm going to treat you right. I don't want to be with anyone else."

I nodded. Undoubtedly some women would've thought what Johnny offered was a far cry from what they wanted. From what they deserved. But I knew Johnny—for him, this was serious. "But you're leaving soon. Really soon. What's the point?" Part of me hoped he was going to say he'd changed his mind about moving, but he'd been talking about his new place moments before.

Johnny squeezed my hand, and I reluctantly met his gaze. Determination burned in his eyes. "I want you to go with me."

My shoulders stiffened. "I already told you—"

"I know, I know, but listen. I'm going to be making good money. You won't need to work. We'll get you a better car. You can come up here and visit your daughter as often as you want. Heck, they can come visit us." He chuckled. "Imagine how much your granddaughter would love visiting the sunny California beaches."

Renee would love it. But Cassie would never bring her. Not if I ran off with a man I wasn't married to and left her when she needed family more than ever.

"Johnny—"

"Look, you don't have to say yes or no right now. I'm going to be down in California getting things ready to move. Then I'm flying to Portland to rent a moving van and pack up my stuff. If you want to join me, I'll pick your stuff up on my way down. You can follow me in your car. If you don't, I'll say goodbye and wish you well."

Did he mean goodbye forever? Was he making me choose, yet again, between going off with him and staying behind to be with my daughter? Irritation pricked at my insides. "Feels like an ultimatum."

"It's not, Angel Eyes," Johnny moved his head slowly from side to side. "It's not meant to be that way, at all." He looked at the candle, its wick growing short, then focused his eyes on me. "We're not getting any younger. The way I see it, you've gone above and beyond for your daughter."

I started to shake my head no.

"You have, Sharon. Your entire life revolves around her and your granddaughter. And from what you tell me, it sounds like she's got a flame burning for that pastor." He raised his eyebrows. "She could be married in a year."

"I doubt that." But honestly, I wasn't so sure.

"It's not like she's a kid anymore. She has her own life." His voice softened. "And you have yours."

My chest burned like the red coals of the fire beside us. Johnny was right. But the thought of leaving made everything in me scream like I was stepping in front of a speeding train. "It's not that simple." My voice sounded gravelly. Johnny made good points—ones I'd already considered. Cassie was going to a support group because of having me for a mother. Later this week I'd have to face my archnemesis so I could continue to go to church with my family. I was fighting an uphill battle. What if I couldn't make it to the top? Where would I land?

Johnny rubbed his finger over the opal on the ring, then he caressed my hand. The gentleness of his touch sent a wave of warmth through me. When he spoke, his voice was sultry, tempting. "You have some time to think it over. No matter which way you decide, the ring is yours. Always."

We finished our dinner. The beef, potatoes, and peppers were cooked to perfection and deliciously seasoned, but the turmoil in my head made eating a challenge. When we were finished, Johnny shoveled dirt on the fire and led me back to the truck. He stopped before opening the passenger door and took me in his arms. I laid my head against his chest. The warmth of his embrace comforted me and made me realize how much the temperature had dropped. Johnny kissed the top of my head. I lifted my chin and gazed up at him, seeing only the outline of his face in the darkness. He leaned in, his lips meeting mine. I was tempted to let myself get lost in this kiss—let it take me anywhere Johnny led us—but thoughts of Cassie brought me back to earth. I broke from our embrace and shivered.

"I guess I better get you home," Johnny breathed, then opened the door for me.

I pulled myself into the truck, and Johnny shut the door. I felt something under my leg. I reached and my hand found the handkerchief Johnny had me cover my eyes with earlier. I opened his glovebox to put it away. A thick envelope fell out, visible in the light that came on inside the compartment. I picked it up. It had the green postcard showing it was certified mail, made out to Johnny Beckett. I looked at the return address. State of Washington. Johnny's door opened and he slid into the truck.

The yellow light flashed with quantum speed in my mind. "What's this?"

Johnny reached over and gently took the envelope from me, opened the center console, and tossed it inside. I noticed there were several other pieces of mail in its depths. "Ah, it's nothing. Stupid legal stuff."

"Legal stuff is usually pretty important. It doesn't even look like you've opened it."

Johnny waved his hand dismissively. "That's because I already know what's in it." He started the engine, looked in the rearview mirror, and put the truck in reverse. "It's a long story."

We drove down the gravel road. I waited for Johnny to offer more information, but all he did was turn on the radio. I didn't know how to lower the volume, so I yelled over the screaming guitars of a Led Zeppelin song. "We have a good forty-five-minute drive back to my place. Plenty of time for a long story."

Johnny dialed down the music using a button on his steering wheel. "It's nothing important."

I shifted in my seat. "You can't ask me to move to another state with you and then not be willing to tell me about your legal problems."

Johnny's lips pressed together. Finally, he shifted his gaze toward me. "If it was important—if it was going to affect our lives together in any way—I'd tell you the whole story." He gave me his most charming smile. "Look, I don't want to end this night talking about legal mumbo jumbo that doesn't matter. But if you want to know all the boring details later, I promise I'll fill you in."

I exhaled. Johnny had never outright lied to me, so there was no reason to think he'd hide something important from me now—other than the fact that he had never been the most responsible person on the planet. The letter was probably some stupid past-due bill for internet service or the like. "Okay, but I do expect more information later."

Johnny's grin grew.

"What?" Was something funny?

"You basically just told me you're at least considering coming with me to California. That's all." He chortled and reached over to take my hand.

Leave it to Johnny to spin an unread legal letter into something good.

Cassie had waited up, like I was a teenager and she was the parent. Thankfully, I'd not only changed into the clothes I'd left in, but also washed off my makeup and slid the ring in my purse. When she asked me why I'd gotten home so late, I told her I'd gone out to coffee with some people from my AA meeting.

"But you don't drink coffee at night."

"It was decaf."

I'd felt too guilty to look her in the eyes, which probably only confirmed her suspicions. She'd walked up to me and sniffed me like she was a dog looking for a criminal.

"You smell like a campfire." Her eyes narrowed into slits.

"What is this? Am I under house arrest or something?"

Cassie folded her arms. "There's something you're not telling me."

"Maybe because it's none of your business."

Cassie's chin dropped and pain flashed in her eyes. "I'm just worried about you."

"There's nothing to worry about. I'm doing good." I put my hands on my hips. "You did the sniff test. Do I smell like liquor?"

"Well...no." Cassie's shoulder's sagged. "But you're being secretive."

I sighed. I wasn't ready to tell her about Johnny yet. "It was just a guy and me having a conversation by his fire pit." That was a version of the truth, but guilt wrapped a cord around my stomach and pulled it tight.

Cassie's face had gone expressionless. "I'm going to bed. If you want to tell me more tomorrow, fine." She walked away, not looking back. "And if you don't, that's fine too."

I knew what fine meant.

Chapter Twenty-Six

FRIDAY ARRIVED BEFORE I WAS READY. The worst thing was, it was my day off and I had nothing to do but wait. Why did Johnny have to be out of town now of all times? It gave me way too much time to mentally prepare myself for everything that could go wrong. What was Samantha going to say about me? Was Cassie going to hate me? Did she already hate me? The tension between us since I came home Wednesday night was palpable.

The thoughts ate at me, making my stomach and head hurt in unison. I needed something to get me through this. I couldn't do it alone. No way, no how. Wouldn't that make it a perfect catastrophe if I showed up for our meeting three sheets to the wind? The thought was almost comical. Talk about flushing any progress I'd made with Cassie completely down the drain.

The ache in my head and the queasiness escalated with each passing hour. About two p.m. I ran to the bathroom and vomited. I washed out my mouth and splashed cold water on my face. My nerves were getting the best of me. I went to my room to lie down, hoping I wouldn't be making any more trips to the porcelain throne. Thirty minutes later I was in the bathroom again, my body convulsing and emptying what was left and then choking as I dry heaved. Why was this happening to me, today of all days? I raised the back of my palm to my forehead. No fever. Somehow, I managed the trek to the kitchen to get a large bowl but didn't make it back with the bowl before my stomach convulsed again. My head was splitting open. I stumbled to my bed, bowl in hand. I collapsed on my bed, the metal bowl crashing to the floor beside me.

My worse hangover had never left me as sick as I was now. My head felt like I had an ax through it. Any movement caused horrible dizziness and nausea. Was I having a stroke? Was it the Ebola virus? I pulled my pillow over my head, blocking out the light streaming through my window. The darkness added a tiny amount of relief. Maybe I had a migraine.

You've worked yourself up to a tizzy. Take deep breaths and remember God is in control.

Mom. If she were here now, she would mediate the tension between Cassie and me. Her calm reassurance and big faith would bring peace.

But she wasn't here. It was time for me to be the matriarch, the one with wisdom and comfort.

I twisted on my bed, pushing the memories away. Mom had been the one I'd run to after Steven died, but even her love didn't stop me from spiraling down a dark pit of self-destruction. Her desperate pleas for me to get help had gone unheeded. Lost on the wind like cries during a winter storm.

You're only as sick as the secrets you keep.

The familiar saying from Alcoholics Anonymous echoed through my pounding head, causing a fresh wave of nausea. I leaned over the bed, heaving into the mixing bowl. I wasn't strong enough. I couldn't face Samantha. Yet if I didn't, there was nothing I could do to save the small gains I'd made with Cassie.

Fatigue and darkness settled over me, and I sank into a restless sleep. What could've been hours later or only a few minutes, the front door opened and woke me up. My eyes fluttered and I attempted to lift my head. Nausea seized my stomach and my mouth went dry. I laid my head back down, willing the sickness away.

After a few moments there was a light tapping on my door. "Mom?"

"Come in." My voice was weak, barely a whisper.

Cassie opened the door and stepped in. I could sense her irritation. Did she think I was taking a nap and not bothering to get ready for our appointment?

"Are you okay?"

"I'm afraid not. I've been sick as a dog all afternoon." I turned my gaze at Cassie without lifting my head, but even that made me nauseated. I swallowed and closed my eyes, taking a deep breath.

Cassie's focus went to the bowl on the floor, which contained little more than a few tablespoons of clear liquid. "I'm sorry, Mom." Her tone had changed, now showing concern. "Is there anything I can get you? Some water?"

"Water would be great."

Cassie left. In a moment she was back, a glass of water in hand. She set it on my nightstand and put her hand on my forehead.

"You definitely don't have a fever. If anything, you feel cold."

I nodded ever so slightly. "I don't know what's going on. It hit me out of nowhere."

"Maybe something you ate?"

Whatever it was, I knew food had nothing to do with it. "I don't know, baby girl."

Cassie brushed my hair out of my face and tucked the blanket around me. "I'll call Pastor Ben and tell him we need to reschedule."

My stomach seized and I lurched toward the bowl.

Cassie stepped back. Thankfully, I hadn't even ventured a sip of water yet and nothing came out of me other than retching sounds.

"We can figure out everything later. You focus on getting better." Cassie made her way to the door slowly, pausing before opening it. "I'm so sorry you're sick. I'll check on you in a little while."

The door opened and closed softly. The stabbing pain in my head eased slightly, and my stomach relaxed. I tried not to think about the coincidence of the easing of my symptoms and the cancellation of the meeting.

Whatever sickness had overcome me was gone by the next morning. The entire weekend passed without Cassie asking me what day we could meet with Samantha. On Sunday I had to work, so there was no need for me to bring it up, no in-my-face reminders of why it was an issue. Cassie was quiet. I wondered what was going on in her head but didn't dare to ask.

Sunday after work, I found an AA meeting to go to. It was in a small room in a community center not far from our house. My urge to drink on Friday combined with my overwhelming emotional reaction to facing Samantha was a blaring red light over the fact that I had failed to go to meetings since our trip to California. Nothing like catastrophe to bring you back where you needed to be.

The room had a stale smell and was adorned with posters of different sorts that outlined services for the needy: supplemental food, rent assistance, crisis centers. One poster listed the twelve steps for Alcoholics Anonymous. Next to it was a poster with a picture of a woman with bloodshot and watery eyes and beads of sweat on her forehead. There was a Band-Aid over her mouth. Above the woman was written, "We're only as sick as the secrets we keep." A cold tremor shot through my body, raising gooseflesh on the backs of my arms.

My feet were frozen to the ground, the people around me disappearing. I waited for Steven or my mom's voice to whisper in my head, but all I heard was silence. Shaking away a feeling of déjà vu, I made my way to one of the folding metal chairs and took a seat.

The meeting went through all the usual motions, led by a young woman with black hair and several visible tattoos. I listened half-heartedly, nodding and responding at the appropriate spots but not truly participating in the meeting. I couldn't take my eyes off the picture of the woman on the wall.

When I got home, Cassie and Renee were there. Part of me was relieved, yet I also wondered how her friendship with Matt was going. She hadn't spoken much about him lately. What right did I have to question her about a possible romantic interest when I'd told her nothing of mine? If I asked her any questions, she was likely to bring up the subject of Samantha. I hated to open that Pandora's box, but if my daughter was hurting and needing someone to talk to, I needed to be there for her.

After putting my purse away and changing out of my work clothes, I joined Cassie and Renee outside. It was pleasantly warm and sunny. Cassie wore sunglasses and soaked up the sun. Renee played with her Barbie car in the grass.

"How was church?"

Cassie shrugged. "It was fine."

I nodded. "Good. How's Matt?" Might as well get right to the point.

Cassie shrugged again, seeming nonchalant. "I only spoke to him briefly."

"I see."

Cassie turned and lowered her chin, looking at me over the top of her sunglasses. "Why are you so interested in Matt?" She smiled playfully. "Do you have a crush on him?"

I rolled my eyes. "He could be my son. But I bet I know someone who *does* have a small crush on him and is trying to hide it."

"Ha!" Cassie looked away, her cheeks flushed. "That would be quite silly of *someone*, all things considered."

"Even smart girls are silly sometimes, Cassie. It's allowed." If she only knew how silly her mother had been lately.

A half-smirk appeared on my daughter's fading-red face. "Not if you're also a recently divorced mom who's made some stupid decisions and is trying to build a new life."

"Hmm." I watched Renee roll the Barbie car across the yard while making engine sounds. "You're thinking about the guy you work with, right? What was his name, Brian?"

Cassie inhaled deeply and then blew air out forcibly. "Yeah."

"We all make mistakes. Under the circumstances, it's no surprise you were swept away by his smooth moves. He was trying to play the knight in shining armor role to take advantage of you." My voice rose in irritation, not at Cassie, but at the memory of the man who thought of my daughter as prey when she was at her weakest. Chills shot down my arms. A dark cloud was in my mind, threatening to release its burden. I wasn't ready for the storm.

"I suppose. I guess sometimes it's hard not to think of myself as damaged goods, so to speak."

I shook my head. Cassie wasn't damaged goods. If the term applied to anyone, it was me, but what kind of example did I set if I labeled myself that way? Not a good one. What would my mom say?

"You're not damaged goods. You're a daughter of the King." As the words came out of my mouth I felt like a fraud, but after they were spoken, my own shoulders were a little lighter, my heart hurt a bit less.

Cassie sighed. "You sound like Nannie."

"Good. She was a wise woman."

"Yes, she was." Cassie nodded. "Have you heard anything else from your MyGenealogy site?"

The sharp change in topics caught me off guard. "No.

Not really." Johnny had done a good job of distracting me from the search for my father. But spending time with him hadn't taken away the unreasonable need I had to find out my father's story.

"I was talking to a secretary at work about it on Friday. I didn't mention it to you before because you were sick, and then it slipped from my mind." Cassie's forehead wrinkled. "I'm sorry."

"Sorry about what?"

"I think I might have a lead. Or the way to get a lead, anyway."

I sat up straighter, a jolt of adrenaline rushing through me. "What?"

"Michael was living in Lassen County, and they have their court records online. If the lady we talked to in Susanville is his power of attorney, I can probably find her name online. Maybe even her contact information."

My mind raced. "That still won't tell us where Michael is."

"No, but we can call or write her and ask again. There might even be something filed that shows where he is living now."

My heart raced. Could I handle another disappointment? I knew the answer. The possibility of finding my father and having my questions answered outweighed the risk.

"Can you look it up tomorrow?" I asked.

"Yes, I think so." Cassie looked thoughtful. "If I find her name but no contact information, I'll run her name through the other program we have. It should yield some results."

"It's worth a shot."

Johnny texted Sunday night and sent me pictures of the house he was leasing.

What did you think of the house?

It was a cute little bungalow with a palm tree in the front yard. It made my heart long for my own home. *It's super cute.*

I'm glad you like it. He added three heart emojis, emphasizing his point.

I tossed and turned when I went to bed, thoughts tumbling through my mind. I couldn't get Johnny's offer out of my head. Though it was ludicrous, the idea made my heart flutter with anticipation, like I was in line for the best rollercoaster at an amusement park. Cassie might have another lead on my father, yet I was afraid to get my hopes up, again. And like a black mark on a perfectly white piece of paper was the unavoidable meeting with Samantha.

It seemed like all three things held the key to my future, and there was only one I had any control over—whether or not I would leave my new life behind and start over with Johnny.

Why was it only in something ridiculous I had any choice?

Cassie came home Monday night with information—and questions.

"Her name is Rebecca Bowers."

My breath caught in my throat. "Bowers?"

Cassie nodded, her eyes gleaming with the news. "Yes, ring a bell?"

"I can't believe it." I searched around the living room for my phone. Where had I laid it down?

"Your first cousin match was an R. Bowers, right?" Cassie followed me through the house while I searched for my phone. Renee sat in front of the television, engrossed in her new favorite show on Netflix.

Dinner was in the oven, but it could wait.

"Yes." I finally found my phone on the kitchen counter, behind the salad bowl. I opened the MyGenealogy app and went to my matches. "Rbowers99" was still there, at the top of my matches. First cousin...at least by name.

"Did you get a phone number? An address?"

"I sure did." Her smile grew wider. She put the piece of paper in her hands down on the kitchen table. The printout was gibberish to me, but Cassie pointed to a specific area. "From what I can tell, she currently lives in Klamath Falls."

"Klamath Falls? Not Susanville?"

"Yep. No phone number, though. Sometimes cell numbers don't show up if they're in someone else's name."

I pulled the dining chair out and sat. My head was spinning, but not in the nauseating way it had on Friday. This was more pleasant. Adrenaline and hope swirled together into a string of possibilities. The paper in front of me came into focus, and I read the information, which included a date of birth for Rebecca Ann Bowers. I did the math in my head. She was only twenty years old. Awfully young for the responsibility of Power of Attorney.

"How do you think she's related? I mean, if she is my first cousin, Anthony would've known about her, right? She'd be his daughter or the daughter of their youngest brother, Richard. And she obviously knows where Michael is, so Anthony would know too, right? Plus, she's awfully young to be either one of their daughters." I rubbed my head, trying to make sense of it all.

Cassie pulled out a chair and sat beside me. "I don't know. I've been thinking about it. There's a lot of possibilities."

"Do you think Anthony lied?"

"No," Cassie sucked in her cheeks. "I considered the possibility, but why would he lie and then give us the address for Michael's house?"

"I don't know." I sighed. "It's confusing, that's for sure."

Cassie sat back in her chair. "I looked up the different possibilities of how Rebecca could be related to you. She could be something other than a cousin. The most likely option is you are a half aunt."

I nodded, staring at the paper. "That would mean...I have a half brother or sister, right?"

"Yes." The look in Cassie's eyes told me she shared the possible joy of finding a sibling—from one only child to the other.

"I suppose anything is possible." I shrugged, unwilling to admit the emotion brought on by the possibility.

"I agree."

"This is all so confusing." I sighed. This lady *has* to talk to us."

"I ordered the official court records, in the hope there would be a phone number in them."

"You think—" I almost said "we," but after Cassie telling me about feeling she was taking on too much when it came to me, I didn't want to assume her help would go beyond her detective work. I cleared my throat. "You think I should call this time, instead of showing up at her doorstep?"

Cassie lifted her hands, palms facing the ceiling. "I think showing up unannounced has mostly worked out so far. But I'd hate to make another trip and have her send us away. Although, Klamath Falls is close enough we wouldn't need to stay the night."

We. Were we in this together again? I didn't want to do anything that made Cassie feel like she was playing the role of mother, or have her going with me simply because she was afraid I was going to find a setback and fall off the wagon.

"Maybe I'll try calling first. If she doesn't answer or return my call, we can always make a trip down there at some point." I glanced toward the living room. Renee was still watching the television. "I'm not sure there's much to see in Klamath Falls. You two don't have to come with me. I can go alone."

Cassie tapped her fingers against the table and stared out the window. "You shouldn't have to do this alone." She turned to face me. "*No one* should."

I straightened, determined to be strong for my daughter. "I haven't always been here for you, Cassie. I know that. We don't have to tiptoe around it. There's no reason for you to hold my hand through this thing." I looked at the table, where Cassie's index finger was still tapping away. "I'm not going to drink if it all goes wrong." At least I wasn't planning on it.

"It's not all about your drinking." Cassie sighed. "I know our past is rocky. We haven't had the picture-perfect mother-daughter relationship. But I also know alcoholism is a disease and you've been fighting it with everything you've got." She leaned toward me. "You've been here for me like a rock since Nannie passed away. And I'm here for you. That's what family is for."

Family. After everything I'd done, I still had my family. A tinge of guilt nipped at my stomach. Why was I even entertaining the idea of running off with Johnny?

Cassie fidgeted in her chair. "There's something else I need to talk to you about—another family matter."

My nerves zinged. Did she know about Johnny? I'd kept the ring from him hidden in my purse. Had she looked through my things? "What is it?"

Cassie inhaled and then blurted out the words. "Pastor Ben asked me when we can reschedule our meeting with Samantha."

I had nothing to say in response. The three seconds of silence spoke volumes.

"Mom, I think we need to get this behind us. You haven't been to church since we talked about it." Cassie's voice was strained.

My mind reeled. How could I explain? "I don't think I can do it."

Cassie sighed. "I know it's hard, but it'll be worth it."

"You have no idea."

The lines on Cassie's forehead deepened. "I know Nannie would want you to do this, Mom. She'd want you in church." She exhaled and looked away. "It seems like you're carrying around this weight and I don't know what to do. I keep feeling like if I don't fix it, then..." Cassie didn't finish her sentence but regarded me with despondent eyes.

Realization made chills run down my spine. She was terrified I'd start drinking again. I'd learned enough from AA to know what Cassie was describing was codependency. The very thing she was trying to overcome by going to the group for adult children of alcoholics. It was the damage done by *me*.

"I'm sorry, baby girl." My voice was barely above a whisper.

Cassie didn't say a word.

I desperately wanted to make things right and I had no words to sum up why everything in me said I couldn't meet with Samantha yet. "Let me think about it. I'll have it figured out by tomorrow night." It seemed all my decisions these days had a "due by" date. Why not add this one to the list?

"What do you mean you'll have it figured out?"

I heard the worry in Cassie's voice, and I imagined the thoughts that went with it.

"I'm not going to look for the answer in the bottle, Cassie." My voice was hard, though I didn't mean it to be.

Two heartbeats of silence, confirming my suspicions of Cassie's fears.

The mood in the room had changed from hopeful and optimistic to uncertain and full of dread.

"Okay. I'll be praying, Mom."

I nodded. "Me too."

PART THREE

"Let us run with endurance the race that is set before us, fixing our eyes on Jesus, the author and perfecter of faith, who for the joy set before Him endured the cross, despising the shame, and has sat down at the right hand of the throne of God."

Hebrews 12:2 NASB

Chapter Twenty-Seven

THE NEXT DAY AFTER WORK, INSTEAD of heading home I drove straight to the Quick-Shop-N-Go and bought a Diet Coke. I told Cassie I would pray, and I would, but I needed to drive, to be someplace where I could hear myself think. The sky was cloudy and gray. The humidity told me a spring shower was on its way. The oppressiveness fit my mood. I knew where I wanted to go, though it didn't make sense.

I drove toward north Springfield, through a subdivision of nice homes I'd never be able to afford. Soon I was on a narrow country road. To my left was a hazelnut orchard, to my right, farmlands. The road curved, and I drove along a line of trees to the parking area for Harvest Lane Boat Launch. Raindrops hit my dirty windshield, making it hard to see. I tried the washer function, but apparently it was out of fluid or broken. Even though it was depressing, the weather was my friend. The parking area was practically empty. I pulled into a spot and turned off my engine. The McKenzie River was still full from the winter snowfall and spring rains. Floating it right now would be dangerous, but in a few short weeks this place would be full of young people with inner tubes and small rafts, putting in to float down the river and soak up the sun.

Steven and I had come here frequently when we were young. Those were the summertime days musicians sang of and script writers wrote about. Young love and freedom. Toes in the icy water as the blazing sun burned our shoulders. I smiled and shook my head at the memory. When I was young, I never dreamt life could go so wrong or get so complicated. I had no idea how quickly life could change.

The rain pounded a steady beat against my car. I waited patiently for the shower to pass, the soothing rhythm of the rain almost putting me in a trance. Once it stopped, I opened my car door and stepped onto the wet ground and walked down to the river. The smell of the new-fallen rain mixed with the lush green aroma of the trees that surrounded me and further soothed my soul. If only Steven were here. Or my mom. Or Dad. Someone who had known me before Jack and Coke became my best friend. Before I had changed. They were the ones who knew who I really was...and what I could've been.

I picked up a rock from the shore and attempted to skip it on the river, but I was out of practice and the current was too swift. The rock went *plunk* and sank. I sighed, refusing to cry. I'd told Cassie I would pray. I closed my eyes, blocking everything out except my pounding heart.

Lord, I don't know if you hear me anymore. I've been lost for so long I'm not sure I can be found. Here's the thing, though. I can't face Samantha. Not at church, under the judging eyes of a man of God in a business suit. Don't get me wrong, I've got nothing against church or men of God. I just don't belong there, you know? But more than that, what I did to Samantha was wrong. I know it. But I don't feel bad. At least not for her. The only person I honestly feel bad for is myself and my family, and I know it's not right, but I can't change it. I've tried. So hard.

Tears streamed from my eyes. Like a gift from heaven, the rain gently fell again, mixing with my tears and washing them away.

Put my tears into your bottle; are they not in your book?

Peace settled over me, remembering my mom reciting the Psalm. I couldn't remember the number of the Psalm or even the rest of the words, but I did remember my Mom's love and comforting words.

Lord, I'm not strong enough.

Was there anything to make me strong? Anything to make me see what I needed to see beyond my own breaking, wretched heart? I thought of the search for my bio dad. Hope, then roadblocks. Dead ends and confusing clues. It was a struggle, yet I couldn't give up. The answer seemed barely within reach, and once found, light would be shed on all the darkness that had haunted me for years. Once I found him, I'd be stronger. I'd know who I really was.

It was my answer.

Before I could change my mind or lose my nerve, I took my phone out of my pocket and tapped out a text to Cassie. *I can't meet with Samantha yet. It's hard to explain why. But I know I can do it after I find Michael. I promise.* I hit send, my chest tight and knees weak. Would Cassie be angry? The answer was undoubtedly yes. The real question was *how* angry she would be, and if our relationship could bear the weight of my weaknesses. I stood in the softly falling rain, the river whooshing by, waiting for my daughter to respond. My phone remained silent.

Chapter Twenty-Eight

WHAT I WANTED TO DO WAS head back to Quick-Shop-N-Go and get something to take the edge off. Surprisingly, though, the urge wasn't as strong as it could've been. My skin wasn't crawling with the need, the emptiness in my chest not as hollow as usual. I could find other ways to kill the time between now and dinner.

I headed home. Once settled inside, I took out my guitar. My playing was getting better, nearly back to where I was when I was younger. Funny that a thing could stay with you, after a quarter of a century of leaving it in the dust and destroying brain cells with alcohol consumption. With the guitar case in one hand, I grabbed a new-to-me songbook and made my way to the dining room. Once settled in a chair, I strummed a few strings, feeling the music, playing with notes. Soon, I was humming along, matching the chords I played. By dinner time, I had "Undeniable Love," the song from my mom's music box, memorized.

Cassie was unreadable when she came home. I focused on putting dinner on the table. Spaghetti, salad, and bread rolls. One of Renee's favorite meals. Renee ran into the kitchen and embraced me in a warm hug. Her love was a steady stream I could depend on. I wanted to tell her about "Undeniable Love," but knew it'd be best to wait until I could play the song for her. Otherwise she'd bug me every ten seconds to hear it.

After dinner was done and Renee was tucked in bed, Cassie approached me. I steadied myself, waiting for the worst. Would she insist I move out? Tell me how I wasn't really a mother to her and never had been? Explain how I was an alcoholic and she was an adult child of one, and now needed years of therapy to lead a normal life?

"The documents I requested from Lassen County came today."

Not what I was expecting. My heart rate spiked.

"Was there a phone number?"

"Yes, there was a phone number for Rebecca." Cassie's voice was flat, unemotional.

My chest tightened. "That's good. Gets me closer to finding Michael, if I can get a hold of her." Closer to meeting with Samantha, as I had promised Cassie.

"Yeah. I'll text you the number. I have it saved on my phone." Cassie spun on her heel to walk away.

"Cassie..." Was that desperation in my voice?

"Yes?" She didn't turn around.

"I'm sorry. I promise I'll be better." My words sounded hollow, without meaning. Ones I'd repeated too many times.

"I know." Cassie's voice was barely a whisper.

A few moments later I was in my room and had a text from Cassie. No explanation or additions. Simply Rebecca's name and what appeared to be a cell phone number. It was too late to call her now, at least that's what I told myself. Tomorrow I'd call her right after I got off work. Janice was working tomorrow, and maybe she could give me a pep talk. Lord knew what I truly needed was someone to hold my hand, but the only person who might've done that was in the room down the hall, so fed up with all I'd done she couldn't even talk to me.

My phone call to Rebecca had to go well.

"Didn't she already turn you away? Even though she knew you were family?" Janice stacked a load of freshly washed towels on our cleaning cart.

I'd expected Janice to be more encouraging. "Well...yeah." When we met Rebecca at Michael's house, we had no idea who *she* was, but the moment we told her who we were—or, at least, who we professed to be—she would've known we were related to her somehow. I remembered the momentary flicker in her eyes when we introduced ourselves, her hesitation. How could she not have been curious about our relationship to her?

"Maybe she thought we were scammers, full of bull. If I call her and talk to her more, she'll see I'm legit." Hopefully.

Janice nodded, and we pushed our fully loaded cart out of the supply room and to the elevator. "I'll say a prayer for you, my friend."

Friend. Those were few and far between most of my life. "I'm not sure how to begin the conversation, when I call." I couldn't outright ask for help.

Janice backed the cart into the elevator. "Just tell it like it is."

"I'm going to blabbermouth it."

The elevator closed. Thankfully we were alone in it.

"It's an awkward situation." Janice shrugged her shoulders. "You're basically saying, 'Hey, remember how I showed up at Michael's house and asked you where he was and you wouldn't tell me? Well, I tracked your phone number down with the help of my daughter, who can look stuff like that up because she works for lawyers, and now I'm asking again.' That's not creepy. At all." Janice laughed, her eyes sparkling with humor but warm with sympathy. "I wouldn't want to be in your shoes."

"I wouldn't want to be in my shoes, but they're the only ones that fit, unfortunately." The elevator dinged and we pushed the cart out into the hallway.

"What'd your daughter say about calling?"

The familiar weight on my shoulders returned, locking

down tight. "She didn't really say much. Just gave me the number. That's about the end of it."

Maybe it was my tone. Or maybe the expression on my face. Either way, Janice didn't ask any more questions about Cassie. "Maybe you should write out what you're going to say when you call, so you're less likely to stumble over your words."

Made sense. I'd thought the same thing.

"What if she doesn't answer? Do I blurt all that out to a voicemail?"

"That's a tough call. I'd say keep it short. Maybe write down two versions."

I nodded, my mind already working on the words.

"If you want, I'll read over what you're planning on saying and let you know what I think."

My guard instantly went up, and I opened my mouth to say no. Then I heard Steven's voice. *A driver is nothing without his pit crew.*

Why was it so hard to trust someone who wanted to help? "I'd appreciate that."

We opened the door to the first room on our list to clean. It wasn't too messy, and the curtains had been left open, revealing the sun shining in a crystal blue sky. Small, tree-covered hills in the distance. It looked like hope.

Baby steps are better than no steps.

Mom's voice instead of Steven's, wrapping me in warmth and reassurance.

I was like a kid with a school assignment, trying to earn an A when I had a record of D's.

Hi, I'm calling for Rebecca Bowers.

This is Sharon Gilbert. You might remember me. My daughter and I showed up at Michael Smith's house looking for him. I don't mean to intrude, but I'm ~~desperate~~ ~~eager~~ really hoping to find him. He's my father. You see, my mother never told him she was pregnant with me, so he never knew I existed. I just want to know who he is. What he looks like. Hear his voice.

How'd I get your number? Oh, well, my daughter is resourceful and was able to find it through some court records. I know this might be kind of creepy, but did you take a DNA test, too? Because I have a first cousin match with the username of R. Bowers, and I was thinking that might be you.

Was it too much? Not enough? Part of me wanted to wad it up and throw it away, but instead I continued, adding alternatives for how Rebecca might respond.

No, I'm not stalking you. I'm just trying to find my dad. Wouldn't you, if you were in my shoes?

I wasn't sure about the last part. I'd definitely need Janice's input.

I understand he's in a care facility, but I'd like to see him. I'd like to bring my daughter and granddaughter also, if that's okay.

I stopped and considered the last part. I wasn't sure if Cassie even wanted to go with me if I found Michael. She might still be too angry. I put brackets around that sentence.

I don't want anything from him. I'm not a gold digger or anything. Maybe, if there's a number I could call, even talking to him on the phone to start out with would be great.

I tapped my pen against the notepad, considering answers to questions Rebecca might ask. How did I tell my story? My husband died in a racing accident and it wrecked me to the point I chose being drunk over being a mom, a daughter, a worthwhile human being? I'd been sober almost two years now, if you didn't count the time I fell off the wagon because my mom was dying and my granddaughter's dad kidnapped her and I was terrified? Any of those details were bound to scare someone so far away, I wouldn't find them again without a canine-assisted search party and a flashlight the size of Texas.

I picked up my pen.

My husband died in a racing accident when our daughter was only three years old. Both of my parents are deceased. My family consists of my daughter and granddaughter. It'd sure be nice to have more family.

Sounded desperate and needy to me, but maybe I needed to sound that way to get this woman to help me. The thought irked me to no end. I tried to imagine being in her shoes. It had to surprise her when we showed up. I'd have been guarded too. Maybe she'd been thinking about us and who we were since then. But she had our phone numbers. If she was curious, wouldn't she have called?

I flipped over the sheet of paper. Now I needed the Reader's Digest version of my story. Something for me to say if I reached her voicemail. When I was done writing, I sighed, but not with relief. It took all I had not to crumple the piece of paper into a ball and start over. Or quit. I sure hoped I didn't get Rebecca's voicemail when I called, because the short version sounded ludicrous.

"This looks pretty good to me." Janice sat across from me at the table in the break room, reading over my scribbled notes.

My knee bounced up and down. "Are you sure? The last thing I want to do is scare this lady off. I'll be up a creek without a paddle."

Janice set the paper down and looked me in the eye. "I honestly can't think of one thing to add or take away. All you can do is hope for the best. Nothing ventured, nothing gained, right?"

I nodded, agreeing, but all I could think was, what will

happen if she turns me away? I took the piece of notebook paper and folded it, putting it in my purse.

"When are you going to make the call?"

Good question. I hadn't talked to Cassie about it yet. She hadn't said a word to me about it since texting me the phone number. My heart skipped a beat. "I don't know." I thought about texting Johnny and letting him know about the lead on my father and my insecurities, but I'd been keeping my conversations with him light and brief. Until I knew for certain what my answer to him would be, I didn't want to complicate things with family drama.

"If you want, I'll sit with you when you make the call." Janice's big brown eyes filled with sympathy.

I averted my gaze. One part of me couldn't handle Janice's kindness. Another part of me knew I needed to do this alone. "I appreciate the offer, but I'd probably only feel more awkward." It was true, another good reason to fly this one solo.

Janice's head bobbed up and down. "I hear you. If you need someone to talk to afterward, you have my number." Janice leaned forward, smiling. "Either way, I'm going to be on the edge of my seat, waiting to hear how this goes. Keep me posted."

I swallowed. "You've got it."

Chapter Twenty-Nine

IT WAS A LONGER THAN USUAL day at work. We were short-staffed and the hotel had been full. I was exhausted when I got home, and it was nearly time to start dinner. I thought about putting the call off until the next day but knew I would never do it if I waited.

Ride the momentum and take the turn before you lose your nerve.

Empowered by the reassuring sound of Steven's voice in my head, I grabbed a Diet Coke, my phone, and the folded-up notebook paper and headed to the backyard, not even bothering to change my clothes. After settling into the chair, I punched in Rebecca's number, saying a silent prayer for heavenly favor before hitting the green button.

The phone rang and rang. My heart fell to my stomach when the familiar ding of the line switching to voicemail came through the speaker. A young woman's recorded voice greeted me. "Hello, you've reached Rebecca Bowers. You know what to do."

No, I didn't know what to do, but I gave it my best shot.

"Um...hello...this is Sharon Gilbert. I'm contacting you about Michael Smith. I think my daughter and I met you when we went to his house in Susanville looking for him." I paused, dead air taking up precious space in the voicemail. I squinted at my script, my vision now blurry. "Look, I'm sorry to bug you, but Michael is my dad and I've been trying to track him down. He doesn't know about me. I'm not looking for anything but to know who he is and what kind of life he had." *And to find out if he ever conquered his alcoholism.* I cleared my throat. "If you would be so kind as to return my call, I can tell you the rest of the story." I said my phone number, even though I knew it would come up on her phone. Even harmless habits were sometimes hard to kill.

I ended the call. Hopelessness fell over me, leaving me feeling both heavy and empty. In my written script, I'd put something about the MyGenealogy DNA test and how I thought Rebecca and I might be related. It was meant to be more proof of who I was, but when I was speaking the words into the void of a voicemail box, it sounded weird and ridiculous. I'd checked the MyGenealogy app first thing in the morning, and it still showed no activity from Rebecca and my message to her as unread. If she hadn't been on the app since I took my test, she wouldn't have seen my name come up as a match, which meant the only way for her to know was for me to tell her—and I'd chickened out.

I threw my phone down on the grass in frustration. Should I call back and leave another voicemail with more information? Or wait for her to call back? *Would* she call?

I felt like a prisoner in my body, itching to get out of my own skin and run. A familiar feeling that had always led me down the wrong path. Grunting as if the effort was too much, I pushed myself out of the chair and bent over to grab my phone. The river would be a great place to be today. All I wanted to do was grab a six-pack of beer and find a dock to sit on. Put my feet in the cold, numbing water and drink the beer to take the ache out of my chest. Feel the sun on my face and bask in freedom, with no reminder of every mistake I'd ever made.

I headed to my room to change my clothes, walking by a basket of clothes on the way. I noticed the blue color of my own t-shirt at the top, the mermaid one Renee had given me at Christmas. An eternity ago. My skin prickled. The idea of freedom my brain conjured up came at a high cost. For someone else it would be okay. A few beers on the riverbank. But I wouldn't stop at a few, and beer wouldn't be strong enough.

In my room I changed into shorts and a t-shirt. My

guitar stood propped in the corner, the base glimmering in a tiny ray of sunshine that filtered through the window blinds. I picked up the guitar and headed outside again. I turned the volume up on my phone, then set it next to me to make sure I wouldn't miss a return phone call. Arranging myself on the front half of the other chair, my left hand found the chords, the familiarity of the strings a salve to my soul. I strummed, closing my eyes and humming as I made my way through the scales, waiting until one struck me with a bolt. Then I would know what song my heart needed to sing. As my fingers moved from the G chord to D, the lyrics popped into my mind and the rest of the chords followed without a thought. Eyes still closed, I sang "Sitting on the Dock of the Bay" softly at first, my voice finding itself along the way. The words rose from my inner core, through my voice box and out of me, circling me in a blanket of comfort and transporting me out of the backyard, even out of myself.

It wasn't until I finished that I realized tears were streaming down my face, falling on my guitar. I wiped the moisture from my face and dried off my guitar with my shirt. I felt lighter, something like peace now residing in my chest, pushing out the pain. The ache remained, my skin still felt too tight, and nothing had really changed except a tiny spark of hope was now burning in my heart.

I looked at my phone. In my musical escape, I hadn't missed any calls. Before disappointment could settle in, I reminded myself that there was a mermaid shirt in the living room that needed to be hung up and a dinner to be made for my family. Gathering my things and heading back into the house, I contemplated if or how I'd tell Cassie about the voicemail I'd left for Rebecca Bowers.

Cassie was emotionally distant when she came home. Renee,

bless her soul, was her usual funny and sweet self.

"I only have one week of school left, Grammy." Her big emerald eyes shone with anticipation.

We were cleaning the kitchen while Cassie ran water for Renee's bath, a chore she insisted on doing before she left for her Adult Children of Alcoholics meeting at the church. I bristled. Could I not be trusted to determine if water was too cold or too hot?

I ruffled Renee's hair. "I know, Sweet Pea. I'm looking forward to picking you up from your summer program every day and getting to spend a couple of hours with you."

"We can go to the pool and the park and have ice cream and play in the sprinkler." Renee stopped loading utensils in the dishwasher to look up at me. "Right, Grammy?"

I chuckled. "Yes, as long as we aren't trying to do *all* of those things on the same day." Even as I said it, a small voice echoed in my head, as if trying to be heard at the end of a long hallway, *don't make promises you can't keep.*

Renee bounced with excitement.

"I'm heading out." Cassie appeared in the kitchen, dressed in jean shorts and a t-shirt.

Renee ran to her mom and squeezed her leg in a hug. Cassie bent over and embraced her, holding her daughter tight. She straightened and looked at me, as if trying to gauge my mood.

"Do you think you could watch Renee Saturday night?"

That was an unexpected question. I would've placed my bet on her asking me if I was working Sunday, and if not, if I could go to church. The tension I didn't even realize I had between my shoulder blades subsided.

"Of course. It's not like I have a hot date." I hoped my attempt at being playful came out right. The truth behind my statement didn't leave me feeling happy. "What do you have going on Saturday night?"

Cassie's gaze flittered to her right. "Oh, just helping with some church stuff."

"On Saturday night?" Renee stood between us, her head going back and forth while we talked.

"It's a youth event the church is having. Sort of a presummer kickoff. I'm helping set it up and checking the kids in and stuff." Cassie twirled a strand of hair around her finger.

"Hmm. So you're helping Matt?" My mouth twitched with a restrained smile.

Cassie shrugged. "Well, yeah. There will be a lot of people helping."

I nodded. "Sounds fun. Renee and I can have a movie and popcorn night."

Cassie bent over and kissed the top of Renee's head. "I'll see you in the morning."

I wanted to walk over and give Cassie a hug, but I still sensed a wall between us, and I was afraid my attempts to knock it down would do more damage than good. "Have a good night."

Rebecca didn't return my call. I checked my phone like an addict needing a fix and never had any new messages, no missed calls.

As the week ended and the weekend approached, the tiny bit of hope I'd held onto slipped away. Should I call Rebecca again? Maybe she didn't check her voicemails. Maybe she accidentally deleted it. Both scenarios sounded highly unlikely. The hard fact was that the lady was ignoring me, shutting me out.

Friday morning, I poured out my worries to Janice as we pushed the cleaning cart down the hall. The hotel had had a busy Thursday night and it would be a long day.

"I'm sorry to hear that, girlfriend." Janice shook her head. "Being left hanging is the worst."

"I'm at another dead end, and I don't even know how to back out of it and find a different path."

"You have her address. Maybe try writing a letter so you can explain yourself in more detail?"

I used the master keycard on Room 121 and pushed the door open. The shades were drawn, and a sour smell wafted through the open doorway. Great. "Yeah, maybe. Seems like a lost cause, though." I didn't tell Janice that part of my urgency was the decision I needed to make about Johnny. I'd wrestled with Johnny's proposition. Was being miffed at him for not asking me to marry him even reasonable? Marriage wasn't Johnny's style. What he proposed about living together—and the promise he was making with the ring—was a serious commitment for him. Besides, it wasn't like a marriage certificate itself meant happily ever after. The growing wall between me and Cassie, along with her relationship with Matt potentially becoming a real thing, made Johnny's statement play like a broken record in my head. *It's not like she's a kid anymore. She has her own life. And you have yours.*

Janice flipped the switch on the wall, throwing light on the disheveled room. "Does your daughter have any ideas?"

My shoulders slumped. Talk about hitting me where it hurt. "Don't know. We haven't talked about it lately."

Janice's sympathetic eyes met mine. "I'd say it might be time to talk to her, don't you think?"

I sighed. "She's been a little distracted lately." It wasn't the most honest description of the feeling I was getting from Cassie, but it was the easiest way to sum it up.

"Mother and daughter relationships are complicated." Janice grabbed the bottle of disinfectant from the cart. "But they are eternal, if you ask me, because at the heart of them is the greatest love we'll ever know here on earth." Janice did her happy-feet waddle toward the bathroom, leaving me alone with the cart and her last statement.

I swallowed the prickly, hot ball of emotion rising in my chest. Janice was right, but she couldn't understand how much more complicated it was in my situation. Most moms didn't make the mistakes I had. How many daughters could ever put such misdoings behind them or think of that love as the greatest known on earth? My mom had left behind that kind of love. What I had to offer was marred and beaten up, held together by duct tape and baling wire.

You can still regain your position in the race. It's not over yet.

Steven's optimistic voice echoed in my head.

I picked Renee up from school Wednesday, as was our new routine. There was only one Wednesday in the school year left, and then it was summer break. I took her to the park, and we both swung on the swing set. Some adults looked at me funny, but I was past the point of caring what people like them thought. Childhood was but a moment of our lives, and I was going to enjoy every single second I had with Renee.

When she tired of the swing, we jumped off together and headed for a picnic table in the shade. It was a warm day, pushing eighty-five degrees. We rested in the shade, drinking water I'd brought with us.

"Did you have a good day at school, Sweet Pea?"

Renee nodded. "We got to show our drawings to the whole class."

I'd almost forgotten about the Father's Day project. "Did everyone like your drawing of the trophy?"

"Yep!" Renee bounced. "Mrs. Stram loved it too, and her eyes got watery when I told her it'd been my grandpa's, but he died before I ever knew him."

I put my hand on Renee's back. "He'd sure be proud of you."

Renee's face lit up with love. "Mrs. Stram said the same thing."

We sat in silence for a moment, the warm breeze blowing through the leaves of an oak tree above us.

"Mrs. Stram was sad. She told us about her daddy. He's really sick." Renee frowned.

"Oh, that is sad." I knew the pain of watching your daddy suffer.

Renee nodded. "He doesn't live here, so Mrs. Stram is going to go get him and put him in a place to live near her. She said he's too sick for her to take care of by herself."

"That's a hard thing to do." I thought of Mom and how she spent her last years in an assisted living facility. And of how I was living on the coast, not there for her the way I should've been. I took a drink of water, but it did nothing for the dryness in my throat.

"Mrs. Stram said it makes her sad, but she can visit him every day now."

A chill ran down my back, ignorant to the heat of the day. The squeals of children playing, the hum of cars passing by, the rustling of the leaves above our heads—all got sucked into a vacuum, and silence surrounded me as the thought settled into my brain.

Why hadn't I thought of it before?

I bounced up out of my seat on the bench. "Are you ready to go home? A glass of lemonade sounds good."

Renee's eyebrows pinched together. "But we've hardly played, Grammy."

"It's too hot, sweetie. Today is a good day to watch a

movie inside." I held my hand out to her and smiled, hoping she would take the bait.

"Okay." Renee frowned but grabbed my hand obediently.

I hid my surprise at how agreeable she was to leaving the playground. Today seemed to be my lucky day.

It's not luck, Mom. A chill ran down my arms. I lifted my gaze to the vivid blue sky. Maybe Cassie was right. Time would tell.

Once home, I poured Renee and myself glasses of lemonade, making sure to put hers in a cup with a lid so she could have it while she watched a movie. Renee picked the new *Aladdin* movie. I put the DVD into the player, then went in my room and grabbed my notepad and a pen. After sitting beside her on the couch, I picked up my phone and opened the Google icon.

"Grammy, aren't you going to watch the movie too?"

I sucked in my cheeks. If I waited until the movie was over to do my search, I'd be on edge the whole time. "Yes, Sweet Pea. I need to look up a few things with my phone. As soon as I'm done, I'll put it away and give the movie my full attention."

I went back to my search. I typed "assisted living Klamath Falls Oregon." To my surprise, there were quite a few. This wasn't going to be easy. I took my pen and wrote down the name and phone number of each facility, adding any notes about them that popped up immediately in the search. Since I had no idea what kind of shape Michael was in and how much help he needed, it was impossible to narrow the results down.

After writing down the list, I chewed on the end of my pen, absentmindedly watching *Aladdin.* There was a difference between assisted living and nursing homes. If

Michael was in bad shape, he would need that higher level of care. I typed "nursing homes Klamath Falls Oregon" into the search bar. Scanning through the list, nothing new showed. My search was complete.

Renee was engulfed in the movie. "Hey, honey, Grammy needs to use the restroom. I'll be right back."

I brought my phone and list with me into the restroom and flipped on the fan. With shaking fingers, I dialed the number for the first facility on my list.

"Pacific Senior Living," a woman's voice greeted me.

I swallowed, hoping I could pull off the ploy Cassie had used for the care facilities in Susanville. "Hi. My name is Sue. I'm calling from…" My heart raced. I'd forgotten to look up the name of a florist in Klamath Falls. *Get a grip, Sharon. Think!* "Um, I'm calling from Happy Days Flower Shop." I rolled my eyes. Really? Happy Days? "We have a called-in delivery here for a Michael Smith. It looks like they want it to go to Pacific Senior Living Assisted Living, but the person who took the order had bad handwriting." I exhaled. What a story. Who would even believe it? "Anyway, I'm just calling to make sure you have a Michael Smith there before I send these out for delivery."

There was silence on the other end of the line. My heart thumped against my chest with such force I was sure the lady on the other end of the phone could hear it.

"That name doesn't sound familiar, but let me check." The woman put me on hold, and classical music came through the speaker on my phone.

Perspiration broke out along my hairline. Finally, the line clicked over.

"I'm sorry, but we don't have a Michael Smith here."

My heart rate plummeted, leaving me dizzy and cold. "Okay, thank you." I hung up before the woman could ask any questions.

One down, eight to go. There was no way I could call all of them during a "bathroom" break, but I figured I had time for one more. I Googled florists in Klamath Falls first, wrote down the name of what sounded like a large one, then called the next facility on my list. After going through a conversation pretty much identical to the previous one, the call ended, and I was still empty-handed.

I'd have to continue my calls tomorrow after work. It was time to return to the couch and watch the rest of *Aladdin*—the story of a goodhearted thief who lied and made a bunch of mistakes but eventually ended up getting the girl anyway. Settling on the couch, putting my phone and list aside, I put my arm around Renee and snuggled her close, wishing with all I had that a happily ever after could happen for a woman like me. If only my life were a fairy tale.

I managed to make two calls the following day during my break but waited until I got home and in comfortable clothes before making any others. My nerves were wound so tight they were about to break. After changing my clothes and getting a Diet Coke out of the fridge, I continued my calls to the care facilities.

By four p.m. I was down to two and nearly out of hope. My heart had gone from racing to hurting. My chest was tight, making breathing an effort. I closed my eyes and forced myself to breathe deeply, pushing through the constriction in my chest. One. Two. Three. Exhale. What would I do if I still had no information after these calls? I'd be out of options, short of showing up at Rebecca's doorstep like some stalker. I didn't see that scenario ending well.

The only sounds were an occasional car driving by and the ticking of the grandfather clock in the corner of the living room. My parents' clock. I stared at its Roman numerals.

How many times had I watched the hands of the clock tick by as I waited for an anticipated event? Christmas Eve and waiting to open the one special gift for the evening. A Saturday morning and waiting for a friend to come over to play. A Friday night and waiting for Steven to pick me up for our first date. Those hands seemed to move painfully slow then. My mom would tell me that I couldn't hurry up time by watching it tick by. Now all I wanted to do was slow it down so I had more time to make up for all of my mistakes.

For everything there is a season, and a time for every matter under heaven.

Dad used to quote that scripture. Ecclesiastes. I couldn't remember the rest of the verse or its address. I missed him so much. His gentle and quiet strength, the fierceness of his love and his beliefs. If only I could be a tenth of what he had been.

My mind ached, trying to remember the rest of the verse. "A time to be born and a time to die." I could recall that part easy enough. I looked around the room as if the walls contained the answers. Where was Mom's Bible? Cassie probably kept it in her room. Feeling guilty for invading her space, I walked to her room and opened the door. The Bible was sitting there on her nightstand. I hurried over and picked it up, taking it into the living room. Thumbing through the Old Testament, I eventually found what I was looking for. Ecclesiastes 3. I read the passage. Among the long forgotten yet familiar words, one line jumped out at me like a blaring red light: *And a time to heal.*

I closed my eyes, my lips trembling. "Lord, if it's not too late for me, I need this. I need to find my birth father. I need to heal. Not only for my sake, but for my daughter's. For my granddaughter. I need this to be the time because I've done everything else I know to do, and I'm still broken. Too broken to fix."

I picked up my phone, cleared my throat, and dialed the

next number. Country Life Care Center. When the receptionist answered the phone, I went through my now familiar speech, doing my best to keep my emotions from coming through in my voice.

"Yes, ma'am, we do have a Michael Smith here."

The young man's easygoing voice jolted me to attention, my grip on my cell phone now tighter. Had I found him? My heart didn't go into overdrive and the room didn't spin. Instead a calm reassurance with a good helping of hopeful expectation came over me.

"If you're delivering flowers, you can leave them at the check-in desk, and they will be delivered to his room. What florist did you say you were with again? It didn't sound familiar."

"Okay, thank you." I ended the call, avoiding the question, thankful I'd blocked my number when I called.

I closed the Bible on my lap and returned it to Cassie's room, the ticking clock reminding me it was time to talk to my daughter.

Chapter Thirty

THE SPACE BETWEEN CASSIE'S EYEBROWS AND her chin nearly doubled as her jaw dropped. "You found him?"

"Well, I can't be certain. But it seems like a pretty good bet, don't you think?"

I continued to chop vegetables while Cassie sliced chicken into thin strips. We were working together to make stir fry for dinner while Renee played in her room. The back patio sliding door was open, and a warm breeze made its way into the hot, stuffy kitchen.

Cassie shook her head. "I'd assumed he would've gone to a facility near his home, but this does make more sense. If Rebecca is family and all he has left, of course she would have him in a care center near her. I can't believe I didn't think of it."

"Don't be so hard on yourself, Baby Girl. You've got a lot on your plate. It's not all on you to figure this out."

Cassie stopped slicing. "I know, but I work for a law firm. My brain should've been thinking in a more problem-solving kind of way." Cassie picked up some spices and sprinkled them on the chicken. "What's your next move? Are you going to call him or show up at his door?"

Good question. I'd looked a little more into the Country Life Care Center. They specialized in seniors needing more intensive care, more of a nursing home than a retirement center. They even had a memory wing for those with Alzheimer's and dementia. I shuddered. *Please, Lord, don't let him be in the Alzheimer's wing.*

The oil was heating up. I nodded to Cassie with her platter of chicken. "Talking to elderly people on the phone is often a challenge. The hearing goes. It makes communicating hard."

"So you think you should just show up and surprise him, like we hoped to do in Susanville?" Cassie dumped the chicken into the wok, and for a few moments the sizzling sound drowned out the conversation.

I shrugged. "Might as well. It's not that far of a drive."

"Renee and I will go with you." Cassie's tone was matter of fact as she stirred the chicken, which was browning quickly. I handed her the platter of veggies.

"You don't have to. I'm a big girl, you know." I offered a halfhearted smile. The truth was, I didn't want to go alone.

"I know we don't have to, but I *want* to. It'll be fun." Cassie's gaze met mine, love and guilt and reassurance all mixed together in the blueness of her eyes.

"You know there's no waterfalls in Klamath Falls. The name is kind of deceiving."

Cassie suppressed a smile. "Oh, I know...but it's okay. There's a great waterfall on the way. You can see it from Highway 58."

I giggled. "Of course." Had she looked it up when she heard Rebecca was in Klamath Falls, or had she visited it before?

"It's called Salt Creek Falls." Cassie turned to me, seeming to read my mind. "It's been on my list."

"I guess we can kill two birds with one stone then, can't we?"

Cassie moved the chicken high on the walls of the wok, then dumped the veggies in the middle. Hot oil sizzled and splattered on the stove. "Hopefully we don't come back empty-handed this time."

With it being so late in the school year, it made sense to wait until Renee was out of school before we headed down to Klamath Falls. Her last day of school was five days after

Johnny was supposed to drive back through and either pick me up or say goodbye. The thought made me sad in a way, but it was also like God was answering my prayer from when I went to the river. I had a solid lead on finding my father. Cassie and Renee were going with me, which was a good sign that my relationship with my daughter was on the upswing, even with the Samantha issue hanging in limbo. I'd promised Cassie that I'd meet with Samantha as soon as I found my father. If this trip was it, then I had no more excuses.

Even with everything looking up, I couldn't let my heart hold onto a perfect outcome. The disappointment I'd suffer if it didn't materialize would be too great. And I still needed to tell Johnny. That was one phone call I was going to put off as long as possible.

Edgy could've been my new middle name. "You're wound up tighter than an eight-day clock," Janice told me one day while we tucked the sheet corners under a king-sized mattress.

I forced a laugh. "I haven't heard that one before."

Janice happy-feeted over to the wastebasket. "Don't take this wrong, but I think it was created just for you and this day."

I sighed. "This waiting for our trip to Klamath Falls has me a little nervous."

"Understandable, girlfriend."

"The problem is, I'm putting too much into it, more than I ever thought I would." I ran a dust cloth over the bedside tables and desk.

"What do you mean?"

I shrugged. "It's going to sound pathetic or like some Hallmark movie or something."

Janice giggled. "Hey, I like those Hallmark movies."

I pursed my lips. I supposed most women did. I probably

would have too, at one time. "I told you about the music box Michael gave my mom, right?"

Janice nodded.

"Well, I bought the chord music for it, and I've been practicing the song on my guitar." I inhaled, not wanting to say the rest.

"That's cool."

I looked away. "Yeah, well, I'm thinking of taking my guitar and playing it for him, assuming I've got the right guy."

Janice squealed. "That's an awesome idea! And you're right—it's Hallmark worthy."

I snorted. "See, I told you."

"If you want to cut loose, my friend and I are going to karaoke tonight. You'd bring down the house with your voice. Trust me." Janice winked at me, then headed for the door, ready to push the cart to the next room.

What was it with this woman and karaoke? Didn't she say she was a churchgoer? "I appreciate the offer, but I'm not really into the bar scene."

Janice twisted her mouth, looking at me thoughtfully. "Hmm. Well, I understand. I'm not much of a bar person myself. I might have a beer or a wine cooler when I'm there. The main reason I go is for Jenny. She has a blast with karaoke." Janice shook her head and laughed. "The girl sings about as off-key as you can get but doesn't give an ounce of care toward what other people think."

This Jenny lady sounded like a perfect match for Janice. Even their names went together. They could have their own sitcom. I smiled at the image of Janice shimmying across a stage while her friend sang off-key. "I'm sure it's a great time. Find a karaoke spot that's alcohol free, and you can count me in."

Janice nodded. "I'll be on the lookout, for sure."

I couldn't put off telling Johnny my decision any longer. Telling him by text message seemed cruel. Thursday night I told Cassie I was going to an AA meeting, but instead drove down to the river. The sun was setting, but the overcast sky muted the color display the sunset had to offer. I dialed Johnny's number.

"Hello, Angel Eyes, I was just thinking about you."

I closed my eyes and inhaled, hoping to breathe in courage. "Really? What were you thinking?"

Johnny chuckled. "Well, for one thing, I was wondering if I need to leave room in the moving van for your stuff."

"I can't go, Johnny." Might as well pull the Band-Aid off and get the pain over with.

Silence on the other end of the line told me my answer wasn't what Johnny was expecting. "Is it the certified mail you found in my glove box? I can explain that."

I shifted in my seat. "I just—"

"It's debt collection. I owe the state of Washington some money, but I'm taking care of it."

I bit my lip. I hadn't called for answers, but the explanation of the envelope I'd found didn't surprise me.

It didn't matter anymore.

"My family and I are heading to Klamath Falls next weekend. I think I have a lead on my biological father. And Cassie still needs me here. She needs someone to watch Renee this summer." The truth was Cassie could easily find another option, but I wasn't ready to leave my family.

Johnny sighed. "Look." His voice was full of tenderness. "I'm not saying you're making the wrong decision, but can you do me a favor? Between now and Saturday, think about if this is what you truly want, or if it's a decision you're making out of guilt about your daughter."

What did that mean? Of course I felt guilty about my past. Who wouldn't? "Johnny, even *if* I decided now was the time to move, I need to find my father." My chest ached. Johnny was hurt. I could hear it in the constriction of his voice. "It's hard to explain why."

"We can go to Klamath Falls on our way to San Jose. It'll be a short detour."

I closed my eyes. No one would ever replace Steven. He had been the love of my life, and no man I'd been with since had ever come close to loving me the way Steven had. But out of all of them, Johnny had come the closest. Under different circumstances, he might even be the one. My next great love. My last love. I owed him a second thought, at least.

"I'll keep thinking about it, but right now, I have to say no."

"We still have a couple of days. I'm heading out of Portland first thing Saturday morning. Let me know if you change your mind."

Our call ended. I lay my head against the steering wheel and cried.

The last Thursday before the end of school was a half day, followed by a three-day weekend, which was dumb if you asked me. Cassie was able to take off work early so she could pick Renee up and take her out for ice cream, as a sort of early celebration of Renee's last day of kindergarten. The attorney she worked for had a big court case the following week, so Cassie wouldn't be able to get off early for Renee's last day of school. I waited at home, knowing it was good for them to have some one-on-one time. I'd have lots of special days with Renee over the summer.

I expected Renee to run in the house with an ice cream

moustache when she got home, but instead the door opened and my granddaughter sulked in behind Cassie, with only a hint of chocolate ice cream on her upper lip.

"What's wrong, Sweet Pea? You should be dancing a jig. You had ice cream before dinner." I knelt down to Renee's height, but her gaze stayed focused on the floor.

Cassie bent over and stroked Renee's long hair. "Honey, it's going to be okay. Grammy will forgive you."

I looked up at Cassie, mouthing a "What?" and completely confused.

"Can you tell Grammy, honey?" Cassie's voice was reassuring.

Renee shook her head violently, eyebrows scrunched together.

Putting my hands on Renee's shoulders, I pulled her into a hug. Cassie was holding Renee's backpack with her other hand, sadness and concern written like a warning sign on her face. Renee melted into my hug and her little shoulders shuddered as she sobbed. "I'm so sorry, Grammy."

My heart skipped a beat, worry growing in me like a weed injected with Miracle Gro. "Sweet Pea, talk to me. What's going on?" I cupped her face in my hands. Huge tears streaked her chubby cheeks.

Renee's lip quivered. "The...trophy...it was in my backpack when I left school." New tears welled in Renee's big eyes. "But it's not there anymore."

Lightning struck my chest. "What? Where is it?" I stood and met Cassie's gaze. "Did she leave it at school?"

Cassie's forehead wrinkled. "We went back to the school, checked the classroom, the lost and found." Cassie held her hands up. "We looked everywhere but can't find it."

"Maybe you left it at the ice cream parlor?" My voice rose an octave, despite the fact I was clenching my fists, desperate to keep my emotions under wrap.

"That's where we discovered it was missing. Renee took the picture of it she drew out of her backpack and noticed the trophy was gone." Cassie's eyes were sad, but not devastated. She didn't understand what the trophy meant.

I closed my eyes, breathing through my teeth, fighting the rage rising in me. "How could it have just disappeared?"

"I don't know. But maybe we can put an ad on Craigslist. It isn't worth anything to anyone but us, so I'm sure if someone finds it, they'll want to return it to its proper home."

I shook my head. "Cassie, that was the *only* trophy I kept all these years."

Renee pulled on the leg of my pants. "I'm sorry, Grammy."

I looked down at my granddaughter, her heartbroken expression pouring rain on the flame of my rage but not putting it out. I gritted my teeth, feeling the burning behind my eyes. If I started crying, it'd only make Renee feel worse. "It's okay, honey. Accidents happen." The words were right, but my tone was unconvincing.

Cassie lifted the backpack and unzipped it. "Renee's drawing of it is spectacular." She pulled a large piece of drawing paper from the backpack. The paper was framed with black cardboard. In the center was a drawing of the trophy. Normally I would have oohed and ahhed over Renee's exceptional artwork. But now all I could think of was, that's it. That's all I have left. Before I knew it, the words left my mouth.

"That's nice—and it's all I have left of your dad now. A picture drawn to leave at his gravesite and get ruined by the rain."

Silence fell like death in the living room. A light sniffling at my feet was the first sound I heard, then I noticed Renee wasn't clinging to my leg anymore. I looked down to see

Renee now holding on to her mother's leg, her forehead against her mother's skirt.

Cassie's face hardened, and darts of fire shot from her eyes. "I think that's a little harsh."

I looked away, sucking in air. Wanting to run. "Sorry. You don't understand."

How could she?

"It's a thing. Memorabilia. Not a person."

"It's all I have left of the love of my life!" And I'd just let my only hope to love again go.

Cassie narrowed her eyes, anger reddening her cheeks. "Really, Mom? It's all you have left of my dad? What about me? Aren't I part of him? Am I not *enough?*"

The hurt in Cassie's expression screamed louder than her words. My heart felt like it was ripped open and stomped on. "Of course you're enough, baby girl." How could I explain to her when she didn't even know the entire story? "It's just that..."

"That I'm not enough, am I? I never have been." Cassie's eyes flitted down to Renee, who still clung to her leg. "I guess no one is."

No. No. No. You're all enough. More than I deserve. I'm the one who doesn't measure up!

I knelt back down and reached for Renee. "Sweet Pea, Grammy is sorry for getting mad." My voice cracked and I swallowed, struggling to make the words come out. "You drew such a beautiful picture. Your grandpa would've been proud."

Renee looked at me with big, emerald, bloodshot eyes. "I wanted to give the picture to you, Grammy, instead of taking it to Grandpa's grave."

I thought my heart had been broken in every possible place over the last thirty years. I was wrong.

"I'd love that. It would be the best gift I've ever gotten,

next to having you and your mama." I put my hand on Renee's back, but she tensed and pulled away from me.

My throat burned. There were no more words to say. None that would erase the words I'd already spoken. I stood, facing Cassie, whose face had become as hard as stone.

Was she done with me? How could she not be?

"I'm so sorry. My reaction was...wrong." My chest ached, the fire of anger still burning. In some ways, it was like I was losing Steven all over again. All because I was trying to make right generations worth of wrongs. Like letting Renee take the trophy to school could somehow undo the loss of a father, or the emptiness of having never known a grandfather.

Don't lose sight of the finish line.

I wasn't even sure I was still in the race.

I was too sick to my stomach to make dinner and pretend like everything was okay. Instead, I went to my room and ordered pizza to be delivered, then texted Cassie that I had done so. No doubt she didn't need the stress of making dinner after our little episode. She didn't respond to my text. I couldn't blame her.

I stayed in my room, too ashamed to leave. If I had to go to the bathroom, I'd find an empty container in my room and use it before facing my daughter. Or Renee. My chest ached at the memory of the hurt in her eyes, her trembling lip. Why had I overreacted? My mom would have never, ever acted that way, even if I'd broken the music box. Why couldn't I be more like her and less like...who? Michael? He had to be the reason I was so messed up.

My guitar sat in the corner of the room, begging me to play it, calling to the aching in my chest. Something deep in me whispered to pick it up and let my fingers find the strings, to let the pain become a melody and let it go. Yet, I couldn't bring myself to pick up the instrument—a gift from Cassie. My caring, thoughtful daughter who'd tried to help me. Who believed my mother had found some biblical confirmation I was supposed to play an instrument, be a musician.

A fifty-four-year-old recovering alcoholic who had nothing to show for her life. I couldn't even take credit for Cassie. My parents had basically raised her. I'd done little more than give birth to her and caused her pain.

That's not true, Sharon. The mirror you're looking in is dim. Keep looking and see the truth.

Was that Steven? Or Mom? Somehow it sounded like both. I curled in a ball on my bed and cried silently. How could so much pain be caused by a piece of metal in the shape of a race car? Even as the thought flitted through my brain, I knew it wasn't the trophy's fault. It was mine and mine alone. I couldn't even explain why it hurt so much.

Yes, you can. It's time you told Cassie. You've kept the secret locked up so long it's grown into a monster.

Tell Cassie? How could I do that now, when she was already angry? I couldn't. I'd never told anyone, not a single soul. My shame had been so great, magnified by the loss. Steven shouldn't have died that night, twenty-seven years ago. He should've placed in the top three. But he lost control. When he swerved, his car was hit hard by another driver at just the right angle on the track to send him rolling. Over and over and over. His car burst into flames before anyone could get to him. My sweet, loving husband was probably burned alive, and I wasn't even there. The love of my life, my little girl's daddy, was lost that night and it was my fault.

You can't carry this anymore, Sharon. You've carried it too long. Tell her.

Maybe this was how it was supposed to be. Wasn't Cassie better off without me anyway? Why not give her one more reason to hate me? I'd have nothing left to lose. The fear of losing would be gone, then, wouldn't it?

Except for finding your birth father.

Yes. But that was different. How could I lose what I never had? Finding him was more about answers, not about my heart.

You're lying to yourself. The mirror is dim, but it will get better.

Resolve and peace settled into my aching chest, into my tired bones. I needed a nap. I shut my eyes and let myself fall into the nothingness of darkness and sleep.

Cassie,

I can't tell you how sorry I am about last night. I hope Renee is okay. Please tell her she did nothing wrong. All the wrong is on me. Tell her, also, that I adored her drawing. She's going to be a great artist someday, of that I'm sure.

I know it's pretty much impossible for you or anyone to understand why I reacted the way I did. I can't even explain why, exactly. But there is something I need to tell you. Maybe you'll understand my reaction a little better, but you'll also never look at me the same. You might even hate me. I wouldn't blame you.

Your dad loved racing and I was right beside him in that passion—until we had you. Being a mom of a newborn changed my perspective. Staying up late on Saturday nights lost its appeal. The hours upon hours your dad spent working on his car felt like time he was stealing from me. From us.

One night I was done. Exhausted and emotional, I confronted him in the garage while he worked on his car, getting it ready for the next day's race. I'd held in my anger and resentment for too long and when I cut loose, I was screaming and downright mean. Your dad didn't fight back. He didn't make excuses. He stood there and let me vent. When I was done, I stormed back in the house and not too long afterward, he came in too. He hugged me and told me he was sorry. He promised to cut back on racing. Not give it up completely but cut back on how many races he entered. It was a compromise I could live with. He stayed in the house and spent the rest of the evening with me. After I put you to bed, we sat on the couch and he held me close and we watched Casablanca. My world felt perfect.

The next day, he went to the races. I didn't go, not even to watch the main events. Not even after he'd given up working on his car Friday night. That's how done with racing I was.

That was the night he had the accident. You're probably thinking I feel terrible because I wasn't there and you're right, but that's not the worst of it. The reason he wrecked was because the brake cylinder came loose. That's why he lost control of his car. Friday night he'd been adjusting it to weld it in. He bracketed it down but didn't finish welding it because I interrupted him and demanded having my way.

So, you see, the reason he died and the reason you had to grow up without a father is because of ME. I did it, Cassie. I could've chosen another night—a less important one—to tell him how I felt. Or I could've talked to him calmly and not made him feel guilty. I could've been there in the pit with him before the race, and maybe I would've reminded him to check everything on his car one last time. But I wasn't, and I didn't, and I lost him forever.

The trophy I gave Renee to take to school was the last one I had left. It was the last race he won before you were born. I was there with him then. In the pits, in the stands, and by his side. Having the reminder of when your dad and I were one, to end up lost—it cut deep. It reminded me of all the ways I failed him. And ultimately, of all the ways I've failed you.

With everything that happened last night, I think it's best if I head to Klamath Falls by myself to look for my father. If I don't go now, I'm going to lose my nerve, and possibly my mind too.

I love you. Now and forever. I know I've failed you in a million ways. As hard as it may be to believe, please know I've always loved you. You've always been enough.

Love, Mom

I tiptoed out the door early in the morning, when the sun was starting to peek over the horizon. I'd packed an overnight bag, just in case, and I put my guitar in its case and threw it over my shoulder. My car sounded incredibly loud when I started it, and I hoped that it didn't wake Cassie. I also hoped it would make it all the way to Klamath Falls.

Traffic was light, and I was soon passing through Oakridge and near the top of the Cascade mountains. Snow still capped the peaks of the mountains abundant with evergreen trees. It was beautiful. After I drove through a tunnel, the sign for Salt Creek Falls appeared. My heart lurched, and I stared straight ahead, afraid of catching a glimpse of the waterfall. It would be too much for my heart to take. Cassie hadn't called or texted me, but I was now out of cell range and probably would be for the next hour at least. Even my radio lost all signals. I was alone, and the only sounds were the hum of the engine and the grind of tires against asphalt.

My Buick was so old the only other music option was cassette tapes. Luckily, I still had quite a few in decent shape. I reached into the middle storage caddy and took out an oldie but goodie: The *Abbey Road* album by the Beatles.

Music filled the car and I sang along, pushing away the darkness that was chasing me out into the tall snowcapped mountains and the crystal-clear waters of Odell Lake, which came into view on my right. By the end of the album, I was on a downhill grade and then merging onto Highway 97—a lonesome stretch of flat land and conifer trees.

Coffee sounded better than soda pop at seven-thirty a.m., but all I had was Diet Coke, and I didn't want to stop at some convenience store for bad coffee. I popped open the cooler in the passenger seat next to me and took out a soda. The car was silent again. I inserted another cassette. This time it was Bette Midler's *Experience the Divine*. The caffeine was kicking in about the time "Beast of Burden" came on. I sang along with Bette and danced behind the steering wheel with enough verve to get a thumbs up from a trucker I flew by in the passing lane.

My spirits were high until Bette started singing "When a Man Loves a Woman." I pushed the eject button so fast you'd have thought the car was going to explode if the song continued. And it might have, in a fiery explosion on the side of the road, because I would've completely lost it. I shouldn't have listened to that tape. Not now. Talk about playing with dynamite.

Thankfully, by then I was able to dial in a country music station. I relaxed, focused on the drive ahead. A green sign said Klamath Falls was only seventy miles away. My pulse quickened. It wouldn't be long now before I was there.

A song came on the radio that pulled my attention. I listened intently, trying to determine which song it was. When the chorus began, I realized it was the song about an alcoholic father, the same one Cassie and I had heard for the first time on our way to Moss Landing. My chest ached at the memory, which now seemed like a million years ago. I reached for the dial to turn the radio off, but stopped myself, mesmerized by the story in the song. At the end of it, the boy in the story was okay. He'd found his way. Would Cassie be okay and find her way too, no matter what became of me? No matter how much I messed up?

My parents were the ones who saved her from me when she was a little girl. Nine years old, to be exact. We were living in Redmond. One night when I'd left Cassie at home alone, my dad showed up and took Cassie away from me. He was too kind to take her and not let me know, though. He tracked me down at the bar and marched in, strong and confident and carrying the weight of a broken heart. I was shocked to see him. He walked up to me and said he had Cassie in his truck, and he was taking her home until I got my life straightened out. Then he left without another word. I shuddered at the shame of the memory.

The DJ came on the radio. "And there's another song climbing its way up the charts by the one and only Andy Bowers, who grew up in Modoc County and got his start playing small gigs in our very own Klamath Falls."

I raised an eyebrow. I wondered if he was related to Rebecca Bowers. I laughed at the thought. No doubt Bowers was a common enough name to belong to more than one family, even in these parts. But who would've thought such talent came from someplace so remote and unheard of?

I checked my speedometer. Feeling lucky—or desperate—I pushed the accelerator down and edged my car to 75 mph.

By the time I was driving along the hill that skirted Upper Klamath Lake, my nerves were overwrought, my stomach was in a knot, and I had to pee. Thankfully, a McDonald's was one of the first establishments on the way into Klamath Falls. After using the restroom, I ordered a sausage

McMuffin and coffee, but I had a hard time getting the food down. I ended up pouring out the coffee and filling my cup with water, deciding too late the last thing I needed was more adrenaline.

I put the address to the care center into the maps program on my phone. It was only ten minutes away. A surreal feeling made me dizzy. In fifteen or so minutes, I could be meeting my father.

I pulled into the care facility at nine-thirty a.m. It was a Y-shaped, one-story brick building with curtains on the windows and not much of a lawn. With sweaty palms, I picked up my guitar case and pulled the strap over my shoulder, the strap to my purse on my other shoulder.

The care center had a button to push for opening the front door but was unmanned. A short hallway with doors that seemed to lead to offices greeted me as I entered. My heart banged like a bass drum as I made my way to a long, tall receptionist desk located where all the hallways seemed to intersect. A group of three people sat or stood on the other side, all young and dressed in brightly colored scrubs.

"Can I help you?" a young man with short red hair and acne scars asked me.

"Yes, I'm here to see my father." Boy, was I being bold. There was still a chance I had the wrong guy.

"What's his name?"

I cleared my throat. "Michael Smith."

The young man nodded. "Yes, okay. Let me see." He pulled a drawer open and took out a file, laying it on the desk and thumbing through it. I saw the name Michael Smith on the files tab, followed by the number 08.06.45. Was that Michael's birthdate? Before I could wonder, the young man shifted the folder so the tab was under the lip of the counter, where I couldn't see it. "And what is your name?"

My knees were Jell-O. If they only let people who were on a visitors list see patients, then I'd made the trip for nothing. "Sharon. Sharon Gilbert. But Smith was my maiden name." A tiny white lie. Smith would've been my birth name if I'd been born under different circumstances.

The young man's head bobbed up and down while he read something in the chart. "I'm sorry. I don't see you listed as family."

Of course you don't. I inhaled, gathering strength. "I'm his daughter."

The young man gave me an apologetic smile. "We don't specifically have a policy about visitors being on a list, but in this particular case, we were asked by the person admitting him to obtain verification of some kind."

My stomach flip-flopped. What kind of "verification" did they need? And what made Michael so special he needed an extra level of security?

"If you could give me some proof of your identity, I think that would work. Otherwise, I need to call his POA for permission." The young man shrugged, obviously uncomfortable with what he was asking.

I slid my guitar case off and leaned it against the reception counter so I could dig through my purse and pull out my driver's license. "Here's proof of who I am, or at least of my name."

The man took the identification, looked it over, and handed it back. "That works. If you could tell me Mr. Smith's birthdate, I think that'll suffice for proving your relationship."

Here goes nothing. "August 6, 1945." I surprised myself with how easily I remembered the numbers on the folder tab. If I was wrong about it being Michael's birthdate, I was done here.

The young man glanced at the chart and nodded. "Bingo."

My breathing stopped. Talk about lucky breaks.

It's not luck, Mom.

I held back the tears that wanted to rise at the memory of my daughter's voice and assurance.

The man looked up at me. "He's in room nine." He motioned to the hall to my right. "The fourth door on your right. If it's closed, just give a warning knock before entering."

"Thank you." I picked up my guitar case and slung it over my shoulder.

The door to room nine was open. I walked in slowly, a parade of butterflies beating their way up my chest and to my throat. There were two beds in the room, one to my left and one to my right. An elderly man was in one of them, sound asleep. The other was empty, but a man sat in a chair near it, staring out the window.

I approached him, clearing my throat to make him aware of my presence. He turned. A wrinkled but healthy-looking man faced me. He wore a faded Carhartt cap, and wide cheekbones kept his face full looking, even in old age. His nose looked larger than I remembered from the picture Cassie had found from his youth. He was dressed in loose-fitting denim jeans and a flannel shirt. My heart stopped when my eyes met his—a reflection of my own brown eyes. He smiled and saluted me.

Had he been in the military at some point? I smiled back and offered my hand. "My name is Sharon."

He nodded, still smiling, and took my hand. "Michael Andrew Smith."

"Nice to meet you."

Michael kept smiling. "You're pretty."

I laughed and my nervousness went down a notch. "Thanks." He seemed coherent. Room nine must not be in the memory care section of the small care facility.

Michael motioned toward another chair opposite the table to his right. Taking his cue, I pulled the chair over and set it at conversation distance from him.

"You're probably wondering who I am and why I'm here." I settled into the seat and put my guitar case and purse on the floor.

Michael lifted one eyebrow. "Did you bring me something to eat?"

I couldn't help but laugh as I shook my head. "No. Sorry."

For the first time in our exchange, Michael frowned. "I'm hungry."

"I can go ask the nurse or someone for food. Would you like me to do that?"

Michael's head bobbed up and down, smiling again.

I sucked in my lips, thinking. This wasn't going as I planned. "I'll be right back." I walked out of the room, leaving my things. I found someone who looked like a nurse in the hallway. I glanced at her name tag: Nancy Kirkpatrick. RN.

"Excuse me, my...um...room nine, Michael Smith. He says he's hungry and would like something to eat."

The nurse smiled. "He's always hungry." Her hazel eyes held sympathy. "It's one of the symptoms of Alzheimer's. The part of the brain that regulates hunger stops working correctly."

The hallway grew longer around me, and all I could hear was buzzing in my ears. *No. He can't!* I blinked several times, trying to focus. "Is that a symptom of early or late Alzheimer's?"

"Both. It can get worse as the condition progresses."

I chewed my lip. Michael seemed normal. At least it seemed like he was able to carry on a conversation. "What should I tell him, then, when he says he's hungry?"

"Just change the subject, and he'll forget he asked."

That didn't sound like the reasoning of a coherent man.

I returned to the room. Michael grinned at me and saluted, again.

It was like déjà vu.

I sat in the chair across from him. "You don't know me, but you knew my mom."

Michael made a chewing motion with his jaw.

"Her name was Eula Brown."

Michael nodded and then held out his hand. "Michael Andrew Smith."

I took his hand. "Sharon Gilbert. Nice to meet you."

"You sure are pretty."

"Thank you." I looked out the window. The view was of the nearly bare, flat-topped hills in the distance. A small green space of grass and well-spaced bushes lined the edges of the care center. This was unfair. Beyond unfair. So many years lost, and now I found him only to find his mind gone? What kind of God does that to a person? But maybe I deserved it after all I had done. I looked at Michael, who was now gazing out the window too, the smile replaced by an emotionless expression. Maybe Michael deserved this too. Payment for sins.

That's not how God works, Sharon. You know better.

My mom had no business telling me about God. Irritation bristled in me, making me twist in my seat. She'd lied to me for years, then confessed before leaving this earth without giving me more information. She'd left me with questions literally no one on this planet could answer—save one—and it seemed the only thing he could remember was his name and his appetite.

I had to keep trying. "Michael."

His focus returned to me, and he offered a smile and another salute. This time he hit the cap on his head, putting it off center. I resisted the urge to straighten it.

"Do you remember Eula? From when you were young?"

Michael blinked several times. "Eula, that's a pretty name."

I nodded in agreement, though in all honesty I'd never found my mom's name pretty. "You remember Eula?"

Michael's forehead wrinkled. "When's breakfast?"

I pushed air through my nose, gripping my patience with every ounce of my being. He had to remember *something*. I leaned down and picked my guitar case up and unzipped it.

Michael nodded toward the case and lifted an eyebrow. "You play that?"

"Yes. Yes, I do." A lightbulb flashed in my brain. "Do you play?"

Still smiling, Michael shook his head. "No. No." He put his hands to his mouth, as if he were holding something, and blew out air. He lifted his eyebrows, eyes sparkling.

"Harmonica? You play the harmonica?" I froze, but my heart took off like a racehorse.

Michael's head jerked up and down excitedly.

Were my musical tendencies genetic? I pulled the guitar strap over my head and wrapped my fingers around the neck of my guitar. "Maybe we can play together someday." Even as I said it, I knew it would never happen.

Michael cocked his head, making an incoherent sound. I exhaled, the excitement of learning my father was musical mixing with the reality that I'd probably never hear him play. "I have a song to play for you."

I played the first few chords of the song, then started over. Closing my eyes, I sang the song from the music box. My voice and guitar echoed in the room.

I can't deny my love for you
It's deeper than the bluest sea
Stronger than the mightiest tree
Darling, say you love me too
Because I can't deny my love for you.

I opened my eyes to venture a peek at Michael. He was

no longer smiling, and his eyes stared into a distance I couldn't see. I closed my eyes again and finished the song. I gave it all I had in room nine.

When I opened my eyes, tears were streaming down Michael's face and he was no longer smiling. He looked right at me, studying me with both intent and desperation.

"Eula. Oh, Eula. I'm so sorry." He wiped at the tears streaming down his face.

I put my guitar down and leaned over, reaching for his hand. It was both strong and feeble. Wrinkled and smooth. "I'm not Eula. I'm her daughter, Sharon." I swallowed. "I'm your daughter, Michael. Eula was pregnant with your child when you left Springfield."

Michael's eyes fluttered and the tears stopped. He looked down at my hand, holding his. He squeezed my hand then lifted it to his lips, brushing it with a gentle kiss. "You're pretty."

I smiled, holding back hope, holding back the emotion that wanted to take over. "I think I look quite a lot like you."

Michael's brow furrowed, his smile leaving his face for a moment, then reappearing as if he suddenly remembered something. "My name is Michael Andrew Smith. Who are you?"

My heart twisted. "I'm Sharon. Your daughter."

Michael let go of my hand and saluted me. "I'm hungry. Are you getting me something to eat?"

I pulled back my shoulders, sitting straight in my chair. I stared at the man who was my father. Whoever he had been, I would never know. And he would never know me. He would never know I even existed.

Every question I had for him would never be answered. Claws of loneliness and regret and bitterness sank into my soul, telling me they were there to stay.

Chapter Thirty-One

THE NURSE NAMED NANCY AND THE young man at the reception desk tried to tell me goodbye as I left, but I ignored them, my disappointment too great for niceties. I stormed out of the Country Life Care Center and straight to my Buick. I put my guitar in the trunk and got in the car, the familiar smell of lingering cigarette smoke and my inadequate attempts to cover it up with air freshener greeting me, reminding me once again of who I was and who I would never be.

It was only midmorning, but it felt like the end of a long workday. Every fiber of my being wanted a drink. And a cigarette. Even in my drinking days I usually waited until noon before I had my first drink, convincing myself that waiting a few hours after waking before my first shot proved that I had control over my drinking. Smoking, however, was a vice with no time restrictions. I pulled my phone out of my purse. No messages or missed calls. Not a single one. Not from Cassie. Not from Janice wondering why I was calling in sick. Not from Johnny. Not from the Rebecca woman I was related to but who wanted nothing to do with me.

Starting the engine and letting the car warm up for a minute, I decided what I would do.

After stopping at the nearest convenience store with a liquor store conveniently located next door, I drove around the outskirts of town, eventually finding a steep road that turned to gravel and took me to one of the bluffs overlooking Klamath Falls and its lake. At the top, I parked my car and got out, taking one of my new purchases with me. I found a big boulder to sit on that overlooked the lake far below. The sky was crystal blue and stretched out before me, touching the tops of gray mountains.

"No waterfalls here, Cassie girl." I sucked in my bottom lip, thinking of my daughter's stubborn determination to see all those waterfalls. She must've gotten that kind of will from Steven, because it sure didn't come from me.

Having found my father lost in the confusion of Alzheimer's, I felt almost nothing at all except a hint of longing, of sadness, thinking of Michael's sparkling brown eyes. He didn't seem to realize he had Alzheimer's. He looked happy, easygoing, and seemed to be a bit of a flirt. Were those remnants of his personality or something that came on with the disease? I guessed I'd never know, and that was the hard part. Never knowing more. His reaction to the song from the music box spoke volumes, yet I wasn't sure what it meant. More mystery.

The finality of it all left nothing but a hollow, empty feeling in my chest. I clutched a pack of Marlboros in my damp right hand, along with a brand-new Bic lighter. I opened the pack, breathing in the sweet scent of tobacco. Even though I hadn't smoked in months, the smell was still inviting. I put a cigarette in my mouth and lit it unceremoniously. Inhaling the smoke burned my throat, but it was a good burn, a welcomed pain.

The sun beat down on my head, the dry heat a nice change from the humidity of the valley. It went well with the cigarette in my hand and the barrenness in my chest. I checked my phone for the second time. In another hour it'd be noon and I could get the brown paper bag out of the cooler in my car and enjoy the company of my long-lost friend. The nonjudgmental companion that was always there, numbing and emboldening me at the same time.

You're putting yourself at the rear of the field. Is that what you want?

No, Steven, but it was where I was meant to be, wasn't it? Cassie was angry with me, and who could blame her? I'd hurt my sweet granddaughter's feelings. The one person on this earth who still believed in me. I had no real friends. I'd pretended like Janice was my friend, but if she really was, wouldn't I have told her I was an alcoholic? I couldn't even manage to be a good keeper of the past. The one trophy of Steven's I'd managed to hang on to all these years was gone forever. Johnny was the only one who still wanted me, and he was a man with secrets. But women like me couldn't choose the highest item on the shelf.

My father would never know me, and I'd never know him.

But I've known you and loved you from the moment you were created.

A cascade of goosebumps flowed through my body, chilling me in the hot sun. I threw my cigarette down, my throat aching. Seeing that it landed on dried grass, I jumped up and stamped it out. The last thing I needed to do was start a fire.

The wind picked up, blowing hair in my face. I climbed up on the rock and brought my knees to my chest and wrapped my arms around them. I'd stay here on this rock, soaking up the sun like a lizard. Get a sunburn. As soon as noon hit, I was grabbing the cooler. Then I would call Johnny and see if he could pick me up in Klamath Falls. He would take me as I was, broken and scarred. I would pretend I didn't see his black marks, the things he didn't want to talk about, and he would pretend like he didn't see mine.

The warmth of the sun lulled me into a dreamlike state, and even with my angst for the contents of the brown bag, I almost lost track of time. It was nearly noon when I checked my phone again. No phone calls or texts.

I sighed, guilt mixing with anticipation. Ten till sounded close enough to me. I hopped down off the boulder, my knees stiff and complaining at the jolt. Leaving my phone on the rock, I made my way to the car and pulled out the cooler in the back seat. The Diet Coke was still cold, promising refreshment. I opened it and took a swig, enjoying the sweetness, then poured half the bottle out onto the dry dirt by the car. The liquid bubbled on the ground before sinking in, a dark warning of what was to come. I set the Coke on the roof of my car and gently lifted the other bottle out of the brown paper bag. Jack Daniel's Old #7 Whiskey. I unscrewed the cap and took a whiff of the sweet scent of the brown liquid. I stared at the contents. This was it. If I poured this into the half-empty Diet Coke bottle, it was all but over for me. My relationship with Cassie and Renee would be toast. I could never return home. But my daughter and granddaughter would be better off without me.

Lord, please take care of them.

My hands began to shake. I had no choice. I'd used up all my strength fighting this demon and finding my birth father. I'd followed Cassie's healthy diet rules as best as I could and worked my butt off as a maid to make a living. I had nothing left in me. Nothing but darkness.

You know that's a lie.

I grabbed the Coke bottle and tipped it at forty-five-degree angle, then slowly poured in the Jack. Even with my best efforts, some of the whiskey spilled down the sides of the Coke bottle, dropping on the dry earth. Oh well.

A sound to my left made me jump, sloshing Diet Coke and whiskey on my shoes. My phone. It was ringing. My heart skipped a beat.

Answer it. Answer it now!

Nothing like hearing your mom's voice in your head when you're making yourself a drink. Cursing, I set the whiskey and Coke on the top of my car and brushed my hands off on my jeans while I briskly walked back to the boulder. It was probably a telemarketer. I'd get rid of them and return to my concoction in a flash.

My phone was vibrating as it rang, edging itself down the rock it was sitting on. I sprinted the last couple of steps, but the name on the screen stopped me as soon as I could see it.

Rebecca Bowers.

I grabbed my phone with one hand. Before I could give it a second thought, I swiped to answer.

"Hello?" My voice sounded winded.

"Hi. May I speak with Sharon Gilbert please?" Rebecca's voice was young and hesitant. Nervous.

"This is she."

What had made her finally return my call? A lot of good it did me now.

"Hey...I'm sorry it took me so long to call you back. This is Rebecca Bowers. It's a long story." She paused, and I heard the murmur of a few voices in the background. "I heard you went to see Michael Smith this morning."

I recalled the questions and hesitation of the young man at the reception desk. Had he called Rebecca and told her I was there? "Yes, I did. I would've talked to you about it first, since you're his power of attorney, but you never returned my phone call." Sarcasm tinged each syllable of my response. I didn't mention the message I sent through MyGenealogy. As far as I knew, she'd never read it.

"Like I said, it's a long story."

"Sure. Well, obviously Michael and I didn't engage in any lengthy conversation. Would've been kind of nice to know the state he was in before I drove all the way down here."

The line was silent a moment, and the only sound I heard was the wind.

"You're still in Klamath?" Was that relief in her tone?

I stared out at the flat lake, the brown and gray hills. "Yeah, for now."

"Could you meet me at a local coffee shop? I can explain

everything better, I think, if we meet in person.”

Now she wanted to meet me? I opened my mouth to say no. I had plans. Which I did. My plans waited for me on top of my car, threatening to be blown over by the wind. I hadn’t texted Johnny yet, but he wasn’t heading to California until tomorrow. I still had time.

For everything there is a season, and a time for every matter under heaven.

I sighed. I supposed the only thing meeting Rebecca would cost me was some of the Jack and a bottle of Diet Coke. I could always stop at the store and get another bottle of soda after our meeting and come back to this exact spot. I liked the view, and there wasn’t another soul in sight.

“Sure. Where would you like to meet?” The hard edge in my voice was anything but warm and inviting. I’d be surprised if the young woman showed up.

“Let’s meet at Leap of Taste. It’s in the older part of town, but they have great coffee and good food, in case you’re hungry.” Rebecca’s voice held a lilt to it now, seemingly unaware of my tone.

I agreed to meet her there in half an hour. Returning to my car, I poured out the whiskey-laden Diet Coke, throwing the empty bottle and the bottle of Jack into the cooler, and then put the cooler in the trunk of my car. After putting the address into the GPS on my phone, I started the engine, feeling as old and tired as my car.

What Rebecca could reveal to me I wasn’t certain. All I knew for now was someone above pushed the pause button on my drinking campaign. Soon I’d know why.

Old town Klamath Falls was quaint, like something out of a movie. Brick buildings from another era lined the streets. What were once probably businesses and banks and such were now mostly specialty shops and restaurants. The courthouse and a couple of lawyers' offices were part of downtown too. Cars lined the street parking spaces, and people milled about on the sidewalks. It seemed like the place to be if you lived in the small town.

I arrived early. The inside of Leap of Taste had all the vibes of the typical Northwest coffee house, complete with the scruffy-looking twenty-something hipsters sitting one table over from moms in expensive yoga pants. A mix-match of tables and chairs were arranged throughout, along with a couple of sofas. The linoleum floor had a large red stripe that led to the coffee counter.

Coffee was the last thing I wanted to drink, but when in Rome, do what the Romans do. I ordered a decaf coffee with nothing in it. The young barista looked at me like I was a dinosaur. I found a small table and sat where I could see the front door.

At exactly noon, Rebecca walked in. She looked even younger than she had when I saw her in Susanville. She was wearing high-rise faded denim shorts with ankle-length black boots and a flowing, sleeveless white top that ended right above the top of her shorts. Her brown hair was down, styled in perfect spiral curls. She was a beautiful young woman.

At least, if nothing else, I could find out how this girl was related to me.

I waved her down, and recognition lit her face. She hurried to my table. "Let me grab a drink real quick. I'll be right back." She was off to the counter before I could respond. No doubt she'd order some frilly latté with extra foam or whatever and would take forever to get back to the table.

My knee bounced up and down under the table. My Jack was waiting.

Rebecca returned quicker than I expected and took the

seat across from me. "I'm sorry this has taken so long."

I wasn't sure if she was talking about returning my call or getting the coffee. "I get it. I'm sure it's unsettling to hear from some strange woman who's trying to track down her long-lost father. Sorry you're in the middle of that mess." I didn't tell her that I believed we were related. It was too odd of a thing to say to someone you've barely met.

Rebecca looked down at her coffee, rotating the steaming cup in her hands. "I was completely taken aback when you showed up in Susanville. Then I got kind of creeped out when you called my number. I had no idea how you got it. With everything going on in my life at the time, I brushed you off as some overly enthusiastic and devious fan."

Fan? Of what? I had no idea what this girl was talking about, but I played along.

"And then I show up at the care facility."

Rebecca nodded. "Yeah, my friend Michelle works there, so she called me. Thankfully I wasn't in class at the time. It finally dawned on me to buck up and pay the renewal fee for the MyGenealogy subscription. I figured if you were who you said you were, there had to be *something* that led you to Michael after all these years." Rebecca shook her head. "I hadn't been on the app in over a year, ever since my best friend bought me the kit for my birthday."

I sat up straight, leaned back. "So you saw my message?"

"Yes." Rebecca's eyes met mine and for a moment we both were silent.

"Is that what made you finally decide to return my call?"

Rebecca nodded and gave me a sheepish grin. "After my friend at the care center called me, I almost contacted the police, but figured the eighty-dollar renewal fee might save me time and energy in the long run. I'm glad I did."

My heart was warming to this girl. "You seem awfully

young to be my cousin."

Rebecca's green eyes sparkled. "You know, that's just how MyGenealogy categorizes degrees of separation."

I nodded. "So I've heard." Cassie had said the same thing, but it was still all gibberish to me.

"If you're Michael's daughter—which, now that I'm looking at your face and after seeing the DNA match, I believe you are—" Rebecca paused, taking a breath, "then you are my aunt, not my cousin."

"Your aunt?" I felt my chin drop.

"Yes." Rebecca took a sip of her coffee.

Something like fireworks erupted in my chest. I could feel the blood flowing through my arteries, heat running through the numbness of my soul. My stressed out, overwrought brain untangled the information, and my eyes widened. "I have a sister?"

Rebecca's face glowed. "A brother—half-brother, to be technically correct. That's why the DNA results say we're cousins. If you and Dad shared the same mother, it would have come up with a closer relation."

I had a brother? But if Rebecca was my brother's daughter, why wasn't her last name Smith? I studied her hands, which were still holding tight to the coffee mug. There was no ring on her finger.

"What's his name?"

Rebecca sucked in on her cheeks. "You really don't know, do you? And here I was, all worried about protecting his privacy." She rolled her eyes and looked away but smiled. "His birth name was Michael Andrew Smith, Jr." Rebecca turned her coffee again in her hands. "But he changed his last name in his early twenties to Bowers. It was his mother's maiden name."

"Why did he change his last name?"

"He said he did it because as a musician, he couldn't

compete with the other Michael Smith." Rebecca's grin widened. It was evident she was proud of her dad and loved him. "But I think it had more to do with finding his own identity. He was still angry with Grandpa back in those days."

The sounds of the coffee shop disappeared as thoughts and emotions swirled within me like a hurricane. My heart hooked itself on Rebecca's statement about Michael, my *brother,* being angry with his—*our*—dad. What had our father done to make his son want to change his last name? My mind was exploding with the revelation that my brother was a musician. I remembered Michael in the care center and how he'd held his hands to his mouth, mimicking playing a harmonica. Music ran in the family.

I managed to utter the easier question first. "My brother is a musician?"

Rebecca leaned forward, lowering her voice. "Yes. If you listen to country music you've probably heard of him. He goes by Andy Bowers."

The name sounded familiar, but with all the buzzing in my brain I couldn't place it. I shrugged my shoulders, feeling guilty. "The name is familiar, but I can't match it to a song or a face."

Rebecca frowned, obviously disappointed. "You can Google it."

"I'll definitely do that, but..." How did I phrase my next question? "If you don't mind me asking, why was he angry with our father? What happened between them?"

"I think it's best if he talks to you about it. He knows more than me." Rebecca took a sip of her coffee and looked away. "Most of my memories of Grandpa are good, but he was a different person before."

Before what? A flame of hope ignited in my chest. It sounded like my father had overcome his alcoholism.

Otherwise, how could Rebecca's memories of him be good? "Do you think he'd talk to me?"

Rebecca turned to me and her mouth and eyes widened, as if she suddenly remembered an important task. "Oh my goodness, yes. That's one of the reasons I wanted to meet you. After checking the MyGenealogy site, I called Dad and told him everything I knew." Rebecca exhaled. "He actually took it well and hardly seemed surprised." Love shone in Rebecca's eyes. "But that's Dad for you."

I felt like I would fall off my seat. I had a brother. And he wasn't disturbed by my existence. "Can I have his phone number?"

Rebecca's brow furrowed. "Well, yes, but since you're down this way, he wanted me to let you know he'd love to see you in person. His house is about two-and-a-half hours south of here."

I opened my mouth to speak, but I was lost for words. I looked at the clock on the wall above the coffee counter. It was half past noon. If I left now, I'd be at my brother's by three p.m. I'd still have time to call Johnny before he left Portland. Or...I could still make it back home today. It'd be a long day. But I sure didn't see myself sleeping until I'd met my newfound brother. He obviously knew my—our—father's story.

"I bet this is a whole lot to take in. Probably more than you bargained for." Rebecca's voice was soft, and her eyes showed sympathy.

I laughed. "This is definitely not how I saw today going." Especially when I was sitting on top of the hill, gazing at the lake, smoking my first cigarette in months. My entire world had changed in one short hour.

A time for healing.

Shaking the chill that ran through me, I nodded. "I'd love to meet my brother."

The address Rebecca gave me was in California, but since Klamath Falls was basically on the Oregon–California border, I wasn't too surprised. She said Andy stayed at his ranch outside of Cedarville, California, when he wasn't touring. The ranch had been in his mother's family for generations, and it was his happy place, his home. It was also where Rebecca had grown up. During the rest of our conversation, I'd found out she was going to school at Oregon Institute of Technology and studying nuclear medicine. They had decided to put Michael in a care facility in Klamath Falls because Rebecca would be in the area for the next two years, and Country Life Care Center was a good facility for memory care patients. Not to mention, it was within driving distance of Cedarville.

"Dad would drive up here to see you, but he's leaving for a tour in a couple of days and has a lot to take care of before he goes. He was up here last week, visiting Grandpa." Rebecca had explained all this to me in an almost apologetic fashion. And she had asked for forgiveness for ignoring my call and assuming I was some kind of desperate and unstable Andy Bowers fan. "You wouldn't believe the things some women have tried," Rebecca had said, her eyes widening.

Once I was in my car, I sat a moment, overwhelmed by the onslaught of information. I longed to talk to Cassie so much my stomach ached. There were still no messages or calls from my daughter. My heart was pulled down by a heavy weight, and loneliness climbed inside my chest and took residence.

I put the address in the map program on my phone and started the car for what promised to be the last leg of my search for my father. My search for truth.

Chapter Thirty-Two

I DIDN'T OWN A WILLIE NELSON CD, and the song didn't come on the radio, so I sang "On the Road Again" to myself, trying to both steady my nerves and lighten my heart. I stopped at a convenience store on the way out of Klamath, but this time it was for Red Vines and a fresh Diet Coke. I didn't want to even open my trunk and dig through the cooler with the other things I'd bought earlier. I'd come so close to falling off the edge, my knees were still weak.

Before leaving the convenience store, I took the pack of cigarettes I'd bought and threw them in the garbage. I didn't need the temptation sitting in the car with me, and I didn't want to show up at my famous brother's house smelling like an ashtray. The forty-dollar bottle of Jack could stay hidden—out of sight and almost out of mind—in my trunk.

As I drove on a pretty straight road south, through pasture after pasture of what I was pretty sure was alfalfa, my mind tried to wrap itself around the day's discovery. I had a brother. A younger brother. He was musical. He was famous. And the most amazing part of all—he wanted to meet me.

What had his life been like growing up? When had his mom and Michael met? What had happened between him and our father? Did he know anything about what happened between Michael and my mom? The last part seemed unlikely, but who knew? Maybe Michael had kept a journal, or pictures. Or maybe there was some memory of my mom that he spoke about when the timing seemed right—like when he heard the song "Undeniable Love." I was certain the memory of my mom was somewhere in Michael's mind, somewhere in his heart. Hopefully he had passed a portion of it down to his son.

So many questions would go unanswered unless Michael was miraculously cured of his Alzheimer's. Andy was my only hope of finding out anything about my father's life. My chest ached at the memory of him, sitting in the chair smiling, unaware of who I was but so friendly. Had he always been a happy, easygoing man?

I'd polished off the entire package of Red Vines by the time I passed a small town called Tulelake. My stomach rolled in protest, angry with me for not eating a real lunch, so I glanced at the map on my phone. No place big enough for a restaurant on the horizon. I took another drink of my Diet Coke.

The farmlands along the side of the road soon turned into red dirt and pine trees as far as I could see, surrounded by low-lying gray hills. Traffic was light on the relatively flat land. Eventually I entered a small mountain range, and then before I knew it, I was in farmland again. I checked my phone. Less than an hour to my destination. My pulse quickened, and I was suddenly a nervous wreck.

Here I was, a middle-aged, haggard woman, wearing worn out jeans and a t-shirt bought from Goodwill, driving a 1995 Buick Skylark in desperate need of a wash, an opened bottle of Jack Daniels in the trunk, going to meet her new-to-her half-brother who'd obviously done something with his life. Something big. He had the money to send his daughter to college. I was so poor I had to live with my daughter, who never went to college and worked her fingers to the bone.

I pulled the car over on a flat, sage-brush-lined turnout. Putting the transmission in park, I leaned back and closed my eyes, trying to slow my breath. Inhale. One. Two. Three. Exhale. Tears burned the back of my eyelids. "Lord, I can't do this. I *want* to. But I don't think I *can*." The only sound was the wind blowing across this land that was foreign to me.

No backing out now, you're almost to the finish line.

I opened my eyes and grabbed my phone. It was late afternoon. Cassie would be getting off work soon. There were still no messages from her. Did she hate me? Was the truth about what happened to her dad the straw that broke the fragile relationship between us?

"If someone forces you to go one mile, go with him two miles." Dad had given me that line a few times growing up. I couldn't remember where it was in the Bible, but he said it meant the same thing as walking a mile in someone else's shoes. I looked out the window at the fields of sage brush, with small patches of green grass or weeds in between. Juniper trees dotted the landscape, their branches short and twisted, adapting to the environment around them.

How many times had I left Cassie with nothing but a note? Each time I felt like it was the right thing to do. The notes were to let her know I wouldn't be gone forever and to assure her I loved her. How much love did she feel though, when she read them? As if in answer, a tumbleweed blew across the road on its own lonely track. Abandoned. Uprooted. Alone.

Tears streamed down my cheeks. I picked up my phone and pushed the speed dial for Cassie's number. The phone rang several times. I sucked on my lips, waiting. The voicemail picked up. I took a deep breath. "Hi, baby girl. It's Mom." I paused, desperate to say the right words. "I'm sorry for leaving this morning the way I did. What I wrote in the note, about your dad, I should've told you in person." I swallowed, fighting to keep my voice even. "And I shouldn't have left. Period. Not without talking to you first." The low-lying hills beyond the sage-brush-covered field reminded me of earlier in the day, when I'd almost drank and lost nearly a year of sobriety. Again. The phone call from Rebecca had saved me. The timing of it was surreal—an amazing stroke of luck.

It's not luck, Mom.

I closed my eyes. "I really wish you were here. I um...found my dad, but he has Alzheimer's, so talking to him didn't go the way I hoped." I laughed, but the sound came out hollow. "Long story short, though, I found out I have a brother. Can you believe that? I'm actually driving to his place now to meet him." I exhaled, the weight on my shoulders a tad lighter. "I love you, baby girl, and I love Renee, with all of my heart. I'll let you know how meeting my brother goes."

I ended the call and reopened the map program on my phone. Thirty miles to go. My stomach growled, reminding me of how long it'd been since I'd eaten a real meal. I didn't want to show up all shaking and lightheaded at Andy's house. Somewhere between here and there, hopefully I'd find some food.

The road took me through a little town called Alturas, but I didn't see any restaurants that looked appealing on the way. Whatever eating spots the town had were probably located off the main highway, and I didn't want to get detoured. A little way out of town, I took a right onto a road called Highway 299 and drove through another mountain range. Pine trees dotted fields of yellowed long grasses and grayish-green sagebrush. The steep, rocky peaks of the range against the crystal blue sky seemed almost magical, beckoning adventurous souls to climb them. Driving past an area where a creek was visible down a small valley, the leaves of Aspen trees shivered in the breeze, playing with the sunlight. The trees, the foliage, the dirt—it was all different than the mountains back home. Everything I saw in this remote area was reminiscent of an Old West movie. It was like going back in time.

As my car descended the mountains, a valley appeared before me so suddenly it took my breath away. A long, tall range of barren-looking gray mountains lined the other side of the valley, their snowcapped peaks touching blue sky. I smiled when a sign showed the name of the place I had descended into, "Surprise Valley."

Once in the valley, some shop-like buildings and houses appeared. A Ford truck coming from the opposite direction met me, obviously not in a hurry. Its driver, an old man with a cowboy hat, lifted his hand off the steering wheel in a small wave and nodded at me as he passed by. I was so surprised, I didn't wave back.

A sign along the road let me know I was now in Cedarville. At a stop sign, I hung a right as the GPS told me to. It looked to be the main street of the tiny town. The road was extra wide, lined mostly by old brick buildings. The parking spaces were vertical to the buildings instead of parallel. A sign on my left caught my eye: The Country Hearth. Given the number of trucks parked in front, it looked like the place to eat. I found a parking spot a few buildings away and pulled in, immediately feeling out of place with my old car and its Oregon plates.

Wood floors and the smell of bacon mingled with the scent of freshly baked pastries greeted me when I opened the door to the restaurant. A tanned woman drawled a warm hello and showed me to a small table, then brought me a glass of water in a half-pint mason jar. I ordered the burger and fries, then stared at my phone while I waited for the food to arrive. Each time I looked up, another person in the small restaurant was looking my way with open curiosity but no apparent distrust. I shifted uncomfortably in my seat. My phone was no help in distracting me. I had zero bars for service. No internet, and if Cassie called, it'd go straight to voicemail. Hopefully she'd know why.

"Are you visiting someone in the valley?" The waitress appeared with my food, which looked and smelled delicious.

I figured telling her who I was visiting probably wasn't the smartest thing at this point. "Just passing through." I grinned to make up for my short response.

"Ah, well, enjoy. Let me know if you need anything."

I polished off my meal and paid at the counter. The food energized me, gave me strength. It was definitely worth the extra half hour out of my day. Now, whether I was ready or not, it was time to meet my brother.

I continued south on Surprise Valley Road. I met three vehicles on the way, and each driver waved as they passed me. By the second one, I had the routine down and waved back. Ten minutes later, I was driving down a gravel road with an arched sign ahead—Bowers Ranch. I was expecting a gate or a guard or something, especially after all of Rebecca's paranoia about rabid fans. Maybe she exaggerated. Or maybe that same protectiveness of their privacy was the reason Andy didn't need a locked gate at his family ranch.

After passing several large metal outbuildings, I pulled up to a two-story white house with a large wraparound porch. Paint peeled from sun-worn shutters and one of the steps up to the porch sagged. Definitely not something a millionaire would live in. A border collie appeared from the side of the house and made its way to my car, tail wagging. Taking a deep breath, I opened the car door and stepped out.

"Hello there! You must be Sharon." A somewhat rugged but friendly-looking man walked out of the house and started down the porch steps. He wore an olive-green t-shirt, dark jeans, and cowboy boots.

I took a step forward, the border collie running circles around me. "Yes, that's me." I waved my hand and then put both hands in my back pockets.

The man approached, a large smile spread across his tanned face. He looked at the dog and whistled. "Daisy, come here, girl." The dog immediately ran to his side. In a few short steps, the man was standing in front of me, offering me his hand. "Andy Bowers."

I shook Andy's hand, which was calloused and warm. "Nice to meet you."

I hesitantly met his eyes. They were the same color brown as our dad's. The same color as mine. In fact, Andy looked a lot like the young Michael I'd seen in the picture Cassie had discovered at Anthony's house.

"Why don't we sit on the porch?" Andy motioned toward the house. "We have a couple of nice chairs and a little table up there."

I nodded. "Sounds good to me."

I followed Andy up the steps to the wide porch and to a set of padded outdoor chairs and a round wooden table.

"Could I get you something to drink? I made a pitcher of iced tea."

"That'd be great, thank you." I sat in a chair, thankful to get off my weak knees.

"I'll be right back." Andy disappeared inside the house. It seemed like he lived alone. How had I not thought to ask Rebecca about her mom? Her siblings?

Andy returned with two glasses of tea and set them on the little table between us. "How was your drive down? Any trouble finding the place?"

I took a sip of tea. "Nope, modern technology is great." I waved my phone in front of me like a flag. "Although I don't have a cell signal out here."

Andy chuckled. "A common problem in these parts if you have certain cellphone carriers." He took a seat in the other chair and leaned toward me, his elbows on his thighs. For a moment I studied his face, looking for myself. The eyes were much the same, as were the cheekbones. His nose was larger, more angular. His jaw and chin were narrow, similar to Rebecca's, creating a more pointed lower face than Michael or I had. His wavy, dark brown hair was long enough it would've touched the collar of a button up shirt, and his hairline started high on his forehead. His eyes were lined with age, and there were deep crevices between his brows, but he looked at least ten years younger than me. Again, I recalled Rebecca's fear of crazy fans, but my brother looked neither rich nor exceptionally handsome. The kindness in his eyes, though, could have won any woman's heart.

"Rebecca told me a little of your story and how you've been looking for your father." Andy's voice was deep and touched with empathy.

I dropped my gaze, staring at my hands, and wondered how Rebecca had portrayed me. "Yes. My mom told me some things before she passed away about a year ago, and I decided I needed to find him."

"I'm sorry about the loss of your mom."

I nodded, still full of nerves, and kept my gaze on the floor.

"I don't know much about my dad's life before he married *my* mom. He was pretty tightlipped about his past. I knew it had been a rough one, though most of it was self-inflicted." Andy's baritone voice carried no judgment, encouraging me to lift my chin and look him in the face.

"He was an alcoholic, from what I've heard." I spoke barely above a whisper.

Andy frowned. "Yep, that he was, most of his life."

Most of his life. That meant he sobered up at some point. "When did he quit drinking?"

Andy was silent for a moment. "About ten years ago. He had a stroke that landed him in the hospital and then rehabilitation. I think the combination of going cold turkey and the reality of his failing health motivated him to finally put the bottle down."

Only ten years ago? He would have been about sixty-five. Andy had spent his entire childhood and all his early adult years with an alcoholic for a parent. Changing his name made more sense. "Were you close to him?"

Andy smiled wistfully and looked away, something in the flat field across from the house seeming to have his attention. "We had a rocky relationship, to say the least. But when Dad quit drinking, he apologized to me and tried to make amends. At first, I didn't forgive him. Too much had happened." Andy's gaze settled on me, his eyes darker. "But God showed me that forgiveness wasn't about what my father had or hadn't done—it was about my own heart and my relationship with Jesus. That's when everything changed."

I blinked several times as Andy's words sank in. How much of what Andy felt could Cassie relate to?

"I didn't mean to go all preacher man on you." Andy chuckled and straightened his shoulders, eyes shining. "But that's the truth of the matter."

"Oh, no, that's not what I was thinking." I tried to fit my thoughts into a question. "After you forgave him, did your relationship improve?"

Andy nodded. "*Everything* improved." The lines between his eyes deepened. "Including, eventually, my song writing."

There was the opening to ask him about his music career, and I couldn't let it pass by. "I've heard you're quite successful." I smiled, not wanting to admit I still couldn't place his name with a song. "I only listen to modern country music occasionally."

"You have no idea who I am." Andy grinned, and he let out a belly laugh. "My poor daughter is so worried I'm going to get chased by the paparazzi or something because I had my first billboard hit song."

"You just started your music career?" He seemed old to get into the country music game.

Andy shrugged one shoulder. "Not exactly. I've been a musician all my life. I changed my name to Andy Bowers when I started, before Rebecca was even born." Andy sighed. "It's been a long, hard-earned road. I spent most of it half broke and bitter at my lack of success. Jesus straightened me out." He smiled. "There I go again."

"No, no, you're fine. I'm a believer too." At least, I had been. Wanted to be.

"I'm glad to hear that."

I shifted in my seat, needing to know more but afraid to ask because it was so personal. This was probably the only chance I'd ever get. "Did you ever have a problem with...drinking? Sometimes it's hereditary."

Andy nodded. "The temptation was there, but I fought it with all I had. I saw what it did to my father, to my mom, and our family. When I got saved, the fight was easier. I wasn't doing it all alone anymore."

I swallowed and clasped the arms of the chair. Did Andy know why I'd asked? Could he see the history of alcoholism written all over my face? He'd gone a different path than me because he saw where the other path led. I had the gene of addiction with no point of reference, no understanding. In many ways, Cassie's and Andy's lives were similar. Maybe someday they could meet.

"Did you hate him?" I held my breath, waiting for the response that would give me a glimpse into Cassie's heart.

"No. I loved him." Andy's heavy eyebrows pushed together. "I went through a stage where I was angry with him, especially in my early twenties. That's when I changed my name. Then, later, I felt sorry for him and had such a sense of loss. He was a charming, loving guy, but his drinking made him unreliable and at times unruly and mean." Andy leaned closer, his elbows once again on his knees, the tips of his fingers pressed together. "When my kids were younger, I was angry because I wanted them to have a grandpa who we could trust. I'd about prayed myself out by that time and kind of gave up on my dad. And God. My wife and I weren't getting along. I spent so much time and money on this music habit of mine and had seen little success. I was too wrapped up in trying to make a name for myself, I didn't see my wife was drowning in loneliness." He shook his head. "I guess instead of having an alcohol addiction, I had a music addiction—or really, an addiction to the stage." Andy sat up, waving his hand dismissively. "I'm sorry. This is all more than you probably want to know."

I tipped my head forward. "No, please keep talking. This is exactly what I came here for."

Andy lifted an eyebrow. "My life story?" He gave me a crooked smile.

"No...understanding." I blew air through my teeth. "Apparently Michael was an alcoholic when he and my mom had an affair. That's why she never told him about me. She didn't want him to be a part of my life. I was raised by another man, a wonderful one, but..." Andy was being wide open honest with me. Maybe it was time I did the same. "Something was always not quite right with me. I can't explain it. Then my husband died tragically when I was only twenty-seven years old." I couldn't speak the words I'd written to Cassie about Steven's death. I'd save that part for another time, another place.

I took a deep breath, hoping to suck in courage. "I started drinking. It was all downhill from there, to say the least." I looked down, guilt fighting to take me hostage as the truth made its way out of my mouth. "I felt cursed."

"I'm sorry, Sharon." The empathy in Andy's voice made me raise my head. "I can only imagine what you've been through." He chewed on his bottom lip. "Your mom didn't tell you about your dad until she was ill?"

"No, I knew my birth father wasn't the one who raised me, but I was told Michael left us, wanted nothing to do with me or my mom. When Mom was dying, she told me the truth—that Michael didn't even know I existed." I swallowed. "Now, I guess he never will."

Andy nodded. "Maybe not in this life. But in heaven he will."

I stared at Andy as goosebumps covered my arms. "He...?"

"Yes, he's accepted the Lord. I think he was trying to follow Jesus his whole life, but the booze got in the way. Who can say at what point someone is saved? But after he quit drinking, he started going to church and got baptized. I think he felt unworthy, until then." Andy lifted the corner of his mouth into a half-smile. "So many of us have it backwards, don't we?"

Was he talking about me? Something lit up in my heart, the wick of a candle touched by a match. "Religion helped you not to drink?"

"Not religion. Relationship. Jesus filled the void I'd been trying to complete with something else all my life."

Mom had tried to tell me the same thing so many times before. I never listened, certain she couldn't possibly understand the struggle inside of me. Hearing the same thing from someone who understood the inner battle, my heart ached with the realization my mom had always been right.

"How...how do you do it? The relationship part?" I felt like a little kid asking someone to show her how to ride a bike.

"It's a choice you make, every day. Where you let your thoughts take you. What you'll allow into your mind and heart. Who you'll talk to when no one else is around."

I saw my husband's face in my mind, young and carefree and full of love. The checkered flag on the horizon. Tears welled up again.

I can see the finish line, Sharon. Hang on tight, we're almost there.

I wasn't ready to let him go.

I cleared my throat. "So, this billboard hit you have, what's the name of the song? I want to download it for my daughter to hear when I get home." I needed to change the subject before I was reduced into a bumbling, tearful mess.

Andy's grin reached from ear to ear. "Ironically, it's called 'When Daddy Came Home.' I wrote it about my own experience with an alcoholic parent and the path of forgiving and making sure the pattern wasn't repeated." Andy gazed at me intently as if seeing into my soul.

A chill ran down my arms. "I...I think I may have heard it on the radio a couple of times." Memory took me back to my drive with Cassie to Moss Landing and the country song that made her cry. The one that had played on the radio as I approached Klamath Falls. The one the DJ said was from a local singer raised in Modoc County. If someone had told me then that my own brother was the one singing it, I'd have called them crazy.

Our conversation continued for almost an hour. I learned more about Andy. He and his wife had divorced twelve years ago. He had a son named Jesse who lived with his mom in Reno, spending holidays and parts of the summer with Andy in Cedarville. Andy had a half-brother, his mother's son from her second marriage. He lived in a house on the other side of the ranch and ran it most of the year. Andy helped when he wasn't on the road, but with his growing success, he'd be on the ranch even less often. Jesse was planning on spending the summer on the ranch, helping his uncle. Rebecca would join them for part of the summer also.

"You and your family are welcome here, any time. I'd love to meet my niece and great-niece," Andy told me, and I knew he meant it.

I was embarrassed to tell him what I did for a living, but he didn't bat an eye at it. I also got up the nerve to tell him I played the guitar. He asked me if I brought it with me. I almost lied but didn't want to tarnish this new relationship. "Yeah, it's in my trunk."

I remembered what else was in my trunk and quickly said, "I should get back on the road."

"I'm glad you came today." Andy eased back in the chair, his hands on his thighs. "Is there anything else you want to know, before you go?"

There was so much I wanted to know about my father's childhood and what happed between him and my mom, but Andy was unlikely to have the answers. "Did Dad..." The word got caught on my tongue, like something bitter you take a bite of and try to spit out. Calling Michael "Dad" didn't feel right. He might have been my biological father, but he wasn't my dad. I started over. "Did Michael ever talk about my mom?"

"I wish I could say he told me their story, so I had something to share with you, but he didn't. Like I said, he didn't talk about the past." Andy frowned. "I'm sorry."

I looked at my hands. "It's okay." My heart dipped, realizing the secrets of the music box would never be known. The depth of the relationship between Michael and my mom would remain a mystery. I looked up at Andy. "Did Michael ever listen to or sing an old song called 'Undeniable Love'?"

Andy cocked his head. "You know, he used to sing a

song with a refrain of 'undeniable love' to himself quite often." Andy sighed and sadness filled his eyes. "Dad was always singing to himself. Sorry to say, half the time, I wasn't really listening. I guess it's one of those things you take for granted until it's too late."

I knew how taking things for granted was, and I didn't want more of it in my life. "Thank you for today, for opening yourself up to me and letting me come see you."

Andy nodded. "I'm glad you made it down. Sorry my pit bull of a daughter delayed things." He gave me a crooked grin, but a tinge of sadness touched his voice. "She's a daddy's girl and has mother-henned me ever since her mom and I divorced."

"She loves you." Cassie's face flashed before my eyes. She was, in her own way, protective of me.

Andy saw me to my car, giving me a shy but warm hug goodbye. As I drove away, dust mixed with the orange of the setting sun, but I could see my brother as clear as day in my rearview mirror, like a light shining brightly in a storm.

Chapter Thirty-Three

I DROVE BACK THE WAY I came, through the quaint little town of Cedarville, over the mountain pass, and back through Alturas. As I did, thoughts cascaded through my mind, kind of like one of Cassie's waterfalls. I'd found my father, but he'd never know me—at least not on this earth. I'd found a half-brother, who was of all things a country musician and had welcomed me with open arms. Unlike me, he'd fought off addiction. He'd turned to Jesus.

My parents had raised me in church. I'd grown up hearing the Bible stories, sitting in pews and singing hymns, going to vacation Bible school. My mom and dad's faith had been strong. I'd mindlessly followed their footsteps, but not created any of my own. When Steven died, I reached the edge of a cliff, with no path to follow. I'd found myself on a cliff again today, overlooking the Klamath Basin, counting down the minutes to noon so I could justify a Jack and Coke. The call from Rebecca had saved me. Talk about lucky timing.

It's not luck, Mom.

My eyes burned as tears filled them. "I think you might be right, baby girl." My chest ached, longing to be filled with light.

Coming out of turn four on the final lap.

I saw Steven, his face determined, steering his car toward the finish line. I saw him at church, sitting beside me in the pew, his face shining with love and concentration as he listened to the pastor preach. Steven, the love of my life, dancing with me to "At Last" during our wedding. He was in heaven now. Had been for twenty-seven years. My heart ached, but for the first time, the ache met peace, and the peace was greater than the pain.

For everything there is a season.

The seeds of faith my parents planted in my heart lay dormant, neglected. My parents were gone, but the faith they'd reared me with remained somewhere deep inside me. Was I ready to pick up that mantle and carry it forward?

Or was it too late?

The lights of Klamath Falls shone in the distance, tiny specks of light against an impossibly black landscape. My stomach grumbled. I also needed gas. Once in Klamath, I drove past the turn off for going home, looking for a gas station with a store. I found one and filled my tank and bought an overcooked hot dog and a bottle of water. Cassie would've reprimanded me for the hot dog, but at least I would have earned points for drinking water instead of Diet Coke.

I checked my phone. I'd told Cassie in my voicemail that I would let her know how the meeting with my brother went. There was so much I wanted to tell her. My messages showed a text from Cassie. My heart skipped a beat. I tapped on the message. It was a long one.

Mom—I got your message and I can't wait to hear how it goes. I've been thinking and praying all day about the note you left. I need you to know it WASN'T your fault my dad died. He's the one who decided to race that night. It was his car, not yours. I love you. Talk to you soon.

I wasn't sure what burned more. My heart or my eyes. My sweet, loving, forgiving daughter. What had I ever done to deserve her? I texted back a short response, letting her know everything was good and I'd give her the entire scoop later.

I left the gas station and decided to drive back through the old part of Klamath Falls on my way back to the highway. Past some old brick buildings with the lights off, I saw a neon sign with a flashing pink "Karaoke" sign beneath it. Part of the pink lighting was missing, so it looked like it said "Karae," but the outline of the other letters was visible because of the neon light of the bar's name, High Desert Bar & Grill.

I took the corner and pulled into the bar's small parking lot. I thought of Janice and her inviting me to karaoke. I owed her an apology for not explaining why I couldn't go to a bar. Recovering alcoholics can't be near alcohol. The temptation to drink would be too strong. I parked at a space near the back of the bar and stared at the neon sign, its bright, artificial light a stark contrast against the black sky, boasting its countless twinkling stars. Inside the bar was a magic potion, a remedy for pain. It would wash away the hurt and the scars. It didn't care about my past. It didn't discriminate when it came to age, sex, and race. It knew my weakness and catered to it, making promises and expecting nothing in return except my loyalty.

It's a choice you make, every day. What you'll let into your mind and heart.

I turned the ignition off, got out of my car, and walked to the back. The sickly-sweet smell of Jack wafted up at me from the cavern of the trunk. Even with the bottle closed, its scent was strong. My hands trembled as I took what I needed out of the trunk and walked to the entrance of the bar.

Blaring music greeted me when I opened the door. Taking a deep breath, I walked in and looked around. The place was full. The smell of grilled meat mixed with the sweetness of alcohol and the aroma of fifty-plus people's perspiration and cologne of choice. A bar was to the right of me, shelves lined with liquor bottles. At the other end was a small stage. A young woman with long, curly black hair was singing a Joan Jett song slightly off-key. The glaze in her eyes and the sway of her hips told me the girl had had one too many drinks. I wove my way through the tables filled with laughing and conversing people who largely ignored the singing of the girl on the stage. Some people looked up at me as I passed, and more than one continued to stare at me like I was a fish out of water. If only.

I approached the karaoke DJ, a young man with a ring through his bottom lip and arms covered in tattoos. Leaning in close, I told him what I wanted to do.

He shrugged his shoulders while looking me up and down. "Go for it, lady, you're next up."

The "Crimson and Clover" song was almost finished, so I didn't bother finding a seat. As soon as the Joan Jett fan walked back to her friends, I weaved through the last couple of tables to the stage. My pulse beat like a wild drum inside my ears. I swung my guitar case off my shoulder and zipped it open, pulling out my Gibson. The guitar my sweet daughter had bought me. For Mother's Day, of all things. For me, who had been about the poorest excuse for a mother a woman could be. I ran my hand along the neck of the guitar, remembering the verse Cassie had found in my mom's Bible, the one my mom had written my name by.

"And so it was, whenever the spirit from God was upon Saul, that David would take a harp and play it with his hand."

I put the guitar strap over my neck and stepped up to the microphone. Joan Jett-fan and I were about the same height, so it didn't need adjusting. The bar had grown quieter, and at least half of the patrons had focused their attention on the stage. On me.

"Hello, folks." My voice quivered, a testament to the bundle of nerves in my throat, in my chest. "The song I want to sing isn't in the karaoke song line-up, so I'm gonna play it for y'all myself." I cleared my throat, feeling all those eyes on me, some curious, some demeaning, others amused.

My fingers found the metal strings, testing the chords.

First a G and then a D. I closed my eyes, grappling with the tune of the song buried in my memory. I strummed a C chord. Yes, that was it. I started over at the G. I closed my eyes and opened my mouth, willing the lyrics from my throat and into the air.

I've wandered far away from God,
Now I'm coming home;
The paths of sin too long I've trod,
Lord, I'm coming home.

My voice cracked and I heard a few sniggers in the audience. My lips trembled. I squeezed my eyes shut and continued.

Coming home, coming home,
Nevermore to roam;
Open wide Thine arms of love,
Lord, I'm coming home.

Murmurs of conversation increased. I ignored them and let my memory take me back to my childhood, standing between my mom and dad, singing in church on Sunday morning. Remembering the love and comfort it brought.

I've wasted many precious years,
Now I'm coming home;
I now repent with bitter tears,
Lord, I'm coming home.

I ventured my eyes open and the first thing I saw was a group of men laughing and shaking their heads. My face burned and my knees shook.

It's a choice you make every day...

Singing the refrain, I lifted my gaze from the table of men and scanned the walls of the bar, searching for something to focus my eyes on other than the people in the crowd. Finding nothing, I closed my eyes again.

I'm tired of sin and straying, Lord,
Now I'm coming home;

I'll trust Thy love, believe Thy Word,
Lord, I'm coming home.

The darkness of my closed eyes filled with light. I saw my mom and dad smiling, their eyes shining with love. My voice rose, accentuating each note of the song.

My soul is sick, my heart is sore,
Now I'm coming home;
My strength renew, my hope restore,
Lord, I'm coming home.

I heard nothing but the song coming from my lips and the chords of my guitar. The voices of the people in the bar had faded away. Inside my chest my heart was burning as if lit by a rampant flame, a fire that could not be extinguished.

My only hope, my only plea,
Now I'm coming home;
That Jesus died, and died for me,
Lord, I'm coming home.

As I entered the refrain for the final time, I stopped playing the guitar and raised my hands in the air, looking up at the darkness of the wooden ceiling. I saw Steven's race car reaching the finish line, the checkered flag swinging down. His face passed before me, full of peace and love, then faded away. Hot tears streamed down my face. My voice somehow grew louder, stronger, reverberating off the walls when I reached the final lyrics.

I need His cleansing blood I know,
Now I'm coming home;
Oh, wash me whiter than the snow,
Lord, I'm coming home.

I dropped my hands and opened my eyes, my vison blurry from the light and tears. Silence filled the room.

From somewhere in the back came the sound of a single person clapping. Soon others joined in, filling the room with the sound of applause. Someone whistled. I lifted the strap of my guitar over my head and bent over to put it back in its case. A middle-aged woman in the front was still clapping, and her eyes shone. Picking up my case, I stepped off the stage. Rock music blared through the speakers, replacing the applause. It seemed no one was wanting to come forward for karaoke.

As I walked away from the stage, the teary-eyed woman approached me. She put her hand on my arm. "That was beautiful," she shouted over the music.

Lost for words, I simply uttered a hoarse "Thank you." I walked briskly to the door, looking straight ahead and avoiding eye contact with anyone else. This wasn't where I belonged.

I exited the bar and breathed in deeply of the cool night air. The sky sparkled with a thousand stars, but the full moon outshone them all. At my car, I opened the trunk and put my guitar in, then pulled the brown paper bag of whiskey and soda out. Closing the trunk, I walked back to the entrance of the bar where a large barrel served as a garbage can. I threw the brown bag in it. The clinking it made as it hit the bottom was a bell ringing freedom. Smiling and light-footed, I went back to my car, started the ignition, and pulled my phone out of my purse. With steady fingers, I typed out a message to Cassie. *I'm on my way home.* Truth be told, in all the ways that mattered, I was already there.

I tiptoed into the house at one-thirty a.m., doing my best to not wake Cassie or Renee. The smell of home welcomed me—the leftover aroma of chicken that must've been made for dinner earlier in the evening, the Cascade dishwasher detergent Cassie used, and the apricot-vanilla scented candle that sat on the table.

The entire drive home I'd contemplated what to say to Johnny. He'd be getting in the moving truck in a few hours and heading south. It was too late to call, but I needed to let him know my final decision before I lost the nerve.

I found my father. It didn't go quite like I hoped. Actually, in a way, it was far better than I ever dreamed. It made me realize how far I've come and how far I still have to go. I know without a doubt I'm supposed to stay here with my daughter.

I paused and wiped away the tears that fell on my phone. Even if Johnny didn't move, I couldn't be in a relationship with him. All the little red flags—the hints he was still drinking, keeping secrets, and not paying bills— were signs he hadn't truly changed. Goosebumps erupted on the back of my arms, remembering his email address: JohnnyBGood. Johnny was wonderful in a hundred different ways, but he wasn't *good*.

For everything there is a season.

Maybe, someday, it'll be time for you and me. But the time's not now.

To my surprise, Johnny texted right back. *Have a nice life, Sharon. I wish you the best.* My heart stung. His response felt brutal, but I knew he was hurting. It was also his way of telling me goodbye—forever. My chest ached, not so much for myself, but for Johnny. He was still running from the pain of life instead of looking it square in the face. He didn't have what I had. No children, no grandchildren. Most importantly, he didn't have the hope that comes from God. I closed my eyes and said a prayer for him.

Bleary eyed, I dug through my purse and pulled out the opal ring. The longing in my heart was almost more than I could stand, but it was a ring I couldn't wear. Standing on my tiptoes, I took my mom's music box off the shelf. Opening the lid, I gently set the ring inside, next to the wooden heart Michael had carved for my mom when they were kids. Finally, I climbed into bed and quickly fell asleep.

I was awakened the next morning by the combination of sunlight shining through my drawn blinds and Renee standing over my bed, peering at me. I smiled groggily at her messy hair and wide eyes. "Good morning, Sweet Pea."

Renee returned my smile and bounced on her toes. "I have a surprise for you, Grammy."

I twisted my neck toward my nightstand, every movement feeling like rusty gears grinding against each other. My phone was on its charging stand and displayed the time: seven-thirty a.m. Who needed more than six hours of sleep? I swung myself up into a sitting position and pulled Renee into a hug. "Waking up here and seeing your smiling face makes Grammy the happiest grandma in the whole world."

Renee giggled and hugged my neck. "But don't you want your surprise?"

I puckered my mouth, as if in thought. "Did you make me breakfast?" I opened my eyes wide, as if I thought that was the answer.

Renee giggled again and wagged her head.

"Hmm. Let's see. Did you make a big blanket fort in the living room for us to play in?"

Renee shook her head again, her grin telling me that she was on to my game. "We can do that later."

I tousled her hair. "Of course. Luckily, I don't have to work today." I was scheduled to work tomorrow, but I was going to beg Janice to take my place. It was time for me to return to church with my family.

Renee grabbed my hand and pulled until I got up. "Come on, Grammy, I'll show you." She led me out the door and down the hall to the living room, then pointed to the coffee table.

Steven's race car trophy sat in the middle of the table, in

all its golden glory. I gasped. "You found the trophy." My throat tightened.

Renee's head bobbed up and down. "It was under the back seat in Mommy's car." My granddaughter's smile spread across her face, lighting her eyes.

I picked up Renee and hugged her close. "I'm glad you found it, Sweet Pea. It is special, but not as special as you. I'm sorry I got mad before."

Renee giggled. "It's okay, Grammy." She squeezed me in a bear hug. "Now can we build a blanket fort?"

Cassie entered from the dining room. She had obviously been standing back, letting Renee and me have a moment. My eyes met hers. I had so much to tell her and many, many things to set right. I wasn't sure where I was going to start or what it would look like. For now, I was overwhelmed with relief to be standing where I was, with the two people I loved most in the whole world. "We sure can build a fort, but let Grammy have some coffee and breakfast first." I nodded toward Cassie, hoping she understood I wanted to talk.

"It's Saturday morning, Sugar Bug, that means you get to watch cartoons." Cassie grabbed the remote from the end table and flipped on the TV.

Renee happily obliged to cartoon watching, and I made my way to the kitchen where coffee was already brewing. I poured Cassie and myself a cup, then took a seat at the dining table. Cassie joined me, wordless, but with the telltale signs of worry and curiosity in the lines of her brow and the way she twisted her t-shirt around her finger.

I told her everything that happened while I was gone, every tragic and beautiful detail. The look of horror on her face when I told her about the whiskey made my stomach knot, but she remained silent while I told her how I ended up being saved by a telephone call, and how lucky I thought I was for the timing.

"Mom, it's not—"

"Luck." I finished her sentence and laughed. "I know that now, baby girl. Without a doubt."

I continued with telling her about my meeting with Rebecca and then my visit with Andy. My brother. Her uncle. The rising-in-fame country music star.

Her mouth gaped open when I said his name. "No way!"

"Yes way. You've heard of him then?" I took a sip of coffee, which was cooling off faster than I was drinking it.

"Yes, I've heard of him. I mean, I don't listen to country as much as I used to, but that song of his we heard on the way to Moss Landing caught my attention, and I downloaded a bunch of his songs on my phone." Cassie shook her head. "This is unreal." Her smile told me she was thrilled with that fact that it *was* real.

I nodded. "He's a super nice guy. Humble and kind." I met Cassie's eyes and found myself tearing up again. "I have a brother. Can you believe that?"

"And he's a musician, like you."

I waved my hand in the air, dismissing her comment. "I'm no musician, I just like to play guitar and sing. He's a professional."

"It's a gift, though. And you share it with him." Cassie's eyes filled with light. "It's in your DNA."

Maybe she was right. I told her about the rest of our conversation. Cassie got misty-eyed when I told her about Michael overcoming his alcoholism later in life, and how Andy had forgiven him and been able to write the song Cassie had fallen in love with.

"God works miracles," Cassie whispered, her eyes momentarily far away. Was she thinking of our relationship? Or something else?

"While we're talking about God, you're not going to believe what I did in Klamath Falls on the way home." I told her the story about the karaoke bar and how I sang an old hymn to a bunch of drunk people. Her jaw dropped closer to the floor than it had when I told her Andy Bowers was her uncle.

"Mom...that's..." Tears welled up in her eyes. "Nannie and Grandpa, if they can see from heaven, have to be beaming from ear to ear."

I bit my lip, looking at the table, too full of emotion to lift my gaze. "I'd like to think they can." I took a deep breath, willing myself to ask the question I couldn't let go. I forced myself to look up, meet my daughter's eyes. "The thing with your dad and what happened with the accident. I know you believe it wasn't my fault, and maybe you're right, technically speaking." I blew air through my teeth. "But Cassie, are you sure you aren't angry? I mean, that I could have been a contributing factor, or that I never told you before?" Both wrongs seemed equally heinous.

Cassie reached across the table, putting her hand on mine. "I've been thinking about that. Remember when we were driving to Proxy Falls, the first time, and I was wondering out loud how the boy I knew could have become so mean and cruel? You said memory is a tricky thing, and sometimes we remember things the way we want them to be, because love blinds us." Cassie leaned in closer. "Mom, do you think you blamed yourself because it was easier than thinking God let it happen? That God somehow took away something so dear to you?"

Something in my chest was breaking, growing, like a seedling pushing through the soil, breaking free. "I...I..." Looking out the window, my mind tried to find words. "I never thought of that." Tears streamed down my face. How many tears had I shed over the last twenty-four hours? But these were good tears. Healing tears.

For everything there is a season.

Should I tell Cassie about Johnny? It seemed like a lot to unload, and without a purpose. Yet, secret keeping was a curse in our family. One that needed to be broken.

I turned back to Cassie. "I have something else I need to tell you. A confession."

Fear flashed across Cassie's eyes. She undoubtedly assumed my secret had to do with drinking.

"For the last few weeks, I've kind of been seeing an old flame."

Cassie blinked several times. "You have a boyfriend?"

"No." How could I explain my relationship with Johnny? "He was passing through, and we spent some time together. But it's over now. He's moving to California today."

Cassie's mouth puckered, but the gleam in her eyes told me she wasn't mad. "I knew something was up."

"How did I end up with such a smart daughter?" I forced a smile and wiped the tears from my face.

Cassie didn't say anything. Instead she reached over and hugged me tight.

Chapter Thirty-Four

EVEN WITH EVERYTHING I TOLD CASSIE, I could tell she was a little surprised that I switched shifts with Janice so I could go to church Sunday morning. Truth be told, I was a little surprised myself. It was like quitting smoking while you were still trying to get used to not drinking anymore. But I knew what I had to do, and the sooner I did it, the better.

The foyer at Cascade Christian Church was buzzing with people as usual. Renee and I got donuts while Cassie said hello to several different women, then made her way over to Matt, who was greeting teenagers. Something like spring sunshine washed over me. I'd be willing to bet my life savings, as meager as they were, that Cassie was falling in love.

"What you smiling about, Grammy?" Renee asked, her mouth full of maple bar.

"Second chances, Sweet Pea." Renee looked confused but then shrugged and kept eating.

I watched the crowd, searching for sleek black hair and olive skin. I spotted her coming from a doorway marked Office. As I was getting up, Cassie arrived, looking content. "Are we ready to go in the sanctuary?"

"You and Renee go ahead. I need to use the little girl's room." I took Renee's used paper plate and disappeared before Cassie could ask questions. After disposing of frosting-covered plates and napkins, I weaved through the crowd toward where I'd seen Samantha. I found her talking to another woman. My insides knotted up.

Lord, help me.

I approached Samantha and tried to make my face emotionless. As soon as Samantha saw me, her conversation with the other woman came to a halt. She looked aghast as I approached, but I didn't let her deter me from my mission.

I now repent with bitter tears; Lord, I'm coming home.

Samantha said something to the woman she was talking to, who looked my way and then spoke to Samantha, seeming sympathetic, then left. Samantha was turning to walk away too, but I grabbed her arm. "I need to talk to you."

Samantha stiffened, and she slowly rotated toward me, her eyes shooting daggers from the darkness. "If you want to talk to me, then commit to meeting with me and Pastor Ben."

I let go of Samantha's arm. "Yeah, yeah, I know. I should've done that a long time ago." I exhaled, willing myself to remain calm no matter what Samantha said or did. "Look, I'm sorry. I'm sorry that my being here hurts you. I'm sorry I haven't met with you and Pastor Ben yet to work this out." My heart was beating like a heavy metal drummer. I wanted to run. But running wasn't an option anymore. I made myself look Samantha in the eye. For the first time I saw the pain in them, hiding behind the wall she'd put between us. "But most of all, I'm truly, truly sorry for what I did twenty-seven or so years ago."

I exhaled. "I've made many mistakes. Horrible mistakes. I wish I could take them back, but I can't." I wanted to explain to her I had no idea Dylan was married when I hooked up with him at the bar. I wanted to explain to her that it was a mistake that caused me to fall headlong into the grips of alcoholism and my self-destructive goal of drinking pain away. But it all sounded like justification. The justification I needed came from above. What I owed Samantha was an apology. Plain, simple, and heartfelt. "I'm truly sorry for the pain it caused you...and for how hard it is for you to see me at church." I exhaled, my nervous energy decreasing as the regret poured from me. "I don't want to cause you suffering, but the thing is, my daughter loves this church, and I want nothing more than to be at the same church as my family." I stopped, took a deep breath. "But if it bothers you too much to see me, I can go to a different church." I pulled my mouth into a half-smile, trying to lighten the mood a fraction and hide the fact that going to another church would break my heart. "You were here first."

During my apology, Samantha's face went from disgust, to shock, to confusion, then...what was she feeling now? I couldn't tell. But tears were falling from her eyes, making lines in her makeup.

"I don't know what to say." Her voice was barely above a whisper. The foyer had emptied, and we were now among only a handful of people in the space.

"You don't have to say anything right now. Here." I reached in my purse and pulled out a little piece of notebook paper I'd written my name and phone number on. Call me a Girl Scout, always prepared. Well, at least today I was. I handed the paper to Samantha. "Call or text me and let me know. And if you still want to meet with Pastor Ben, I'm good with that too. Whatever helps."

With nothing left to be said, I spun on my heel and walked into the sanctuary. The music was booming, and everyone was on their feet, clapping hands and singing. I walked down the aisle, looking up and down the rows for Cassie. Finally, I spotted Renee, who saw me also and jumped up and down at the end of an aisle near the front, waving at me to come. I joined my family, who had saved a seat for me.

The worship band was playing an upbeat song, one popular on the radio. One I knew the words to, thanks to spending time on the road with Cassie. I clapped my hands, joining in on the worship. I had no idea how Samantha was going to respond to my apology. I didn't have any control over it either. For today, I would enjoy worshipping with my family and sing my heart out.

By the time we got home, summer was showing what it promised in the days ahead—hot, humid days and lots of sunshine. I was looking forward to it with an excitement I hadn't felt in a long, long time. I'd be spending extra time with my granddaughter. Cassie would lead us to a waterfall or two, I could bet on that. We'd have to get a grill so we could cook outside and enjoy the summer evenings. I'd play music and sing with Renee. Maybe Cassie would join us as well.

After we'd had lunch and Renee was down for a nap, I told Cassie I needed to talk to her. Concern etched her forehead, guarded her eyes. My heart pinched at the reminder of how it was going to take time to undo the damage done to trust. It'd be okay, though, as long as I kept looking up.

We settled on the couch. The drapes were drawn on the windows to keep the sun out and the cool in. An oscillating fan sat in the middle of the room, circulating the air. It was cozy, quiet. Safe. I didn't need to beat around the bush.

"I talked to Samantha at church."

Cassie's eyes widened and the color drained from her face. "When?"

"Before I went into the sanctuary and joined you and Renee."

The room was silent, save the hum of the fan.

"What..." Cassie pulled on a strand of her hair, twirling it around her finger. "Um...what did you guys talk about?"

I cleared my throat. "I apologized to her for what happened in the past and told her how sorry I was. Then I told her I wanted to keep going to Cascade Christian Church because you and Renee go there, but if it made her uncomfortable to have me around, I'd find another church. I don't want to go anywhere else, but I'm the villain in her story. I think it's the right thing to do."

Cassie dropped her hands to her lap, her face somber. "What did Samantha say?"

"Nothing, really." I exhaled. "I think she was shocked. But I also told her I'd talk to her with Pastor Ben present, if that helped." I looked away, toward the fan. I couldn't undo the damage I'd already done. All I could do was try to do right from here on out.

"She's not going to ask you to leave." Cassie's voice was soft, barely above a whisper. "I'm sure of it."

I tilted my head and smiled. "You're always optimistic."

"I do try to be, but it has nothing to do with optimism. I know some of Samantha's past and what she's going through." Cassie's eyebrows knit together. "She's been through a lot."

Haven't we all.

"I don't blame her for hating me." That was true. If the roles were reversed, I'd be full of rage every time I saw her face.

"Her husband cheated on her a lot. The time with you was the first one she found out about."

"Swell guy."

"She stayed longer than she should have." Cassie continued, her eyes distant. Something told me there was a part of Samantha's story Cassie could empathize with. "They were trying to have children. Or at least she was. But it never happened." Cassie shrugged. "Finally, she'd had enough and divorced him. By the time she remarried, she was too old to have children. The granddaughter you see her with at church is actually her step-granddaughter."

My chest ached, realizing the life Samantha had led. The betrayal. Lost dreams. Loneliness. When she saw me, she saw more than some cheap mistress—she saw everything she'd lost. Wasted years. She was still hurting, after all this time.

At time for healing.

A chill ran down my arms, and my chest burned with love and sorrow for Samantha. In so many ways, we had a lot in common. Who would've thought?

"I hope she's willing to talk to me some more."

Cassie reached for me, squeezing my arm. "I'm sure she will." She smiled, her eyes glistening. "God's in this. I can feel it."

"Me too, baby girl. Me too." And I meant it.

After our talk, Cassie went to her room for a nap. I stayed in the living room, not feeling particularly sleepy, and enjoyed the quiet stillness of the afternoon. Cassie had left her Bible—Mom's Bible—on the coffee table. I picked it up, admiring its worn edges. Oh, how I missed my mom! It'd been nearly a year since she passed. Would it get easier in year two? Year three? Or would the ache of her absence be something I never got used to? How I wished I could talk to her now about everything that had happened on my trip to Klamath Falls and Cedarville. About everything that was happening in my heart.

It'd been a long time since I'd read any Scripture. I needed to start. I thumbed through the pages of the Bible, noting the many underlined and highlighted passages. Some of the margins contained one- or two-word notes my mom had written in her small, fluid handwriting. Mom had lived in this book.

In First Samuel, I found my name written in the margin,

like Cassie had told me. It was next to the underlined verse:

"And so it was, whenever the spirit from God was upon Saul, that David would take a harp and play it with his hand. Then Saul would become refreshed and well, and the distressing spirit would depart from him."

I ran my finger over the verse and Mom's writing of my name. My mom had searched for answers and hope in these pages. How many times had she prayed for me? Even when I had looked too far gone, beyond hope, lost forever? I knew she never quit praying. Where would I be without her prayers? What would've become of Cassie? Renee?

There was no way to thank her. Even if I could, mere words were inadequate.

I thumbed through more pages, landing in Psalms. Here, there were more underlined and bracketed passages than any other of the Old Testament chapters I'd seen. At Psalm 103:17, I came upon another note in the margin. Cassie's name. Underlined next to it was the verse, "But the mercy of the Lord *is* from everlasting to everlasting. On those who fear Him, And His righteousness to children's children."

To their children's children...to their grandchildren. Those who fear Him. Mom had underlined the word "fear" in red, and I knew why. Dad had told me many times that in almost all the passages of the Bible where the word "fear" was used when talking about God, it actually meant love—an awed, respectful love. I leaned back on the couch, cradling the Bible in my lap like a lost treasure. Righteousness. Could a woman who'd wasted years of her life being an alcoholic and failing at her responsibilities ever be righteous?

I need His cleansing blood I know,

Oh, wash me whiter than the snow.

With Jesus, I could be—no, I already *was*—as unbelievable as it might seem.

I ran my fingers over Cassie's name in the margin, like I had my own. How long ago had Mom made this note? What was she thinking and praying at the time? Was she afraid Cassie would turn out like me? Like her biological grandfather?

Would I find Renee's name in this Bible?

It's your turn now.

A soft, affirming voice, as gentle as a breeze. A combination of my dad and my mom and Steven.

Love.

I thought of what Renee's future held. The gene for addiction, the curse, came from both her mother's and father's sides. She was fatherless. Only six years old and yet so much stacked against her. I blinked back new tears.

It was time. A time for healing. And a time for me to start being the prayer warrior my mom had been. To pray relentlessly over my family. In righteousness and love and faith. To use my musical gifts to sing songs of praise. Underline some Scriptures. Make my own notes in the margins. "Lord, help me be like my mom."

You already are, Sharon. You already are.

STUDY QUESTIONS

1. At the beginning of the story, Sharon decides to trace her family tree after learning her birth father never knew about her existence. What sorts of feelings do you suspect drove her quest? Have you known someone who searched for family after learning part of their history is missing? What were their findings? Did it affect their life in a negative or positive way?

2. Music is a theme throughout *One Way Home*. How do you think music "saved" Sharon? Has music played a part in your spiritual journey?

3. Sharon's past meets her head on when she runs into Samantha at church. What do you think of Sharon's reaction? Have you ever had something from your past that you'd rather forget pop up into your present life? How did you deal with it?

4. Throughout the story, Janice tries to befriend Sharon. Have you ever tried to befriend someone who didn't let their guard down? Is there anything Janice could have done differently?

5. Sharon's relationship with Renee brings joy and light into her life, and Renee seems to benefit from her relationship with Sharon as well. How important is the role of a grandparent in a child's life? Under what circumstances should a grandparent not be involved in their grandchild's life?

6. When Cassie tells Sharon that she has "seemed angry lately," it takes Sharon by surprise. Why do you suppose she wasn't able to see this anger in herself? What was the emotion behind her anger?

7. Sharon struggles with temptation as she battles her previous addiction to alcohol. When Johnny re-enters her life, how do you think she should have handled his return? How did you feel about her lying to Cassie about him, and how afraid were you for her to return to the life she once lived? Can you think of a Scripture that speaks to this kind of temptation? What signs were there that Johnny hadn't changed in important ways?

8. Sharon found her father, but he couldn't answer her questions because of Alzheimer's. How might the story have been different if Michael didn't have Alzheimer's disease? How do you think he would have acted toward her? Do you think Sharon still would have found her way back to God?

9. When Sharon finds her half-brother, she learns not only more about her father, but also what it's like to grow up with an alcoholic parent. How do you think that changed her view of herself? Of Cassie? What do you think gave Sharon more hope—learning that her father eventually overcame his alcoholism, or hearing that her brother found strength to fight the alcoholism curse through his relationship with God?

10. Were you relieved when Sharon decided not to go to California with Johnny? Do you think there is anything that would compel Johnny to really change? What is the significance of Sharon putting the ring he gave her inside the music box?

11. Throughout the story, Sharon keeps secrets. She reflects on how her mom kept secrets and how she now sees Cassie keeping secrets from Renee. Near the end she says, "Secret keeping was a curse in our family. One that needed to be broken." What do you think of her statement? Should some things be kept secret in our families, or should we bring everything into the light? What is the price of keeping secrets versus the price of being honest?

12. What do you think is going through Samantha's mind when Sharon approaches her and apologizes for the past? How significant is it that Sharon offers to find another church if it will make Samantha more comfortable? Do you think that was the right thing to do? What does this action say about how Sharon has changed?

Author Note

Writing *One Way Home* was a vastly different experience than writing *One Woman Falling*. With my first novel, I was able to draw the emotions and the plot largely from my own experiences. Cassie, the main character, was quite a bit like me (or at least how I once was). With *One Way Home*, I had to get myself into Sharon's head. Sharon's character was initially based on my own mom, but Sharon took on a life of her own even during her smaller role in *One Woman Falling*. How could I write from the point of view of a recovering alcoholic? While alcoholism has weaved its way through my life, I haven't experienced the addiction firsthand.

I started with research, including listening to the memoir *Drunk Mom* by Jowita Bydlowska. It was dark, raw, and insightful.

When it came to the desire to find one's birth father, I had some experience with that, but I wasn't sure if what I had felt was "normal." The memoir *Inheritance* by Dani Shapiro helped me to understand how much the need to know the truth about your lineage can drive a person to take action.

While both of the above memoirs were useful in helping me understand Sharon, the book that made it all come together for me was *The Soul of Shame* by Curt Thomas. While reading *The Soul of Shame*, I came to understand Sharon's real problem wasn't addiction, it was shame—and shame was something I definitely *could* relate to and write about.

If Sharon's story struck a chord with you or you found yourself able to empathize with her struggles, I highly recommend reading Curt Thomas's book. Shame is a spiritual disease—incredibly insidious and destructive—stealing our hope and God's best for us.

Don't let it write *your* story.

I'd love to hear from you if this story touched your life in any way, or if you'd like me to pray for you for any reason. You can connect with me at the following links, and you can sign up for my newsletter as well.

Website: melaniejcampbell.com. You can read my blog, find links to my writing, and sign up for my newsletter on my website.

Facebook: www.facebook.com/meljeancampbell
Twitter: @MelanieJean_27
Instagram: melaniecampbellauthor

Now, a Sneak Peek at Book Three

ONE LAST STAND
Cassie's story continues

Chapter One

I BEELINED THROUGH THE WALKWAYS THAT connected the brick and stone buildings of the University of Oregon. The campus was beautiful luscious green landscaping and a mix of old buildings and new. There was an atmosphere of both history and academia here, and it made my heart zing with excitement. If only I didn't feel like I stuck out like a sore thumb. Scanning the faces of the people I walked by, the ones who looked over the age of thirty were few and far between. Not to mention most were dressed casually in shorts and t-shirts, while I wore my gray slacks and a short-sleeve rayon blouse.

I glanced at my phone. In ten minutes my parking meter would run out of time, and no doubt I'd end up with a ticket. Picking up my pace, I forced myself to ignore the text notification on my screen. Other people might be able to jog-walk and text at the same time. I wasn't that coordinated.

I'd used my lunch break from Wardwood, Rosen, et al. to see an academic advisor before I registered for fall term classes. The advisor, who was, thankfully, a kind and middle-aged woman, had helped me figure out my schedule for the entire school year. Returning to college at the age of thirty-two was daunting, especially as a single mom working full-time, but the pleasant woman assured me it wasn't impossible.

Breathless by the time I made it to my Explorer, I checked my phone again. My chest fluttered. Matt wanted me to text and let him know all about my appointment, but now I only had ten minutes to drive back to work, park, and stuff food in my face so I didn't pass out from low blood sugar before five p.m. I quickly pecked out a message letting him know it'd gone great and promising to fill him in on the details later. Maybe I could sneak another text at some point in the afternoon. Thankfully, my boss, Cynthia, was supportive of my back-to-school endeavors. She'd even said I could decrease my hours a little as long as I kept up with my work. But she was a stickler about being on time. The last thing I wanted to do was return late from lunch on my first official school business.

I chomped down a protein bar while I weaved my Explorer through the parking garage. My mind was swirling with the information the advisor had given me. I sighed, wishing I had time to talk to someone before I had to be at my keyboard. Once parked, I speed-walked to the Park Place building. Once on the eighth floor, I used my key card to get in the back door of the office, thankful to avoid Lana, the official purveyor of office gossip. I checked my phone again— eleven fifty-five a.m. I had a few minutes to spare. Maybe I could shoot Matt another quick text, but first, I needed something to wash the protein bar down. I popped into the nearly empty break room.

"What's the scoop, college girl?" Missy's familiar voice made me smile. Her tanned arms were full of two cases of Snapple tea. It reminded me of our first conversation in this exact place, over two years ago. It was amazing how much my life had changed since then. How much *I* had changed.

"I think it's something I can handle. And if I stay on track, I could have my degree in Human Services in three years instead of four."

Missy set the cases of tea down and lifted her hand for a high-five. I met her hand with mine, and my heart soared. My life was all high-fives these days.

I opened the fridge and grabbed a peach iced tea, popped off the cap and gulped half of it down.

Missy laughed. "Thirsty much?"

I exhaled, shaking my head. "Protein bars make a dry lunch."

"Well don't let yourself starve. I've heard those pastor types like the curvy girls." Missy winked. Though I knew she was joking, heat ran up my cheeks.

"Funny." I chuckled. "You know I'm not giving up on getting you into a church building one of these days."

Missy's eyes held their typical mischievous twinkle. "Oh, I'm sure I'll be in one for your wedding."

I rolled my eyes, but my heart lurched. "I hope you don't wait *that* long." I held up my ringless left hand. "No ring. No proposal. I think we have a ways to go before the wedding bells."

Missy puckered her lips. "I've seen the way Matt looks at you." She lifted her eyebrows. "He is head-over-heels."

I bit my bottom lip but couldn't suppress a smile. Matt and I had been dating for nearly a year. We talked about marriage, but we definitely hadn't made any plans. Lots of couples in our day and age talked about and planned their wedding and marriage before there was even a proposal, but Matt wasn't like that. He was so old-fashioned he had even asked my mom for permission to date me before he broached the subject with me. It was one of the many things I loved about him—and another example of how incredibly good God had been to me since my divorce from Derrick.

I glanced at the clock on the wall and jumped. It was after one p.m. "I need to get to my desk."

Instead of sending Matt another short text, I decided to wait until I got off work and call him. The five p.m. traffic would afford me plenty of time to talk before getting home, and he didn't have any church responsibilities on Tuesday nights. Once out of the parking garage, I pushed his number on my phone and waited for the Bluetooth in my car to pick up.

"So it went well?" His voice was calm yet inquisitive. The sound of someone who genuinely cared.

"Yes. Oh my goodness. Better than I expected." I excitedly poured out all the details. My first term would have two online classes and one early morning class. Cynthia had already okayed me coming in late on Monday, Wednesday, and Friday so I could take that class. We still needed to run it by her boss, Brian, but he'd likely be fine with it. My stomach burned when I thought Brian's name. I'd forgiven him for how he'd lied to me and used me when I first started working at the firm. In the end, he'd helped me get custody of Renee, so it would seem the strikes against him were even. But the truth was, seeing him every day was a regular reminder of how naïve and foolish I had once been.

"That's wonderful, Cassie. I'm so happy to see you following your dreams." Matt's voice was so tender, it brought tears to my eyes. He treated me with the kind of love I'd longed for all my life but never believed I'd have.

"Thank you. I can't even put into words how excited I am about going back to school. And I'm so glad I have my mom living with us to help with Renee. If I was totally on my own, I don't know how I'd do it."

"You'd find a way, with God's help."

I took the exit to Springfield. Soon I'd be home. Mom would have dinner cooking and Renee would probably be helping her in the kitchen. I knew Matt was right—if my mom hadn't gotten sober and devoted herself to being here for Renee and me, God would've still found a way. But it undoubtedly would have been harder. I was pretty certain I wouldn't have had the time or energy to date anyone, even Matt.

"How was your day?" I asked. Our entire conversation had been focused on me, and I longed to hear more of Matt's voice. His job as a youth pastor kept him busy.

"It was good, really good." Matt's voice trailed off.

"Are you sure?" His "goods" didn't sound convincing.

"Positive. It was a typical day. But I wanted to ask you if you're free Friday night? I'd like to take you to a nice dinner...to celebrate."

"Since I don't start classes until the fall, I'm pretty sure I can go out Friday night." I tittered, but my stomach knotted. When I did start school, my time with Matt would have to be cut back. We'd already talked about the time issue, though, and Matt assured me that the quality of time—and who you spent it with—was more important than the amount.

"Good! How does six sound?"

"Works for me." I parked, got out of my Explorer and headed toward the stand of mailboxes by my house. Mom always forgot to check the mail when she got home, her focus being on Renee. "I can't wait."

We said good-bye and I dropped my phone into my purse, then reached into the mailbox. The stack of paper I pulled out was thin, and I sorted through it as I walked to the front door. Junk mail. Power bill. I needed to switch to online statements. Then there was a hand-written envelope. I looked at the writing. It was made out to Renee. That was odd. I looked in the upper left-hand corner for the sender, then froze in place. Chills ran down my neck.

No.

It couldn't be.

Adrenaline zinged through my veins and my head spun. The sender's name was written in even, block-like handwriting. Derrick Peterson.

My daughter's alcoholic, long absent, ex-convict father had written her a letter.

What did he want?